Books by Amanda Skenandore

BETWEEN EARTH AND SKY

THE UNDERTAKER'S ASSISTANT

THE SECOND LIFE OF MIRIELLE WEST

Published by Kensington Publishing Corp.

THE
SECOND
LIFE
OF
MIRIELLE
WEST

AMANDA SKENANDORE

KENSINGTON
PUBLISHING CORP.

www.kensingtonbooks.com

KENSINGTON BOOKS are published by
Kensington Publishing Corp.
119 West 40th Street
New York, NY 10018

Special book excerpts or customized printings can also be created to fit specific needs. For details, write or phone the office of the Kensington Sales Manager: Kensington Publishing Corp., 119 West 40th Street, New York, NY 10018. Attn. Sales Department. Phone: 1-800-221-2647.

The K logo is a trademark of Kensington Publishing Corp.

ISBN-13: 978-1-4967-2652-0 (ebook)
ISBN-10: 1-4967-2652-9 (ebook)

ISBN-13: 978-1-4967-2651-3
ISBN-10: 1-4967-2651-0
First Kensington Trade Paperback Printing: August 2021

10 9 8 7 6 5

Printed in the United States of America

For Kristin,
Because you asked,
And because I would have anyway.

CHAPTER 1

———≫•◦•≪———

Los Angeles, California
1926

Such fuss over a little burn. Some salve and a gin rickey, and Mirielle would be right as rain tomorrow. But Charlie had insisted on ringing the doctor. *Look how it's blistered,* he said. Off in the nursery, the baby was crying. Mirielle's head beginning to pound. She didn't have the energy for another quarrel.

Dr. Carroll had set Mirielle's broken arm when she was six. Delivered all three of her children. Cared for her after the—er—accident. So she knew well how to read his expressions. The affable smile he wore when he greeted her in the great room and asked after the baby. The shrewd glance when slipping in a question about her moods.

But his expression upon examining her hand made her insides go numb as if she were sixteen again and trussed up in a corset. The way his lips clamped shut and pushed outward, causing his graying mustache to bunch and bristle. The furrow that deepened between his eyebrows. The slow, deliberate way his features reset themselves.

Mirielle pulled her hand away. She'd seen his face morph that way before. But this was just a little burn. Mirielle wasn't dying.

"The spot on the back of your hand," he asked. "How long has it been there?"

She glanced at the pale patch of skin at the base of her thumb. What the devil did this have to do with her burned finger? "This little thing? Can't say I remember."

"And when you scalded your finger curling your hair, you didn't feel any pain?"

She shook her head. It was the smell that had alerted her. Like meat in a frying pan. She ought to have let the hairdresser give her a permanent last week when she'd bobbed her hair. Then Mirielle wouldn't have had to bother with the iron. Or the doctor. "It's just a burn. A trifle. I thought you might prescribe some ointment. Maybe a little whiskey while you're at it."

Still that serious expression.

She reached out and batted his arm. "Oh, come on. That was a joke. You know I can't stand that cheap medicinal stuff."

He mustered a weak smile while brushing off the sleeve of his jacket where she had touched him. "Is your husband home?"

"He ran off to the studio. Be glad you missed him. Charlie's been in a bum mood ever since his last picture. That reviewer at the *Times* sure did—"

"Mirielle." His eyes fixed her with unsettling intensity. "I'd like you to go to County General."

"The hospital? Whatever for?"

"There's a dermatologist there, Dr. Sullivan. I'd like him to have a look at your hand. Perhaps your driver can—"

"Of course." Her insides squeezed all the tighter.

"I'd take you myself but . . ." His steady gaze became skittish.

"I'll ring for the driver as soon as I finish making my hair."

"No, best go right away. I'll telephone ahead so they'll expect you." He gave her arm a hesitant pat and forced another smile. "Perhaps I should give them an alias when I call."

Mirielle almost laughed. It'd have to be an awfully slow day in the newsroom for anyone to care about her going to the hospital for a silly little burn. But then, maybe Dr. Carroll was right. She and Charlie had been fodder enough for the press these last few years. She drained what remained in her highball and glanced at the framed posters hung about the great room. Every one of her husband's motion pictures was displayed, from his very first to his latest flop. "Tell them to expect a Mrs. Pauline Marvin."

The dilapidated county hospital on Mission Street bustled like a hash house on a Sunday morning. Nurses and orderlies in starched white uniforms scudded from bed to bed in the vast ward beyond the admitting desk.

"Miri—er—Pauline Marvin," she said to the nurse at the desk. "I'm here to see some doctor or another. Sullivan, maybe? He's expecting me."

The woman didn't look up but waved a hand toward the crowded waiting area. "Have a seat."

Mirielle clutched the lapels of her fur-trimmed coat, skirting the coughing, groaning masses. Children squirmed on their mothers' laps. Farmers picked at the dirt beneath their nails. Off-duty waitresses and shop clerks and telephone operators hunched over scandal magazines. CINEMA STAR DENIES PLASTIC OPERATION! one of the headlines read. THREE MEN DANCE CHARLESTON TWENTY-TWO HOURS STRAIGHT!

She stood against the far wall and glanced at the clock. Ten thirty-five. She'd wait until ten forty and not a minute longer. Already she'd wasted too much time on this silly errand.

Another nurse soon arrived at the admitting desk. She whispered something to the first, who looked up in alarm and pointed at Mirielle.

"Mrs. Marvin," the second nurse called. She wore the same uneasy expression Dr. Carroll had donned after examining her hand. "Follow me, please."

The nurse escorted Mirielle down a long hallway to the back of the building, up three flights of stairs, and into a small room with a single bed. "Wait here."

She filled a washbowl with liquid and placed it on a rickety metal table outside the door. The sharp smell stung Mirielle's nose from clear across the room. "What the devil is that?"

"Disinfectant."

Dr. Sullivan arrived shortly after and examined her hand, glancing but a moment at the burn before focusing on the back of her thumb. "How long have you had this lesion?" he asked.

Lesion? Mirielle flinched at the ugliness of the word. It wasn't a lesion at all, only a lightened blotch of skin.

More questions followed. Had it appeared gradually or suddenly? Had she noticed other lesions on her body? He bade her undress and prowled around her. She was used to men looking at her, but not unclothed and not in this way—lips flat and eyes narrowed as if she were a vexing word puzzle in the *Saturday Evening Post*. Raise your right arm. Raise your left. Sit down. Hold out your feet.

She complied until he hollered to the nurse for a scalpel and specimen slides.

"Hold it right there." She reached for her stockings and chemise. "Just what do you mean to do?"

"Don't dress. You've got other lesions too. One on your back, two on the medial aspect of your thigh, one on your—er—derrière. I need samples to examine under the microscope."

She craned her neck to see the offending spots. "Are you sure it isn't just poor circulation?"

"Stand still," he said by way of answer. He scraped the edge of the scalpel over a small, irregularly shaped area of pale skin on her thigh.

Mirielle felt nothing. Not pain or discomfort. Not even a tickling sensation. Had she not been watching, she wouldn't have known the blade was on her at all. He smeared the flecks of skin and tissue onto a glass slide, then moved to the next spot.

"Is it cancer?"

"I'd rather not speculate. But you'll have to remain here until we have a definitive diagnosis."

"At the hospital?"

"Yes, here in the isolation ward."

"That's impossible. I've got children. A ten-month-old who's teething."

He passed the slides off to the nurse, then rolled up his shirtsleeves and scrubbed his hands and forearms in the basin of disinfectant by the door. "Better for them that you remain here." Then, he shut the door, locking her inside.

Morning passed into afternoon and afternoon into evening. Mirielle's mouth was sticky with thirst. Her head throbbed anew. Were she at home, at least she'd have a softer bed to lie on. Curtains to blot out the light. A record on the phonograph to drown out the noise. She closed her eyes, and the din rising from the wards below became that of the cook bustling in the kitchen, her daughter returning from school, the baby babbling in the nursery.

Mirielle got up from the lumpy hospital bed and rattled the doorknob. She banged and yelled for the nurse. How worried Charlie must be. Perhaps Dr. Carroll had telephoned. Set his mind at ease. With any luck, Mirielle would arrive home just as the cook was finishing dinner. She'd find Charlie in the parlor, drink in hand after another long day haggling with Mr. Schulberg to cast him in another picture, and the girls already tucked in and asleep. Surely, Charlie would be a dear and fix her a drink too. Light ice and a heavy pour.

But the sky outside the small, unwashed hospital window darkened, and still the doctor didn't return. The cawing seagulls quieted. The palms and eucalyptus turned from green to bruised purple to black. The distant HOLLYWOODLAND sign faded to shadow against the disappearing hills. She tried to open the window to stir the room's stale air, but the sash had been nailed shut.

An orderly brought her a newsprint-wrapped sandwich and paper cup of water, setting both down on the dirty floor just inside her room as if he dared not come inside. She hollered after him, but he knew nothing of her tests, or when the doctor might be back.

Hours later, Mirielle wrapped herself in her coat atop the narrow bed and tried to sleep. Thoughts of cancer and smallpox ran rampant in her mind. Would she wake in the morning with boils covering her skin? Or to news that a tumor was eating her from the inside out? She felt fine. Tired, yes. And certainly in need of a nightcap. But not ill. She twisted the silver bracelet around her wrist. Funny now that death might truly be at hand how Mirielle found herself wanting to live.

CHAPTER 2

Mirielle did her best to smooth and style her hair when she awoke at dawn. No one had bothered to hang a mirror, as if a fresh face and neat coiffure were somehow unimportant. Luckily, she had a compact stowed in her purse for such emergencies. The sink water tasted of rust, but she filled her paper cup and choked down a few sips. Her hands trembled for want of a real drink. Noise rose from the floors below—the click-clack of footsteps, the creak of wheelchairs, the rattle of gurneys—but the rooms around her were quiet. She perched on the edge of the pancake-thin mattress, coat on, hat and gloves at the ready. Whatever her diagnosis, she was going home as soon as it was delivered.

When her door finally opened, it was her husband accompanied by a nurse, who didn't follow him inside.

"Charlie, thank God! You won't believe the night I've had." She stood and pulled on her gloves. "Not a wink of sleep. And these nurses, dimwitted as oysters and just as common."

His lips grazed her cheek in a perfunctory kiss. "Calm down, dearest. I'm sure the doctor will explain."

"You don't know anything?"

"I couldn't get more than a few sentences out of the fellow who telephoned. Only that you were here pending some test or other, and I should come first thing in the morning."

He tossed the newspaper he'd been carrying under his arm onto the bed, and they sat. The mattress sagged beneath their weight. A smudge of shaving cream had hardened beneath Charlie's ear. She wiped it away.

"Helen didn't sleep?"

He shook his head. "Wailed like a banshee until after midnight. The nanny finally got her to suck on a brandy rag and fall asleep."

"And Evie?"

"Off to school as I left." Charlie's gaze cast about the small room, his upper lip curling and nose wrinkling. "This place is filthy. Why did Doc send you here? California Lutheran is in far better shape." He pulled out his hankie and wiped the corners of his mouth. A habit of his when his patience grew thin. "And closer to the studio."

"I'm sure he wasn't thinking of what would be convenient for you. And never mind me. I had to sleep in this place last night."

"I've got a meeting with Mr. Schulberg at ten o'clock." He pulled out his pocket watch and burnished the glass face against his coat after glancing at the time. "Ten sharp."

The bedframe creaked. The patient in the room below hollered for his bedpan. The nurse who'd escorted Charlie to the room splashed fresh disinfectant into the bowl by the door.

"We've got the Gleesons' dinner party tonight, don't forget," Charlie said.

"Can't you beg off? I'm certain I won't feel up to it. Not after this ordeal."

"We begged off last time, remember? Besides, he's got a script I want to look at."

Mirielle sighed. Mrs. Gleeson was a first-rate bore. The idea of spending the evening in her moldering parlor with imitation pâté and watered-down gin rekindled yesterday's headache.

"Choose a short cigar when he offers, will you? I don't want to sit there all night grasping at things to say while you men puff away."

Charlie pulled out his watch again. "Say, nurse?"

No answer.

"All this because of a burn?" he asked her.

"And this." She showed him the patch of pale skin on the back of her hand.

Charlie removed his gloves. He brushed his thumb over the spot, sweeping down and along the thin scar hidden beneath her silver bracelet. Then he drew her finger closer to his face and examined the burn. "You didn't—er—burn yourself on purpose, did you?"

Mirielle yanked her hand away. "Of course not."

Silence yawned between them. Charlie picked up the paper, perused the front page, then flapped it open to the sports section. Mirielle didn't care which horse had won in the Excelsior or how the U.C.L.A. freshmen fared at the latest track competition. Her gaze drifted to the window instead. But the cloudless blue sky reminded her of summer. Of picnics on the beach and lawn parties and children splashing in the pool. Splashing until they didn't. She turned her attention back to the dingy room, crossing her arms over her chest to still the tremble.

"There's a leper here at the hospital," Charlie said some while later.

"A leper? That's ridiculous. People like that exist only in the cinema."

He tapped the paper and held it wide for her to see. WOMAN LEPER ADMITTED TO COUNTY GENERAL the headline read. "Says she's here until they can arrange transport to some leper home in Louisiana."

"Good God," Mirielle said. "Does it give a name?"

"A Mrs. Martin, I believe. Do we know any Martins?"

"No, I don't think—" She grabbed the paper from Charlie and scanned the article. Not Martin. Marvin. A Mrs. Pauline Marvin. Mirielle's entire body went cold. She dropped the paper. The pages fluttered apart, landing on her lap and across the floor. "Charlie, that's me."

CHAPTER 3

$\Longrightarrow\!\!\!\Longrightarrow\!\!\!\cdot\!\!\!\Longleftarrow$

They said their goodbyes at the hospital. Too risky for Charlie to be seen at the train station with her. The nurse secreted her down an empty stairway and out the back, snapping, "Don't touch anything," when Mirielle reached for the handrail. Outside, the early morning air was cold and pregnant with mist. Beneath the thin silk of her dress, Mirielle's skin prickled with gooseflesh. But at least she was out of that quarantine cell. Charlie waited in the alleyway beside his shiny roadster, the seat piled high with her wardrobe trunks and hatboxes, as if they were spiriting away on some delightful holiday. It made the truth all the more bitter.

He kissed her quickly on the cheek, then shrank away, out of reach. It was the sort of distance her grandmother would have called chaste. But Mirielle wasn't some blushing debutante and he a bashful stag. They'd never been those things—blushing and bashful. When, in their ten years of marriage, had they come to stand so painfully far apart? She wanted to blame the disease—a disease she didn't have no matter what the doctors said—but she remembered months back sitting beside him in the front pew at the funeral. Their knees had brushed, a whisper of a touch, and she recoiled like he were a stranger. Maybe that had been the beginning.

She caught the scent of smoke carried on the heavy air and saw an orderly with his cigarette at the end of the alley watching them. Charlie saw him too and angled his hat down to obscure his face. The hospital and its ancillary buildings crowded around them, keeping them shadowed in the fledgling dawn. But soon, the sun would rise, revealing them to whoever looked out their window.

Charlie checked his watch and cleared his throat. They'd already worked out the details of her departure—what excuse he'd make to family and friends, where she might secretly send him letters, which of her hats and dresses and shoes she needed for the journey. What else was there to say?

"And the girls?" she asked at last. Part of her wished he'd brought them, despite the doctor's warning. She needn't touch them, only blow kisses and tell them goodbye. A final look to imprint their faces on her memory.

"They're with the nanny," he said, tugging on the cuff of his suit jacket and surreptitiously glancing at his watch again. "Evie misses you. Helen, too, I'm sure."

Hearing their names made every part of her ache. She hadn't nursed Helen in months, not since the accident, but even her nipples tingled with pain. Perhaps it was best he hadn't brought them.

"Sure could use a drink."

Charlie frowned, but withdrew a flask from the inside pocket of his suit, handing it to Mirielle after a quick look around. Pigeons roosted on the eaves above them. Rats rustled in the nearby trash cans. The orderly smoked his cigarette. Otherwise they were alone.

She unscrewed the cap and took a long pull. This was the good stuff, smuggled down from Canada, and the fire it lit in her empty stomach a welcome friend. Another sip and soon enough her pain would dull.

She handed the open flask back to Charlie. He brought it to his lips, but stopped short of drinking, replacing the cap and tucking it back into his pocket with an almost imperceptible wince.

"Good grief! I'm not sick. These doctors are buffoons."

"I know," he said, even as he wiped his gloves on his trousers. So much for being a great actor.

Nearby, a motor growled to life, and a moment later the ambulance appeared.

Mirielle's gut clenched. She took a step closer to her husband. To Charlie's credit, he didn't back away. Suddenly there were a million things she wanted to tell him. *I love you. I'm sorry. I know it was my fault.* But the words remained on her tongue, souring with the aftertaste of booze. At last she said, "Help the orderlies with my luggage, won't you? I'd hate for them to break anything."

She was swept up into the back of the ambulance as soon as the last bag was loaded. She pressed a gloved hand to the window and mouthed *goodbye*. Charlie mouthed something in return, but she couldn't make it out.

Tears building in her eyes, she turned away and didn't look back as the ambulance carted her over the river toward Central Station. The HOLLYWOODLAND sign and distant hills reflected the burnt glow of sunrise. They passed Little Tokyo and the gaping lot where construction was set to begin on the new city hall. Charlie had boasted it would be the tallest building in all of California, though she hadn't cared a wink at the time. Now, the idea of the city changing in her absence made the alcohol in her stomach roil. Or maybe it was the layered smell of sweat, vomit, and disinfectant that clung to the ambulance walls. Regardless, she needn't worry. A little luck and she'd be back before they broke ground.

A train whistle sounded over the wheezing of the engine, and Central Station came into view. The ambulance rolled past the depot and onto the tracks, rattling Mirielle like a shaker of salt. It stopped beside an open boxcar. The orderly got out and began tossing her luggage into a careless heap on the ground.

"Hey!" Mirielle said, clambering out of the ambulance when it was clear no one was coming to help her down. "Careful." She picked her way over to the orderly, trying to keep the dirt from spilling into her calfskin slippers. "I'll need a few of these with me in my sleeper car. This one and . . . that one." She pointed to a leather and silk valise still in the back of the ambulance.

The man grunted and threw the bag atop of the rest. He wiped his hands on a rag, then gestured grandly to the open boxcar. "Your sleeper awaits, madame."

Mirielle turned around and peered into what she'd thought was a luggage car. Light penetrated only a portion of the inside, leaving the rest in shadow. A few empty crates and a wooden barrel were all she could see.

"There must be some mistake," she said, turning back to the orderly. But he was already climbing into the ambulance. She waved to get his attention. "Excuse me!"

A cloud of dust bloomed in answer as the ambulance drove away. Some gall! She swatted the dust from her dress. Clearly, that loafer had no appreciation for crêpe-de-chine silk.

"Hurry now, and see to your luggage, ma'am," a voice said from behind her.

Mirielle turned back to the train. A stout, older woman in a white nurse's uniform had come to the lip of the boxcar and was squinting down at her through thick glasses. "We depart in five minutes."

She looked past the woman into the car again. There weren't any cushioned benches or polished card tables or private sleeping berths. There weren't any seats at all.

"I'm afraid there's been a mistake. I'm meant to—"

"Oh dear, you're not the leper from County Hospital?"

"Well, I came from County Hospital but I'm not . . . my diagnosis hasn't been confirmed. I'm only—"

The nurse gave a relieved smile. "No mistake. Best get your things aboard."

"You cannot mean for me to ride like a hobo the entire way to Louisiana."

The nurse cocked her head, as if traveling across the country in a dirty boxcar were completely natural.

"This is preposterous," Mirielle said. "Who's in charge here?"

"Well, I suppose at the moment the railroad police. Shall I fetch them?"

Mirielle glared up at the woman. The sun, fully risen now, flooded the rail yard in light. Voices sounded from the nearby platform, just visible between the cars. Workers loaded and unloaded freight from neighboring trains. The longer she stood here, the greater the chance someone would recognize her.

Starting with her hatboxes and traveling bags, Mirielle loaded her luggage into the boxcar, stowing it just inside the door. She expected to stay only a few days in Louisiana—how long could it take to straighten out her diagnosis, after all?—and had instructed Charlie to pack only the barest necessities. A dozen or so day dresses with shoes to match. A few of her cotton tennis dresses and an evening gown or two. One of her tweed coats and a worsted wool sweater in case the Louisiana climate was unfavorable. Her red-squirrel-fur coat just for good measure. Then there were her bust flatteners and brassieres, girdles and petticoats, stockings and chemises. Twenty or so pairs of stockings and her satin kimono. Hats, handbags, stoles, scarves. And then, of course, the items from her vanity: cold cream, whitening cream, vanishing cream, eyebrow cream, talcum powder, toilet water, perfume, hair curling fluid, rouge, lipstick, and face powder.

Really, she'd been quite modest in her requests. But as she dragged the first of her three trunks toward the car, she wondered if perhaps she could have done without her parasol, riding cap, and ten sets of silk pajamas. The train whistle blared, hurrying Mirielle along. She tried to hoist the trunk into the car, but only managed to raise it a few inches off the ground before the handle slipped from her grasp.

"Let me help you, señora."

"Thank you, I—" She looked up and caught sight of the man who'd offered his assistance. He was an older man with dark brown skin and graying black hair. Dark, eyebrowless eyes peeked from a puffy, deeply creased face. When he reached out and grabbed the handle of her trunk, she saw an outcropping of ghastly lumps covering his forearm.

Mirielle shrank back and stifled a scream with her hand. This was a pest car. He was . . . a leper. How many others were aboard, hiding in the shadows?

The man jumped down and grabbed her other two trunks, hauling them into the car before Mirielle could regain her wits enough to protest. It was as if she were living out a scene from *Ben-Hur*. She'd read the book as a girl, and just last month Charlie had dragged her to the theater to watch Mr. Niblo's version of the film. The train car was like the awful dungeon where Ben-Hur's mother and sister had been locked up, wasting away for years. Their hair turned white. Their fingernails loosened from their flesh. Their skin was overtaken with scales while their lips and eyelids were eaten away by the disease. Was that what awaited her in Louisiana?

She shuffled back. Her heel caught on a train rail and she fell.

The Mexican man came over to her and held out his hand. Mirielle shook her head, but he grabbed her forearm and hauled her up anyway. "Here's not the place to run, señora," he whispered to her.

Run? What was he talking about? She followed his nervous eyes around the crowded yard. At least half a dozen railroad police milled about.

"But I'm not—"

Their train's whistle shrieked again. The man climbed back inside the car. He'd touched her coat sleeve when helping her up. Now it was covered with germs. The entire train car must be teeming with them. Maybe she *should* run.

Another look about, and it seemed as if the police were drawing nearer. If she caused a scene, someone would surely recognize her. Her and Charlie's names would end up splashed across every newspaper and gossip rag in the city again. Never mind that she didn't have the disease. Those blockhead journalists never let the truth get in the way of a good scoop.

The train's wheels whined, and it lurched into motion. A backward glance at Los Angeles, and Mirielle hurried to the boxcar, grabbing the iron rail beside the opening, and scrambling inside.

CHAPTER 4

⟫•⟪

Mirielle was only just aboard when a rail worker jogging beside the train slammed closed the boxcar door, plunging her into darkness. She felt along the splintery wall until her foot struck something soft.

"Oy!" a woman's voice said.

Mirielle stumbled backward. "Excuse me."

The train listed, and she lost purchase on the wall, tripping over her feet and nearly falling.

"You really should sit down before you hurt yourself, ma'am."

Mirielle recognized that as the nurse's voice. Somewhere nearby she also heard a rasping noise, measured and guttural, like the surf after a storm. She backed away until she ran into the sharp, solid edge of a trunk—hopefully her trunk—and sat down atop it.

A whisper of light stole through cracks in the siding. After a minute or two, her eyes adjusted to the dim. The trunk beneath her was her own, and the rest of her luggage nestled nearby. The rasping noise came from a man laid out on a cot against the far wall. Each breath he drew seemed a struggle. The nurse perched beside him on a low, three-legged stool—the only proper piece of furniture in the entire boxcar. The Mexican man sat on the floor in the far corner, and the woman Mirielle had run into squatted atop her tattered valise. She looked older than Mirielle, though not by much, stocky and puffy-faced with a rag tied about her head. Her hands were marked with lesions. Not pale and innocuous like the one beneath Mirielle's thumb, but scaly and raised, as if lumps of red clay had dried and crusted on her skin.

Though no one's limbs were missing nor their fingernails peeling from their flesh like in *Ben-Hur*, Mirielle couldn't help but shudder. She pulled a handkerchief from her handbag and wiped her sleeve and the toe of her shoe before tossing it to the ground. When the Mexican man's eyes met hers, she looked away, focusing instead on the woodgrain maze of the floorboards.

The train sped along, and Mirielle felt her insides tear, as if only part of her had climbed into the boxcar and the rest remained firmly planted in Los Angeles. A few weeks and she'd be home again, she reminded herself. The girls would hardly miss her. She clasped her hands. They still trembled a bit, but the worst of drying out was over. When she returned home, maybe she'd go easy on the hooch.

The train stopped in the late afternoon, and the boxcar's door rolled open. Mirielle squinted and shielded her eyes from the sudden onslaught of light. Her backside ached, and her neck was stiff from keeping her head turned away from the others. She had to pee, and her stomach churned with hunger.

"Ya got fifteen minutes," a gruff voice called from outside. "Get out and do your business."

The Mexican man jumped out and stretched. The woman and the nurse descended next and Mirielle behind them. Sand spilled into her shoes as her feet sank into the ground.

A few detached train cars sat scattered about the yard. Beyond them, desert: wiry sagebrush, towering saguaros, and far-off mountains. She started toward the depot, its pitched roof visible above the train. YUMA, read a hanging shingle. Even from here at the tail end of the train, she could hear the bustle of the platform—hurried footfalls and dragging luggage, cheerful hellos and choked goodbyes.

Before she'd waded but a few sinking steps beyond the boxcar, the nurse stopped her. "Don't stray too far now."

"I'm just dashing off to the dining car. I'll be back in a jiffy."

"I'm afraid that area's off-limits. Your supper's right here." The nurse held out a plate of beans and a slice of bread.

Mirielle hadn't expected caviar, but this disappointed even her low expectations. "Don't be a cluck. I haven't even got a fork."

"That's what the bread's for."

She waved away the plate. "Never mind supper. I've got to use the ladies' room."

But they—the lepers—weren't allowed in the lavatories either, according to the nurse. She gestured toward an uncoupled boxcar some distance off and suggested Mirielle might relieve herself behind it.

Mirielle gaped at her. Surely she wasn't suggesting Mirielle pee in the uncivilized open. They weren't animals, after all. But the nurse's solemn expression didn't falter.

A wistful glance at the depot and Mirielle stomped toward the uncoupled boxcar. With her bladder about to burst, she had no choice but to hike up her dress and squat behind the rusty wheels. On the way home, she'd insist on a private sleeper. That was, once the doctors at the Marine Hospital figured out she didn't have leprosy, and this whole awful mess was behind her.

With a few minutes left before departure, she wandered to the last set of tracks. More sand spilled into her shoes. A bur snagged in her stocking, poking her through the silk. But after so many days locked in that dingy hospital room and then the suffocating boxcar, the sun's warmth felt good on her skin. The sky above was blue as the topaz cocktail ring Charlie had given her on their third anniversary. Beyond the cactus and sagebrush, a streak of dust appeared in the distance, smudging with the dull brown of the horizon. Was that a man? Running?

A mule brayed behind her, and a wagon rumbled past. She watched until it too became a cloud of dust, then trudged back to the boxcar.

She returned to find the nurse cowering before the railroad deputy.

"I thought he was right here. I . . . I cannot keep my eye on all of them at once. I'm their nurse, after all, not their jailer."

The deputy's pale brown eyes flickered from the nurse to Mirielle. His expression puckered with disgust. He spat and turned back to the nurse. "Just get the rest of your goddamned lepers back inside and don't let any more escape."

The nurse waved Mirielle into the car. Only the rasping man on the stretcher and the woman with the headscarf were inside. Had the Mexican man fled? Mirielle guessed by the nurse's stricken expression he had. She followed her gaze to the expanse of desert beyond the tracks.

The dust she'd seen earlier had settled. Had the man managed to outrun the wagon? Mirielle found herself hoping he had. Soon the wagon took shape amid a newly blooming cloud of dust. As it drew closer, Mirielle saw the Mexican man shuffling behind, struggling to keep up with the pace of the mules. A rope stretched between the wagon's undercarriage and the handcuffs about his wrists. His face was bloodied and swollen, his pant leg ripped. It fluttered about his calf, parting with each step to reveal a long gash down his shin.

The nurse shooed Mirielle away from the doorway as the wagon approached. The train's engine had been stoked, and steam billowed from the chimney. The wagon stopped beside the boxcar, and the railwaymen untied the runaway. They tried several times to unlock his handcuffs, but blood had gotten into the lock, and the key wouldn't work.

"Ain't got time to fuss with this," the railway deputy said as he and the others hoisted the man into the boxcar. "They'll have to cut them off when you get to where you're going." They rolled the door closed as the handcuffed man was still wiggling his way inside like an inchworm, nearly smashing his foot.

He crawled to his corner and struggled to a seated position. The handcuffs had chafed his skin raw. Dirt, blood, and drying spittle rimmed his lips. Mirielle waited for the nurse to tend to his wounds— the gash on his leg, the cuts and bruises on his face, the cactus thorns buried in his flesh. But the man on the cot, whose breathing had grown raspier since their departure in California, claimed her attention.

The Mexican man coughed and smacked his lips. He'd likely breathed in more dust than air as he struggled behind the wagon. Mirielle fled his gaze but could not ignore the continued hack of his cough. She tottered to the barrel of drinking water in the corner. Its dark, glassy surface trembled with the movement of the train. She'd avoided drinking from the barrel for fear of catching the others' sickness. The man's dirty lips would only foul it more. But they were still two days out from Louisiana, and neither one of them could go without water for that long.

Mirielle took a deep breath, filled the ladle, and drank. Then she refilled it and took it to the man, spilling half the contents on her dress as the train rocked and listed.

He cupped the ladle in his soiled hands and drank. "Gracias."

Mirielle met his eyes and nodded. He might be a leper, but he was also a man and didn't deserve what the railwaymen had done to him. She fetched him more water, then found the handkerchief she'd discarded and wiped the blood and dirt from his face. Her heart hammered as she worked. Fear-tinged sweat crept along her hairline. It was hard to tell whether age or disease had caused the deep creases in his skin. Either way, she was careful not to touch him without the handkerchief.

Next, she carefully plucked the thorns from his legs. Mirielle certainly wasn't a nurse, but she knew a thing or two about cacti from outings she'd taken with her son in the California hills.

The man winced but otherwise didn't make a sound. How long had he been a leper? How many times had he tried to run? His graying hair suggested a man well into his fifties. His hardened eyes suggested a man older still. One who knew the meanness of the world.

At least they had that in common.

CHAPTER 5

$\Longrightarrow\!\!\!\Longrightarrow\!\!\!\diamond\!\!\!\Longleftarrow\!\!\!\Longleftarrow$

After two and a half days, the train finally arrived in New Orleans. Mirielle and her traveling companions waited inside the boxcar while voices of disembarking passengers drifted past. Then their car was uncoupled from the others and pushed to a barren section of the rail yard. The door rolled open just as an old, war-model ambulance squealed to a stop before them. U.S. MARINE HOSPITAL was stenciled in fading white paint across its side. Two men in plain wool work suits jumped down from the front seat, eyeing Mirielle and her companions before conferring with the nurse. They moved the sickly man from his cot to a stretcher and carried him to the ambulance. Mirielle was too tired from the harrowing train ride to do anything more than follow behind.

The western horizon glowed orange like the fruit-laden citrus trees at home. The rest of the sky had drained of color. The ambulance had only just lurched into motion when the crackle of fire rose above the motor's din. Smoke tinged the air. A sharp turn and their boxcar came into view through the window. Flames crawled up its sides, incinerating any trace of them and their germs.

Mirielle's legs were stiff and eyelids drooping when the hours-long ride from the train station ended. She stumbled out of the ambulance and looked around. The Louisiana air was damp and colder than she'd expected. The darkness of this desolate place unnerved her. She longed for the streetlights, flashing marquees, and lighted storefronts of Los Angeles. There, you could see and hear and feel life pulsing all around. Here, it rustled and croaked in the shadows, subdued and menacing.

The ambulance's headlamps cast their light on a towering plantation home, the kind Mirielle had read about in novels and seen in moving pictures about the antebellum South. It glowed like a specter in the surrounding darkness, a jutting veranda and corniced pillars casting long shadows across its white façade.

"This is the hospital?" she asked the driver, as he unloaded her luggage.

"Nah, ma'am," he said in a heavy drawl. "That there's the administrative building and sisters' residence."

Before she could ask whom he meant by sisters, two women with lanterns shuffled from the plantation house. Their dresses looked like something her grandmother would have worn, overly starched and oppressively long. Beads clattered from their belts. Perched upon their heads was some strange ornamentation one could scarcely call a hat. It looked like a giant seagull with outstretched wings.

"One stretcher case and thems three who can walk," the driver said to the women.

"Very good," one replied. "Take him straightaway to the infirmary. We'll see to the others." The woman turned, gracing Mirielle and her companions with a closed-lip smile. Raising her lantern, she regarded each of them in turn, her brow furrowing when her eyes lit on Mirielle. At last she said, "This way."

She started across a wide side lawn toward a distant hedgerow. Beyond the hedge lay a vast cluster of buildings, just visible in the muted moonlight.

"Excuse me! When will the porter be round for our bags?" Mirielle asked.

The woman turned around. Her gaze fell on the pile of luggage at Mirielle's feet and her lips flattened. "We haven't a porter, my dear. This is a hospital, not the Hotel Ritz."

"I'll say," Mirielle whispered under her breath.

"Take whatever you can carry. I'll send an orderly for the rest in the morning."

"The morning? What if it rains or wild animals climb inside?"

"What sort of animals did you have in mind?"

Mirielle glanced at the shaggy outline of trees in the darkness. "I don't know. Wolves, bears, snakes."

The woman gave a mirthless laugh. "We haven't any bears or wolves here, and God willing it won't rain. Now grab what you need and come along."

And snakes? The very idea made Mirielle's skin prickle. She looked down at the hatboxes and valises and trunks, trying to decide which to take. She wasn't sure where Charlie had packed what. Her pajamas were likely in one of the trunks. Her hairbrush in one of the valises. Her toothbrush and dental paste in—

The woman gave a loud *ahem*. "We haven't all night."

Mirielle grabbed two of her bags, hoping one of them contained her nightly ablutions, and followed the two absurdly hatted women along a dirt path. They passed the waist-high hedgerow and shuffled up a ramp that led to a covered boardwalk with screened-in sides. Lamps with cheap industrial shades dangled from the awning. The walkway branched and turned in so many directions Mirielle felt as if she'd landed in a maze. Buildings of various shapes and sizes butted up to the walkway, their whitewashed siding set aglow as the moon slipped free of cloud cover.

The group split at one of the intersections. The Mexican man followed the quieter woman down a long corridor, his wrists still shackled and gait limping. Mirielle trailed the others on a serpentine path, arriving at last at the ladies' infirmary. Hospital beds lined both sides of the long narrow building. A few were occupied with sleeping figures Mirielle was loath to look at. The rest of the beds were empty, made up in the stark, precise manner one would expect at a nunnery. Fitting, she realized, as now that they were inside, she could see the strand of beads dangling from her guide's waist was a rosary.

"We'll begin the intake process in the morning," the woman said, showing Mirielle to a bed.

"We can't start now? I'm in an awful hurry to get home."

"The doctors have long since retired for the evening. We wake them only in cases of emergency."

"This is an emergency! I've been misdiagnosed. I don't belong here."

One of the patients sleeping nearby stirred. The sister frowned.

"I'm afraid you don't get to decide what is and what is not an emergency. Try to get some rest, and we'll speak again in the morning."

Before Mirielle could argue further, the woman turned and left. Mirielle watched her go, glaring at the back of her winged hat. She rummaged through the bags she'd carried. The first contained an assortment of gloves, scarves, and jewelry. Inside the second, Mirielle found half a dozen pairs of shoes and, wrapped in cloth and tucked away at the bottom, the silver-framed photograph that used to sit on her vanity. Thoughtful of Charlie to pack it, even though she wouldn't be gone from home for long.

The sweet faces of her family staring back at Mirielle through the glass made her weary body ache anew. She sat, the thin mattress bowing beneath her. She slipped off her shoes, dragged the scratchy cotton blanket atop her, and fell asleep with the photograph cradled to her breast.

Mirielle awoke the next morning to find the same woman who'd escorted her to the infirmary the night before pulling up a stool beside her. A crisp white smock was draped over her gown. The giant hat atop her head was as stiff as plaster. Mirielle sat up and smoothed her disheveled hair. She must look the part of a hobo, so wrinkled and dusty her dress. Must smell the part too.

"Is the doctor in yet?" she asked.

"He's assisting in the operating room, but I expect him here presently."

"Ma'am, listen, like I told you last night—"

"You may call me Sister Verena."

"Sister, there was a misunderstanding in California. The doctor there couldn't tell his head from his ass."

Sister Verena frowned. "However accurate your vulgar assessment may be, I still must complete the intake form."

"Is there a nurse I can talk to? This medical stuff may be beyond your—"

"I am a nurse. Head nurse." She looked pointedly at Mirielle and readied her pen. "Now, may we begin?"

Mirielle flapped her hand in assent and turned her head to the window. The sky outside was cloudy, painting the gnarled trees and stringy moss in diffuse gray light.

"How old are you?"

"Thirty-two."

"Where were you born?"

"Los Angeles."

"Have you ever lived overseas?"

"I already told the doc in California all this. Nothing in my history is out of the ordinary."

"That's for us to determine. Have you ever lived abroad?"

Mirielle turned back to face her. "No, never. And while you're at it, write down that I never had a family member who was a leper or knew a leper."

"Are you married?"

"Yes."

"Children?"

"Yes."

"How many?"

"Three—er—two." Mirielle glanced down at her folded hands. "Two."

Sister Verena scratched down her answer. She asked a few more banal questions then said, "And what name would you like to go by here at Carville?"

"What name? My name. Miri—"

"Most patients prefer to take a new name. We're very guarded with our records, but with so many residents and personnel and visitors, well, word could inadvertently get out. For families on the outside, the stigma can be devastating."

"I'm not a patient or a resident!" Mirielle didn't realize she was shouting until the others in the room craned their necks to look at her. She lowered her voice and bit out, "I don't have this disease."

"Very well," Sister Verena said, straightening the edges of her papers and putting down her pen. "We'll call you patient three-sixty-seven for now."

CHAPTER 6

An orderly brought Mirielle breakfast—eggs, grits, and canned peaches—on an enameled stoneware plate. Certainly an upgrade from the cold food served on paper plates on the train. Lunch came too before the doctor finally arrived. He donned a white jacket over his black officer's uniform and strode to her bedside with a broad smile. Sister Verena followed a step behind. When he sat down on the stool opposite Mirielle's bed, she could see the fatigue in his red-rimmed eyes. The front thatch of his thinning brown hair stood on end like the head plumes of a quail.

"Welcome to US Marine Hospital Sixty-Six, ma'am," he said, extending his hand. "Carville, if you like. I'm Dr. Jachimowski, but most residents call me Doc Jack."

As Mirielle shook his hand, she realized he was the first of the many doctors and nurses she'd encountered over the past several days who deigned to touch her. His warm palm and unfaltering smile eased the tightness that had wound about her rib cage. "Pleased to meet you, Doctor. Are you the resident expert?"

He chuckled. "I'm one of them. Dr. Ross, the Medical Officer in Charge, spent decades fighting the disease in India and is one of the foremost leprologists in the world. He deals mostly with administrative matters, but you'll see him around from time to time. We have other specialists too—an ophthalmologist, a dentist, an orthopedic surgeon—who come up regularly from the city. We also—"

"Yes, but you can tell true leprosy from other ailments. I mean, you must see it all the time. You're the man who can prove those blockhead doctors in California diagnosed me wrong."

His smile tottered. "Yes, I'm your man. Let's take a look. Nurse, can you bring us a screen?"

Sister Verena set up a folding screen around the bed, and Mirielle undressed at Doc Jack's behest. He examined her skin while Sister Verena took notes in Mirielle's chart.

"Flat, reddened macule on the left lateral shoulder, approximately five centimeters diameter . . . flat hypopigmented macule right flank three centimeters . . . flat reddened macule lower right thigh, medial aspect, one and a half centimeters . . ."

Each time he called out a new finding, Mirielle's pulse revved like an over-gassed engine. Seven lesions in total, where the doctor in Los Angeles had found only five. "Couldn't these be birthmarks or poor circulation?"

"Hmm," Doc Jack said, in a way that offered little reassurance. "We'll know soon enough."

He produced a small stick with a wisp of cotton at one end and asked her to close her eyes. "Let me know when and where you feel the cotton touch your skin."

"Yes, my forearm," she said almost as soon as she'd closed her eyes. "Right forearm."

"Good."

Then came the tickle of cotton on her left calf, her right palm, the small of her back. She felt like a schoolgirl again, standing before her teachers reciting the capitals of the forty-five states. Right shoulder . . . right cheek . . . the number of seconds between each touch lengthened . . . then nothing. "Are we done?"

"Almost," the doctor said.

She screwed her face in concentration and waited. Sister Verena's pen scratched atop her paper.

"Left knee," she almost shouted when she felt the brush of cotton again.

"Are you sure?" Doc Jack asked.

"Yes . . . er . . . I think so. Can you do it again?"

"We've got all the data we need. You can open your eyes."

Mirielle wrapped her arms around herself, feeling for the first time self-conscious of her nakedness. "Can I dress?"

"Not quite yet. I'm going to take a few tissue samples from the spots I found, just like they did in California. It shouldn't hurt more than a little."

Sister Verena wheeled over a small steel table with a scalpel and several laboratory slides on top. Mirielle watched the doctor cut a small slit in the discolored spot beneath her thumb and then scrape the blade along the wound. It didn't hurt at all. Nor did the next or the next, though Mirielle's stomach roiled, and she had to look away. Only when he cut into her earlobe did she feel the sting of pain, and then only a little.

"All done," Doc Jack said, wearing his friendly smile again. "You can go ahead and dress. Nurse Verena, will you take these slides to the laboratory?"

"Yes, Doctor." She wheeled the table away, Mirielle's slides rattling against the steel.

"How long till we know?" Mirielle asked the doctor.

"A few days."

"Days? I have a family, a baby who needs me." Without thinking, her hands went to her breasts, long since dried of their milk. "I have to get home."

His tired eyes regarded her, and she convinced herself it wasn't pity but simple kindness that made them soften. "I suppose I could go examine the slides myself. Give me an hour, maybe two."

"Thank you."

He started to shuffle around the screen, but Mirielle called out to him. "Doc Jack."

He turned around.

"The man with the handcuffs, is he okay?"

"Took near an hour to saw the darned things off him, but yes, he's fine."

"And the other man?" Mirielle hesitated. Did she really want to know? "The man who came in on the stretcher."

His smile faded. "We did an emergency tracheotomy on him this morning, but he was already bleeding into his lungs and didn't come through."

Mirielle nodded as the doctor left, feeling suddenly queasy. Her fingers trembled as she fastened her girdle and brassiere atop her chemise, and shimmied back into her dress.

* * *

Doc Jack returned just over an hour later as promised. Sister Verena trailed behind him, her stiff skirts rasping as she walked. The doctor smiled at another patient as he crossed the room toward Mirielle. Said a cheery hello to another one of the sisters. A good sign, Mirielle decided. But when he pulled the stool up to her bedside and sat, he was no longer smiling.

"I examined your slides very carefully, and I'm afraid the doctors in California were correct. You are infected with the *Mycobacterium leprae* bacillus."

The infirmary began to sway as if an earthquake were upon them. Mirielle put her hands out on either side of her and clutched the mattress. "Bacillus?"

"I'm sorry, that's how we refer to the microorganism, the germ, that causes leprosy."

"But that's . . . that's impossible. I feel completely fine."

"Lucky for you, we caught it at a very early stage. With the proper treatment, it may never advance. . . ."

Mirielle tried to unscramble his words and reassemble them in a way that made sense. "The passengers on the train and I had to drink from the same water barrel. I may have accidentally touched one of them too. Maybe those are their germs on the slides, not mine. If I could shower, brush my teeth, then you could test again and it would be negative."

"That's not how the disease develops. It takes years to incubate . . . er . . . grow inside you. Many patients here contracted the disease as children and didn't show signs—"

"I have to go." Mirielle stood and reached for her bags. "Home. This isn't, I can't, you've made a mis—"

Doc Jack stood too and laid his hand on her arm. "I'm afraid you can't. Leave, that is. Carville is the best place in the world to be for the treatment of leprosy. We've got the best personnel, and we're trialing new remedies all the time."

"There isn't a cure?"

He squeezed her arm, then sank his hand into his pocket. "Well, no. Not exactly. We have medicines and therapy that help in certain cases and can—"

An orderly rushed into the room and yelled between panting breaths, "Doc Jack, you're needed in the men's infirmary."

"I've got to go, but I'll see you again soon. Nurse Verena can answer all your questions."

Mirielle shuffled backward until the underside of her knees hit the creaky bed frame. No cure? She sank onto the mattress and looked around for a basin in case her undigested lunch rose any farther up her throat.

"Do you have any more questions?" the sister asked.

Questions? Mirielle had a million but couldn't form them into words. She shook her head.

"And a name?"

"What?"

"I need a name to put on your chart, dear."

Mirielle closed her eyes—hoping that would stop the room from spinning, stop the vomit burning its way up her esophagus, stop the charade that had suddenly become her life.

CHAPTER 7

"This is Mrs. Pauline—" Sister Verena untucked Mirielle's chart from beneath her arm and glanced inside. "Pauline Marvin."

The name sounded ridiculous said aloud by Sister Verena. Was it too late for Mirielle to change it? Then again, the entire situation was ridiculous. A different name—something more generic and less personal—would hardly change that.

The sister nudged Mirielle toward a small group waiting outside the infirmary. "Your traveling companions, I believe you know."

"I'm Hector," said the Mexican man, meeting her eyes a moment before returning his gaze to the ground. His tattered and dusty clothes had been changed for clean ones, and his wrists were wrapped in gauze.

"Olga," said the puffy-faced woman.

But these weren't their real names. Surely they'd been pressed for an alias too. Who had they been before? A twinge of regret stirred inside Mirielle at not having spoken to them on the train when they weren't yet so cleaved from the world.

Like Mirielle, they both held a hospital-issue pillow and sheet set.

"And this is Frank Garrett," Sister Verena said, gesturing to a man Mirielle didn't recognize. "Mr. Garrett has been a patient here for several years and is very active in the colony. He'll give you a tour of the facility before showing you to your assigned houses." She flashed her closed-lipped smile, then turned back to the infirmary.

"Call me Frank," the man said, extending his hand.

Mirielle gasped and backed away. It was hardly a hand at all. The skin was rough and scarred. A short nub extended above his knuckle where his ring finger ought to be. The other fingers curled inward. His left hand, hanging idly at his side, looked similarly misshapen.

Her stranglehold on her pillow and bedclothes tightened. The stories were true. Lepers' fingers and arms and legs just fell off. Would they find body parts strewn and decomposing about the facility? Would her limbs shrivel and fall off in the same way?

"Quite a sight, no?" he said, raising both of his hideous hands to eye level. "Claw-hands, we call 'em here. Makes it tricky to hold a pen, but don't challenge me to a crawfish eating contest." He made a twisting gesture with his claws.

Hector chuckled. Mirielle backed away.

"*Mais*," Frank continued, his drawling voice still light. "Happy to meet ya, Mrs. Marvin." He started down the screened walkway and waved a claw for Mirielle and the others to follow. "Say, sure do like your name. Puts me in mind of a serial I watched years back."

He stopped and gestured to a T-shaped building. Windows ran the length of every side, each shaded by a canvas awning. Like all the buildings and walkways, brick piers raised it several feet above the boggy ground. "That there's the dining hall and kitchen. Meals served up at seven, eleven, and four thirty. You'll hear the bell. If not, you'll see the line. We line up at Carville for just about everything from soup to soap." He turned and smiled at Mirielle and Olga. "Feel free to grab a tray and cut in line, ladies. We do try to be gentlemanly here. Most of us, anyway."

They continued on, Frank pointing out the tennis court and laundry, the laboratory and operating room. Not only were his hands fit for a sideshow, but he talked funny too. Fast yet lazy-sounding, as if he couldn't be bothered to enunciate his vowels or bring his tongue forward to make a *th* sound. It was different from the Southern drawl others spoke with. Creole perhaps. Or Cajun. Was there a difference? Mirielle didn't know and didn't care. She only wished she didn't have to pay such damned close attention to make out what he was saying.

Other residents passed them on the walkways, some in wheelchairs, some on bikes, some on foot. All gawked shamelessly at Mirielle and her companions. Frank seemed to know everyone and belabored the tour with needless introductions. Mirielle didn't listen to the other residents' names or reach out when they offered her a hand. She'd been promised a room somewhere in the long quadrangle of bungalow-style houses surrounding the dining hall and just wanted to get there. Wanted to close the door and block out this place.

"Pauline Marvin?" one of the passing strangers asked when Frank introduced them. Lumps of various sizes crowded his face such that she could barely see his lips and eyes. "Like in that old show?"

Frank slapped the side of his leg. "That's what I was thinking. You remember the name?"

"Nah," the man said. "Had Pearl Sutter and Charlie Wes—"

"For Pete's sake! My name's got nothing to do with those old pictures," Mirielle said.

"Sheesh," the man said, eyeing Mirielle before taking off on his bike.

"Sorry, *chère*," Frank said, though in his hillbilly way of talking it sounded like *sha*. "Didn't mean to get your feathers up."

"My *feathers* are not up. I simply want to get to my room."

"I hear ya. We're almost there." He started walking again, leading them deeper into a web of covered boardwalks. "What a howl those shows were. *The Pitfalls of Pauline*? Nah, that ain't right. *Pauline's Perils*? . . ."

The Perilous Pursuits of Pauline. Mirielle had snuck out every week the summer she turned nineteen to watch the latest episode. Her grandmother found the whole moving picture industry intolerably common, but Mirielle loved it from her first glimpse at a nickelodeon on the pier. Pearl Sutter was at her best in *The Perilous Pursuits of Pauline,* and her handsome costar wasn't too shabby either, though at the time Mirielle hadn't recognized his name. The films were shot in New Jersey. It wasn't until the following spring that Charlie switched studios and came out to Hollywood. They'd met at a party—one, like the pictures, she'd had to sneak out to attend—but she always joked that their first meeting had been a dingy theater on Adams Street during a screening of *The Perilous Pursuits of Pauline.* No one here needed to know that, though. Certainly not Frank.

The tour stalled again at the recreation hall and attached canteen.

"You can usually find me here behind the counter working the soda fountain," Frank told them. "Or sorting the mail. Letters have to be dropped off by ten a.m. sharp so it can go through the sterilizer before the postman comes." Frank paused. "Don't hurt to offer a little prayer that it ain't incinerated in the process."

"The mail is sterilized?" she asked.

He brushed a strand of dark, wavy hair away from his face. Clearly, he didn't know the fashion nowadays was for short hair, parted at the side and slicked back *à la* Valentino. "Yes, ma'am."

"And sometimes letters get incinerated?"

"Not too often," he said with a wink.

She pursed her lips and looked away. The canteen consisted of little more than a counter and stools; a few shelves stocked with cigarettes, candy bars, and canned goods; and a spattering of mismatched tables and chairs. A mousetrap with a moldy bit of cheese sat in one corner. Gold and green crepe paper bunting hung from the walls, torn and drooping, with a hand-painted sign hanging askew. *HAPPY MARDI GRAS!* it read. A few flecks of matching confetti littered the floor.

"Ready to move on?" Frank said as if she'd been the one holding them up.

She brushed past him to the exterior walkway, but couldn't go any farther on her own. One white building looked so much like the next, interconnected with what must amount to over a mile of caged-in walks. Mirielle felt like a rodent in a maze, the kind tortured with experiments until it lost all its hair and gnawed off its own tail.

The tour stopped at another intersection. "There's Union Chapel for those of ya of the Protestant persuasion," Frank said, gesturing with a claw-hand to a plastered building with a square belfry and amber-tinted window. "Got your regular services Sunday mornings and Bible lectures Wednesday evenings."

He pointed out the Catholic chapel too, not more than a few dozen yards away. Both buildings faced away from the colony toward a narrow dirt road and smooth-sloping levee. The Mississippi River bounded the reserve on three sides, Frank told them, but the levee blocked any view of the water. Between the chapels and the road rose a cyclone fence crowned with several strands of barbed wire. It marched link upon link as far as she could see.

Frank was saying something about the daily mass schedule, but she interrupted him. "Is this a hospital or a prison they're running here?"

He looked from her to the fence and back. "Ain't you heard? There are lepers here." He waited a beat, then chuckled at his own pathetic joke. Mirielle tightened her hold around her pillow and bedsheets for want of strangling him. They continued down the walkway, Mirielle last among them. She no longer bothered to glance up when they passed other patients. She didn't nod or offer her fake name in reply to theirs. She was afraid of what she would see if she looked at them—more scaly skin and sunken noses, more missing legs and shriveled hands, more reddened and despondent eyes.

They rounded a corner and stopped before a long line of houses. She prayed the tour was over and one of these houses were hers.

"Don't forget to come out for our next meeting of the What Cheer Club," Frank was saying, walking backward to address them, his awkward gait slower than her daughter Helen could crawl. "We host holiday parties and social—"

"Enough with the jokes!" Mirielle slammed her foot down on the walkway. "We're tired and just want to get to our damned rooms."

Frank stopped. Olga and Hector turned and looked at her.

"My God," Mirielle went on, the dam of her rage breaking. "The lines, the mail, your crippled hands"—she swept her arm toward the cottages and walkways and hospital buildings—"none of this is funny. And this What Cheer Club. Do you take us for saps? What does anyone here have to be cheerful about?"

Frank looked down, ran his craggy fingers through his untamed hair, then raised his chin. His ice-blue eyes met her gaze squarely. "We're alive. That's one thing."

"Alive? You said it yourself, we're . . ." Her mouth struggled to form the word. "Lepers. We might as well be dead."

"That ain't how I see it."

She picked up her luggage and brushed past Olga and Hector to stand directly before him. "Well, maybe you should get your eyes checked—there's a joke for you!—now, what number is my room?"

He shook his head, then muttered, "House eighteen. Irene, she's your orderly, her. She'll show you which room is yours."

Mirielle stomped past him. The cottages butted up to the walkway, each with a number painted above the door. Most had their doors propped open, rocking chairs and potted plants cluttering the porch-like nook that jutted beyond the walkway.

An old woman sat hunched in one of the weathered rockers outside of house eighteen. Lesions marred her face, and a gauze bandage covered her left cheek. Pink fluid had bled through the fibers and wept from beneath the edges down her face.

"What you lookin' at?" she asked as Mirielle approached.

"Are you Kathleen?"

"You mean *Irene,* and no, I ain't."

When she didn't say anything more, Mirielle shimmied around her and went inside. A hallway ran the length of the house, with doors lining either side. The floorboards creaked beneath her. The wall paint bubbled with rot.

"Third door on the right, newcomer," the woman called after her.

The room was empty save for a narrow, iron-framed bed, a side table, a straight-back chair, and an unvarnished wardrobe. A cast-iron radiator hummed alongside the wall. Mirielle's luggage sat in a heap in one corner. The day's gray light spilled in through an undressed window. Mirielle stepped inside and closed the door. She dropped everything and stared at the tiny room, too shell-shocked to cry.

CHAPTER 8

A few hours later, a knock sounded on the door. Mirielle didn't bother to get up from her undressed bed to answer. "Go away."

She hadn't unpacked anything except the framed picture of her family, which she'd set on the rickety bedside table. Everything else lay untouched—her luggage a towering pile in one corner, her bedclothes and pillow a heap on the floor.

The knocker entered uninvited. "Welcome to Carville!"

She was a tall woman, thick through the waist, with henna-dyed hair graying at the roots.

"Are you Iris?" Mirielle asked.

"Irene. Orderly of this here palace."

"Are you a . . ."

"Leper?" She reached out and patted Mirielle's shoulder. "Baby, we're all lepers here."

Mirielle jerked back so quickly she fell off the narrow bed, landing on her rear on the opposite side. "I'm not a . . . a . . . I don't . . . I can't possibly have the disease."

Irene walked around the bed and held out her hands to help Mirielle up. Save for a few red patches on her face and neck, her skin was unblemished and her limbs whole. Reluctantly, Mirielle took her hands. With surprising strength for a woman hot-footing it toward fifty, Irene hauled Mirielle to her feet.

"I know it's hard, baby. Took me months to accept it. Cried myself to sleep two weeks straight and then some." She gave Mirielle's hands a squeeze before letting go. "Let's get you something to eat."

"Is it dinnertime?"

Irene cocked her head to one side, revealing a large ear with a scarred, drooping lobe. As if on cue, a bell tolled somewhere off in the colony. "It is now. That's the supper bell. Come on."

"I'm not hungry."

" 'Course you are." Irene took her arm and dragged her from the room.

After several twists and turns in the walkway, they arrived at the dining hall. Irene yapped the entire way, but Mirielle didn't register a word. They cut in near the front of a long line and shuffled with their trays down the food counter. Kitchen staff heaped peas and fried potatoes and roasted chicken onto a plate and deposited it on Mirielle's tray. Bread and butter, a glass of milk, and some gummy substance she guessed to be cobbler soon followed.

With their trays brimming, she and Irene crossed the dining hall toward a crowded table of women. Heads turned, and people stared as Mirielle passed.

"Folks don't move fast here, except at mealtime," Irene was saying. "Once you hear that bell ring, you'd better watch out." She nodded for Mirielle to take the last seat at the table, then squeezed in another chair for herself. "Listen up, ladies, this is Pauline."

After a chorus of hellos, Irene introduced each of the women, most of whom lived in house eighteen, including the old, bandaged woman Mirielle had met on the porch. None of their names stuck in her addled mind. All she noticed was their disease. A few had islands of lesions across their skin—dry, thick patches more or less circular in shape. One had pea-sized blisters up and down her arms. Another hadn't any eyebrows, only thickened, red skin in their place. The woman to Mirielle's left had trouble grasping her fork as several of her fingers curled inward like Frank's. The woman across the table couldn't fully close her eyelids, while her cheeks and lips drooped pendulous and flaccid, giving her a strange, doleful expression. Still others had no discernible marks of the disease at all.

"Is it true you're from California?" a woman with only a few pale rings scattered across her skin asked.

"Yes."

"You ever meet any of them moving picture stars?"

Mirielle choked on a sip of milk. "No."

"Too bad," the woman said, and turned back to her food.

The women asked other questions too. Personal ones. Was she married? How long? Children? Boys? Girls? How many? How old? Did any of them have the disease?

"Of course not," Mirielle said to this last question.

Several women at the table snorted and smirked.

"All right, that's enough with the questions," Irene said, scraping the final bits of chicken and potatoes onto her fork. "Let the poor gal breathe, will ya?"

Their conversation turned to speculation about Hector and the other newcomers to which Mirielle offered nothing. Instead, her thoughts wandered back to her examination. How many times had Doc Jack brushed her with cotton that she didn't feel? Had the numbness in her burned finger spread? Her entire body felt fuzzy, as if she were a figure in one of her daughter's drawings—one hand and half of the body messily erased, the rest without definition or adornment, abandoned before completion in favor of a tea party with her dolls.

She looked down at the fork buried in her untouched food. If she jammed the tines through her hand, would she register pain? What about through her heart? Never mind Doc Jack's tests and microscope. A few tiny—what had he called them? Bacilli?—wouldn't keep her from returning home.

"There you are," Irene said loudly, drawing Mirielle from her thoughts. "What did I tell you about being late for supper?"

A young girl approached their table. Her stockings slouched around her ankles and her black and white saddle oxfords were speckled with mud. The air left Mirielle's lungs. There were children at Carville too? Several seconds passed before she remembered to breathe in again.

The girl squeezed in between Mirielle and Irene, setting her supper tray down with a thud.

"No radio privileges, that's what I told you," Irene continued. "Remember?"

The girl nodded.

"Good. You gonna be late again?"

She shook her head and forked a heaping bite of potatoes into her mouth.

"Polly, this is Jean," Irene said.

"Nice to meet you," Mirielle managed after another shaky breath.

Jean turned and looked at her. She chewed loudly, her lips smacking. Her dark hair was plaited in two braids, one of which had started to unravel. Freckles dotted her nose and cheeks along with reddened patches Mirielle guessed to be the disease.

"How old are you?"

Jean swallowed and flashed a wide smile. One of her molars was missing and another partially grown in. She held up nine fingers.

Mirielle's ribs contracted around her heart. Her son would have been nine years old too. "When's your birthday?"

In lieu of answering, Jean took another bite of potatoes.

"She can't talk," one of the women across the table said.

"That ain't true," Irene said. "She don't talk. There's a difference."

Mirielle's ribs squeezed even tighter. How awful for a child so young to suffer like this. She looked around the dining hall for other children and spotted nearly a dozen. Were their parents lepers too? Thank God her own children were hundreds of miles away, safe and sound in the nanny's capable care.

With an unsteady hand, she picked up her glass of milk and took a sip. As she set it back down on the table, a flash of movement within the liquid caught her eye. Something brown and slimy writhed inside the glass. Mirielle screamed, pushing away from the table so quickly her chair nearly toppled.

"What is it, baby?" Irene asked.

Mirielle pointed at the glass, then grabbed her napkin and wiped her tongue.

"Milk gone sour?" Irene picked up the glass and sniffed.

"There's something in there."

Irene frowned and plunged her fingers into the milk. A moment later, she withdrew a squirming, bug-eyed tadpole.

The other women at the table laughed, Jean the loudest.

Irene grabbed Jean's hand and dropped the slimy creature into her palm. "You take this out to the fountain right now then get Mrs. Marvin another glass of milk. And don't you even think about going to the rec hall tomorrow to hear the radio."

Jean pouted and rose loudly from her chair.

"Sorry, baby," Irene said to Mirielle. "Jean can be a little ornery sometimes."

A little? Mirielle wiped her tongue again, then balled up her napkin and threw it onto her plate. Good thing she wasn't hungry. Who knew what else the girl had put in her food.

Conversation continued around her. Jean brought her another glass of milk, but Mirielle wasn't about to drink it. She knew it would be rude to leave while the rest of the women were still eating, but Mirielle didn't care. She grabbed her tray and had started to stand when one of the women asked, "Say, were all them trunks and bags the orderlies carted in this morning really yours?"

"Yes. Only the barest necessities. I won't be staying long. I'm not . . ." Not what? A leper? Doc Jack's tests had proven she was. *Mycobacterium leprae*, he'd said, when he might as well have handed her a bell and shouted *Unclean, unclean!* "I'm not sick."

"You will be." The woman with the bandaged face sneered. "We were all pretty once, dollface."

"Hush, Madge," Irene said, and then to Mirielle, "Don't pay her no mind. The disease gets on differently for everyone."

"My doctor back in Chicago told me I'd be here two months tops," another woman said. "So alls I brought was one lousy suitcase."

Mirielle sat back down. The doctor in California had told her and Charlie the same thing. A few months at most and she'd be home. She was glad to hear it confirmed. Two months in this wretched place without Charlie and her daughters seemed a terrifically long time. But this woman gave her hope. She, like Mirielle, had few outward signs of the disease, and was surely now nearing the end of her sentence. "How much longer do you have?"

"Have for what?"

"Of your two months?"

Everyone at the table laughed.

"Honey, that was five years ago. And I got no hope of leaving anytime soon."

"Five years?"

"That's nothing," another woman said. "I've been here seven."

"If I'd have known then what I know now," the woman from Chicago said, "I'd have brought my whole house with me."

Irene patted Mirielle's knee. "It's not as bad as all that. Every month Doc Jack and the sisters will scrape a little of your skin onto some slides and look at them under the microscope. If you go twelve months in a row without any signs of the germ, they hand you a diploma and you're free to go."

"A diploma?"

"A certificate from the public health office that says you're no longer a public menace."

Mirielle frowned. Menace? That was almost as ugly a word as *leper*. "If you only need twelve negative tests, how come you've all been here so long?"

Several of the women smirked. Jean giggled around a mouthful of cobbler.

"Twelve *in a row*," Irene said.

"How long you've been waiting for your diploma, Madge?" the woman from Chicago asked before turning and whispering to Mirielle, "She's a real old-timer."

Madge spat a piece of chicken grizzle onto her plate then turned her mean, watery eyes on Mirielle. "Twenty-one years."

CHAPTER 9

The next days passed in a blur. A visiting dentist inspected Mirielle's teeth. A technician in the laboratory took blood samples. A nurse vaccinated her against smallpox. She met again with Doc Jack, who told her more about the disease and prescribed her twice-weekly injections of chaulmoogra oil and the same putrid medicine taken in capsule form with meals. The capsules made her stomach roil and, more often than not, came back up just as quickly as she swallowed them, leaving her throat burning and her mouth tasting of rotten fish.

In between meals and appointments, Mirielle kept to her room. The conversation she'd first had with her housemates played round in her mind like a worn-out record. *We were all pretty like you once . . . no hope of leaving anytime soon . . . If I'd have known then what I know now . . .* Twenty-one years Madge had been at this wretched facility. A lot of good it had done her. No wonder she had the disposition of a boiled lobster.

Mirielle couldn't stay for one year, let alone twenty more. She had her daughters to raise. How many times in the months before coming to Carville had she brushed Evie off her lap and told her to go play? How many times had she heard Helen cry and waited for the nanny to soothe her? What kind of a mother had she become? It would take twenty-one years and twenty more, just to make it up to them.

* * *

At lunch on her fourth day, Mirielle felt the familiar stirring in her stomach and hurried outside to vomit. All three of her pregnancies combined hadn't made her as sick as those awful chaulmoogra pills.

Next to the dining hall sat a sunken tea garden and fountain. She hurried over and splashed her face with water. A chill spread over her skin, but her nausea slowly subsided.

Just as she was about to go back inside and brave a few more bites of lunch, a low whistle sounded from behind her. She startled and turned around. A middle-aged man was seated at one of the concrete tea tables nearby.

"Ain't you a choice bit of calico," he said, eyeing her without compunction. The skin on his face was thick and coarse. His nodulous forearms reminded her of a Gila monster. He stood, and Mirielle backed away, bumping into the lip of the fountain.

"Don't believe we've had the pleasure of meeting. You must be new around here." He took a step forward and extended his hand. She let it linger in the air between them.

"What, you afraid I'm contagious?" He kept his hand outstretched a moment more before letting it drop to his side. "Got news for you, doll, so are you or you wouldn't be here."

Mirielle raised her chin and started to walk away.

"What's your rush?"

"I'd rather sit and watch my hair grow than talk to a man as fresh as you."

He chuckled. "My apologies. Been in the can the last four weeks so my manners are a bit rusty."

Mirielle paused halfway up the steps that led back to the dining hall and turned around. "There's a jail here?"

The man seated himself again on the bench beside the tea table, stretching his legs out before him and crossing his ankles. "You bet-cha."

She couldn't help but snicker. "Whomever for? Residents caught speeding their bikes on the walkways? Patients who refuse to take their chaulmoogra pills?"

"Stay awhile, and I'll tell you."

Mirielle hesitated, then descended the stairs and sat on the lip of the fountain. "Well?"

The man smiled. His teeth were the color of urine. "What's your name?"

"Miri—Pauline Marvin."

"Perdy name."

"So, why were you in jail?"

"Whoa, slow down, doll. You're supposed to ask my name now. It's only polite."

"Maybe I don't care."

He leaned forward. "Gonna tell you my real name, not the made-up name the nuns call me." He paused, smiled again, and leaned closer. "My real name's Samuel Hatch. Ever heard of me?"

Mirielle scooted as far back as she could without falling into the fountain. "No."

"I'm the reason this whole joint exists. Caused such a howl a few years back in Washington, D.C., they had no choice but to make a national leper home to lock me up in."

She thought a moment and remembered her father mentioning something about a leper who'd snuck into some ritzy Washington hotel to get the attention of Congress. He'd been an avid reader of both the *Times* and the *Examiner,* her father, and often read the most sensational stories aloud at breakfast. It surprised her now that she recalled the story. Most mornings, she'd come to the table half-asleep, her hair still smelling of cigarette smoke and last night's perfume.

"That was over a decade ago. You've been here ever since? In a jail cell?"

"Nah. Been here since seventeen, but that ain't the reason I was locked up." He patted the concrete bench. "Why don't you come sit next to me?"

Mirielle frowned. He could be crazy. Dangerous. And no doubt his breath smelled as awful as his teeth looked. But curiosity got the better of her. She sat not beside him, but on the opposite bench so the concrete tea table was between them. He swiveled around to face her.

"Go on," she said. "I haven't got all day."

He laughed. "All we have here is time. Years of it. Time to sit and rot and wait for our deaths and ponder over our lives before."

Mirielle suppressed a smirk. A leper-philosopher, wasn't that just dandy.

"I noticed your wedding band. Do have children, Mrs. Marvin?"

The sudden earnestness in his eyes disarmed her. "I do."

"Me too. Three daughters and a son." He looked down. "They're grown now. Married, I expect."

"You don't keep in touch? Don't they know you're here?"

"Oh, they know."

He told her how he and his family had been chased from one town to the next as soon as anyone learned about his disease. For years they'd drifted, living hand to mouth on the outskirts of society. Eventually, the health authorities would catch up with them, and he'd be locked away in an isolation ward. All the while his disease was getting worse and harder to hide.

"No one in your family got sick from you?" she interrupted.

"This gazeek ain't as contagious as they'd like you to think. Youngsters are especially susceptible, they say, but none of my kids ever came down with so much as a bump. Didn't matter none, though." His once earnest eyes turned mean. "Did you know our condition is lawful grounds for divorce, Mrs. Marvin?"

Mirielle touched the silver bracelet around her wrist. That might happen to others, but she and Charlie were different. They'd already endured the worst kind of hardship. If anything, her illness had brought them closer together. She stood. A breeze ruffled the garden's sculpted hedges and overarching palm fronds. Foolish to have let his pitiful ramblings waylay her.

"I ain't told you why I done it yet," Mr. Hatch said.

"Done what?"

"Raised such a fuss in Washington."

She started for the stairs. "I don't care."

"No one wanted me, see? Everyplace I went, every devil's den they locked me up in just wanted to pass me off to someone else. Let the leper be someone else's problem. If they're gonna insist we be segregated from the rest of the world, least they can do is take care of us."

"Is this why they locked you up in jail here? Because you yap so much?"

"Got a gal I see on the outside. She don't care who or what you are so long as you leave a few clams on the nightstand."

Mirielle stopped. What did he mean, *on the outside*? She turned back. "You see her where?"

He flashed his yellow teeth. "Why? You wanna come along?"

"Not a chance, buster. What I mean is does she come here, or do you go there?"

"If you think them sisters allow whores in during visiting hours, you're dumber than you are pretty. 'Course I go to her. At a bawdy-house outside of Baton Rouge. That's why I was thrown in the can."

"For sneaking out?"

"For not coming back."

"They let you out?"

"No, but I could of made it back before the pinhead watchman realized I was gone. Nah, I snuck out to see my Lulu and stayed gone three months this time till some chump in the city turned me in."

"This time? You've snuck out before?"

"Lots of times. I get so sick of this place, I start to go a little mad and forget how shitty life is on the outside. Hell, half the time I get to wherever it was I thought I wanted to go and end up just turning myself in."

He seemed half-mad right now, but Mirielle returned to the table and sat down beside him. "How do you do it?"

CHAPTER 10

That night, Mirielle waited until after she heard the heavy thud of the night watchman's boots atop the walkway in front of the house before sneaking out. She carried a bulging valise in each hand and another tucked beneath her arm. It had taken her several hours to pick through her belongings, deciding what to take and what she could bear to leave behind.

Light streamed from beneath a few of her housemates' doors, but no one stirred as she crept past. She exited the house out the back where a screened porch opened to a short flight of stairs. The ground was damp and boggy from afternoon rain. Mud suctioned onto her patent leather shoes. But the covered walk was too noisy and well lit to traverse. She tiptoed behind the houses toward the front of the colony. Clouds blotted out the stars and muted the moonlight.

Mr. Hatch had told her of a hole in the east corner of the chain-link fence that surrounded the facility. A hole just large enough to shimmy through. Her heart thudded against her breastbone, fueled by equal parts fear and exhilaration. In three days' time, she'd be home again. It was just a matter of getting there. Then she and Charlie could figure out what to do next. Her disease hadn't progressed at all since her visit to the doctor in Los Angeles. Perhaps it was—how had she heard it phrased?—permanently arrested. She'd also heard tell among the residents of doctors on the outside willing to treat lepers without quarantine. Either way, sitting around Carville wasn't helping anything. Her daughters needed her. Charlie needed her. And she needed them.

Dozens of old oak trees dotted the wide lawn between the last houses and the fence. Moss drooped from the boughs, the color of old bones in the darkness. Her valises had grown heavy, and mud squished between her toes inside her shoes. When she reached the fence, she felt along the links for a break. The cold metal scratched the pads of her fingers. Every sound made her start and freeze. She groped along the entire length of the fence from the east corner to the hedgerow that marked the edge of the patients' side of the reserve. Nothing. Not a single break or hole. She retraced her steps, squinting in the near blackness, running her fingers over the metal links as low to the ground as she could manage without crawling.

By the time she'd made it back to the eastern corner, the cloud cover had parted, and moonlight brightened the grounds. But even with the light, Mirielle couldn't find the hole Mr. Hatch had described. Had he lied to her? Had the hole been repaired?

Mirielle's chest tightened, and her eyes smarted. Helen's first birthday was barely a month away. She set down her bags and tugged absentmindedly on her bracelet. Surely, God hadn't kept her alive just to be parted from her daughters. She picked up the valise that held her silver-framed photograph, grabbed ahold of the fence, and started to climb. The metal rattled with her weight and bit into her palms. It snagged on her skirt and tore her stockings, but she kept climbing. Slow. Lurching. Her fingers ached as she neared the top. Holding on with one hand, she heaved the valise up and over the strands of barbed wire crowning the top. It landed with a thump in the weeds on the far side. Now what? How did *she* get up and over?

A breeze swept down from the levee, shaking the fence. She clutched the metal links and closed her eyes until the breeze died down. Then, she released one hand and shrugged her arm out of her coat sleeve. She could use the coat to blunt the barbs. The breeze stirred again, catching the dangling fabric and whipping it back. She grabbed hold of the fence, just as the fingers of her opposite hand began to lose purchase. Her coat slipped down her arm, flapping like a cape from her wrist. Before her fingers could grasp the coat, the wind tugged it free. It fluttered like a lame bird to the ground.

Mirielle considered climbing down to retrieve it, but her hands already trembled with fatigue. If she didn't climb over now, she'd never make it back up. She inhaled the cold night air down to the bottom of her lungs and reached for the top strand of wire. It sagged with the force of her grasp. She loosed one foot from the fence and planted it several links above the other, then shifted her weight and sprang upward, hoping the momentum would carry her over the fence. But she hadn't counted on her skirt catching on the barbs, caging her legs so she could not swing them over. For a moment, she teetered at the top, barbs poking and slicing through her skin. Then she fell. Her flailing arms hit first. The bones of her left forearm snapped. Her backside and skull struck the ground next. She heard herself howl, and her vision blurred.

Mirielle wasn't sure whether she'd passed out, or simply shut her eyes against the pain and howled on. But when her eyes opened, two white buzzards circled above her. No, not buzzards. The sisters and their hats.

"Hush now, dearie," one of them said. "You'll wake the entire colony."

A light flashed in her face, and a male voice said, "What's going on here?"

"Another absconder, I'm afraid," the other sister said.

"No, no." Mirielle tried to shake her head but the motion made her nauseous. "I just . . . tripped."

"Help us get her to the infirmary," the sister said.

The blinding light switched off, and two hands grabbed her beneath the armpits and hoisted her up. Pain blazed from her forearm. She yelped again.

"Can you walk?" the man said. Mirielle recognized him as the night watchman.

Her legs were steady, but the world swayed. Every part of her hurt—her back, her head, but most especially her arm. She took an unbalanced step. "I think so." She took another, teetered, and fell back into the man's arms.

With her good arm looped around the watchman's neck, she managed to limp to the infirmary. Lights were on in several of the houses. Nosy residents pressed their faces to their window screens. Her dress, she realized, was torn and bloodied from the barbed wire, filthy from the mud. But it wasn't as if they hadn't seen worse. Take a look in the mirror if you want a show, she would have yelled, had it not hurt to speak.

The sisters had run ahead and prepared a bed for her. They cut away what remained of her dress and stockings, swabbed her many gashes with alcohol, and helped her slip into a hospital gown. Soon Doc Jack arrived, eyes bleary and hair standing on end, and with him Sister Verena, her long blue dress as crisp and sharp as her gaze.

Doc Jack checked Mirielle's eyes with a small flashlight, then probed along her spine and the back of her head. "Some bruising in the lumbar region and at the base of the skull but nothing more serious," he said to one of the sisters who'd found her and now sat scribbling in Mirielle's chart. Then to Mirielle, he said, "You're lucky. A minor concussion. A broken arm. You could have broken your neck."

His eyes were kind, his tone gentle, but Mirielle looked away and said nothing. She didn't feel lucky. Her arm felt as if it were on fire. Her dress and stockings were ruined. Tomorrow her name would be whispered over every breakfast tray. More importantly, she was still trapped in this hellhole. Helen would turn one without her.

Doc Jack gave Mirielle a shot to help with the pain while he and Sister Verena reset her arm. The medicine fogged her mind and blunted the pain, but she still winced and yelped when Doc Jack reset the bone.

"You shouldn't have tried to run away," Sister Verena said once the procedure was complete, wrapping her arm in gauze then strips of plaster-soaked muslin. "What devil possessed you to think you could scale a barbwire fence?"

Mirielle couldn't tell whether Sister Verena really believed a devil possessed her or if that was simply her fuddy-duddy way of calling Mirielle stupid. Either way, she hated her. Sister Verena had no idea what it meant to be a mother, how the pain of your children's absence was worse than a thousand broken arms.

"I was just out for a nightly stroll when I slipped," Mirielle said. It was a ridiculous lie, but she wasn't about to satisfy Sister Verena with the truth.

"So that blue fabric caught in the barbed wire isn't from that immodest costume you call a dress?"

Mirielle looked her square in the eye. "No."

"And the two bags Watchman Doyle found by the fence are not yours?"

"Nope."

"As you say, then. Must be somebody else's. I'll tell Mr. Doyle to take them straight to the incinerator." She applied the final strips of muslin to Mirielle's cast and stood.

"Wait."

Mirielle's shoes and dresses could burn. But the photograph. That was irreplaceable.

"They're mine. There's another bag on the far side of the fence by the road."

Sister Verena lifted her chin and smirked. "I thought so."

CHAPTER 11

————»•◄————

Mr. Hatch may have lied about the hole in the fence, but he hadn't lied about the jail. No sooner had Mirielle's cast set than she was whisked away to a small, cement building at the far edge of the colony. Her cell was fitted with the barest adornments—a bed, a table, and a thatch-backed chair—all of which creaked and wobbled. The room's lone window, a sliver of a thing high up in the wall, let in meager light and no breeze. Her only companions were a mouse who lived in a crumbling section of the wall near the corner, and Watchman Doyle. Of the two, she preferred the mouse.

Her only reprieve was twenty minutes each afternoon when she was permitted to wander the fenced-in jail yard for exercise. Mirielle relished these short snatches of fresh air and insisted on going out even if it rained. Most days, Irene stopped by. She came straight from her shift in the pharmacy, smelling like fifty-cent perfume and week-old fish. They'd chat for a few minutes through the chain-link fence, Irene doing the lion's share of the talking. Then Irene would slip her a candy bar or magazine when the watchman wasn't looking and say a cheery goodbye.

The rest of the time, Mirielle fixated on escape. Not from the jail, but from the entire wretched colony. She'd have to wait for her broken arm to heal, of course. And this time she'd take only one bag . . . two tops. Instead of carrying them by hand, she'd sling them on her back so both hands would be free to climb the fence. If she wrapped her leather duster around the top strands of barbed wire—carefully this time, not as an afterthought—she could scramble over without a scratch. From there, it'd be easy as pie to get home. No one would suspect a fresh-faced, smartly dressed woman of being a leper. She'd catch a ride in a jiffy and be at the train station in New Orleans before anyone at Carville realized she was gone.

Lying on the lumpy mattress in her cell, she imagined herself back home, the French doors in the great room thrown wide, a sea breeze fluttering the gossamer curtains, an ice-cold gin fizz in hand. Her favorite record played on the phonograph. Laughter sounded from the nursery where the girls played. The briny smell of oysters Rockefeller wafted from the kitchen. Charlie's roadster rumbled up the drive. Home. She just had to escape and make it there.

One afternoon a few weeks into Mirielle's jail sentence, Irene handed a letter through the fence instead of the usual rumpled magazine or half-melted Oh Henry! bar. "I asked Frank to set aside your mail. This came yesterday."

Mirielle grabbed the letter without bothering a glance in Watchman Doyle's direction. There was no return address, but her silly alias—*Mrs. Pauline Marvin*—and the colony's post address were written in Charlie's hand. She traced his tidy lettering before bringing the envelope to her nose. It smelled only of paper, not the spicy scent of Charlie's aftershave she'd hoped to inhale.

"From your hubby?" Irene asked.

Mirielle nodded.

"When my old man was off fighting in the Philippines, I was just as lovestruck as you. God, how I missed him." She toyed with the gaudy gold and ruby ring on her index finger. "Did I ever tell you the story of how he won this for me in a poker match in Dallas—"

Mirielle gave a small cough.

"Aw, hell. Here I am yappin' when you must be wanting some time alone with your letter." She gave Mirielle a wink. "I'll come around tomorrow, baby, in case you got a reply you want me to smuggle out."

Mirielle thanked her, then sat down in the shade of a nearby tree with her back to the jail and tore open the letter.

March 14, 1926

Dearest Mirielle,

  In the quiet hours since your departure, I've thought often of our time together. Surely you know, those early days were among the happiest of my life. Our afternoons at the seaside with the children. Those fancy-dress parties and tea parties and raucous parties in the Hills. How you glowed then! Not even Douglas could boast a more enchanting wife. And what a wonderful mother you were. Everyone loved you then, I most of all.

  But how quickly things fell apart after Felix's death. Neither one of us has known happiness since. I thought Helen's birth might be a chance at a second life for us. But your accident so soon after robbed us of that. My picture failed—the one you didn't even bother to come out and see—and there were grumblings around the studio to drop me. And you, you couldn't understand because you've never endeavored for anything in your life. Never had to struggle.

  I'd put everything I had into my work at the studio. I realize now it was a vain attempt to make up from without for being undernourished within. You'd gone into yourself and were nothing but a shell of a woman, moving from sofa to liquor cabinet and back again without any concern how your blueness was killing us. Even when you were up—playing mahjong with the other studio wives or drifting among the crowds at a party—you were a phantom. Not even Helen's cry or Evie's laughter could stir you. It got so I preferred to go out alone and make excuses for your absence or linger on set long after everyone else had gone home. Loneliness was better than your desolate company. Anyone who saw beyond the glib presentations we made of ourselves could guess at my bravado and your intractable melancholy.

  I do not begrudge you your sadness. How could I when I feel it so deeply too? But your indifference, your impatience, your selfishness—these things all but ruined us. And I worry they may ruin us still. I know you deplore your current situation, but you must follow the doctor's advice and remain

*at Carville until you are well and fully healed. Think what
news of your disease would do to our family. My career
would be shot. The girls hated and sorely teased. We'd have
nothing when already you've left us with so little.*

*I hope you will not hate me for saying so, but I see your
illness as a gift. And I plead you don't squander it. The
woman I met all those years ago shined as much from within
as without. She had passion and pluck. She cared about
people and things beyond her own misery. Here, at last, is a
hardship you cannot drink away. Perhaps, in your struggle,
you can find that woman again.*

*Your husband,
Charlie*

Mirielle stared at the letter dumbfounded. The paper was from
Charlie's stationery, the handwriting unmistakably his own, but the
words . . . surely they hadn't come from his pen. *Selfish, indifferent*—
what kind of man said these things to his wife when she was unjustly
locked away and suffering from a terrible disease? And what did he
mean by saying you *were* a wonderful mother? That she no longer
was?

She started to crumple the letter before realizing there was a
second page behind it. She peeled the pages apart and saw it was
a drawing. Several stick figures standing beneath a crayon-shaded
blue sky and an oblong yellow sun. Mirielle smoothed the crinkled
edges and traced the waxy figures with her finger. Charlie was easy
to spot with a square hat and polka-dotted bow tie. Evie too. She'd
drawn herself with long braids and a pleated skirt. Next stood Mirielle, holding baby Helen in her arms. All four of them wore broad,
U-shaped smiles.

Mirielle smiled too. From the branches above, a bird warbled. A
white butterfly flitted above a nearby patch of clover flowers. Charlie
was wrong. The past year and a half since Felix's death, she hadn't
been as awful as he'd made her out to be in his letter. Maybe not an
ideal wife, but certainly still a good mother.

Her eyes drifted from the butterfly back to Evie's drawing. A fifth
figure, a woman, stood spaced apart from the others. A maid? The

cook? Mirielle examined the woman more closely. She held what looked to be a cocktail glass. Her short coiffure matched Mirielle's peroxide-lightened bob far better than the long, dark hair of the woman holding Helen. Instead of a smile, she wore a frown.

Mirielle had mistaken the nanny for herself. She was the figure apart.

Watchman Doyle hollered from the jail steps that break time was over. Mirielle ignored him. The birdsong that only moments before had sounded so lovely now scratched at her ears. With tear-rimmed eyes, she crammed the letter back in the envelope, then carefully folded the picture and slipped them both in her pocket.

CHAPTER 12

$\blacktriangleright\!\!\!\gg\!\!\circ\!\!\ll\!\!\blacktriangleleft$

Mirielle lay in bed, tossing Charlie's crumpled letter up and down like a baseball. Pale light filtered in through the tiny window, and gray clouds blotted out any trace of sky. It could be noon. It could be nearing evening. She couldn't tell and didn't care.

She'd lost count of how long she'd been holed up in this dingy room. Charlie's letter had arrived three weeks into her jail sentence, but how many days had passed since? Two days? A week? She tossed the wad of paper up, swiping at it when it began to fall. She missed, and the crumpled letter struck her in the nose.

It didn't hurt. Nothing seemed to hurt anymore. Not her broken arm. Not her stiff back. Not her once pounding head. Only her inner parts hurt, as if someone had turned her inside out and scoured her with a Brillo pad.

The letter rolled to a stop beside her on the lumpy mattress. She picked it up and teased it back into a rectangle, smoothing it against the hard surface of her cast to flatten the wrinkles. The paper was worn thin now from having been wadded and unwadded so many times. The ink was smeared too. But it didn't matter. She'd committed nearly every line to memory. The smudged letters were only placeholders, a path to follow with her eye as Charlie's voice sounded in her mind as if it were not a letter at all, but a phonograph recording. Sometimes his voice was plaintive. Sometimes angry. But the words never changed.

He couldn't forgive her for Felix's death. And how could she blame him? It *had* been her fault. But those other charges he'd heaped so insensitively upon her—selfish, indifferent, unaccomplished—of those she was entirely innocent.

Her hand closed around the paper, crumpling it again. He ought to have said these things before when she had the means to act on them. Coward.

She threw the ball of paper so high it struck the ceiling. Flecks of yellowed plaster rained down. She caught the paper this time and tossed it back into the air just as the main door to the jail swung open. Mirielle knew well the sharp whine of its hinges. Charlie's letter landed on the bed and rolled off onto the floor. She didn't bother to retrieve it.

Could it be suppertime already? Her lunch sat untouched on the small table beside the wall. The only things she'd taken from the tray were her chaulmoogra pills. Those she'd thrown into the corner in the hopes of poisoning her cellmate. But the mouse seemed to have better sense than the patients here, for it hadn't touched a single pill.

Clipped footfalls sounded on the floorboards, and a gruff voice said, "Which cell is the absconder in?"

Mirielle heard the scrape of chair legs as Watchman Doyle scrambled to his feet. He coughed and cleared his throat. "Ah, er, Dr. Ross. Good afternoon."

No reply from the doctor.

The watchman cleared his throat again. "Ah, right. The absconder. Cell three."

Mirielle stood. Her bobbed hair had grown out to an unruly length and hung flat and messy around her face. With her arm shackled in a cast, she could barely manage to shampoo it, let alone curl or wave it. Her bangs—too short to tuck behind her ears—tangled with her eyelashes. Even during her bluest of moods, she'd never dreamed of leaving the house or meeting a stranger in such a shabby state back in California. Now, she didn't even bother to open her compact. Whoever this Dr. Ross was, she could meet him with an unpowdered nose.

Her cell door opened. The flood of light temporarily blinded her, and she shielded her eyes with her cast arm. A short, compactly built man strode in.

"Mrs. Marvin, I'm Dr. Ross, the Medical Officer In-Charge here at Marine Hospital Sixty-Six."

Watchman Doyle hovered in the doorjamb until Dr. Ross dismissed him with a nod. To Mirielle he said, "May we talk a moment?"

"Do I have a choice?"

He removed his white officer's hat and tucked it beneath his arm. Four gold stripes decorated his shoulder boards. "No, ma'am."

She sank back onto her bed and motioned to the thatch-backed chair across the room littered with bedraggled magazines and candy wrappers. The doctor did not sit. He glanced about her cell—the untouched lunch tray, the scatter of chaulmoogra capsules in the corner, the rumpled quilt on which she sat—and frowned. "Mrs. Marvin, let me get right to the point."

"By all means. Between meals and my twenty minutes of afternoon exercise, my social schedule's rather full."

His thin-lipped frown deepened. "You've been at this facility less than a month, and already violated rule six of the hospital rules and regulations by attempting to abscond. As you can see, we don't take lightly to such behavior. Sister Verena tells me you're aloof toward the other residents and noncompliant with your treatment regimen. Furthermore . . ."

He droned on, but Mirielle didn't listen. Instead, she watched the way his neatly trimmed mustache bobbed like an inchworm as he spoke. His black uniform was impeccably pressed, the gold buttons polished, not a speck of lint or stray thread to be found. She pitied his wife and the pains she must take each morning before sending him off.

Charlie was a fastidious dresser too, but they had help to look after the laundry. Clothes on the floor were gone by midmorning and back, neatly pressed and hanging in the wardrobe, the next day. She'd happily take the maid's place now, though, if it meant being home. She imagined the smell of shaving cream clinging to Charlie's shirt collars, the smudge of crayon on his cuffs rubbed off from one of Evie's drawings. Her stomach twisted as if she might be sick with longing.

"Mrs. Marvin."

"Hmm?"

That frown again. Dr. Ross threw a sour glance at the chair, then dragged it over to the bed, brushing off the seat before sitting. Magazines and sticky candy wrappers scattered onto the floor. "Mrs. Marvin, I know diagnosis with a disease such as leprosy can be devastating but—"

"Oh, you know, do you? And how's that? Were you torn from your family and locked away in some Podunk hospital in the middle of hell?"

"I've worked at leper colonies all over the world and I assure you, Marine Hospital Sixty-Six is the most up-to-date and idyllic facility there is. Be grateful you weren't cast overboard and expected to swim to the desolate island of Moloka'i or dragged to a shanty colony in India or South Africa."

Mirielle straightened. "Grateful? I'm imprisoned"—she gestured to the cement walls around them—"literally imprisoned with the most grotesque and pitiful human beings I've ever seen. Cast aside to die. My daughters, who knows how many hundreds of miles away, are without a mother. My husband—"

"You cannot outrun this disease." The reproach in his voice was gone, but the words were enough to strike her mute. "I've seen enough people in your position that I can tell you're thinking of absconding again. Maybe you've already planned your escape." He glanced at the bulky plaster cast around her arm and gave a slight smirk. "Who knows, this time you might succeed. For a while. But the disease will eventually catch up to you. And when it does, you'll wish you were here."

Now it was Mirielle's turn to smirk. "I'd never wish myself here. Not for all the gold and diamonds in the world."

His deep-set eyes flickered to the table where Evie's drawing sat propped against the wall on display. "And your family?"

What could Mirielle say to that? She hated Dr. Ross for bringing them into this—Charlie, Evie, Helen—but he was right. Just as Charlie was right. She *had* been distant since Felix's death. Selfish. But she could be the wife and mother she'd been before if given a chance. She just had to get out of here to prove it.

"You're lucky, Mrs. Marvin. Your disease was detected early.

With proper rest, a good diet, healthful activity, and adherence to your treatment plan, you may well be able to arrest the disease before you too are counted among the grotesque and pitiful."

"So I'm just supposed to sit around and hope that someday I'll make it to twelve negative skin tests?"

"Hope, yes. Sit around, no."

Mirielle rolled her eyes. He sounded just like that altruistic fool Frank.

"Why don't you take a job around the colony?"

"Thanks, but I'm not really the working girl type."

He stood and tugged on his jacket until the fabric lay smooth. "There are two types of patients at Carville: those who count themselves among the dead, and those who have the pluck to claim their place among the living. The choice is yours."

Mirielle watched as he started for the door. There was the word again, *pluck*. Had she ever really possessed such a quality? And how the devil could she muster it now in a place like this?

"But there isn't a cure."

Dr. Ross stopped in the doorway of her cell and turned around. "No, there is not."

No cure. Sister Verena and her housemates had all told her the same thing. Chaulmoogra oil might help manage the disease, but did not make it go away. Each time she asked, Mirielle had hoped for a different answer. Each time she'd manage to talk herself out of believing the bleak truth. Like when the doctor had pronounced Felix's death. For days her mind had rejected the idea. He wasn't dead but sleeping. Tomorrow he'd be up galloping around the house again. Not until they'd closed the lid on his coffin and lowered it into the ground did she believe it. Not until she heard the plink of dirt against the wood. It still came back to her—that sound—in her dreams and sometimes even her waking hours. *Plink. Plink. Plink.*

She pressed the cool plaster of her cast against her stomach and wrapped her other arm tightly over it. No cure. No chance to make amends.

"Not at present, anyway," Dr. Ross said.

Mirielle looked up. "You think there's a possibility of finding one?"

"This isn't a leper colony of old, Mrs. Marvin, no matter how provincial it may seem to you. I'm not here out of some over-pronounced sense of charity. I'm a scientist. I believe we can beat this disease."

"How?"

"We're experimenting with new treatments all the time. We're finding new ways to study the bacillus. If there's a cure to be had, this is the place that will find it."

"You really believe that?"

"I wouldn't be here if I didn't."

Mirielle glanced at Evie's drawing, then back to Dr. Ross. "I want to help."

March 30, 1926

Dear Charlie,

I know you didn't mean those awful things you said in your letter. I haven't been myself of late, that's true. But a grieving mother has a right to be a little blue. You make it sound like I was tight from morning to night and didn't care a wink about the rest of you. So I had a drink now and then. It was easier to face the day full of gin or champagne. But that doesn't mean I didn't care for you. At any rate, Carville is completely dry, so you needn't worry on that account any longer.

And it hardly seems fair for you to say I never struggled. After Felix's death, every day was a struggle. You were lucky to have your work. I hadn't any refuge.

You'll be pleased to know I'm working now, though. The big bug himself at Carville came to see me and asked for my assistance in fighting this disease, which, by the way, isn't so terribly contagious as Mr. Niblo and his little film would have you believe. Of course I said yes and from here on out shall be endeavoring alongside the doctors and nurses to find a cure. Very important work, as you can well imagine.

My disease, I have been assured, is a very mild case, and I shall be home in a year when all my tests are negative. Sooner if we find a cure. And then you'll see I'm the same woman you fell in love with and married.

Your wife,
Mirielle

P.S. What excuses have you made to the girls for my absence? I suppose others are asking too. Best we keep it simple. Say I've gone east to take care of an ill relative— a great-aunt in Chicago or some such fancy. You must tell the girls every day that I love them and that I think of them constantly. This, at least, is the truth.

CHAPTER 13

———⊰•⊱———

Mirielle stood in the doorway of the dressing clinic, loath to cross the threshold. When Dr. Ross said he had the perfect idea how she could help, this was not what she'd had in mind. Already the smell of liniment and rotting flesh threatened to unsettle her breakfast. But the words in Charlie's letter—*You've never endeavored after anything in your life*—propelled her inside.

She avoided the patients' wide-eyed stares. Some sat on low stools, soaking their feet in basins of water. Others perched on chairs scattered about the room as the sisters bandaged their raw and ulcerated limbs.

"You're late," Sister Verena said, coming up beside her.

Mirielle fought back a grimace. She hadn't pictured Sister Verena around when she imagined helping to find a cure. "I wasn't sure what to wear."

Sister Verena eyed Mirielle's satin crepe day dress as if it were a burlap sack. "Indeed."

"This won't do? I thought the royal blue was a suitably serious color, while still complementing my complexion, of course. I simply can't wear dark yellows or lavenders with too much pink in them. They wash out my cheeks such that not even rouge can save me."

"You'll need to wear a uniform. Report to the materials office and tell them you'll be assisting in the clinics." She gave Mirielle's outfit another withering glance. "They'll provide you with more *suitable* attire."

A uniform? Uniforms were for maids and waitresses and street sweepers. But Mirielle decided it best not to argue and left in search of the materials office. After several wrong turns, she found it tucked between the laundry and the water treatment plant. When she explained why she'd come, the man at work there rummaged through several racks of woefully outmoded clothes before handing over a heap of scratchy white blouses and skirts.

"This is the uniform?"

The man nodded.

"But shouldn't someone take my measurements first?"

"These are factory-made garments, ma'am. No measurements needed. Alls they come in is small, regular, and stout."

Mirielle's face puckered. "And which did you give me?"

"I got a good eye for lady's sizes." He winked. "You're a regular."

Mirielle scowled. "Regular indeed."

Back in her room, she changed out of her satin dress and into the cotton uniform. The skirt hung clear to her ankles, and the blouse had no shape or softness. The sleeves were too short and the collar scratchy. The cuff was too narrow to button around her plaster cast. No matter how tightly she fastened her girdle, the skirt flared at her hips like a bell. One look in the filmy bathroom mirror and Mirielle cringed. Even her grandmother—when she was alive—had dressed more smartly than this. But for a chance to see Charlie and her girls again, Mirielle would wear anything.

On the way back to the dressing clinic, she passed a group of men seated where the walkway abutted the porch in front of house twelve. The Rocking Chair Brigade, Irene had unaffectionately called these men, warning Mirielle about their perpetually sour dispositions and propensity for gossip.

"You thinking about taking the vows and becoming a nun?" one of the men said as she passed. Several of the others snickered.

"All you need is one of them goofy hats," another said.

"Not that it's any of your beeswax," Mirielle said. "But I've taken a job in the hospital. I'm going to help find a cure for this wretched disease."

"That so?" said the first man. "Well, thank God you're here. Ain't like they've been looking for a cure for the last half-a-century."

Mirielle raised her chin and kept walking.

"Careful you don't chip a nail now."

"Or smudge your perdy makeup."

"And look out that you don't get any of the gazeek on you."

Mirielle made the mistake of glancing back. The man who'd last spoken was covered hairline to collar with rough, lumpy nodules.

"Otherwise, you'll wake up with a face like mine."

There was a sniggering quality to the way he spoke, and several of the men laughed, but his dark, flat eyes were humorless. Her brisk step flagged. Could she really accelerate her own disease by working with others whose illness was more advanced?

"That's better," Sister Verena pronounced when Mirielle arrived back. "Did Dr. Ross explain what your role and responsibilities would be?"

Mirielle shook her head.

"I thought not."

"I told him I wanted to help find a cure, and he said he'd find me a position where I could do that."

Sister Verena pursed her lips. "Dr. Ross oversees all aspects of the facility, but his role is more . . . administrative. As Sister Servant and head nurse, I'm in charge of day-to-day operations of the infirmaries and clinics." She paused and didn't continue until Mirielle gave a short nod.

"You'll report to me or, in my absence, Sister Loretta."

Wasn't that swell, Mirielle thought. She bobbed her head again for Sister Verena to continue.

"Tuesdays, you'll work here in the dressing clinic. Mondays and Wednesdays in the ladies' infirmary. Fridays in the pharmacy and every other Thursday in the shot clinic." She strode the length of the room as she spoke, and Mirielle followed after her. "You'll be tasked with simple things. Cleaning and dressing wounds, rolling bandages, preparing supplies for disinfection, answering patient call bells, helping change their linen . . ."

Mirielle stopped, and Sister Verena spun around. "Is something wrong?"

"How's any of that going to lead to a cure?"

"Do you have advanced schooling in chemistry?"

"No."

"Biology, pharmacology, medicine?"

Mirielle looked down. Her shoes gleamed with the fresh polish she'd given them last night while envisioning herself surrounded by glass tubes and beakers like the photographs of Marie Curie she'd seen in *Vanity Fair.* "No."

"Do you have any skills whatsoever related to the medical profession?"

"I cared for my children when they were sick." She raised her eyes and met Sister Verena's gaze, doing her best to look assured.

"Then you should do very well at the tasks I've laid out for you." She pointed to two men soaking their feet. "Dry their legs so Sister Loretta can rebandage their wounds and then prepare fresh water for the next patients."

Mirielle sighed and grabbed a stack of towels from the nearby linen cupboard. Sister Verena thought her useless, incapable of even menial work. Just like the men in the Rocking Chair Brigade. Just like Charlie. Well, she'd prove them all wrong.

She marched over to the first man but hesitated before bending down. Several of his toes were missing, and open sores covered his legs. This is what the men in front of house twelve had meant by the gazeek. The poisonous microbes that caused their disease. She imagined them like teeny-tiny jellyfish floating in the water and clinging with their tentacles to the man's skin. The minute she touched him, they'd latch on to her too, adding to the gazeek already inside her.

He looked at her expectantly. She glanced from his face to his ruinous feet and shook her head. There had to be some other position for her. She'd never make it to twelve negative tests or survive until they found a cure doing this work. But before she could stand and slink away, a soft, fleshy hand patted her shoulder.

"Let me show you how it's done, dearie." Sister Loretta squatted down beside her with impressive ease for one so ancient. She smiled at Mirielle and grabbed a towel. "All right, Ronnie, here we go." She spread the towel wide, and the man raised his leg. "The skin's especially fragile after soaking, so dab, don't rub. And don't forget between the toes."

With gentle, careful movements, she dried one leg, then the other. The smile she wore never faltered. "Many patients suffer nerve damage and can't feel much anymore, so a light touch is best. And when you get fresh water, make sure it isn't too hot or you're liable to cause a burn."

Mirielle nodded, remembering her own incident with the hot curling iron.

When Sister Loretta finished dabbing between what remained of the man's toes, she draped the towel over her arm and moved the basin aside so the man could lower his legs. Milky, fetid water sloshed over the basin's side. Mirielle dropped the towels she was holding and lurched back like a crab, smacking her cast on the hard floor. Pain radiated through her arm.

Sister Loretta mopped up the spilled water as if it were nothing.

"Aren't you afraid?" Mirielle asked. "Of catching the gaz— the disease?"

"I came to Carville back in 1904." She glanced at Mirielle, her expression serene. "You were probably just a little girl then. The Daughters of Charity had already been here a decade taking care of patients. Not once in all those years has anyone on staff gotten the disease."

"Really?"

"We wash our hands and do our best to keep the place clean. It's not a very hardy germ. Feebly contagious is all."

"I don't need to worry then? I mean, about making my own condition worse."

Sister Loretta stood. "A little care, and you'll be just fine, dearie."

Mirielle nodded and gathered up the towels she'd thrown aside. She glanced at the basin of water, trying to rid her imagination of all the tiny, jellyfish-like germs swimming inside. After all, how many times had she waded in the ocean without being stung? She tucked the towels under her arm and picked up the basin, bracing it against her cast. She could do this. A little care, and she'd be fine. With each slow step to the hopper, she repeated Sister Loretta's assurances in her mind.

She flinched with the splash of water when she upturned the basin over the hopper, but a strange satisfaction bloomed inside her watching the water swirl down the drain and all those tiny germs along with it.

CHAPTER 14

The next day, Mirielle spent the afternoon hastening from bed to bed in the ladies' infirmary. No sooner had she refilled a glass of water or fluffed a pillow than another patient's bell rang. Everything was made doubly hard with her arm still in a cast. Her feet ached when she returned to her room, and she would have ignored the call to supper had Irene not barged in and dragged her to the dining hall.

Fastening the buttons of her beastly uniform the next morning, Mirielle began to second-guess this helping business. How was fetching someone an extra blanket or emptying their bedpan getting her any closer to home?

When she arrived at the small, one-room X-ray building for her shift, a long line had already formed along the walkway outside. Twice weekly the building doubled as the shot clinic. Her fellow residents looked resigned, if not a bit wary as they stood waiting. Mirielle tugged at her ill-fitting collar, then shimmied past and went inside.

The hulking X-ray equipment had been pushed against the walls to provide room for a dressing screen and a small table crowded with supplies. Doc Jack sat on a stool behind the screen while Sister Verena inspected a set of needles each the size of an ice pick. When she was through with her inspection, she handed Mirielle a record book.

"Listed here is each patient's prescribed dose of chaulmoogra oil. Call it out when they enter and I will prepare the syringe. You must also keep the supply table stocked and needles cycling through the boiler for sterilization. Do you think you can manage that?"

Mirielle grabbed the book and rolled her eyes. Of course she could manage it.

The first patient entered and told her his name. She opened the book, balancing the spine on her cast arm, and flipped through the pages until she found his record. "Eight cc's."

The man shuffled behind the screen and unbuttoned his drawers while Sister Verena drew the medicine into a syringe. A sluggish air bubble drifted upward through the oil when she tapped the glass. She handed the syringe to Doc Jack, who wiped one side of the man's rear with betadine, then jabbed in the needle. A rush of queasiness washed over Mirielle as she watched the plunger descend. When Doc Jack removed the needle, a syrupy mix of blood and oil oozed from the injection site.

Mirielle unbuttoned her collar and fanned herself with the record book to keep her breakfast down while Doc Jack mopped up the mess with a cotton square. He taped another square over the site and said, "All done," at the same time as Sister Verena said, "Next dose."

Mirielle turned back to the line of patients. The man in front grunted out his name, and she thumbed through the record book, her stomach still swimming. Soon it was all she could do to keep up with names and doses, never mind the dwindling supply of cotton squares and the pile of sticky needles in need of sterilizing. Morning passed in a blur, and her queasiness faded. She bustled between the back table where the boiler sat and the line of waiting patients, juggling the open record book in one arm and fresh supplies in the other.

The lunch bell brought only a brief reprieve. Soon patients were lining up again. Most seemed to remember exactly where they'd stood before the bell and filed into line without fuss or jostling. But Jean, the young girl who lived with Mirielle in house eighteen, cut in near the front. Several of the adults behind her cussed and grumbled.

"Brat," one of them said.

"Get back to the end of the line, or I'll drag you there by the ear-lobe," said another.

"Hey," Mirielle said, setting down the record book and moving toward the ruckus. "Leave her alone."

After the tadpole incident, she'd kept her distance from the girl, though she suspected the crayon markings that had mysteriously appeared on her cast when she woke this morning and the tangle of worms between her sheets two nights before to be Jean's handiwork. But that didn't mean the other patients had any right to bully her. She was a child, after all. Only a few years older than Evie.

"Ain't no one allowed to cut in line," a fellow with Jack Dempsey–sized arms said. His red, disease-thickened face made him look all the more like a man who'd just come from twelve rounds in the ring.

"That doesn't mean you get to call her names."

"I can do whatever I damn please."

Another man stepped out from his place in line. "*Mais*, Dean! Ya in a hurry to get your ass poked today?"

Mirielle recognized him—first by his blunt, misshapen hands, then by his vivid blue eyes—as Frank, the tour guide she'd yelled at her first day at Carville. He waved over Jean with one of his claw-hands. "Anyway, I promised I'd save a spot for her."

Jean skipped to his side, a grin, sweet as it was sinister, stretched across her face. Dean scowled but quit his griping, and Mirielle returned to the tiresome record book.

"I see ya found a way to skip the line," Frank said when he and Jean made it to the front several minutes later. "Looks good on ya, the uniform."

Mirielle didn't return his smile. "No one looks good in matte white."

He chuckled. "You're about as good at taking a compliment as ya are at absconding."

Ignoring his steady gaze, she balanced the record book in the crook of her cast arm and flipped through to find their names. She'd called out Jean's dose to Sister Verena and was looking for Frank's when a flash of movement caught her eye. Before she'd realized what was happening, squares of cotton were floating in the air. They clumped together in a small cloud as they left Jean's outstretched hand, then dispersed as they fluttered downward like huge square snowflakes. Jean giggled. She skipped past the dressing screen and out the door. Cotton squares landed everywhere—on the X-ray equipment, on the floor, on Doc Jack's head.

"Ahem," Sister Verena said, setting down her syringe and brushing the white squares off her shoulders and the pointy wings of her hat.

Mirielle bent down and began scooping the cotton off the floor. Frank squatted beside her.

"I've never met an ornerier child in my life," she muttered. Her children would never misbehave like that.

"Don't think too badly of her," Frank said, helping Mirielle with the mess. "Been here three years and she ain't heard nothing from her family. Not a visit or a letter. Her daddy, he dropped her at the front gate and didn't look back, him."

Mirielle glanced at him, then back to the cotton squares scattered across the floorboards. The ever-present ache she felt for her daughters deepened. Did they know how hard she was trying to make it back to them? Or did they feel as abandoned and forgotten as Jean?

CHAPTER 15

From the outside, the pharmacy looked like one of the patient houses: a long, single-story structure adjoining the walkway. But instead of beds and side tables and living room sofas, it was crowded with cabinets and balance scales and gurgling equipment.

Mirielle lingered in the doorway, delighting in the strange sounds and smells. This was the sort of place she'd imagined in jail. This was the sort of place they'd find a cure.

She introduced herself to the sister in charge, Sister Beatrice, and followed like a chick at the woman's heels as she showed Mirielle around. An industrial-sized mixer sat on a counter churning ointment. Disinfectant bubbled in a double boiler nearby. Percolating jars of pale, yellow liquid crowded a bench along the opposite wall. At the back of the room, open shelves crammed with medicine bottles stretched to the ceiling.

"What are we working on today?" Mirielle asked. "Something new?"

"Why, yes. Have a seat and I'll get the supplies."

Mirielle grabbed a stool and sat at a large, marble-topped table in the center of the room. If *Vanity Fair* came to interview Mirielle about how she, a lowly patient, found a cure for leprosy, this was where they'd set up for the cover photo. She'd sit just where she was now, angled toward the camera, holding a beaker and smiling. How proud Charlie would be of her then.

The uniform would have to go, of course. She'd need a haircut and maybe a permanent too. It wouldn't be hard to persuade a beautician to visit the colony once everyone was cured.

Irene, who also worked in the pharmacy, arrived just as Sister Beatrice shuffled to the table with a stack of iron trays.

"Sorry I'm late," she said. "I had a little dispute to settle back at the house."

Pennies to dollars it involved some prank Jean had played on another of their housemates. At least Mirielle wasn't the only one the girl terrorized. She hadn't forgotten what Frank had said yesterday about Jean's father. As cruel as Charlie's letter had been, at least he hadn't forgotten her.

Irene sat beside Mirielle at the table. The white cotton uniform fit her worse than it did Mirielle. The fabric pulled and bunched around her wide hips, and the buttons at her bust strained to stay fastened. So much for factory-made garments, stout sizes and all.

Sister Beatrice drew Mirielle's attention back to the iron trays. Each one was lined with shallow pockets. Capsule molds, she told Mirielle. Next the sister brought over a hot plate and set a pot of gelatin atop it. Once the gelatin melted, Mirielle and Irene's job was to coat each of the molds in the hot liquid.

The task proved far less glamorous than Mirielle's imaginings. More than once, she burned her fingers with the molten gelatin, not always realizing she'd done so until seeing the red and blistered skin. Her bulky cast constantly got in the way. Irene didn't burn herself once. She yapped nonstop as she worked, hardly looking at the molds, and still managed a more even coating than Mirielle did with her trays.

Irene talked in stories. "I remember this one time when . . ." Or, "Back in my younger days . . ." There wasn't a clear chronology or connection from one to the next, and Mirielle had a hard time keeping up. Sometimes, Irene would stop in the middle of a story and veer off in an entirely new direction. Other times, she'd pause midsentence, tap on Mirielle's cast and say, "Careful, baby. Watch out for them drippings," and Mirielle would look down to see she'd burned herself yet again.

By the time they'd finished all the trays, Mirielle had caught enough fragments of Irene's stories to piece together her history. She'd grown up in farm country somewhere in the eastern part of

Texas. Married young. Had a son. Lost her husband in some war. Not the Great War. Cuba? The Philippines? Mirielle couldn't remember. After his death, Irene and her son moved to the city. She married again. Divorced. One husband, she'd wed for love. The other, a "real son-of-a-bitch," she'd wed for money. But Mirielle wasn't sure who was who or in which order they'd come. Eventually, Irene and her son had ended up back in East Texas where they'd started, this time with means to buy and run their own farm. Their own "hunky-dory ending." Until the disease.

When the gelatin cooled and set, Sister Beatrice brought over a large jar of chaulmoogra oil. The rancid-fish smell Mirielle had come to know so well spread through the room the minute the sister removed the lid.

"I thought we were working on something new today," Mirielle said.

Sister Beatrice smiled and held up a can of cocoa powder. "We are."

"Cocoa powder might be the key to fighting the disease?"

"Oh, I doubt that," the sister said, "but it might make the chaulmoogra go down easier."

"And hopefully stay down," Irene said under her breath.

Sister Beatrice gave Mirielle and Irene each a glass pipette. She instructed them to fill the capsules with oil and top them off with a pinch of cocoa before sealing them with a drop of hot gelatin. Irene got right to work, but Mirielle set down her pipette and buried her face in her hands.

"What's wrong, baby?"

"Cocoa? Cocoa!" She slammed her cast down on the table, regretting it the moment after when pain shot through her arm. The jar of chaulmoogra oil rattled, and her pipette rolled toward the edge. Irene caught it before it could fall to the floor and shatter. "I thought we'd be doing something important today."

"We are. How many times have you puked up your chaulmoogra pills and your lunch with it? Heck, half the folks around the colony would just as soon grease their hair with this stuff as eat it."

"It's still not a cure. Nothing I'm doing—not here or in the infirmary or that horrid dressing clinic—is helping me get home."

"That ain't true."

Mirielle swiveled around to face her, reaching out with her good hand and clutching Irene's. "I've got to get home. You're a mother. You understand."

"You knock out twelve negative tests, and you got your parole."

"I can't wait for that. A year, maybe longer. And some people never make it to twelve. What if I'm one of them? A cure is the only sure bet."

"It ain't that simple. And it ain't gonna happen overnight. In the meantime, what you're doing does matter."

Mirielle let go of Irene's hand, picked up her pipette, and plunged it into the jar of oil. "How does filling capsules or changing bedpans or ticking off names in a ledger matter?"

"For one, if you're anything like me—and you are—you'll go crazy if you don't stay busy."

Mirielle counted out ten drops then moved on to the next capsule. Already Irene was wrong. They were nothing alike. Never mind Irene's misguided fashion sense or her cheery personality. Mirielle didn't know the first thing about busy, unless one counted mahjong in the afternoon and a dancing party in the evening as busy. And she certainly didn't see why busy was a desired state. The past four days had been the busiest of her life, and all she wanted to do today when she was done was crawl into her bed and sleep for a week. Busy was what gave people wrinkles, premature gray hair, and a nervous laugh.

"Maybe I'm not cut out for this . . . work thing."

Irene spun around. "You tellin' me you never worked? Not a day in your whole life?"

"I hosted a charity luncheon for the Red Cross during the war."

"Baby, that don't count as work. I was milking cows and collecting eggs before I could walk. After my first marriage, I slung hash for five years straight at an eating-house in Dallas. It sure beats mucking out a barn. Them customers could get handsy, though."

"You were a waitress at a hash house?"

Irene shrugged. "What of it? A gal's gotta eat as surely as a fella does. And I had my son to look out for. You tellin' me you wouldn't put on a uniform and serve a man breakfast if it meant feeding your girls."

"Of course I would," she said, and tugged on her abysmally loose and scratchy collar. "I'm wearing a uniform now, aren't I? It's just . . . I still don't see how it helps."

"The uniform?"

"No, this." She waved her pipette like a pointer at the mess of cocoa powder and oil and gelatin before them.

"Listen, everyone gotta find their own meaning in what they do. For some folks, it's keeping busy. For some, it's serving God. For some, it's just plain surviving."

Mirielle looked down at the marble table. It reminded her of her vanity at home. The swirls of black and gray through the glittering white stone. How had she ended up here? What she wouldn't give to be dipping into face powder instead of cocoa, smelling her favorite *eau de la violette* perfume instead of fishy chaulmoogra oil.

Irene gave her a gentle nudge with her elbow. "I ain't saying someday you ain't gonna help find the cure to free us all and get you home. But there's gonna be a heck of a lot of days between now and then you gotta show for, baby, and they ain't all gonna be pretty. Best you have some reason to get up in the morning or one of these days you just won't bother. They don't call it the disease of the living dead for nothin'."

Mirielle gave a slow nod, then straightened and dipped her pipette back in the oil. "I wanna prove Sister Verena wrong. My husband Charlie too. They both think I can't stick with anything."

Irene flashed her a conspiratorial smile. "That's a good start."

April 14, 1926

Dear Charlie,

How are Evie and Helen? Send another of Evie's drawings with your next letter, will you? And you must write the moment Helen starts walking or says her first word. I hate to think that when I return home she'll be talking and waddling about and I will have missed all those precious first moments. You'll teach her to say mama, won't you?

I miss you all, but you'll be happy to know my work here keeps me terrifically busy, occupying my hands while you occupy my thoughts. For several hours any given day, I am beside the nurses and doctors in saving the lives of my fellow patients. It's all very important and exciting. I'm told I am a quick study and bring a sense of cheer and style to this otherwise desolate facility.

Consumption and pneumonia are bigger killers here than the disease itself, though it certainly does its share of damage. And people's limbs don't just fall off either. That's plain hooey. Many patients suffer injuries to their hands and feet on account of nerve damage. Without watchful care, these injuries can fester and end in the amputation of a toe, a finger, or even an entire leg. Other patients suffer muscle weakness or even go blind. But fear not, I am still in the utmost health. Not a new spot or symptom since I arrived.

I could continue on for pages about all that I am doing but simply haven't time. Hugs and kisses to the girls. Should any of our friends wish to write while I'm away tending to my sick aunt, please ensure they can do so care of you.

Your Wife,
Mirielle

CHAPTER 16

———➤◦◄———

Mirielle stood with her back to the mirror and craned her neck, straining to see her reflection. Was the lesion on her shoulder darker? No, that was just the blotchy glass. The spot on her lower back, however, was bigger than it had been last week by half a centimeter. At least from this angle. When she looked over her opposite shoulder, the spot appeared smaller.

But neither her vantage nor the mirror could account for the new lesion on her neck. She'd noticed it in jail, but blamed the cell's musty bedclothes and bad air for the irritation. Then, after she was released, she blamed the scratchy collar of her uniform. But now, after nearly a month, there was no denying what it was.

She ran her index finger over the spot. It was scarcely larger than a dime but red and rough to the touch. A few strands of pearls or a fur stole would be enough to hide it. A little face powder might do the trick too. But she couldn't help thinking again of *Ben-Hur*—the horrified face of the guard when he discovered Ben-Hur's mother and sister in the dungeon, the way the crowds scattered at the cry of "*Leper!*" "Not a sound," his sister said when they'd seen Ben-Hur sleeping. "He belongs to the living—we to the dead."

Was that true? Was Mirielle only fooling herself with her hopes for a cure? Did she too belong to the dead? It certainly felt that way when she looked around the colony. And not because of ruined faces and missing limbs. It was in their eyes. Even those who could see had an emptiness to their stare.

Not everyone was that way. Not Frank or Irene. Even Jean had a glint, albeit a mischievous one, in her eyes. But perhaps they were fools too.

Mirielle wrapped herself in her kimono, cinching the silk ties tight about her waist, and returned to her room to dress for the day. One thing could be said for her dreary uniform: it saved her the trouble of sorting through her dresses and hats and shoes to pick a suitable ensemble. Doc Jack had recently removed her cast. Her lower arm was still tender, but at least she could now button both sleeves.

When she arrived at the dressing clinic, several patients were already soaking their feet or gritting their teeth as the sisters examined and redressed their wounds.

"Fetch me some Ichthyol ointment please, Mrs. Marvin," Sister Verena called before Mirielle even had the chance to hang up her raincoat.

She shrugged out of her coat and grabbed the ointment from the cabinet.

"Is it too much to ask that you be on time?" Sister Verena said when Mirielle handed her the jar. She was seated beside a patient in a wheelchair. One of his legs was missing at the knee. The other, outstretched and propped atop a stool, was covered with sores.

"This isn't the right ointment. How many times do I have to tell you, Ichthyol is the purple ointment, not the white." She handed the jar back to Mirielle. "I suppose a minim of focus is too much to ask as well."

Mirielle stalked back to the cabinet and swapped the white ointment for the purple. Nothing she did was enough for Sister Verena. What did that even mean, *minim*?

For the next several hours, Mirielle dried feet, emptied water basins, and fetched supplies. Near the end of her shift, Hector came in. He limped when he walked, and the skin around his wrists was still faintly red from the handcuffs. He sat down on one of the low stools, and she filled a basin of water for him.

Mirielle had seen him only a handful of times since their arrival, and always just in passing. Like Irene, he seemed taken with this notion of busyness and worked several odd jobs around the colony. When he wasn't at work, he kept to the company of other Mexicans, but today, as always, he doffed his hat and nodded at her.

"*¿Cómo está,* señora?"

Mirielle had to stop herself from reaching up to hide the lesion on her neck. "Just peachy," she said dryly. "You?"

"*No estoy mal.*"

She watched him unlace his shoes, remove his socks, and tuck them neatly beneath his stool. He rolled up his pants—hospital issue, Mirielle could tell by the dull fabric and uneven seam, but a vast improvement to the tattered trousers he'd arrived in. When he started to remove the old bandages that covered his feet and legs, he winced.

"Here, I'll help." Mirielle scooped a palmful of water from the basin. "Sometimes getting the gauze a little wet helps to loosen it." She dripped the water onto his bandages and began to peel and unwind them. It was slow, halting work. Whenever she met resistance or felt the dressing sticking to his skin, she scooped up more water. At first, Hector sat rigid, his jaw clenched and knuckles white. But soon, his shoulders and hands relaxed.

Mirielle relaxed too. She tucked a towel beneath her knees for cushioning and rolled up her shirtsleeves. His skin was rough and chapped with several outcroppings of nodules that oozed milky fluid. One of the gashes he'd incurred during his flight in Yuma still hadn't healed. She worked with particular care around these areas so as not to cause him any more pain.

"I'm not really that peachy, to tell you the truth. I awoke to find toothpaste in my slippers this morning. Courtesy of that pesky Jean, no doubt. And this job. It's not one bit what I expected. I thought I'd be . . . well, I guess I don't know what I thought, but not this." She looked up at him, awaiting some response, but he only smiled. Probably didn't speak much English. She continued. "Everyone's got their strengths, right? Well, this isn't mine. I'm good at . . . dancing and looking nice and throwing a swell party."

She finished unbandaging his right leg and guided his foot into the basin of water. Then she started on the left. "I guess when I say it that way, it sounds pretty frivolous. Not that you understand me. But I was a good mother too. Before, anyway. I've got two daughters and miss them like mad. My littlest one just had her first birthday. Who knows"—her voice faltered and she wiped her eyes on her sleeve—"who knows if she'll even remember me when I get home. But I will get home. It's the one thing I'm sure of."

She peeled away the last of his dressings and ushered his other foot into the water. He gave a long sigh and wriggled his toes.

"I think you are very good at this," he said.

Mirielle looked up at him. "You speak English?"

"I was born in California, same as you."

"Oh . . . er . . . sorry, I assumed . . . How do you know I was born there?"

"I recognize you from the magazines. Your husband's last movie was *muy graciosa*, very funny."

Mirielle's stomach tightened. She glanced quickly around, but no one else was close enough to have heard him.

"He'd love you for saying that. The critics didn't think it was *muy graciosa* or even a little *graciosa*." She looked down at the smooth depression at the base of her finger. She never wore her wedding band when she worked at the clinic. "I . . . I didn't even see it. You won't tell anyone, will you? I mean, who I am. Who my husband is."

Gossip spread quicker here than a flask of gin at a dry party. One indiscretion and the entire colony would know her real name by suppertime. A spiteful resident, a letter to a tabloid editor, and the entire country would know she was a leper.

"Your secret is safe with me, señora."

Maybe it was the warmth in Hector's eyes, or their shared journey in that stuffy boxcar, but Mirielle trusted him. "Thank you."

She gathered up the used bandages and toweled off the damp floor. Her gaze snagged again on the long gash across his leg that hadn't healed since their arrival. "How come you tried to run away?"

"I could ask you the same question."

"You've got a family too?"

"*Sí*. Three boys and a girl. They're grown now, though."

"You were trying to get back to them." She looked out the rain-speckled window at the low, gray clouds. The grounds of Carville stretched for acres beyond the warren of houses and medical buildings. But sometimes it felt as claustrophobic as her jail cell. What good were tennis lawns and baseball diamonds, soda fountains and movie projectors when you couldn't see your children?

"I was not running back to them. I'm not welcome there anymore."

His words drew her attention from the window. "Where were you trying to go, then?"

He shrugged. "Somewhere I could get work."

He told her how he'd met his wife, and they'd married young. Life had been good for a while. They owned a small bean farm south of Seventieth Street. Then came the disease. Fast too. Not like for some who go years with nothing more than a little numbness and a few spots. Word got around, he told her, and no one would buy their crop anymore. They lost the farm. His kids were expelled from school. They moved north to San Gabriel, but soon people were talking there too. The health department came around and threw him in the pest house. Meanwhile, his wife and children were shunned and starving. Nobody wanted a leper's wife picking their fruit, scrubbing their floors, not even mucking their stables. Nobody wanted a leper's kids playing with their own. He escaped, and they moved again. And again. Without treatment, the disease got worse, impossible to hide.

"No one else in your family got sick?" she asked.

"*Gracias a Dios*, no. But, by the end my wife was afraid to look on me." He broke from Mirielle's gaze and stared at the blank wall behind her. "I overheard my oldest boy say he wished I'd hurry up and die so they'd all be free of me. After that, I left."

He told Mirielle about the odd jobs he worked along the coast while she dried his feet, dabbing at the beads of water that clung to his red, waxy skin. He stitched together flour sacks and slept beneath them when it rained, sending nearly all his wages back to his family.

"Even with me gone, life is still hard for them," he said. "Without the farm, they have nothing. I didn't know there'd be work here. It isn't much, but it's something."

Silence stretched between them as Mirielle finished drying his feet. The tenderness in his voice when he'd spoken about his family affirmed how much he still cared for them. The desperation in his eyes when he'd fled in Yuma made sense to her now. She felt it too, hotter now than before, as if she'd swallowed part of his story and taken it on as her own.

Mirielle handed him his shoes. "Once there's a cure, we can both go home."

"I hope I make it that long, señora." He glanced down at his ulcerated legs.

"You will."

He limped across the room to where Sister Verena waited with her ointments and fresh bandaging. Mirielle grabbed the water basin and carried it to the hopper. She caught her reflection in the trembling water—hair frizzy, nose shiny, lesion flaunting itself red and ugly above the collar of her blouse. Hopefully, she'd make it that long too.

CHAPTER 17

⇒►·◄⇐

That night, Mirielle sat on the worn but cushy sofa in house eighteen's living room. Her back ached from hours of schlepping water and leaning over stinky feet. The chaulmoogra pills she'd taken with supper rumbled in her stomach. When she burped, the strange taste of chocolatey fish lingered on her tongue.

She tried not to think about what awaited her tomorrow in the infirmary. More bedpans, no doubt. And call bells. And cranky patients who wanted their pillow readjusted every five minutes. She could just not show up. Sleep in and take a long, hot bath while her housemates were gone to lunch. But then Sister Verena would have the satisfaction of being right about her. Charlie, too. Besides, Hector had told her she was good at the job. When she'd unwrapped and dried his legs, she hadn't once flinched or gagged like she had her first days in the clinic.

She rubbed her stiff neck and tried not to think about how nice it would be to have an ice-cold gin fizz in her hand and a jazzy record playing in the background. Irene owned a Victrola phonograph cabinet and kept it in the living room for anyone to use. But someone—likely Jean—had broken the turntable. Mr. Li, a Chinese man who lived in house thirty and could fix anything, according to Irene, was waiting on parts to repair it. So Mirielle had only the chirp of crickets carried through the open window to fill the silence.

She'd heard of people coming to cities like New York, Chicago, Los Angeles and suffering a nervous breakdown because of the constant noise. Mirielle felt just the opposite. The country silence strained her nerves. No wonder an entire house at Carville was reserved for those who'd gone mad.

She slipped off her shoes and curled her feet beneath her on the sofa. One of her housemates had left a rumpled magazine on the side table. She picked it up for something to do. A young starlet with glossy black hair and honey-brown eyes stared up at her from the cover. They'd met once at a party, hadn't they? Mirielle couldn't remember. There were so many of this type of girl in Hollywood— young, pretty, hopeful. You could see the ambition in their eyes like daggers. She and Charlie laughed about it. The way these girls fawned over him and anyone else they thought had pull at the studios. They were mad about each other then, she and Charlie, as close as any two people could be. Now the thought of him alone at these parties, surrounded by fawning ingenues, made her unsettled stomach roil all the more.

The longer she stared, the more daggerlike the cover girl's eyes became. Mirielle pulled the collar of her blouse over her lesion and flipped open the magazine to rid herself of those eyes. Ads for typewriters and toothpaste filled the first few pages. Then the table of contents and a full-page spread announcing Paramount Pictures's upcoming release, *A Kiss for Cinderella*. She didn't have to flip back to the cover or check the contents page to know the magazine was months out of date. She remembered Charlie talking about the picture just after Christmas. That was true of everything at Carville, though, dreadfully provincial and months, if not years, behind the times.

But it beat listening to crickets. She'd just turned to the first article and begun reading when the creak of floorboards caught her attention. She looked up and saw Jean standing in the doorway. Irritation prickled her skin. How long had Jean been there gawking? What mischief was she up to?

She flashed Mirielle a shy smile, and Mirielle's irritation retreated. Her daughter Evie had the same spattering of freckles across her nose and the same naughty habit of sucking on the ends of her braids. It seemed a trifle now, though, and Mirielle's throat tightened thinking of all those times she'd scolded Evie when she ought to have let her be.

"You don't have to stand there," Mirielle said.

Jean hovered a moment more in the doorway, then bounded over and hopped onto the sofa next to Mirielle. The seat cushion groaned. She pointed to the magazine.

"Just a gossip rag," Mirielle said. "Stories about actors and actresses. Reviews of the latest pictures. Nothing a little girl would find interesting."

Jean frowned and jabbed a finger at the pages.

"Don't you have paper dolls or spinning tops or some such toys to play with?"

Jean shook her head. Mirielle knew that wasn't true. She'd stepped on the crayons and rusty jacks Jean left lying around. But she couldn't blame the girl for being bored when her entire world amounted to a tangle of hospital buildings and a few acres of swamp.

"All right. You can listen along."

The first article was about an actress who'd retired from the screen after suffering a nervous breakdown. In her final days, she couldn't manage more than three to four hours' work a day and fainted from sheer weakness many times on the set. "Not surprising," Mirielle interjected. "Those studios run their actors ragged."

She paused, remembering Charlie's last film, the one he'd started not long after her accident. He'd all but lived at the studio. He blamed that on Mirielle's moods, but she knew the big producers were just as much at fault.

Jean nudged her, and Mirielle continued to read. The actress's doctors sent her to some mountain spa for absolute rest and quiet. Here, Mirielle paused again and snickered. If that place were anything like Carville, all that quiet had likely made her condition worse.

" 'It was terribly pitiful to see such a mesmerizing woman grow so thin and anxious,' " Mirielle said, reading a comment made by one of the actress's old screen pals. " 'Her once lovely complexion had become like that of a lep—' " Mirielle choked on the word.

She glanced at Jean, who lay with her head on the opposite armrest, jogging one foot in the air and sucking on the end of her braid. Hopefully, Mirielle's mumbling had been enough to conceal that hateful word. She closed the magazine and set it facedown on her lap. "That's enough Hollywood gossip for tonight. I'm sure it's past your bedtime."

Jean frowned, but peeled herself off the sofa and trudged to her room. When she was gone, Mirielle flipped back to the article and tore out the page, wadding it into a tiny ball before throwing it in the trash bin.

What would these same Hollywood socialites think if they knew there'd been a bona fide leper in their midst? What terrible things would they say then? For a moment while reading, it had been almost like she were home. The crisp, briny air. The squawking seagulls. The glitz and excitement. But that word had pierced her like a giant hook, its barb snagging her flesh, pulling her back to the muggy air and shrieking crickets and utter drabness of Carville. How long could Charlie claim she was visiting a sick aunt before friends and reporters became suspicious?

CHAPTER 18

Three days later, Mirielle sat in the pharmacy filling jars with Ichthyol ointment, that silly gossip article still haunting her. Even Irene's constant gum flapping didn't prove enough distraction.

Leper. Didn't people know what a hateful word that was? Did they care? She'd spent nearly an hour in the shower that morning and gone through half a bar of soap trying to scrub off the shame that article, that word, had doused her with.

It didn't help that now her hands were stained purple and smelled like rotten eggs from the god-awful ointment. She tried rubbing her hands on the apron tied over her skirt, but the blotchy color remained. Carville had literally seeped into her, insidious as the disease itself, when all she wanted was to be free of them both.

Irene, who'd somehow managed to keep her hands clean, wagged her head. "You look a mess. All that water you wasted this mornin' and you're just gonna have to shower again."

Mirielle looked down at her hands. Tears blurred her vision while laughter pressed at her diaphragm. The laughter won out. Irene heehawed beside her. A stern look from Sister Beatrice, and they both quieted. Mirielle wiped an errant tear from her cheek. This set Irene chuckling again. "You got purple on your face now too."

Mirielle scooped a glob of ointment from the mixer and smeared it across Irene's chin and down the front of her white uniform. Irene's eyes widened to the size of silver dollars. She stopped chuckling, and they both stared at the streak of color across her blouse.

Before Mirielle could apologize—what on earth had gotten into her?—Irene reached into the mixer and flung a gob of ointment at Mirielle. It struck her just below the collar, splattering up her neck and across her blouse. She gaped a moment at the mess, then lunged for the vat of ointment at the same time as Irene. Her laughter roared again, this time uncontrollable as she pawed Irene with her gooey, smelly fingers. Nothing was off-limits—not their hair or skirts or shirtsleeves or earlobes. A pass of Irene's ointment-covered hand across her face, and Mirielle caught a sharp, sulfur taste on her lips and tongue. But even this didn't stop her. She hadn't laughed this hard since before Felix's death. Hadn't made a mess like this since she was five years old and had gotten into her grandmother's rouge.

A loud stomp finally quelled their playful mayhem.

"Jesus, Mary, and sweet Joseph!" Sister Verena said. "What is going on here?"

Both Mirielle and Irene dropped their arms to their sides and froze. Mirielle hadn't heard Sister Verena arrive.

"Sorry, Sister," Irene said. "We . . . er . . . things got a little out of hand."

"I'll say. This is a pharmacy, not a sandlot."

Mirielle knew she ought to remain quiet. Sister Verena looked like she'd swallowed a bee and wanted to take the sting out on someone else. But the laughter Mirielle had hastily gulped down bubbled at the base of her throat, inching upward, so she spoke. "It was my fault. I started it. I thought"—something between a burp and giggle escaped her mouth—"I just thought Irene's uniform could use some color."

A few more giggles escaped before Mirielle could silence them. Irene gave her a sidelong glance, her tightly closed lips straining to resist a smile.

"We'll clean it all up," Mirielle said.

"That you will. And since you claim responsibility, Mrs. Marvin, I'll be deducting the cost of the wasted ointment and new uniforms from your pay."

"Yes, Sister," she said, her voice squeaky with the threat of still more laughter.

"And I'll see you in my office once this mess is cleaned and you're"—her narrowed eyes traveled the length of Mirielle's purple-blotched uniform—"presentable again."

Before Mirielle could find her voice, Sister Verena turned and left. Irene grabbed a bucket of soapy water, and together they wiped away the globs of ointment speckled across the room.

Even after a generous lather of soap and a dose of rubbing alcohol, Mirielle's skin remained spotted with faint reddish-purple splotches. Face powder helped to conceal it, but only a little. She changed out of her stained uniform and donned her simplest outfit—a two-piece suit of lilac wool-crêpe. It hadn't any beadwork or ribbons or flounces, and the skirt hung well below her knees. She'd done enough today to provoke Sister Verena; she didn't want to challenge her definition of "presentable" too.

Sister Verena's office sat in a closet-sized room in between the two much larger buildings that served as the men's infirmary. While most of the other whitewashed doors throughout the colony were scuffed and dirtied from use, Sister Verena's gleamed as if Mirielle were the first to rap upon it.

"Enter," Sister Verena called.

Mirielle smoothed down her suit and opened the door.

"Ah, Mrs. Marvin." Sister Verena gestured to a straight-backed chair in front of her desk.

Mirielle suddenly felt like she had at finishing school when the headmistress had caught her with a case of cigarettes. She'd been holding them for a friend and hadn't intended to smoke one. Everyone knew cigarettes stained your teeth and made your breath awful for kissing. But she'd been punished nevertheless. Twelve swats with the headmistress's paddle. She sat now in the straight-backed chair and tried not to fidget, half expecting Sister Verena to pull a paddle from beneath her desk.

Instead, Sister Verena steepled her hands and drummed her fingers together, her gray eyes trained on Mirielle. For several moments, only that slow, steady thrumming filled the silence. Then the sister spoke. "Today's incident notwithstanding, you've taken to your work in the hospital better than I'd expected."

Mirielle cocked her head. "I have?"

"Mmm," Sister Verena said in answer. "Some people don't have the fortitude for it. We've even had to redirect sisters to other callings when they couldn't face the daily horrors here." She leaned back in her chair and stilled her fingers. "I'm not saying you're particularly swift or proficient yet, but you do seem to have a certain . . . grit."

In her life, Mirielle had been complimented for a whole host of things—her pretty smile and silky hair, her stylish clothes and flashy jewels, her grand house and well-mannered staff—but no one had ever suggested she had any merits beyond the external presentation of herself.

"Grit?" It was an ugly word to say. Guttural and clipped. But in hearing it again, she quite liked the sound. Lawmen had grit. Mountain climbers and airplane pilots. She straightened in her chair. "Thank you."

"None of that matters, though, as you still don't seem to care about anyone but yourself."

Sister Verena's words shattered any fantasy of scaling mountains. "But I do! I care about Irene and . . . and Hector. Why, a few nights ago I read Jean a bedtime story."

Sister Verena gave her an incredulous look, as if she somehow knew the "bedtime story" Mirielle referred to was really an article from the gossip section of *Picture-Play.*

"What about today? Think of those patients who will suffer when we run out of ointment. And the women in the infirmary loath to ring their bell because you haven't a kind word or even a smile for them when you answer. Or those in the dressing clinic who watch you carry away their towels between two fingers as if they were lice-infested."

"Some of them smell as if they've never seen soap before," Mirielle said, hoping Sister Verena might manage a laugh. Instead, her frown only deepened.

"I simply do not see how you can stay on in the position when—"

A knock at the door saved Mirielle from hearing the words she'd been dreading since the pharmacy. Without this job, how could she prove to Charlie she was a changed woman? How could she help find a cure?

Sister Verena grumbled something under her breath before saying, "Enter."

The door opened, and Frank stepped inside. He looked as if he'd just come from the canteen—shirtsleeves rolled, hair tousled, a dirty dishrag slung over his shoulder. "Sorry for busting in on y'all's conversation." He smiled at them both, then handed Sister Verena a box the size of a book. "These came for ya with today's shipment."

The box rattled as she took it, and her sour expression melted away. "I wasn't expecting these until next week."

"Thought ya'd be glad for it."

Sister Verena tore away the brown paper wrapping and lifted the lid. Inside were hundreds of colored candy hearts. She put on the glasses that hung from her neck on a chain and rooted through the candies, reading the mottos stamped in the center before at last selecting one and placing it on her tongue. She closed her eyes and breathed a delighted sigh.

Mirielle's lips clamped around a laugh. She glanced askew at Frank, who seemed to find nothing funny or peculiar about the sister's childlike enjoyment in a candy handed out at St. Valentine's dances and kiddie parties.

Sister Verena popped another in her mouth before holding the box out to Frank.

"Don't mind if I do." He used his contracted fingers like pincers and plucked a yellow heart from the box. He tossed it in the air and caught it on his tongue.

Sister Verena gave a tittering laugh and, as if with an afterthought, held the box out to Mirielle.

She took a candy and turned it over in her palm. *Be Mine* was printed in the center. Felix had loved these as a young boy. Had delighted in reading every candy aloud before eating it. She could almost hear him chirp *Ask Dad, Sweet Talk, I Love You*. She chewed the small candy quickly, all but choking as she swallowed.

"*Mais*, I'll leave y'all to it." He stepped outside, but turned back before closing the door. "Say, ya coming to the What Cheer Club meeting Monday, Mrs. Marvin?"

The What Cheer Club? What kind of Southern gibberish was he talking? Then she remembered him jabbering about some do-good social club the first day she'd arrived. She glanced at Sister Verena and then back to Frank. "Why, yes. I'm most looking forward to it. You know how much I care about—er—spreading cheer."

His vivid blue eyes narrowed shrewdly. "Glad to hear it. I can count on your help with the July Fourth celebration, then?"

"I'm your gal." She stood and turned to Sister Verena. "Thanks for the chat, Sister. I hate to keep you from your candies. You can rest assured, I've taken everything you've said to heart." She flashed her most innocent smile. "See you Monday in the infirmary?"

That serious, flat-lipped expression returned to Sister Verena's face. She wiped a small crumb of candy from the white bib that overlay her habit. "I'll expect you promptly at seven, not nine or nine thirty as you're used to sauntering in. Since you'll be leaving early to attend Mr. Garrett's club meeting, that is."

Mirielle's smile wobbled but held. "Seven it is."

CHAPTER 19

⟞⟞●⟝⟝

Sister Verena kept her busy in the infirmary all the next day. No sooner had Mirielle answered a call bell or jotted down a patient's temperature than Sister Verena was calling to her to sharpen needles or roll bandages or remake the empty beds. When the bandages weren't rolled tightly enough, or the corners of the bedclothes weren't tucked in just so, Sister Verena made her start again. By one o'clock when she was finally dismissed, Mirielle was actually looking forward to the What Cheer Club meeting. At least it would give her a chance to sit down.

When she arrived at the rec hall, the meeting was already underway. The heavy door slammed behind her. Frank, who was seated on a low platform in front of several rows of chairs, stopped talking, and the few dozen people in attendance craned their necks to look at her.

Mirielle smiled and waved that they should continue, but the clap of her heels atop the pinewood floors reverberated through the hall almost as loudly as the door. Frank remained silent as she picked her way past several empty chairs to a seat near the front beside Irene.

"You ready and comfortable now, Mrs. Marvin?" he asked.

"Yes, quite. Thank you."

Frank resumed reading through last month's minutes, and Mirielle looked around. The gamblers who usually haunted the far corner of the hall playing cards and shooting dice had cleared out. Few, it seemed, had decided to stay for the meeting. The windows on either side of the hall were open, a light breeze sweeping out the cigarette smoke and peanut smell that lingered after last night's movie. Even so, the air was hot and sticky, and she wished she'd brought her fan.

Irene leaned over. "Happy surprise to see you."

"Surprise? Don't I seem like the do-gooder type?" she whispered back.

"Baby, you seem like a lot of things, but a do-gooder ain't one of them."

"I'll have you know—" A grumble sounded behind them, and Mirielle realized she was no longer whispering. She lowered her voice and continued. "I hand-delivered a check to the Votes for Women Club when I was sixteen."

"Turnin' out your velvet-lined pocket and marchin' in the streets ain't the same thing." Irene pulled a palm leaf fan from her bag and waved it in front of her face. "Did Sister Verena force you to come?"

"No. I came of my own accord, thank you very much." She grabbed Irene's fan and turned it on herself. "But I do need to do something to get her off my tail."

"Something y'all wanna share?" Frank said, looking directly at Mirielle and Irene.

Mirielle shook her head. Irene turned to him and smiled. "Why, yes. Polly here was just tellin' me how anxious she is to help out."

Mirielle jabbed Irene with her elbow. Irene snatched back her fan and continued to smile.

"Glad you're eager to contribute, but could ya kindly—"

"You can help out by quitting your yapping," someone behind them called, cutting Frank off.

"Why don't Polly help by turnin' her nose down once and a while," said another man in the crowd.

Irene swiveled around. "Who said that? I got two fists that can show your nose somethin' right now."

"What, Little Miss Uppity can't stand up for herself? Too afraid she'd chip a nail?"

"Why don't we have a bake sale. Polly can bring the humble pie."

Irene started to climb over her chair, flashing those around them a peek of her red girdle straps. Mirielle grabbed her arm. She'd heard far worse things whispered about her in Los Angeles tea rooms and cabaret clubs. "Don't bother with them. They're just jealous."

"I'd sooner be jealous of a pig," someone said.

"You look like a pig, so no surprise there," came a voice from the far back.

Mirielle remained forward-facing, refusing to let her chin drop while more insults were flung, some directed at her, some at others. But inside, she felt the sting of the words.

Frank rapped the side of his hand on the small table in front of him. When that didn't work to quiet the group, he took the Coke he'd been drinking and banged down the bottle. "That's enough! This club ain't a place for bullying and name calling. *Mais!* Don't we get enough from the rest of the world?"

The shouts and grumbles ceased. Irene turned around with a huff, whipping her fan back and forth in front of her.

"There, that's better," Frank said. "Now, I expect there are some apologies to offer up around here."

"Sorry," someone said behind her.

"Apologies, Polly," said another.

Frank's eyes shifted to her.

"Apologies accepted," she said. His gaze didn't lift. If anything, it grew more pointed. She took hold of her necklace and twisted the beads around her finger. The silence of the room was as stifling as the heat. "Oh, all right." She turned around and faced the rest of the club members. She'd passed them all on the walkways or in the dining hall. Many of them had come for a dressing change or shot of chaul-moogra oil during one of her shifts. But she hadn't taken the time to ask any of their names or where they were from.

"I'm sorry if I've seemed a little . . . aloof."

"A little?" a man in the back row said. Another bang from Frank, and the man sank down in his seat.

"Well, maybe more than a little. But I'm new here and all this"— her throat tightened—"is a little overwhelming and not at all what I'm used to."

"I'll say," a man seated a few rows back said. "I heard the devil himself stopped by Carville but left the very next day, preferring Hell to this shithole."

Frank banged his bottle again, though Mirielle heard him chuckle with the rest of the group. The tension in the room, thick as molasses only moments before, was gone. Mirielle faced forward. Irene grabbed her hand. Mirielle didn't realize she'd been shaking until she felt the steadiness of Irene's palm against her own.

The meeting continued with a report on the canteen's income and expenses. She hadn't known the store was patient run or that proceeds funded club activities—like the upcoming July Fourth celebration—as well as a small stipend for the blind patients.

When Frank explained the plans for the celebration—a special flag-raising ceremony in front of the administration building that the patients could watch from beyond the hedgerow and a picnic supper under the oaks—Mirielle raised her hand.

"That's all?" she asked. "Where does the celebration come in?"

Frank drank the final swill of his Coke and looked at her with a bemused expression. "If ya got other ideas, by all means, share 'em."

"You'll need decorations, for starters. Linens, centerpieces, perhaps some sort of streamers. And music. And if there's going to be music there ought to be dancing too. Fireworks, if we can get them. Games for the children. Ooh, and what about a punch fountain in the center of the yard."

"Ya volunteering to arrange all that?" he asked between chuckles.

"Well, no. I'm more of an ideas woman. But I'm happy to weigh in on color choice and fabric."

"That sounds right lovely, Mrs. Marvin, but I'm afraid the club don't have the money or the manpower for that kind of a party."

"What about asking the Hot Rocks to play?" a woman two seats over from Mirielle said.

"Yeah," echoed another.

Frank leaned forward. "Ya know, that ain't a bad idea. Summer's a busy time for the canteen. I bet we could even throw a little scratch their way for their trouble."

"Who are the Hot Rocks?" Mirielle whispered to Irene, imagining some newly famous jazz band from New Orleans or Baton Rouge.

"A couple of fellows from the colony who got instruments and get together to play sometimes. They're good."

Mirielle doubted that. But even bad music was better than nothing.

"We could ask the materials office if they've got any old sheets that we could dye and use for decoration," another woman said.

"Great idea, Norma. I'm gonna put ya in charge of that," Frank said, then with a glance at Mirielle, "I'm sure some of the other club ladies would be happy to help."

"I don't sew. One of those things I just never could set my mind to. Better to ring a tailor." She looked around and, seeing no one else in agreement, added, "Or stop by the department store . . . or just tighten your belt."

"Stop talking, baby," Irene whispered.

Mirielle nodded.

"How about ya plan a couple of games for the youngsters then," Frank said to her. "Maybe a treasure hunt or frog race."

"Why that's perfect," Irene said, just as Mirielle began to shake her head. "You got two girls. Must'a been to dozens of kiddie parties with them."

A stab of panic seized her. The breeze had died down and the hall was hotter than ever, but her hands and feet went cold. She hadn't gone to such a party in months. Not even Evie's seventh birthday. The thought of balloons and laughter and children running about made her stomach sour. Where was the nanny, that's what everyone had asked. But Mirielle should have been watching too. Should have heard the splash. Should have seen him fall.

She blinked, and the balloons were gone. The laughter. The sunlight glinting off the pool.

Frank took up his pen. It was specially constructed with an extra-wide grip so he could hold it in his crippled hands. "Mrs. Marvin in charge of children's games."

Before Mirielle could find her voice, the meeting was adjourned and people were standing to leave. She wiped the sweat from her hairline with a clammy hand and approached Frank. "Put me in charge of something else," she managed after a deep breath. "I'll write to my husband and have him send us an entire crate of fireworks."

Several of the remaining club members looked over with interest.

"That'd sure be swell," one of them said.

"I ain't seen a firework in fifteen years," said another.

"See," Mirielle said, "that'd be more help than some silly kiddie games."

"Unless your husband's Mr. Coolidge himself, fireworks may be a tall order. And, as I recall, the kiddie games was your idea." Frank stacked his papers into a tidy pile and stood. When he looked at her again, his gaze softened. "Tell ya what, why don't ya ask your husband to send us some treats for the kids' treasure hunt. Lollipops. Baseball cards. Maybe a few seashells. I'll help ya with the rest."

"And fireworks!" one of the club members called as he was leaving.

"And fireworks," Mirielle muttered, turning to leave herself. Charlie had to know someone who could get them fireworks. All the best parties in the Hills had them these days. But the games. She shouldn't have even mentioned it. She hadn't been thinking of Felix at the time but Jean, and how some simple, old-fashioned fun might do her good. Her heart banged as loud as her shoes as she crossed the room. Loud as the door when it again slammed shut behind her. Were she at home, she'd be on her second drink by now. Maybe her third. That always seemed to quiet the pounding. Here, her only hope was to wait it out.

CHAPTER 20

That night, Mirielle skipped supper, blaming the chaulmoogra pills she'd taken with lunch for an unsettled stomach when Irene came to fetch her. House eighteen was quiet, with everyone off at the dining hall, and Mirielle opened her window and cracked her door to let the air drift through her room. If it were this hot in early June, what would July and August be like? She'd ordered an electric fan like some of her housemates had, but it had yet to arrive. And even the catalog's very best model couldn't turn the swampy Louisiana air into the fresh, crisp air she remembered from home, no matter how quickly its blades whirled.

She lay down on her bed, the springs whining and the quilt bunching beneath her. More than an hour had passed since the What Cheer Club meeting and still her heart raced as if she'd just climbed a dozen flights of stairs, or danced the Charleston for three songs straight, or jumped headlong into the swimming pool to save her drowning son. Of course, she hadn't paid attention to the thud of her heart then or the weight of her waterlogged clothes. She'd realized only after. The commotion of voices. Charlie and another person now in the pool with her. A few squeals of laughter across the yard from an ongoing game of pin the tail on the donkey. An orange balloon, somehow cut loose, drifting heavenward.

Her hands trembled now like they had her first days dry at County General. She drew her knees to her breast and folded in her arms. Her eyes closed against the waning sunset. She clutched her left wrist so tightly the grooves of her bracelet bit into her skin, into her scar.

Mirielle didn't remember falling asleep, but when she woke, daylight had drained completely from the sky outside her window. Her hands no longer trembled, and her heart beat slow and steady against her breastbone. Panic's seizing grip had loosened, leaving sorrow to fill the deep imprints left behind.

She got up and turned on her light. Footfalls pattered throughout the house. Soft voices sounded. A faucet turned on and off in the bathroom. She glanced at the small silver clock at her bedside. Only eight o'clock. She'd never passed so quickly in and out of the darkness before. Was she starting to heal, or had she simply grown callused?

Without bothering a glance in her handheld mirror, she grabbed her stationery set and headed for the living room. Two of her housemates chatted on the front porch. The others were still out or readying for bed, leaving the living room all to her. When she turned on the lamp, she found a plate of potato salad and a ham sandwich resting on the side table. The scrap of paper beside it bore her name, *Polly*, written in Irene's large, curling script.

She sank down onto the sofa, legs curled under her, and set aside her stationery. She could eat a few bites at least, just to show her gratitude. Her first mouthfuls went down easier than expected, so she tried a few more. Hardly five minutes passed before she'd eaten the entire sandwich and forked down all the potato salad. She even ran her finger over the plate and licked clean the mayonnaise.

After Felix's death, friends had sent expensive gifts of fruit and cheese and sweets, as opulent as they were impersonal. Surely someone had eaten all that food. Maybe Mirielle had choked down a bite of Camembert or candied pineapple herself. Or had it gone to waste? Thrown out with the withered flowers and condolence letters.

She set aside the plate and took her stationery to the wobbly writing desk in the corner of the room. A month's time was plenty for Charlie to procure and send a crate of fireworks. She'd ask him to send noisemakers for the children too. And bonbons. And a dozen of those lollipops you could get at Ocean Park Pier that were the size of a bread plate. Felix had loved those lollipops. Evie too, though Mirielle hadn't bought her one in ages. The first thing she would do once she was home and settled was take the girls to the pier. Never mind the crowds. Never mind that the sun would spoil Mirielle's makeup and bring out Evie's freckles. Never mind that Felix's ghost would be there with them too. Charlie had written about second chances. Mirielle's homecoming would be their second chance, and this time she wouldn't mess it up.

No sooner had Mirielle uncapped her pen, than she felt a tap on her shoulder. Jean stood behind her, holding a copy of *Picture-Play*. She waved the magazine and nodded to the couch.

"I can't read to you right now," Mirielle said, turning back to the desk. "I'm writing an important letter."

Jean stomped her foot and threw the magazine atop Mirielle's gold-edged stationery paper. The corners of the magazine were furled, and the color photograph on the cover beginning to fade. But at least it was a newer issue than the last one they'd read. Only two months behind the times instead of six.

"Maybe when I've finished with my letter," she said, turning back the cover to peek at the contents. *Producer's Wife Caught in Leading Man's Love Nest*, the title of one article read. That was hardly news. The affair had been going on for years. *Prohibition Agent Interrogates Celebrities in Connection with Bootlegging Racket*, another read. That was true too, but hardly suitable for a nine-year-old girl.

"I can't read you this, Jean. Sister Verena would have my head. Besides, this magazine's for grown-ups. Half of what's printed is lies anyway. Don't you have any children's stories?"

Jean shook her head.

Mirielle glanced at the wall clock, then capped her pen. "All right, come on. I think we have enough time before curfew." She took Jean's hand and started for the door.

Outside, crickets sang in the surrounding darkness, and moths beat against the walkway screens. The air had cooled and smelled of night jasmine.

She'd expected Jean to pull away the minute she touched her. But Jean held fast to her hand as they walked, refusing to let go even when a bike or wheelchair rolled past, pushing them to the side. Mirielle had all but forgotten what it was like to feel a smaller hand in her own.

A building little bigger than a shed sat between the two chapels at the east end of the colony. Frank had called it the reading room when they'd passed by on their tour of the grounds. In the three months since, Mirielle had never ventured inside. The dilapidated, slanting exterior offered little hope that it housed anything more than moldering newspapers and maybe a few mice.

A gust of musty air struck them as Mirielle opened the door, but when she switched on the light, a tidy room with several shelves of books appeared. Jean let go of her hand and ran her fingers over the spines of the books.

Mirielle sat down in one of the two mismatched armchairs. "Go ahead, pick one."

Jean surveyed the books for several minutes, taking out a few and flipping through their yellowed pages, before sliding them back into place on the shelf. Mirielle knew there was a small schoolhouse in the colony. One of the patients taught class for the children during the day, and another taught night school for adults who'd never learned to read or write. Jean attended day school, but sporadically. Mirielle often saw her rummaging through Irene's garden or building Lincoln Log towers in the living room when she ought to be at class.

"Can you read?" Mirielle asked, rising from the chair.

Jean only shrugged.

"Here, let me help you pick one." She perused the titles, finally settling on a book with scrolling rose canes and a little girl pictured on the cover. "*The Secret Garden*. Have you read it?"

When Jean shook her head, Mirielle tucked the book under her arm and turned out the light. A mouse's squeak sounded, and she hurried to close the door behind them.

Back at house eighteen, Mirielle read aloud two chapters before closing the book and handing it to Jean. "That's enough for tonight."

Jean gave a squeak not unlike the mouse they'd heard earlier and thrust the book back into Mirielle's hand.

"If you pout or throw a tantrum, I won't read to you again for a week."

Jean snatched the book and rose from the sofa. Mirielle stood too and returned to the writing desk. She penned a few lines—the first, as always, asking after the girls, then trumpeting her grand, if not heroic, efforts to turn the piddling Fourth of July picnic into a roaring party befitting the day. She was working her way to asking for fireworks when the stroke of a hand through her hair startled her.

She spun around to see Jean standing again behind her chair. "You about scared my stockings off. Why aren't you in bed?"

Jean stroked her hair again. "You're never gonna get out of here, you know."

Mirielle's spine prickled. "So you can talk?"

"Only their favorites get to leave. They's the ones that get all the good medicine."

Mirielle recoiled from Jean's touch and rattled her head. "All this time you've been quiet as death when you speak perfectly well?"

Jean shrugged. "I only talk when I want to."

"Who's picking favorites? Everyone around here I see is getting the same stinky chaulmoogra pills."

"Sister Verena and them others. Iodide's the best. But only a few patients get it. The sisters don't like you, so you're never gonna." She reached out to touch Mirielle's hair again, but Mirielle caught hold of her hand.

She gave Jean's fingers a gentle squeeze and then let go. "That's not true. The sisters want us all to get better."

"Everyone thinks that in the beginnin'. By the time you learn, it'll be too late." She stared at Mirielle, her muddy-blue eyes strangely calm. Then she gave a quick shrug, said in a more childish voice, "Night," and skipped from the room.

Mirielle watched her go, rubbing the gooseflesh from her arms.

CHAPTER 21

Jean had to be wrong about the iodide. During her hours in the dressing clinic, infirmary, and pharmacy Mirielle had come across dozens of treatments beyond the awful chaulmoogra pills. Ointments of mercury and trichloracetic acid, solutions of arsenic, injections of carbolic acid for particularly large and stubborn nodules. But she'd never seen anyone receive iodide.

Perhaps it was the shock of hearing Jean speak that kept the idea swirling in Mirielle's mind. She'd never questioned which patient got what medicine. It always seemed appropriately correlated to the degree of their disease. The sisters did show particular fondness for the Catholic patients, especially those who attended the myriad of masses and rosary recitations and other ceremonial nonsense that kept the little chapel busy all hours of the day. And it was plain as a hat on a rack that Sister Verena disliked her. Was Mirielle naïve to think all patients received the same care?

To settle the issue in her mind, she snuck into the pharmacy a few days later before her shift in the infirmary. The door was unlocked, but the room empty. Shelves of medicine bottles lined the far wall. Most were pills and solutions she knew: aspirin, morphine, castor oil, codeine elixir, quinine, licorice root. Others had strange, scientific names like sodium sozoiodolate or pyrogallic acid. One shelf, stocked with boric acid, Lysol, and witch hazel, wasn't medicines at all but antiseptics.

She'd scanned most of the labels when a small bottle on the top shelf caught her eye: *Iodide of Potassium*. Mirielle dragged over a footstool and was just about to climb atop it when the clap of boots and rustle of starched skirts sounded behind her.

"Mrs. Marvin? What are you doing here?" Sister Beatrice asked as Mirielle spun around. "You're not scheduled to help out in the pharmacy until Friday."

Mirielle flashed an innocent smile even as a trickle of sweat dampened her brassiere. "It isn't Friday? I must have gotten my days mixed up."

The Bunsen burner in the corner hissed, and Sister Beatrice scuttled over to check the flame. "It can happen easy enough around here," she said over her shoulder. "Just be sure you don't mistake Friday for Saturday and forget to come back."

"I won't."

While Sister Beatrice's back was turned, Mirielle climbed on the stool and reached for the bottle of iodide. She had to stand on her tiptoes and coax the bottle forward with her fingertips before she succeeded in grabbing it. She pocketed the bottle and jumped down just as Sister Beatrice turned back to her.

The trickle of sweat felt now like a river, pooling between her breasts. But she managed another smile and said, "See you Friday then," before hurrying from the room.

"You're late again," Sister Verena said when Mirielle arrived at the infirmary.

The bottle of iodide in Mirielle's pocket felt like one of those hideous bullfrogs that appeared on the lawn after it rained. The soft rattle of pills like the bullfrog's tremulous croak. Any moment it might jump free of her pocket and expose her.

"I . . . er . . . thought it was Friday and went to the pharmacy instead."

"Perhaps you ought to invest in a calendar then."

"Yes, that's an excellent idea," she said.

Sister Verena's eyes narrowed.

The pills seemed to rustle and croak even though Mirielle stood completely still. She dropped her arm to her side to cover the bulge of her pocket.

"Well, don't just stand there and waste more time. Put an apron on and get to work."

Mirielle nodded and walked as smoothly and steadily as possible to where the aprons hung on a wall. With each step, the pills jangled.

But Sister Verena had already crossed to the opposite end of the infirmary to suction the secretions bubbling out of a patient's tracheostomy tube when Mirielle turned around with her apron on. She got to work taking patients' temperatures and refilling their water glasses, doing her best to avoid both Sister Verena and Sister Loretta as they bustled to and fro.

It couldn't hurt to take the pills, Mirielle decided, as she progressed from bedside to bedside with the thermometer and pitcher of water. The doctors wouldn't stock medicine if it were dangerous. At worst, it would do nothing. At best, her lesions—the loathsome one on her neck in particular—would disappear. Maybe then they'd release her home early without having to wait out twelve negative skin tests or the discovery of a cure.

When she went to the sink to refill the pitcher, she snuck a water glass for herself. After a glance over her shoulder to be sure no one was looking, she took two of the small, white pills. There was no hideous aftertaste or immediate roiling of her stomach. Maybe Jean was right; maybe they did save these pills for the favorite patients, if for no other reason than they went down better than chaulmoogra oil.

She stuffed the jar with cotton so the pills wouldn't rattle and returned to her work, already feeling healthier and more spry. As the morning passed, she found her hand slipping into her pocket again and again to check that the medicine bottle was still there. She figured how many pills she'd take each day and where in her room she'd hide the bottle. It gave her something to think about while she turned down bedclothes or waited for the thermometer to cook beneath a patient's tongue. These menial tasks brought her no closer to home, to a cure, so she had to hope the iodide would.

Lunch arrived. After serving the patients, Mirielle took her plate outside and ate her shrimp gumbo and rice leaning against the walkway railing. The air—hot and sticky as it was—smelled of newly cut grass and blooming roses. A vast improvement over the infirmary's smell of Lysol and liniment.

She forked a bite of gumbo into her mouth and chewed. Her taste buds smarted at the fiery seasoning, but the plump shrimp and fluffy rice went down easier than it had when she'd first arrived. That was what, three months ago? Yes, three months and ten days. After Felix's death, time's edges had softened, one day, one week, one month, bleeding into the next. Here, the days had taken on shape again.

A flutter of blue wool hurrying toward the infirmary caught Mirielle's eye. From a distance, the sisters' huge cornets really did look like birds caught mid-flight. The wool and wings took shape into a woman—one of the sisters whose name Mirielle didn't know. She bustled into the infirmary and reappeared with Sister Verena only a minute later.

"I must go assist in the operating room," Sister Verena said to Mirielle. "I trust you will be able to keep yourself occupied under Sister Loretta's eye."

A chuckle tried to work its way past the gumbo Mirielle had just swallowed. She choked and coughed instead. Sister Loretta's eyes were so bad she couldn't see an elephant standing in front of her without her thick glasses. Even then Mirielle wondered.

"I'll do my best not to go to pieces on her."

Sister Verena frowned and hurried away, the other sister shuffling to keep up.

Back inside the infirmary, Mirielle cleared away the lunch trays while many of the women napped. Even Sister Loretta, seated at the nurses' desk in the corner, had let her eyelids close. But when Mirielle came to collect the last tray, she found her housemate Madge awake and scowling. An ulcerated and infected nodule on her leg had brought Madge to the infirmary over a week ago. The wound had healed, but Madge continued to spike fevers.

"You came for my tray last on purpose," Madge said to her. "Just so I'd have to sit with these dirty dishes in front of me longer and inhale that sickening shrimp and pepper smell."

"You ate almost your entire plate of gumbo."

"That don't mean I like the smell."

Mirielle collected her tray, shoved it into a slot in the food cart, and wheeled the cart toward the door. The kitchen staff would grumble if she didn't have it ready when they came by to collect it.

No sooner had she left the cart, than Madge's call bell rang. Mirielle flapped a hand at her so Madge wouldn't wake the entire infirmary with the sound. But she continued to ring the bell until Mirielle made it clear across the room to her bed.

"No need to hurry, dollface. I'm only suffering," Madge said.

"I was just here. What do you want?"

"I dropped my book."

Madge's book lay splayed on the floor beside her bed.

"You and I both know you're perfectly capable of bending over to get it."

"What if I fell from my bed? I could break an arm."

Mirielle bent over and picked up the book. "Trust me, you have to fall a lot farther than that." She dropped the book in Madge's lap and turned to go. Not three steps gone, and Madge's bell rang again.

"Shh! You're going to wake the entire colony." She grabbed the bell from Madge's hand and set it on the far side of her nightstand.

"I don't like this book. Fetch me another from the reading room."

"I can't leave Sister Loretta here alone."

"Sure you can. Besides, what do you have better to do? Powder your nose? Repaint your lips? I suppose that's one good thing about being in here. I don't have to wait for hours on end while you preen about in the bathroom."

"Excuse me for giving a darn about the way I look."

Madge snorted. "Like that matters when you're here waiting around to die. You think the grim reaper's gonna care a damn what you look like when he comes for you?"

"I shall not be dying here," Mirielle said, feeling all the more certain for the weight of the medicine bottle in her pocket. "Besides, a girl feels her best when she looks her best."

Another snort.

"You should try it." Mirielle pulled a strand of Madge's hair from behind her ear. It was softer than she expected. Rich brown streaked with gray. "Your hair is actually quite lovely. Have you ever thought about a bob?"

Madge batted her hand away. "That's nonsense."

"I could cut if for you. I've watched my stylist do it dozens of times."

"I'd rather read a bad book."

"Suit yourself."

Mirielle turned away but had only made it a few steps again when she heard Madge's gravelly voice. "I guess a little trim wouldn't hurt."

She sharpened a pair of scissors from the supply cabinet and rummaged through the infirmary's cubbies and drawers until she found a comb. A lice comb, but it would have to do. She'd never actually cut anyone's hair. Not even her children's. The nanny saw to that. But she mustered a confident stride to Madge's bedside, lest the woman change her mind.

"Sit up straight and hold still. I'll have you looking like Mrs. Castle in no time."

First came the detangling. Madge's hair was so crimped and knotted, it was plain no one had run a brush or comb through it in days. Mirielle took care to be gentle, starting with short strokes at the bottom and working her way to the top.

"It's got to be washed, there's no way around it," Mirielle said, and piled towels around Madge's shoulders before dousing her head with water and scrubbing her oily roots with soap.

To her surprise, Madge didn't complain or protest but gave over to Mirielle's fingers with a contented sigh. After rinsing away the soap and combing the hair smooth, Mirielle grabbed the scissors. Her first snips were tentative. Madge's hair reached the middle of her back. She remembered the shock at seeing her own long, beautiful hair scattered around her the first time she'd cut it short and hoped Madge didn't have the same vain attachment.

With Sister Loretta and the other patients still dozing, Mirielle took her time. A snip here and there, then a step back for assessment. At first, the sides were jagged, and Mirielle had to cut the hair a little shorter than she'd intended to even them out. But when she finished and stepped back for the final time, she beamed at the result.

"It suits your face so well."

Madge patted and fingered her hair, her face puckered. "Get a mirror. I want to see."

A quick glance at the sleeping patients and Mirielle hurried back to her room. She grabbed her silver hand mirror and, after a short hesitation, her rouge and lipstick too.

Madge wanted the mirror right away, but Mirielle insisted on a few more passes of the comb first. "You messed up my masterpiece with all your fingering."

When she pulled the makeup out of her apron pocket, Madge gave a dismissive wave. "I don't need that shit. Who've I got to impress?"

"It's not about impressing anyone. It's about feeling your best. Now keep still." She dabbed two fingers in the rouge, but hesitated before smearing it across Madge's cheeks. Her skin was thick and uneven from nodules that had ulcerated and then healed.

A few of the women in the surrounding beds had woken—likely from Madge's fussing—and Mirielle could feel their stare upon her as her fingers hovered over Madge's face.

Just do it already, she told herself. It wasn't as if she didn't have the disease too. As if the same bacteria that had ruined Madge's face didn't also live inside her. She brushed her fingers over one cheek-bone, then the other, blending out and downward. Twenty-one years Madge had been locked up here. She'd probably never worn makeup before in her life.

"There. Now for some lipstick."

When Mirielle finished, she handed Madge the mirror. Madge held the glass inches from her face then back at arm's length. Her eyes remained narrowed and her lips pinched.

Maybe Mirielle had gone too far with the makeup. Maybe she should have only trimmed Madge's hair instead of shearing it off at the shoulders. "You don't like it."

A tear leaked from Madge's eye, and Mirielle hurried for a han-kie. She'd only been trying to help. Maybe Charlie was right. She was incapable of imagining someone else's needs beyond her own.

When she returned with the hankie, Madge was still holding the mirror before her face.

"Your hair will grow back in a jiffy, you'll see. And I can wipe away the rouge and lipstick." Mirielle dabbed the corner of the han-kie in Madge's water glass. But when she reached out to wipe off the makeup, Madge pulled away.

"I look . . . I look like a cinema star." She turned to the other patients, who were now sitting in their beds gawking. "Don't I?" Madge didn't wait for their reply but gazed back at the mirror. "A goddamned cinema star."

Mirielle had seen her smirk and sneer but never actually smile before. Mirielle smiled too.

"Do me next!" the woman one bed over said.

"No, me!" said another. "I want to look just like Theda Bara."

"No, you don't," Mirielle said. "She's got an awfully big nose. And an ego to go with it. But I'll see what I can do."

The afternoon passed more quickly than any since her arrival. She didn't notice the changing light as the sun crossed the sky. She didn't notice the tick of the wall clock or ache in her feet. She didn't notice Sister Verena's return until a sharp *ahem* cut through the women's happy chatter.

"Blessed Virgin! What is going on here?"

Mirielle froze, her fingers enmeshed in another patient's hair and soapsuds up to her wrists.

"I leave for three hours and you turn the infirmary into a . . . a beauty parlor." She said it with the same repugnance one might utter *cat house*. "Where is Sister Loretta?"

Sister Loretta gave a soft snore from the corner.

"Jesus, Mary, and Joseph!"

Mirielle dried her hands on her apron, choking back a laugh. The only other time she'd heard Sister Verena curse—a nun's version of cursing, anyway—it had meant trouble.

"I thought it might lift the women's spirits. A fresh haircut. A little rouge. It's so dreary in here all the time and—"

"Is nothing serious to you? This is a hospital. The women here are . . ." She paused, glancing beyond Mirielle at the women sitting up in bed before saying the word *dying*. But everyone heard it in the silence. And any cheer that had blossomed in the room while Mirielle flitted from bed to bed with her scissors and comb wilted. "The women here are ill. They're in need of rest and medicine, not haircuts and rouge."

Mirielle wiped her hands on her apron, her gaze locked on Sister Verena. "Maybe they're in need of both."

"Because you think that is precisely why you've no business working here. It was a mistake from the beginning."

"I feel better today than I have all week," Madge said.

"Me too," said another patient, patting her new bob.

The woman whose head was still lathered with shampoo spoke up too. "You can't sack Mirielle. She hasn't finished with my hair."

Sister Verena's gaze flickered from one woman to the next, her flinty expression softening into resignation.

"A woman feels her best when she looks her best," Madge added, and Mirielle couldn't help but smile.

"Oh, all right," Sister Verena said at last. "But you're not to shirk your other responsibilities to play beautician."

"Yes, Sister."

"And no more lipstick. I'll not have you turn my infirmary into a den of immorality." She stomped away before Mirielle could get herself into more trouble asking about kohl or face powder. Better to take her victories where she could and keep the lipstick in her pocket. Right beside the iodide.

CHAPTER 22

Mirielle continued to take the potassium iodide pills for three days straight. She stashed a few pills in her pocket or purse and swallowed them alongside her chaulmoogra oil. By the fourth day, she was sure the lesion on her neck had flattened and become less red. By the fifth day, the pale patch beneath her thumb that had started this whole mess all but vanished.

So on the sixth day, when her legs began to itch, she thought little of it, blaming the heat and muggy Louisiana air. She took her pills as usual and went about her day. Everyone in the infirmary who was well enough to sit up wanted their fingernails buffed and hair styled. Sister Verena kept her busy sharpening needles, emptying bedpans, and changing dressings too.

The next day, while she stood inside the X-ray room, helping Sister Verena ready shot after shot of thick chaulmoogra oil, her legs itched all the worse. It was sweltering in the small room, the electrical fan sputtering in the corner no match for the summer's heat. When she bent down to scratch her legs, she felt dozens of tiny bumps through her silk stockings. Someone in house eighteen must have left the screen door open last night and invited in the mosquitos.

As the morning progressed, the itching turned to an aching. The line of patients awaiting their shots seemed never to shorten. She shifted her weight from foot to foot and at last dragged over a crate to sit on, but the throbbing in her legs only grew worse.

She awaited Sister Verena's chastisement. *Can't you stand still?*

Must you sit? But instead she said, "Are you quite well, Mrs. Marvin? Perhaps you'd like to take the afternoon off."

Was this a trick? Something to lord over Mirielle's head later? "No, I'm fine. Quite capable of finishing my shift."

The supper bell rang just as Mirielle finished packing up the needles and cotton and empty bottles of chaulmoogra oil.

"I'll send one of the men to fetch the supplies back to the infirmary," Sister Verena said to her. "Go eat."

Trick or no, Mirielle nodded. But she hadn't any appetite and went to her house instead. On her way to her room, she stopped in the bathroom, swallowing the iodide pill she'd stowed in her pocket with a few palmfuls of water. She splashed water onto her cheeks too, relishing the coolness against her skin. When she turned off the faucet and straightened, she caught sight of herself in the mirror. Her face was flushed. The spot on her neck, just yesterday flattened and pale, had swollen into a bright red boil.

She hurried to her room and tore off her stockings. Tiny boils covered her legs. She touched one. It was hot and painful. Mirielle recoiled and flung her skirt down to cover the sight, for once grateful for the uniform's ridiculous length. What was happening to her? An allergy of some sort. The harsh detergent they used in the laundry had always bothered her. Or maybe it was the bath soap. She'd run out of her favorite soap from home and been forced to use the plain, hospital-issue soap until Charlie obliged to send her more.

She changed out of her uniform into her nightgown, refusing to look at her sore, bumpy legs. Never mind waiting on Charlie. Tomorrow she'd buy different soap at the canteen before she showered. She lay down on her bed without turning down the sheets or quilt. A little air would do these bumps good. And she was hot anyway. Tired too. Sunlight slipped in beneath the thin silk curtains she'd made from a skirt the laundryman had ruined. Her bedside clock read five thirty. Just a little nap then. Tonight was movie night at the rec hall, and she'd promised Irene she would come. The projector they had was a relic that broke down every other reel. The films they showed were ancient—three, four, sometimes ten years old. And never the good ones, the ones she'd watched in nickelodeons and vaudeville halls when her father and grandmother thought she was sipping tea in some society girlfriend's parlor. *Star of Bethlehem, Ivanhoe, Jane*

Eyre—pictures that had made her fall in love with the cinema long before she ever met Charlie.

She fell asleep thinking of those movies. Jane and the handsome Mr. Rochester. The three wise men on their camels following a shining star through the desert. But in her dreams, those images morphed. She was Esmeralda in *The Hunchback of Notre Dame*, averting her eyes from the grotesque Quasimodo. Then, just as suddenly, it was she whose limbs and back were twisted, whose skin was coarse and hairy, whose face was that of a monster. It was from her that others hid their eyes. She was Nosferatu, Frankenstein, Mr. Hyde. Soon it was not enough for the others in her dream to look away. They pointed and snickered. They gasped and scowled. Those few who dared come close kicked and pinched her. They grabbed her shoulder and shook her.

"Polly," they said, and she swatted them.

"Baby, wake up."

Mirielle jolted awake, her arms flailing against the strong hands that held her shoulders. "Get away!"

"It's me, baby. Irene."

Irene? Irene. Mirielle sat up and flung her arms around her. "I was having the most awful dreams."

"I'll say. I could hear you clear across the house."

"I can't go to the pictures tonight. I can't."

"The pictures? Baby, you missed the picture show. A hoard of buffalo couldn't have woke you." She unwound Mirielle's arms from around her neck. "Missed breakfast too."

"It's morning?"

Irene nodded.

Mirielle rubbed her temples. Her head ached. Her fingers were stiff and sore at the knuckles. She'd slept all night but didn't feel rested. Morning meant it was now Friday. Friday meant . . .

"Oh, futz! We're not late for our shift in the pharmacy, are we? Sister Verena will have my hide when she hears about it." Mirielle swung her legs onto the floor to stand. The rush of blood sent her boils throbbing. They were bigger this morning. Redder. One or two oozed pale thick liquid. She hurried to cover her legs with her nightgown, but Irene had already seen. She bent down and touched one of the boils. Mirielle winced.

"How long you had these?"

"It's just a reaction to the soap." Even as Mirielle said it, she knew it wasn't true. She'd seen hundreds of bumps and sores like this at the dressing clinic.

Irene stood and put a hand on Mirielle's forehead. "You're burning up. Let's get you to the infirmary."

"No. I can't. I'm fine." Her voice was thin and unsteady. She tried to stand, but the pain in her legs was unbearable, and she sank back onto her mattress.

"You sit tight. I'll fetch a wheelchair."

The path to the infirmary had never felt so long. Around every twist and bend in the walkway, they passed someone new who stared at Mirielle in the wheelchair the same way passersby in the street stared at Charlie, their eyes saying, *Is that him? Impossible. It couldn't be.* The Rocking Chair Brigade were not content to stare but clamored for news as Irene pushed her by.

"What's happened, Mrs. Marvin?"

"Are you ill?"

Excitement tinged their voices as if they'd gotten the scoop on a story sure to make the front page.

"Bugger off, you old fops," Irene said to them over her shoulder.

Mirielle wished she could stand and stomp on every one of their feet. Or kick them between their legs so they doubled over and saw stars. What if the next time she passed this way she didn't have feet or legs with which to kick at all? What if these boils got infected and the doctors had to amputate?

"You can have my shoes when they take my legs," she said to Irene, as the infirmary came into view. Her eyes were dry, but there were tears in her voice. "The gold ones with the satin bows. And my alligator-skin pumps you like."

"Oh, hush. No one's gonna take your legs, and my feet are too damn big for your shoes anyway."

At this, Mirielle did cry. Such beautiful shoes and they'd go to waste. Just like all the lovely things in her former life.

In the infirmary, Sister Loretta helped settle Mirielle into one of the beds then hurried off to find Doc Jack. It felt strange to lie beside women only two days before she'd been tending to. She hadn't had the energy to dress but had thrown her kimono on over her nightgown before Irene returned with the wheelchair. Now she yanked its satin lapels tightly closed and pulled the rough bedclothes up to her neck, as if in doing so she could somehow disappear.

"Unhappy surprise to see you in the infirmary without your work apron, Mrs. Marvin," Doc Jack said when he arrived. "Let's see what the trouble is." He motioned to Sister Loretta, who stood beside him, and she pressed a thermometer into Mirielle's mouth. "May I?" He motioned to the blankets covering her legs. Mirielle nodded, careful not to dislodge the thermometer from under her tongue.

She expected Doc Jack's eyes to widen or mouth drop open when he saw the ugly crop of boils. But his face remained placid. He pressed his fingers against a few, and Mirielle let out a cry through her nose.

"A dozen or so lesions on both legs in various stages of eruption. Erythemic and hot to the touch," he said to Sister Loretta, who then scribbled the assessment in Mirielle's record.

Mirielle whimpered again.

"Don't worry, dear. They'll disappear soon enough."

Sister Loretta plucked the thermometer from her mouth and examined it, holding it only inches from her glasses. "One-oh-two, Doctor."

"What's wrong with me?" Mirielle asked.

Doc Jack pulled up a stool. "I think you're experiencing what we call a leprous reaction. Something has exacerbated the disease."

"Will I die?"

"No, that's very unlikely. Sometimes a reaction can trigger acute nephritis, which can lead to kidney failure and death, but we'll keep a close eye on you here in the infirmary." He patted her knee as if what he'd said should be somehow reassuring. "Sometimes patients go blind if iridocyclitis develops, but that's only if the illness goes untreated."

"Why did this happen?"

"Many things can bring about a reaction. Poor diet, intercurrent disease like typhoid or influenza, pregnancy, overmuch stress. Anything that lowers your body's resistance to the disease."

Mirielle frowned. Ever since leaving the jail, she'd taken care to eat well and get enough sleep. And she certainly wasn't pregnant. She couldn't even remember the last time she and Charlie had made love. Thinking of him added a new dimension of pain. When she'd woken from the morphine-induced twilight sleep of childbirth, he'd been beside her. When she'd come to after her accident, he'd been clutching her in his arms. Now she was alone.

"And my legs? These dreadful boils will really go away?" She hadn't the strength for tears, but her voice warbled like a frightened child's.

"A few days or a week and I'm quite certain they will." Doc Jack must have read the panic on her face for he leaned closer and patted her knee again. "Don't worry. Why, there are some leprologists who think reactions like this are a good sign and find their patients better off afterward. Some even prescribe iodide of potassium to induce a reaction."

Mirielle's heart tripped on its own rhythm. "Iodide?"

Doc Jack nodded.

"Do you ever prescribe it?"

"We experimented with the drug a few years back but I was never convinced of its efficacy. The possible side effects of a reaction are too grave, you see. And patients don't always improve afterward."

Despite the pain in her knuckles, Mirielle's hands curled into fists around the sheets. "Does that mean my next skin test might be positive?"

Doc Jack stood and looked at her with the same expression of condolence she'd seen him give other patients in the infirmary before delivering bad news. "I'm afraid so."

Mirielle's entire body went cold. She'd only just gotten her first negative. It took conscious effort to nod as Doc Jack continued to speak. Jean knew of the danger of iodide. Mirielle would bet her bottom dollar on it. How foolish she'd been to trust the girl! Mirielle's mind was still foggy, and tiredness was creeping back upon her. As soon as Doc Jack left, she drifted to sleep, dreaming of monsters anew.

CHAPTER 23

$\longrightarrow\!\!\bullet\!\!\longleftarrow$

For the next week, Mirielle remained in the infirmary, battling aching joints, erupting boils, intermittent fevers, and above all, boredom. It was strange to lie in bed while sisters and orderlies bustled around her. She found herself hesitating before reaching for her call bell, reluctant to ask for more water or fresh sheets. Was it fear of rebuke for yet another call? Embarrassment at not having the strength to perform simple tasks herself? Mirielle couldn't put her finger on it. But she sat with chapped lips in sweat-drenched sheets until she could no longer stand it. More often than not, the sisters and orderlies were kind and swift in answering, and Mirielle regretted the many times she'd tramped to a patient's bedside and spoken brusquely.

She understood now too how slowly the minutes passed when four white walls and an under-stuffed mattress comprised your entire world. The occasional birdsong through an open window, the bleat of rain upon the roof, the footsteps and chatter from the walkway— these were both welcome distractions and painful reminders of her confinement. Only Irene's daily visits saved her from going mad. The woman could prattle on about anything—the weeds in her garden, the latest Montgomery Ward catalog, even last night's supper— and, for once, Mirielle was happy to listen.

Frank stopped by too, though strictly speaking, men were not allowed in the ladies' infirmary. He slipped in one afternoon when Sister Verena had been called away and Sister Loretta was dozing in the corner to deliver a letter to another patient. On his way out, he pulled up a stool and tarried at her bedside.

The Hot Rocks had agreed to play at the July Fourth celebration, he told her, and Dr. Ross would permit dancing. Mirielle had never been one to feign modesty, but she pulled the covers to her chin as he spoke, fearing how red and raised and ugly the lesion on her neck must be. Her hair was likely a fright too. She tried to smooth the wayward strands in a subtle, natural way so he wouldn't think she was primping for him.

"Well?" he said.

"Hmm?"

"Have ya given it any thought?"

Mirielle rattled her head. Even though he talked like a bush hound, his voice had a pleasant, almost lulling sway. "Thought to what?"

"The treasure hunt for the kids."

"Oh." Mirielle crossed her arms and looked away. Jean wasn't the only child at Carville, but Mirielle was in no mood to plan anything the girl might enjoy.

"Think on it," he said, standing to leave. "And be sure to get well. Ya got a frog race to judge too, remember?"

When she didn't have the distraction of visitors, Mirielle steamed and stewed. Never in her life had she known such a rotten girl as Jean.

On her eighth day in the infirmary, Mirielle's fevers at last relented and Doc Jack permitted her to leave under two conditions. One, she was to rest a week before returning to work. Two, she must return to the infirmary each day for a quick checkup and dose of Fowler's solution. Doc Jack promised the concoction of arsenic and potassium bicarbonate would help the boils on her legs heal—and it had. Only a few pinpoint scars and bumps remained. But the medicine had to be carefully dosed to avoid arsenic poisoning.

Imagine if Jean had told her to take that instead of iodide, she thought as she walked back to house eighteen. Mirielle would be dead. The morning sunshine stung her eyes. The riot of colors and sounds around her almost too much to take in. Mirielle had been terrifically foolish to have listened to the girl and try to treat herself alone.

She stopped and leaned against the walkway railing. She'd only done it to get back to her daughters, to Charlie, sooner. Now, if her next skin test came back positive, she'd be here all the longer.

Mirielle brooded about it the rest of the walk back to her house. She brooded while she showered off a week's worth of sweat and sickness, and brooded while she dressed. Irene stopped by while Mirielle was fastening the straps of her shoes and asked if she wanted to play a game of rummy. Mirielle shook her head. She was too angry to speak, too bent on finding Jean.

No more bedtime stories. No more shoulder shrugging at her antics. She'd give the girl an earful and be done with her. Mirielle wasn't her mother. She had her own daughters to think of, far away as they may be.

As soon as her shoes were fastened and hat pinned, Mirielle started off. She searched the house and surrounding lawns, the rec hall and canteen. Jean had a fascination with the goat and monkeys they kept by the laboratory for experiments, and Mirielle searched there too. When she came to the reading room and found it empty, she sat down on one of the worn armchairs to rest a moment. Her stamina had waned after a week in bed. Church bells tolled the hour, two long peels from Sacred Heart's belfry. But earlier she'd heard both chapels ringing—one atop the other—to call the residents to Sunday service.

Mirielle stood and marched toward the oak-shaded lawn at the southeast corner of the colony. Church wasn't the only to-do on Sundays. Though visitors were allowed any day of the week, few ever came. Those who did, usually came on Sundays.

Picnic tables sat beneath the sweeping oak boughs and dangling moss. Those lucky few residents who hadn't been hauled across the country or forgotten by their families congregated here with their visitors. But Jean was not among them.

Mirielle hovered a moment, leaning against the splintery lip of one of the picnic tables. Before today, she'd avoided this shady lawn on Sundays. No need to be reminded that no one had come to call on her. Now that she was here, it was impossible not to imagine Charlie in a dapper suit and fedora seated at one of the tables. She pictured herself beside him, so close the scent of his spicy aftershave tangled with her perfume. Evie played in the grass nearby. Helen squirmed on Mirielle's lap. In between her thumb sucking and cheerful babbling came the word *mama*.

Mirielle drew her arms around herself, a tight squeeze to stanch the longing, then let them drop to her side. Such imaginings were impossible. Children under sixteen were forbidden to visit, and the trip across country was unmanageable, even if Charlie were to undertake it alone.

As she turned to leave, Mirielle spied Jean high up in one of the trees at the edge of the lawn. She sat on one of the thicker limbs, swinging her legs and chewing on a piece of straw. Mirielle's festering anger boiled up again. She stomped to the base of the tree. "Jean, you climb down this minute."

Jean glanced down, her expression morphing from wide-eyed surprise to jaw-clenched obstinacy. She shook her head and returned her gaze to the picnic tables.

"You're already in a heap of trouble, missy. Don't try my resolve."

Jean continued swinging her legs. She bit off a piece of straw, chomped it between her teeth, then spat it out. Mirielle watched it fall to the ground, her hands tightening into fists. "Climb down now, or you'll be sorry."

She heard Jean snicker and had to dodge another falling piece of saliva-coated straw. "If you're not down by the time I count to ten . . . well . . . I'm coming up to get you. One, two, three . . ." Mirielle prayed Jean would come to her senses and clamber down before she reached ten, but Jean didn't move. Obstinate girl! Mirielle grabbed on to the lowest branch, testing the strain of her weight on her newly healed arm before walking her feet up the furrowed trunk.

The soles of her patent leather shoes skidded down the bark. She let go of the tree and tore off her shoes. Then, after a glance toward the picnic tables, she unfastened her stockings from her girdle and yanked them off as well. Her bare feet found better purchase, though anyone who looked would catch a glimpse of her underclothes. She scrambled precariously up the tree one branch at a time. "If I fall and break my arm again, I swear you'll be in a cast too," she mumbled as swamp moss tangled with her hair and bark scratched her palms.

When she finally reached the bough where Jean sat, she looked down. With so much anger propelling her upward, Mirielle hadn't realized how far she'd climbed. The ground lay at least fifteen feet below. She closed her eyes and wrapped her arms around the trunk until a rush of dizziness passed.

Jean sat at least ten feet out from the trunk.

"You have one more chance to climb down," Mirielle said to her. "Otherwise I'll tell Sister Verena what you've done, and you'll lose your radio privileges for a year."

The girl stuck out her tongue at Mirielle and crossed her arms.

Mirielle stomped her foot, then tried not to flinch as the limb shuddered and swayed. "You're nearly ten years old. Stop acting like a toddler."

To this, Jean only crossed her arms more tightly and looked away.

Mirielle glanced down again, then quickly up. Her pulse thudded in her ears. Grabbing an overhead branch, she planted her toes outward and stepped away from the trunk. She knew women in the pictures who did their own stunts. If they could do such daring feats, so could she. She took another few steps. A breeze off the river fluttered the hem of her skirt. An ant crawled onto her hand and down her arm, but she dared not let go to swat it away. The farther she walked, the more the limb beneath her wobbled and groaned. Fear of falling ate away at her anger and bravado. She'd made it halfway to Jean when the groaning sound sharped into that of a splintering crack. Mirielle froze. Her heartbeat was deafening now. The breeze a lash upon her nerves. She inched a foot or so back toward the trunk, then let go of the branch above her and slowly sat down, still several feet from Jean.

Minutes passed, and neither of them said a word. Mirielle listened for another cracking sound but heard only the flutter of leaves and her uneven breathing.

"Why did you tell me to take potassium iodide when you knew it would make me sick?" she said at last.

Jean shrugged, continuing to stare at the milling residents and their visitors.

"I could have gone blind. My kidneys could have failed and I would have died."

Jean gave no reply.

"You want me dead, is that it?"

Jean's muddy-blue eyes cut to Mirielle, then down. She balled her hands in her lap and shook her head.

"Have you gone mute again?"

Another shake of the head.

"Then why!" It came out more a scream than a question, and Jean startled, grabbing the branch to steady herself.

Mirielle sighed. The overload of adrenaline, first from anger, then from fear, had left her jittery.

"I didn't want you to go away," Jean said, so soft it was almost a whisper.

"What are you talking about? I'm stuck here same as you."

"Someday you will. It's all you talk about." She lifted her chin and raised her voice, speaking in a nasal pitch. "'Back in California . . . When I get home to California . . .'"

Despite her anger, Mirielle chuckled at Jean's impersonation. "It's my home. I have two daughters younger than you and miss them terribly."

"See. You will leave. They all do." Jean stared back at the residents on the lawn, her eyes rimmed with tears. Mirielle followed her gaze, remembering what Frank had told her about Jean's father. How he'd dropped her at Carville's gate and never looked back. What must it feel like to watch others with their families after being abandoned? No wonder Jean misbehaved.

Mirielle scooted as close to Jean as she dared, leaving several feet yet between them. "Do you climb up here every Sunday?"

"Nah, usually I'm down there with *mon père*." She jutted her chin toward the lawn. "He comes to visit just about every Sunday. Our house ain't but a few hours south across the river. He's a boat maker."

She'd heard Jean speak so little, Mirielle had never noticed the faint Cajun sway to her speech. "You're lucky to get visitors," she said, even though she knew Jean was lying. "What about your mother?"

"*Maman*'s dead."

"I'm sorry. My mother died when I was young too."

Below them, two of Carville's other children—black girls a few years younger than Jean—scampered over picnic tables and around tree trunks, giggling and hollering. The man who'd come to visit them ran after them in a game of tag while a woman looked on, smiling and fanning herself with her hat. One of the girls had pale lesions up and down her arms. The other had lost most of the fingers on her right hand, giving it a mitten-like appearance. Otherwise, they were identical.

"When they find a cure, we'll all leave and go home to our families," Mirielle said.

Jean snorted.

With the man sweating and clutching his side, the twins stopped their game and skipped over to the woman—presumably their mother—who produced two red lollipops from her handbag. The twins squealed.

"They have lollipops twice that size at the boardwalk in Los Angeles," Mirielle said, seeing the longing in Jean's eyes. She inched her butt along the branch, fearful of another cracking sound but determined to get closer. When she made it to within an arm's distance, she reached for Jean's hand, but Jean leaned away.

"I hate lollipops."

"Oh? They have all kinds of flavors. Cherry, orange, lemon-lime, even cola-flavored. I've asked my husband to send some for the July Fourth party."

"Really?" Jean's face brightened.

"Fireworks too. And there will be music and dancing and even a frog race. But you've got to cut out your antics and do your schoolwork, otherwise I'll tell Sister Verena not to let you attend."

Jean wadded up the last bit of straw she'd been chewing and tossed it to the ground. "What good is it if I can write my letters pretty and add up a bunch of numbers if I'm just gonna be stuck at Carville all my life?"

"You're going to get out," Mirielle said, feeling a renewed sense of determination. Her work wasn't just about proving Sister Verena and Charlie wrong; it was about stopping the disease. For all of them.

Below them on the shaded lawn, many of the visitors were taking their leave. The twins' parents hugged them, then shooed them toward the colony's maze of houses and walkways. An elderly woman kissed her husband goodbye. A mother, her son.

Absentmindedly, Mirielle reached again for Jean's hand. To her surprise, Jean took it. "Someday the both of us are going to make it home," Mirielle said. "But first, you've got to show me how the devil we're going to get down."

CHAPTER 24

The week of rest Doc Jack prescribed Mirielle before she was allowed to return to work passed more slowly than a dry dinner party. Though she'd bemoaned the hectic hours and grizzly sights, the stench of urine and chaulmoogra oil and unwashed feet that went along with her position, she'd never stopped and thought about what she might otherwise be doing to fill the time. It took less than two days to reorganize her wardrobe, buff her shoes, polish her dresser set, trim her hair, and manicure her nails. Irene coaxed her into helping weed her garden. Madge taught her how to play penny-ante poker. Jean came to her each night with a book. But that still left her with far too many hours for her mind to wander. To wander back to Charlie, Evie, Helen, and, inevitably, Felix.

Without a gin rickey or champagne cocktail to blunt her thoughts, they spiraled downward until Irene barged into her room, gardening shears in hand, or Jean called to her from the living room for help with her schoolwork.

On the fifth day after Mirielle's discharge from the hospital and their talk up in the tree, Jean asked her bluntly, "How come you always fingering that bracelet?"

"It was my mother's."

"And you been wearing it since she died?"

"No, I put it on after . . ." She couldn't very well tell Jean she'd put it on after her accident, after the bandages came off and the red scar haunted her. "I wear it as a reminder of my son."

"Can I have it when you die?"

Mirielle winced, then laughed. "No. But tell you what, I've got a necklace you can wear to the July Fourth celebration. If you're good."

That was enough to turn Jean's attention back to her arithmetic sets. When Mirielle reached for her bracelet again, she caught herself and folded her hands together instead.

On the last afternoon before returning to work, Mirielle went to the canteen to await the mail delivery. Her letter to Charlie requesting candy and fireworks for the July Fourth celebration had gone out two weeks ago. Surely she ought to have a reply by now, if not a box of goodies.

She sat at the counter and ordered a Coke. Frank grabbed a glass between his palms and set it beneath the soda fountain's spout. After adding a few cubes of ice, he pressed down on the lever, and fizzy soda spurted into the glass. He'd poured her dozens of drinks in the months since she'd arrived, but the dexterity he managed despite his crippled hands never failed to amaze her.

Grunts and shouts sounded from the far end of the adjoining rec hall, where several of the patients crowded to gamble. She sipped her Coke and watched them.

At home, she'd been the best mahjong player of any of her friends and left their afternoon games with a full purse. But those afternoons had been civilized affairs. Cake and tea—or a mint julep if she were lucky—and dulcet-toned gossip. A few of the women smoked. But not these rancid-smelling Murads sold in the canteen.

How many games had she missed in the months she'd been gone? What kind of gossip had been spread around about her hasty departure? She imagined they'd discussed every possible ailment the sick aunt Mirielle was caring for might have, from consumption to syphilis.

They might have written her, Mirielle's friends. Perhaps Charlie had forgotten to forward their letters. They worried after her, surely. Or had their luncheons and garden parties and mahjong games gone on the same without her?

She glanced at the wall clock and checked the time against her watch. The canteen's clock was four minutes slow, and the mailman nine minutes late. Everything else at Carville ran with military precision—the thrice daily meal bells, the once-a-week afternoon call for laundry, the ten o'clock curfew—why should tardiness be permitted with the mail?

She drank down the last of her Coke and rolled the empty glass back and forth between her palms. Frank began to whistle as he polished the bar with a damp rag. It was a slow, swinging melody, the notes clear and silvery. She didn't recognize the song but felt its sorrow in her bones. She stilled her hands and listened. Frank was taller than most men at Carville. His dark wavy hair would look swell if smoothed down and parted in the center or slicked back in a pompadour. Either he didn't know the latest fashions or didn't care. Even so, were it not for his hands and the lumpy skin on his forearms, he could pass for handsome.

The gamblers' shouts and laughter rose and fell behind Frank's whistling the way the crowd's chatter underscored the orchestra at the downtown cabarets. When they first started going around together, Charlie would whistle in between songs when they were dancing, stepping and turning as if the music had never ended, keeping any other fellows from cutting in. Mirielle would laugh and follow his lead, even hum along if she knew the tune.

Now, she shivered. "Can you cut that out?"

"Huh?"

"The whistling."

Frank turned to her, his blue eyes guileless. "Sure. Sorry, *chère*."

But the silence was worse. Mirielle pushed her glass to the back of the counter. "Frank, I'm—"

The arrival of the mail cut short her apology.

"Howdy," the mailman said, setting a fat stack of letters, magazines, and catalogs on the counter alongside two paper-wrapped packages. She snatched up the letters and scanned each of them for her name, flipping those of other residents into a messy stack for Frank to sort. The fewer letters remaining, the more her ribs squeezed around her heart. When she got to the end, she splayed the half-sorted letters out haphazardly across the counter and looked again.

"*Mais!*" Frank said. She knew he liked to sort them into neat, alphabetized piles—A's at one end of the counter, Z's clear down at the other, each letter facing the same way.

"I'll be done in a second."

None of the letters and neither of the packages were addressed to Mirielle West. Then she remembered Charlie would be using her silly Carville name. She scoured the letters again, playing tug-of-war over the last of them with Frank until she could plainly see that none were addressed to a Mrs. Pauline Marvin either.

"Sorry," she said, handing over the last envelope, which was now crumpled at the edges and slightly ripped. "It's just that I'm expecting . . ." Heat crept over her skin from beneath the collar of her dress and up into her cheeks.

"Ain't news to me," he said.

She helped him sort and straighten the letters, again regretting the silence. After the magazines and envelopes and catalogs were stacked in tidy piles, Mirielle lingered at the counter. "You've got a real swell whistle. I'm just in a bum humor today," she said.

"Wanna talk about it?"

Mirielle shook her head. "But I wouldn't mind another tune."

Frank smiled and started whistling again, a faster, more cheerful song. Mirielle's mood lightened with the airy notes. A letter or package from Charlie would come tomorrow, and she'd laugh about how manic she'd been today.

She listened to that song and half of another. As she turned to leave, the coverline of a magazine snagged her eye. She brushed aside the stack of letters atop the magazine. *Picture-Play.* A young, familiar face stared back at her. She always did take a lovely photo, Vilma. Beneath the main coverline— *MISS BANKY'S GOT IT. HAVE YOU?*— ran several others. The last line, the one that had caught Mirielle's attention, read, *WIFE OF LEADING MAN CHARLIE WEST SENT TO NUT FARM.*

Mirielle's lungs froze mid-inhale. Her eyes leaped from word to word a second time. A third time. A fourth. She grabbed the magazine, flattened the face of Vilma Banky against her chest, and ran from the canteen.

CHAPTER 25

The next day, Mirielle arrived at the dressing clinic early, hoping the bustle of unwrapping bandages and changing water basins and scrubbing feet would prove sufficient distraction from the horror she'd read the day before. If she wasn't careful and attentive, she could peel a man's skin off with his bandages, or reopen healing wounds. The disease left many patients without feeling in their limbs so they couldn't tell her if she was hurting them. Once, on her second day in the clinic, she'd looked down after cleaning the old and crusted ointment from a woman's legs to find the basin water bloody from too hard a scrubbing.

Today, it took more effort than most to focus her attention, though. She felt on edge and constantly breathless, as if her lungs hadn't fully expanded after yesterday's events.

As the morning progressed, the clinic grew hot and crowded. The air smelled like week-old laundry, and Mirielle's uniform clung sticky to her skin. But for once, she hid her worries behind a smile and embraced the busyness. Unravel this dressing, clean those feet, fetch more ointment from the cupboard, more gauze, more soap. Crouch down, stand up, hurry out to the hopper.

Not until after lunch did the clinic slow down. The hair about her face was frizzy and her damp apron smudged with remnants of liniment and blood. She leaned against the wall before an open window and let her head loll back, hoping to snatch a breath of fresh air and cooling breeze.

"I hope I have not come too late, señora," a voice said.

Mirielle raised her head. The smile she'd been trying at all day came easy to her face. "Of course not, Hector. Sit down. I'll get some warm water."

She unwrapped the gauze from his legs and helped him lift his feet into the basin to soak. The nodules that had covered his legs like a mountain range were shrunken now, the ulcers scabbed over. Even the long gash he'd suffered in Arizona had finally knit together.

Her next pull of breath came easier than the one before. So many patients came through the dressing clinic each time she worked, it was hard to remember one's ailments from the next. The missing toes, weeping lesions, and infected wounds that had so horrified her at the beginning no longer made her flinch or gape. If some got better, others got worse, and for all her careful undressing and gentle scrubbing, for all the ointments and medicines the sisters applied, Mirielle had never been certain they were making a difference.

But clearly with Hector they had. And Mirielle, with her small, monotonous ministrations, had helped. A strange feeling settled over her. Pleasant and uplifting.

"How good your legs look."

"*Si*," he said. "Every step they used to ache. Now I feel as if I could run a race and win."

He looked above her head at the window, and she wondered if he too were thinking about the Yuma desert and how he might fare against those heartless railwaymen today. But healthy as his legs had become, he still hadn't the advantage of youth or wagon. What hope was there then if you could outrun the disease but not the hate and stigma?

As quickly as it had come, that pleasant feeling fled. She wiped her eyes on the sleeve of her blouse, but a few tears slipped past and dropped into the basin, rippling the water like rain on a lake.

"¡*Ay*! What's wrong, señora?"

"It's nothing." She looked up at him and tried to find her smile again.

"You must miss your family. Tell me about them. Your girls."

Mirielle hesitated, then sat upright and wiped her hands on a clean corner of her apron. "Evie, she's seven, and such a sweet girl. Helen's fourteen months this Friday." She told Hector about Evie's inquisitiveness, how every day since she was two, she'd had a new question. She liked butterflies and earthworms and the sea anemone they found in tide pools at the shore just as much as she liked her dolls. She told him Helen had Charlie's hazel eyes and had laughed and crawled before any of her siblings.

"She'll be talking soon too, I suppose," Mirielle said. Though likely not the word *mama*.

She didn't tell Hector about Felix. Or the many times in the months since his death when she'd brushed Evie off her lap and told her to go play in the nursery or heard Helen cry from her crib and waited for the nanny to soothe her.

Hector sighed, thinking about his own children, she imagined. The children who'd grown to wish him dead.

"And your husband?" he asked after a moment. "He must be missing you, no?"

A fresh wave of tears overtook her. After a bleary glance around the room to be sure no one else was within earshot, she said, "Those goddamn scandal rags! Someone told those gossipmongers that I've been committed to an insane asylum. Charlie must be terrifically embarrassed. And what can he say? The truth is worse."

Hector pulled a handkerchief from his pocket and handed it to her. "You think it could hurt his career?"

"Think of Roscoe Arbuckle or Mabel Normand. Their careers were never the same."

"But this is madness we're talking about. Not murder."

"In Hollywood, it's all the same thing." She dabbed at her eyes and blew her nose, too embarrassed to admit it was her reputation she was concerned with as much as Charlie's. No matter how quickly she was cured or granted parole, she could never tell people the truth about where she'd been. So instead, they would think her a lunatic, whisper about her when she left the room, point and snicker behind her back. Los Angeles's beloved society gal who'd lost her marbles, been whisked away in a straitjacket, and—gasp!—confined to a padded cell.

Her friends, if she could even call them friends anymore, would keep their distance. Their neighbors in the Hills would think twice before inviting them to parties. The publicity folks at Paramount would forbid her from attending Charlie's premieres, lest talk of her madness overshadow the picture's debut.

She tucked Hector's hankie into her pocket, promising to return it once she'd laundered it, and grabbed a towel to dry his feet and legs. With each careful pat, she tried to rekindle the joy she'd felt earlier at seeing his wounds so much improved.

When she finished, he laid a hand on her shoulder and squeezed. "*Lo siento*, señora. Someday this too will be behind you." He glanced down at his healing legs. "We cannot survive without hope."

CHAPTER 26

—————◦—————

Mirielle tried to carry Hector's words with her over the next few days. If he, a man who'd lost everything to this disease, could still have hope, so could she. Each day after her shift in the infirmary or shot clinic or pharmacy, she went straight to the canteen, steeling herself against what Charlie's letter might say about the rumors of her madness. Was this the final straw? Would he blame her for this too?

Whatever he said, whatever damage the story had caused, she would make it up to him. Just as she would somehow repair her reputation. It was an easy lie to believe. She'd been so blue after Felix's death, so indifferent, one could easily suppose a mental breakdown would follow. When she returned from Carville, she'd make a great show of being her old self, fun-loving and serene. Little by little the story would fade. A new scandal would take its place. People might not forget, but their interest would wane.

Or so she resolved to convince Charlie, when three more days passed without a letter. She brought her stationery box into the living room after supper and uncapped her pen. It seemed positively archaic that the colony didn't have a telephone. It would be so much easier to broach this issue with Charlie over the line. To be able to judge from his voice the extent of the damage. She'd heard that Dr. Ross had a telephone in his office in the big house. But she'd have to sneak past the hedgerow and break inside if she wanted to use it. A feasible option, were the sisters not housed on the second floor.

If Sister Verena spied her with as much as a toe beyond the hedge, Mirielle could count her job at the hospital gone.

She did wonder what it was like in the sisters' quarters. Did they wear their habits until bed or did they unpin their huge hats and shake their hair free as soon as they were up the stairs? Did they spend their free hours kneeling in prayer or did they draw or knit or play cards like other women? It was hard to imagine Sister Verena at a card table playing hearts or rummy. Harder still to imagine her puffing a cigarette and raising the ante in a cutthroat game of poker.

Mirielle chuckled at the thought. The page before her was still blank. She wrote a few lines, crossed them out, and started again. A few more lines and her pen flagged. Better just to start anew. She crumpled the paper and tossed it aside. Her legs, still healing from the boils and lesions that had erupted during her reaction, itched, and she tucked them under the chair to keep from scratching as she wrote.

She'd managed only to write the date and *Dear Charlie* when Jean bounded into the room. She opened the record cabinet built into the base of the phonograph and thumbed through the discs.

"Which ones do we want?" Jean seemed to have only two volumes: mute and loud.

Irene came into the living room dressed in a green-and-white-checked apron dress. They'd spent the afternoon in the pharmacy together, but Irene had since remade her hair and painted her lips. "Oh, let's just bring them all."

Jean began pulling the records from the cabinet.

"Careful now." Irene bent down to help her, reading the names of the records aloud as she pulled them out, along with comments like, "oh yeah, that's a goodie," and "here's a peppy one."

Mirielle couldn't write with all the noise, but at least they seemed to be taking the records somewhere else to play them. She heard the record cabinet door shut and Irene's knee joints pop as she stood.

"Say, I bet Mrs. Marvin's a swell dancer," Irene said to Jean. "Why don't you ask her to come along?"

Mirielle swiveled around in her chair as Jean approached.

"Wanna come?" Jean asked.

"Where are you going?"

"Mrs. Hardee's gonna learn me to dance for the party."

"Teach me," Irene corrected.

"Teach me." Jean leaned closer to Mirielle. "She's too old to know any of the flapper dances, though. Do you know 'em?"

Mirielle laughed. "I may have danced the Charleston and the shimmy a time or two."

"Hot dog! You'll come along then?"

"I can't. I've got a letter to write."

Jean frowned. "You're always writing damned letters."

"Don't use that word," Irene said.

"You say it all the time."

"That's the privilege of being a grown-up. Ain't much else to recommend it. Now come on, let's leave Mrs. Marvin alone."

Jean dragged her feet from the room. Irene followed, stopping in the doorjamb and saying over her shoulder, "We'll be up in the observation tower if you change your mind."

Mirielle turned back to the writing desk. It wasn't that she was always writing letters, but that she was so slow—damned slow, as Jean would say—that it seemed like she never finished. Irene's and Jean's voices rang from the walkway, followed by a peal of laughter.

How long had it been since Mirielle last danced? Christmas, she supposed. An obligatory party with all the studio bigwigs. Charlie had made her promise she would dance and smile, not just mope about the bar all night. Dance she had—two songs were sufficient for keeping up appearances—and smile too, but anyone could see it was a pinned-on smile, an accessory no different from her string of pearls or feather hair clip.

But before that, before Felix's death, she'd loved to dance. Dinner parties and society balls and downtown cabarets. She loved the music, the commingled scent of sweat and perfume, the rush of air over her skin as she whirled. It was a chance to clear her mind and exist only in the physical. In the here and now.

Mirielle capped her pen and placed the sheet of paper—still blank save for the date and Charlie's name—back in her stationery box. She was in no mood to dredge up apologies for someone else's venomous pen. *Unstable for years*, the *Picture-Play* article had said of her. *A real Hollywood tragedy.* She'd read the article a dozen times over the past days. Each time the words stung anew. The humiliation. Couldn't she be free of it for just one evening?

*   *   *

The observation tower was a rickety structure that stood just inside the fence between the Protestant chapel and hedgerow. Mirielle had never climbed the thing. The wooden framework looked soft and weathered. It creaked with the slightest breeze. She'd been told the view from atop was worth the trouble of its two dozen stairs and that just last year a government surveyor had pronounced the structure sound. Mirielle, however, remained skeptical.

The setting sun hung orange above the horizon, and the air felt like a sponge. A breeze ruffled the tops of the nearby trees. Music and laughter drifted down from the deck above. Mirielle grasped the handrail and climbed.

The view was more spectacular than the others had described. Mounting the last few steps, she could see the entire colony spread before her—the long parallel walkways and attached houses, the quadrangles of green lawn in between, the tangle of medical and utility buildings, the broad roofs of the dining and rec halls. Beyond the neatly trimmed hedgerow lay the big house with its antebellum façade and farther on two rows of cottages for the personnel. At the far end of the colony, the dairy barn and silos were visible and the ring of pecan trees that stood guard over the cemetery. When she reached the deck and looked in the opposite direction, the wide, smooth surface of the Mississippi glimmered in the waning light. It bounded Carville on three sides like the sinuous body of a snake, the steep levee, rutted road, and wire fence curving alongside it.

Though she'd lived beside it for months, this was her first glimpse of the mighty river. The play of fading light off its glassy surface reminded her of the ocean. But the smell was different, the sound, and her chest squeezed. She'd forgotten how much she missed the briny air, the caw of seagulls, the white-capped waves rushing to the shore.

"You came!" Jean said, pulling Mirielle back to Carville before she could fully remember the feel of hot sand beneath her feet.

Jean and Irene weren't alone in their escapade. The young twins were there as well, dancing with Frank and Mr. Li, the colony's resident handyman, to the lively song. They paid no mind to the shudder their clomping feet sent through the old wood. Jean grabbed her hand and tugged her to the center of the deck.

A foxtrot played from the portable phonograph someone had lugged up. It took Mirielle's feet only a moment to find their place in the song. She placed a hand on Jean's shoulder before remembering she was to dance the part of the man and moved it to the small of her back. Jean knew only a few steps and leaned clumsily into Mirielle's lead. She tromped on Mirielle's toes and twirled right when she should have spun left. But the smile on Jean's face—wider than Mirielle had yet seen—was worth all the lurching and twisting of arms and scuffing of shoes.

The air wasn't any cooler here than it had been below, but the occasional breeze rolled over them, providing some relief. The deck's planking felt more solid than Mirielle had first thought, and when the next song played, a quickstep, she turned and chasséd without worrying her feet would break through the ancient wood. She coached Jean through the basic steps, then allowed her simply to follow, laughing with her when their legs tangled. They danced the waltz and the Charleston and the shimmy and the shag. They switched partners, and Mirielle danced with the twins, Mr. Li, and even a playful one-step with Irene.

Though she winded more quickly than she had before her leprous reaction, and hadn't danced many of these steps in nearly two years, Mirielle felt fully alive for the first time since coming to Carville. The music hummed through her limbs from the tips of her fingers to her toes. The breeze tickled her sweat-dappled skin.

After a dozen or more songs, she begged off the next dance to catch her breath. A waist-high railing enclosed the deck with a bench jutting out from two sides. She sat down and leaned against the rail. The sun had set, but a full moon had taken its place, casting a bright, silvery glow on the river and surrounding trees.

Several records rested upright against the phonograph. The more classical orchestra records Mirielle recognized as Irene's. The rest were a motley assortment of ragtime, jazz, and hillbilly music. Some of the bands she recognized. Others, like Fiddlin' John Carson or the Skillet Lickers, were as foreign as Chef's gumbo had been the first time she'd seen it on her plate.

When Frank sat down beside her, she held out one of the records. "I've got a stirring suspicion this honky-tonk music belongs to you."

He took the record from her and smiled down at it. "Don't knock it till ya try it."

"This phonograph yours too?"

Frank nodded. "I reckon this ain't like them fancy, fancy ballrooms you're used to, but ya can't beat the view."

He was right. A bird landed on the river, causing a shimmering ripple across its surface. Outcroppings of trees and a patchwork of farmland spread out in the distance, painted shades of deep blue and purple in the moonlight. The air smelled of earth and foliage and the faintest hint of jasmine.

"Good to be outta the sisters' sight too," he said.

"They don't approve of dancing? What a surprise."

"Inviting in the devil, I believe is how Sister Verena puts it."

They both smiled. The song ended, and Frank lifted the tonearm. He replaced the jazz record with the hillbilly one she'd handed him. A lively mix of fiddle and steel guitar played, soon joined by a rough, nasally voice. The lyrics—something about a turkey hiding in the straw—were absurd, but Mirielle couldn't help tapping her heel in time with the jaunty beat.

"Yeehaw," Irene shouted, and whirled one of the twins about the deck. Jean and the other twin locked hands with Mr. Li and spun about in a high-stepped dance of their own improvising.

"How 'bout it?" Frank said, standing and extending his hand.

Mirielle's foot stilled. She gaped at his shrunken, curled fingers too long before remembering herself and muttering some excuse about still catching her breath. Frank shrugged and went to join Mr. Li and the girls. But she'd caught the flash of hurt in his eyes before he turned away.

She swiveled on the bench, turning her back to the stomping and hooting dancers, and looked over the railing. What was wrong with her? In her work at the dressing clinic and infirmary, Mirielle had cared for deformities far worse than Frank's. Dancing with him wouldn't make her any more a leper than she already was. Why, the sicklier of the twins had hands like rough mittens, her fingers almost fully absorbed into her scarred and lumpy palms. Mirielle hadn't hesitated to dance with her.

Perhaps it was the echo of shock from her first day at the facility, the horror Frank's hands had seemed to her then.

He didn't ask her to dance again. Mirielle was glad for it, still uncertain she could bring herself to accept his hand. But the shine of the night was gone. Troublesome thoughts crept back into her brain.

Soon, mosquitos chased them from the tower. Irene's lipstick had settled into the cracks and corners of her mouth. The twins' braids had turned frizzy. Jean's cheeks were flushed. Mr. Li carried the records and Frank the phonograph. They parted at the first fork in the walkway—the twins to one of the three colored houses; Frank and Mr. Li to the small cluster of detached cottages at the far end of the colony; she, Jean, and Irene to house eighteen.

Frank didn't look at her when they said their goodbyes, his eyes sliding past as if she weren't there. She'd refused men dances before—though with a bit more grace—and afterward not thought a wink about it. But tonight's incident stayed with her as they trudged home along the deserted walkway. His fingers bent like talons. His skin like melted wax. His handsome face earnest and then stung.

She wished he hadn't soured the night by asking. What if she'd been too winded or simply didn't like the hillbilly tunes—either could have been true as far as Frank was concerned. But Mirielle knew vanity and fear had gotten the better of her. Frank knew it too.

June 22, 1926

Dear Mirielle,

You'll understand my delay in writing when you hear my great news! I'm to star in a feature production set to be released next spring. It's a full seven-reeler, and sure to be a great financial success. Mr. Schulberg was reluctant at first to have me for the part, owing no doubt to the disappointing reception of The Man from King Street, *but Cecil won him over. Set construction is already underway at the lot. I am to play opposite Gloria Thorne. She's rumored around the studio to be quite irascible and demanding on the set, but she's such a doll at parties I cannot imagine it so. At any rate, I'm glad to have her name attached to the picture as it can only further assure our success. Filming's set to start in three weeks, and I've been terrifically busy with preparations.*

I'll write you again once we begin production with all the news. You mustn't share too much for I suppose word can leak even from a leper colony. Evie sends her love, and I imagine Helen would too if she could rightly speak. She's walking now even without the nanny's hand to steady her and soon I think shall be running, so eager she is to keep up with her sister.

I hope you are well and getting the proper rest.

Your Husband,
Charlie

P.S. I couldn't make sense of your request for fireworks. What could someone in your situation want with such things? Perhaps you meant it as a joke. Surely it would be dangerous for people not in full possession of their extremities to operate anything with fire.

CHAPTER 27

⟫•◦⟪

Charlie's letter arrived five days before the Fourth of July celebration. She read the last line and stared at the paper dumbly before reading it all again. A joke? Too dangerous for people not in full possession of their extremities? What did he imagine Carville to be—a place for spastics and idiots? Clearly, he hadn't understood when she'd written about the disease, about how the tiny germs attack the nerves and can leave people's extremities insensitive to touch. She hadn't meant to imply it affected a person all over or it happened to everyone. Certainly not that it rendered them incapable of striking a match, lighting a fuse, and stepping away. If Charlie could see the daily feats of the patients here—wheeling themselves around when they'd lost their legs, playing baseball with only stumps for hands, growing flower gardens without the benefit of sight—he'd have sent the fireworks in a jiffy.

His letter hadn't even mentioned the toys and trinkets and lollipops she'd asked him to send for the children. Did he think that was a joke also? What good was a treasure hunt if there were not booty at the end?

Her only consolation was that he hadn't mentioned the scandalous article in *Picture-Play*. The date of his letter—almost two weeks after the magazine's release—ensured that he'd at least heard of the story. Likely he'd been plagued by telephone calls and harassed by reporters. *Is it true?* they'd have hollered, swarming his car as he left the lot. *Has your wife really gone insane? Lost her mind? Fallen mad?* At least, it didn't seem to have hurt his reputation at the studio.

Was it out of kindness that he didn't mention the story? Perhaps he thought she didn't know. In his mind, Carville must be a desolate and dreary place populated by those not yet dead, but close enough to the grave to smell the freshly exhumed dirt.

It wasn't an entirely unfair assumption. She'd certainly thought it desolate and depressing herself at first. And there were plenty of residents who thought it so still. The Fourth of July party was meant to help change that. And now they wouldn't have fireworks to celebrate as the rest of the country did. They wouldn't even have lollipops.

The edge of the letter crumpled as Mirielle's fingers tightened. She'd promised fireworks. What would the other residents think of her? And how disappointed Jean and the other children would be when they got to the end of their treasure hunt and found no treasure. If Mirielle were at home, she could direct her driver to the best sweet shops downtown and return with a smorgasbord of candy sticks, butterscotch patties, gumdrops, coconut bonbons, fruit jellies, and chocolate kisses. They'd stop by the pier too for lollipops of every flavor. Here, all Mirielle had was the rinky-dink canteen. But it would have to do.

Without bothering to smooth its edges, she stuffed Charlie's letter back into the envelope and grabbed her purse. Two dollars and five cents jangled inside. Hardly enough for a smorgasbord. Maybe Frank would let her put the rest on credit—not that she relished asking him, or seeing him at all. This money business was maddening. She'd never given a wink about what things cost before coming to Carville. But it wasn't as if she could just walk into a bank anymore or pluck a few clams from Charlie's billfold.

As she left the house, she could hear Jean playing with her Lincoln Logs in the living room. She liked to build high towers only to topple them with the lob of a tennis ball. More than once, Mirielle had stepped on one of the scattered logs, but it beat finding toothpaste in her slippers or slugs in her pockets. Since their chat in the oak tree, Jean's behavior had greatly improved. She was talking and reading and attending school. Occasionally, Mirielle would draw back the bath curtain to find tadpoles in the tub. Madge would deal a hand of poker only to realize all fifty-two cards in her deck were spades. Irene would open the lid of her phonograph and a family of grasshoppers would jump out. But these were harmless antics and kept house eighteen lively, if a bit messy.

Thanks to Charlie, though, Mirielle had failed to hold up her end of the bargain. She stamped down the walkway straight to the canteen. Barn dance music sounded from the radio in the rec hall, reminding Mirielle of the observation tower. In the week since, she'd avoided Frank as best she could in a tiny colony like theirs. She suspected he was avoiding her as well. He glanced up from the cash register when she entered the canteen, but didn't smile. Several residents sat at the counter, sipping soda and flipping through newspapers or chatting with those beside them. She hoped they'd keep him busy enough not to notice the music and be reminded of that night too.

Shelves lined the far wall of the canteen where Frank stocked canned goods, cigarettes, dime-store beauty products, and candy. Anything else residents wanted to buy had to come from mail-order catalogs and took weeks to arrive. Exactly what one might find on the shelves varied. Some weeks it was creamed corn and Campbell's soup, other weeks pork 'n beans. Camels and then Murads. Oh Henry! bars, then the next week peanut brittle. But today there was little of anything on the shelves.

Mirielle looked behind the remaining cans of spinach and tubes of Colgate dental cream, finding only four Hershey's bars and a box of Cracker Jacks. Maybe this week's stock hadn't been shelved yet.

"Where's all the sweets?" she asked Frank at the counter. She'd meant to sound nonchalant, but a strange nervousness buzzed in her stomach, and her words came out like an accusation.

"This week's shipment ain't come in yet."

"When will it arrive?"

Frank shrugged. "Supposed to come yesterday."

"But surely before the Fourth."

"Hard to say. Mightn't come at all. Wouldn't be the first time."

"You're kidding!" Mirielle's raised voice drew several sidelong glances. "What kind of operation are you working with?"

"The kind that's willing to do business with lepers."

She handed over the Hershey's bars and Cracker Jacks for Frank to ring up. It was only enough for a few squares of chocolate and a couple of kernels of popcorn for each kid, but she'd buy more tomorrow when the shipment came in. *If* it came in.

"How are the clues for the treasure hunt coming along?" he asked her, using the knuckle of his index finger to depress the cash register's keys.

"Fine." The clues were the least of her worry now. She ought to tell him that her husband hadn't sent any candy for the kids. Or fireworks. But she couldn't bring herself to form the words. Not yet.

Three days later on the afternoon of July second, Mirielle and Irene finished their shift in the pharmacy and headed toward the canteen to meet with Frank and a few other residents about the party.

"You've been awfully quiet today, baby," Irene said as they walked. "You feeling okay?"

Mirielle nodded. All afternoon they'd been diluting disinfectant, and the sharp smell of it clung to her uniform. She wanted to go back to her room and change, but if she did, she'd likely lose her nerve and skip the meeting entirely. The stock of goods for the canteen still hadn't arrived, and all Mirielle had to show for her grand plans for the party were a dozen silly treasure hunt clues, four candy bars, and a single box of popcorn.

A mix of disappointment and embarrassment had stirred inside her all day, building to a kind of dread. She'd managed only a few bites of her lunch, and Sister Beatrice had to remind her three times of the proper ratio of water and Lysol. Now her feet dragged and shoulders slumped.

When they got to the canteen, Irene ordered them each a Coke, and they waited with the others at a back table until Frank finished helping the customers at the counter. The Hot Rocks were excited to play, Frank reported when he joined them. Mr. Li and a few other residents had built a simple bandstand out of scrap lumber from the woodshop. Norma and her housemates had dyed several yards of old fabric to make bunting for the stage. Hector would cut the lawn to a fine stubble the morning of the party so they'd have a place to dance. Irene had met with Chef, and together they'd planned a feast of barbecue, beans, and cake.

Everyone's eyes turned to Mirielle. Her mouth felt dry, and she took a long sip of Coke. The bubbles danced in her empty stomach.

"I've got the treasure hunt all planned out," she managed to say, and told them about the course she mapped out—starting under the oaks and ending at Union Chapel with stops along the way at the monkey cage, tea garden, observation tower, grain silo, tennis courts, powerhouse, and the stretch of walkway between house thirteen and the cookshop referred to as Pork Chop Walk. At each location, she'd hide a clue leading the children to the next spot.

"And at the end?" Norma asked.

Mirielle took another gulp of soda. "I . . . my husband couldn't . . ." She looked down, feeling all the more foolish for the tears threatening in her eyes. "I haven't got but four Hershey's bars and a box of Cracker Jacks."

"It something," Mr. Li said.

"Not nearly enough. Not what I promised. And . . ." She took a deep breath and looked up. "No fireworks."

No one looked surprised. Instead, they regarded her with sympathy, as if this was something they'd known would happen but hadn't had the heart to tell her at the start. Everyone except Frank. His expression was dark and inscrutable.

"I'll do some askin' around," Irene said, giving Mirielle's hand a squeeze. "I'm sure I can rustle up some more candy and trinkets."

"Me too," Norma said.

Mr. Li fingered the brim of his cap. His round face was like a prune, the skin furrowed and thickened with plaques. Before coming to Carville, he'd run a prosperous furniture shop in San Francisco. When his disease had been discovered, he'd told Mirielle, he'd been locked in a boxcar without food or water and shuttled back and forth between county lines for days before a hospital finally agreed to take him. "Maybe I can do something in the way of fireworks."

"Don't get yourself in trouble like last year," Frank said.

"No, no," Mr. Li said with the hint of a smile.

How someone could manage anything close to fireworks locked inside the colony with only two days' notice, Mirielle didn't know. But if anyone could, it was Mr. Li.

"Thank you," she said, her voice a bit steadier. "I was afraid you'd take me for a heel, promising such things and coming up, well, empty-handed."

"You ain't the first to be disappointed by the outside world, baby," Irene said.

"My husband's got an awful lot to bother with right now. That's all. He just got a new—" Mirielle stopped before blurting out *picture contract*. Only Hector knew who her husband was and what he did. Best keep it that way. "A new job. Anyways, thanks for understanding."

Frank leaned back in his chair and crossed his arms. "What about the frog race?"

"Won't I just stand at the finish line and name whichever frog makes it there first the winner?"

"It's serious business, racing."

"I'm certain I can judge a silly old frog race," she said.

"And what about the bullfrogs?" Frank asked. "How many did ya get? Big, big ones, I hope. And they gotta be the same size."

Mirielle tugged on the collar of her blouse. She didn't remember him saying anything about her finding the frogs. "I . . . er . . ."

"Ya did get the frogs, didn't ya?" Frank said.

"Um . . . no."

Frank shook his head. "*Mais*, that's a shame. The kids will be heartbroken."

"But I . . ."

He really should have told Mirielle this was her responsibility. It wasn't as if she'd organized a frog race before. She looked down at the last few sips of soda in her glass. Tiny bubbles troubled the cola's surface. She pushed the glass away, no longer the slightest bit thirsty. "How was I supposed to know to get frogs?"

"Ya thought they'd just magically appear?" Frank said.

She looked to Irene for support but got only a shoulder shrug.

"It's all right," Frank said after an uncomfortably long silence. "We'll go tomorrow night."

"Where?"

"Where else? The swamp."

CHAPTER 28

━━━•◦•━━━

"You're going dressed like that?" Irene said to her the next night.

Mirielle had donned a loose-fitting tennis dress that belted at the hips. "Isn't this sporty enough?"

"City folk." Irene shook her head and handed over a pair of green galoshes. "At least wear these."

Mirielle slipped them over her pumps and hurried out. Frank leaned against the trunk of a pecan tree just beyond the ring of houses at the far edge of the colony waiting for her. An empty flour sack was slung over his shoulder. He eyed her dress with disapproval, then switched on the cap lamp strapped around his head. "Come on."

They traipsed across the cow pasture toward the wood. Her feet slid back and forth inside Irene's too-big galoshes. Mud and cow manure clung to the soles. More than once, she stepped clear out of them, wheeling her arms for balance until she managed to fit her foot back inside and pry the galoshes from the clinging ground.

Frank kept a pace ahead of her. The night was black as onyx, and she had to all but run to stay near the pool of light cast by his cap lamp. They skirted the tangle of trees that marked the edge of the forest. It smelled of boggy soil and rotting wood. Moths scudded in and out of Frank's light. A twig snapped high in one of the nearby trees.

"Just a possum," Frank said, likely in response to her quick draw of breath.

Another snap sounded from the wood. "How do you know? What if it's a panther stalking us. Or an alligator."

He stopped so abruptly, Mirielle almost ran into him. The beam of his light blinded her. He switched it off, and blackness enveloped them. Mirielle preferred the blinding light to this.

"For one, gators don't climb trees," he said. "And there ain't no panthers in these parts. Listen."

When he didn't continue talking, Mirielle realized he meant for her to listen to their surroundings. At first, all she heard was silence. How she missed the noise of the city—car engines and bicycle horns and police whistles. She missed the light too. Even on a moonless night, Los Angeles glowed, a faint but permeating yellow from the collective twinkle of street lamps and car lights.

Her ear caught the sound of crickets chirping. An owl hooting. The splash of water in the distance. At the rustling of leaves, she looked up. Her eyes had adjusted to the dim, and she saw the pale underbelly of a possum as it scurried along a tree limb.

"See?"

She nodded.

They stood only inches apart. The scent of him—soap and sandalwood and zinc liniment—blended with the woody smell of the forest. "You grew up in a place like this?"

"Yep. Lovely, ain't it?"

That was going a bit far. But the buzzing and the hooting and leaf chatter did have a soothing, almost songlike quality to it. "We needn't worry, then?"

He turned from her and snapped his cap lamp back on. "I didn't say that, but certainly not on account of a possum."

She followed as close behind him as the clunky galoshes would permit. Not far on, the tree line curved away, revealing an expanse of flat darkness. When Frank's light shined upon it, patches of water glimmered back at them amid lily pads and duckweed.

He led her to a flat-bottomed skiff tied to a nearby tree. They pushed it into the water, and he climbed aboard. Mirielle hesitated. Lake water lapped against her galoshes. She cast a wistful glance over her shoulder. The colony was but a few pinpricks of light in the distance. When she turned back to the skiff, Frank extended his hand to her. "Come on."

Something splashed into the water at the far side of the lake.

"I don't think I can do this."

"Ya have to." When she didn't take his hand, he said, "Think of Jean and them other kids."

Mirielle sucked in a deep breath and grabbed Frank's hand. His skin was dry and bumpy; his fingers twisted nubs beneath her own. She let go the minute she was aboard, wiping her hand on her skirt before registering the insult.

"Sorry . . . I . . . It's not . . ." She stopped herself before saying something that would make the insult worse and sat down.

"Ya ain't the first." He sat opposite her and handed her the cap lamp. "Scan the surface of the water. When ya see a pair of eyes shine back at ya, reach out and grab."

"What? Me?"

"I gotta row."

"But how do I know it will be a bullfrog?"

He gave a faint smile and shrugged. "A gator will be too heavy to pull outta the water."

She glared at him but took the lamp, tightening the straps so it fit snuggly across her forehead. "This is the last time I volunteer for one of your stupid What Cheer events."

"Shh. You'll scare away the frogs."

With the oars' handles sandwiched between his hands, he paddled them with slow, smooth strokes around the perimeter of the lake. Amid the soft ripple of water, she heard a strange vibrating noise—like that of an airplane propeller, but much quieter—rise and fall among the duckweed.

"What's that?" she whispered.

"The bullfrogs' breeding call. A bit far on in the season for that. Late bloomers, I guess." He drew the oar through the water. "Keep your eyes on the water. There's gotta be some close."

"I am."

"Anything?"

"No." But then she saw them, two beady eyes just above the water's surface. Mirielle hesitated, grimacing, then reached out quickly and grabbed. A huge, slippery bullfrog writhed in her hand. It puffed its jowls and croaked. Its long legs kicked and splashed as she pulled it out of the water. "Take it!"

Frank tucked the oar beneath his arm and opened the flour sack. "Here. Drop him in."

Mirielle happily let go, and the frog tumbled to the bottom of the sack. It croaked again and stared up at her. Its dark skin was slick and spotted. The frog jumped, and Mirielle lurched back, nearly falling off her seat, but Frank closed the bag before it could escape.

"Not bad," Frank said when he'd stopped chuckling. "He's at least eight inches."

"How many more do we need?" Mirielle asked, wiping the mud and slime from her hand.

"A dozen or so should be enough."

A dozen? There weren't even that many children. Frank's cheery voice made her want to throttle him. Easy to laugh and smile when you weren't the one grabbing at a pair of glassy eyes in murky water.

The next frog twisted free from her grasp before she could drop it in the sack. The one after, Frank deemed too small and made her throw back. By her fourth catch, she'd gotten the hang of spotting their glinting eyes and holding on to their slippery bodies.

After her tenth catch, she quickly spied another frog and reached out. Before her hand touched the water, Frank pulled her back. Two nostrils joined the eyes above the water. Below the surface, Mirielle made out the long slender form of an alligator.

"Just a t-li'l guy," Frank assured her. "Couldn't have done worse than a nip." But he paddled them clear across the lake then let the boat drift through the marsh reeds, catching the last two himself.

With their bag full, he rowed them to shore. However *t-li'l* the alligator had been, Mirielle was glad to be finished. Her back ached from hunching over the water, and dozens of mosquito bites welted her skin. Frank, who'd come better dressed for the hunt in pants and a long-sleeve shirt, seemed in no hurry.

As soon as she felt the bow of the skiff catch on the muddy shore, she stood, realizing her mistake only as the boat began to wobble. She flung out her arms in a vain attempt to balance herself, succeeding only at further rocking the boat. Frank reached out to her, too late, and she toppled into the muddy lake.

The water, though neither cold nor deep, sent a shock through Mirielle. Her hands and rear hit bottom quickly, settling into the mud. A sharp pain radiated down her recently broken arm, and her fingers tingled. When she sat up, her head was above water. The cap lamp dangled from her ear, no longer shining. Slimy water weeds tangled in her dripping hair. She coughed and cradled her arm. Not broken, she decided, but damn sore.

Frank leaped from the boat and helped her to her feet. Her tennis dress clung wet and muddy to her body. The night air, cooler than when they'd set out, made her shiver. Then something flapped against her thigh. Mirielle yelped and hiked up her skirt to find a fish caught in her girdle strap. Frank laughed as she batted it free.

"It's not funny." She stomped to the shore and emptied her water-filled galoshes.

"It's not. Of course. It's just . . ." His words trailed into more laughter as he peeled a lily pad off her back. "At least the frogs didn't go over."

Mirielle humphed and started toward the colony, leaving the boat and bullfrogs to him.

CHAPTER 29

The children delighted in the July Fourth treasure hunt. Jean led the charge, and they made it around the colony, ending at Reverend Philips's tin lizzie parked in front of Union Chapel in forty minutes flat. They dumped the box of treasure on the gravel drive. The marbles and ribbons and handcrafted toys Norma and Irene had rustled up tumbled out alongside Mirielle's candy. The children cheered and divided up the spoils. No one, save Mirielle, seemed to notice the missing lollipops.

The frog race was less of a success. They staged it at the baseball diamond. Each child selected a frog and lined up behind third base. But instead of hopping orderly down the baseline to home plate, the frogs leapt this way and that. Two ended up on the pitcher's mound. One in the dugout. One the outfield. One of the twins' frogs wouldn't hop at all. At last, a boy named Simon managed to chase his bullfrog to home plate, and Mirielle declared him the winner. Residents on the sideline who'd laid bets with one another grumbled, but the children laughed and scooped up their frogs for a rematch under the oaks where Chef was barbecuing.

After supper, the Hot Rocks gathered with their instruments, and the music began. Mirielle sat at one of the picnic tables surrounding the newly mowed lawn, watching the dancers. It wasn't Jelly Roll Morton at the Apex, but the band played far better than she'd expected. They started with a waltz, and several of the older residents whirled across the lawn. With far more men at the colony than women, those ladies keen to dance were never without a partner.

Frank came and sat beside her. Tonight, he'd applied pomade to his wavy hair in a not-so-successful attempt to slick it down. His neck was ruddy with razor burn. "What a fine, fine time the kids had today. So can I count on ya for the turkey race at Thanksgiving?"

"Not a chance."

He laughed. "Truth be told, I didn't think you'd come along to the swamp. Certainly not catch frogs."

"You think just because I'm a woman, I'm scared of a little mud."

"You ain't any woman, Polly."

"Right. I'm an uppity girl from the big city who couldn't possibly know a thing about catching frogs."

"As I recall, ya did mistake a possum for a panther."

She batted his shoulder and faced the lawn. The band played the final notes of a one-step then started in on a jig. Jean and the twins scurried to the dance floor.

"Ya weren't much of a boatman either," Frank continued.

"That was your fault."

"My fault?"

"You should have told me not to stand so quickly."

"How could I know ya were gonna do something so stupid?"

"Because I'm an uppity city girl!"

Frank laughed, and Mirielle too.

Their laughter had just petered out to an awkward silence when Hector strode up to them.

"You going to dance with Señora Marvin or just talk her ear off?" he said to Frank.

Frank cleared his throat. His eyes were suddenly skittish of her. "I am a mighty good talker."

Mirielle regretted that moment on the observation deck when she'd declined his offer to dance. She'd behaved worse than a debutante.

"Well then, señora," Hector said. "May I have the honor?"

Mirielle took his hand and followed him to the lawn. They danced a foxtrot and then a Texas Tommy two-step. He hadn't Charlie's finesse but knew the basic footwork. It was enough to make her forget for the length of a few songs who and where they were.

"This is a nice party, no?" he said as a new song began. "I hadn't expected to dance again. Especially not with a beautiful woman."

Mirielle's hand fluttered from his shoulder to the lesion on her neck. It had shrunk to the size of a dime again and was only slightly raised. But it was the first thing she saw whenever she looked in the mirror. "You're a peach for saying so, Hector."

He put her hand back on his shoulder and smiled in that kindly way that reminded her of her father. She had to admit, even if she didn't say it aloud, it was a nice party.

By the end of the song, a grimace battled Hector's smile.

"Are your legs hurting again?"

He shook his head. "It's nothing, señora. I am an old man and we tire easily."

"Why don't you sit down and I'll get you some lemonade."

"Thank you, no. I think I'll go back to my room and lie down." He kissed her hand in a grand, old-fashioned gesture, and shuffled toward the houses, rubbing his lower back.

She watched him go, then turned back to the lawn full of dancers. The band struck up another fast-paced melody. Sister Verena stood at the periphery scowling. A few of the other sisters hovered wide-eyed beside her. Clearly, they hadn't been taught to dance the collegiate shag at the nunnery.

Everyone else delighted in the song, though most of the older residents retreated to picnic tables where they tapped their feet and watched. Irene danced with a fellow from house thirty several years her junior. She winked at Mirielle as they kick-stepped past. Frank danced with a blond woman named Hattie, who worked in the lab. He was a better dancer than Mirielle had realized atop the tower.

Halfway through the song, Jean grabbed her hand and tugged her into the swarm of dancers. They hopped and kicked and lunged and turned through the basic steps Mirielle had taught her, laughing as they entangled themselves.

Mirielle's dress clung to her skin by the time the song ended. Jean raced off to dance the next number with one of the twins. Mirielle crossed to the edge of the lawn and leaned against the broad trunk of one of the oaks to catch her breath. A twinge of guilt stirred beneath her breastbone. Not for dancing. Charlie wouldn't mind. But for laughing. For enjoying herself at this humble affair without him or the girls.

A boom sounded, followed by a popping noise. Then a glimmer of light exploded above the small clearing between the oaks and the barbed wire fence. Jean and the other children squealed. Mr. Li squatted in the clearing beside a smoking cylinder. The flicker of a match and another boom. The night sky shone with flashes of light.

Would Charlie take the girls to the Ocean Park Pier to watch the fireworks tonight like they'd done in years past? He'd need to remember cotton for Helen's ears, otherwise she'd cry at the noise. And not to let Evie go barefoot on the pier or she'd end up with splinters.

Mirielle's heart ached in their absence. She sat on an exposed root, her knees drawn up against her chest, watching one last firework burst in the sky before the staff confiscated Mr. Li's explosives.

CHAPTER 30

Carville buzzed with talk of the Fourth of July party for several days after. The Hot Rocks were local celebrities now and had already promised to play for Thanksgiving and Christmas. Even the frog race was lauded as a success. Smiles about the colony seemed more commonplace too. *Hello*s along the walkway. Fewer people griping as they waited in line for their chaulmoogra injection. Maybe Frank was right. Maybe it was not only their bodies that needed healing but their spirits too.

At the dressing clinic a week and a half later, Mirielle was unwrapping the bandages from a resident's arm when he asked, "You were the one who got all them bullfrogs for the kids, weren't ya?"

"For the race, yes."

"It true you had to beat back gators to catch 'em?"

Mirielle couldn't help but smile. Gossip spread the same at Carville as it did anywhere. And for once, it was nice to be aggrandized instead of slandered. "We came across an alligator or two."

Dried pus cemented the last strip of gauze to the man's skin. She loosened it with water and teased away the bandage one corner at a time.

"You ought to start up a business, selling frogs for people to fry up on their hot plates. It'd sure beat whatever chicken Chef cooks up."

"I'll keep that in mind," she said, though she'd sooner wear cotton stockings than go back to that swamp.

At the end of the day, as Mirielle bagged up the day's refuse—

scraps of gauze, empty tubes of liniment, soiled dressings—and lugged it outside to be taken to the incinerator, she realized Hector hadn't come in. Last week, the wounds and nodules on his legs had again improved. Could it be that now they'd healed completely?

But that evening at supper, Mirielle didn't see him in the dining hall. Probably eating in his room after a long day's work, she told herself. She sat down beside Irene at their usual table and listened as her housemates talked about a runner nicknamed the Flying Finn and some world record he'd just broken. It was big news on the radio. Even if he were more handsome than Valentino, as Irene insisted, the however-long meter dash was a topic of little interest to Mirielle. She did laugh, though, when Madge suggested Irene ought to make him husband number three.

Jean seemed not to care about the racer either. While the women talked, she made a tower of potato salad on her plate with a waterfall of peas cascading down one side. Were it Evie, Mirielle would have told her not to play with her food. But what harm was there in it? She plucked a cherry tomato from the dregs of her salad and nestled it on top of Jean's tower. They both giggled, even as Mirielle felt a pang of regret. She ought to have played more and scolded less as a mother. When she got back home, she'd make a point of allowing more horseplay, even at the dinner table. Mrs. Post and her book of etiquette be damned.

When everyone had finished eating, they loaded up their dirty dishes and dropped their trays at the counter. Madge had suggested a game of bridge on the back patio once the sun set and swampy air cooled. Mirielle agreed Jean could be on her team if she promised to sit through a whole game without complaining she was bored. On the way out, Mirielle glanced at the bulletin board affixed to the wall beside the door.

The service schedule for both chapels was pinned to the board along with handwritten advertisements for everything from bicycle parts to haircuts. At the far side was the infirmary list—a register of names updated whenever a patient was admitted or discharged.

Mirielle stopped, causing a backup of grumbling residents behind her. Hector's name was on the list.

Instead of heading to her house, Mirielle hurried down the walkway to the men's infirmary. There were all kinds of reasons a patient was admitted to the infirmary. Some were frighteningly serious like pneumonia, blood poisoning, or laryngeal affection, where nodules crowded the windpipe and a patient slowly suffocated unless a tracheotomy could be performed. But others weren't so deadly, Mirielle reminded herself. A mild reaction, overtiredness, eye inflammation.

Except in special circumstances, women weren't allowed in the men's infirmary. Thankfully, Sister Loretta was the only nurse on duty.

"Why, Mrs. Marvin, are you here for your shift?"

"Tomorrow," she said. "And in the ladies' infirmary."

"That's right." She took Mirielle's hand and patted it. Her age-spotted skin was always soft and cool. "These long summer days get me so confused."

"I came to ask after Hector."

"Nephritis, I'm afraid."

"How severe?"

"It's too soon to know, dearie."

"Can I see him?"

Sister Loretta glanced around as if to be sure Sister Verena wasn't there, then nodded. "Bed fifteen. Just a quick visit, mind you."

Mirielle walked down the center aisle of the room past several beds before reaching Hector's. The overhead lights had already been turned off for the evening, but twilight stole in through the open windows.

In bed fifteen lay Hector, asleep. Mirielle pulled over a stool and sat down, but did not wake him. Five months had passed since their journey from California. How frightened she'd been of him, of everyone in the boxcar. How little she'd known about the disease.

She tucked his blanket around his shoulders and made sure his water glass was filled. His face looked puffy, his closed eyes like overstuffed pillows squeezed into their sockets. Not a good sign. Edema like this happened when the kidneys weren't working and the body couldn't get rid of fluid, Sister Verena had taught her. But Mirielle had seen women with swelling like this improve suddenly, their bedpans dry one minute, overflowing the next.

Before leaving, she leaned over and kissed him lightly on the cheek. A few days and he'd be just fine. Doc Jack was treating him. And Sister Verena. As much as Mirielle disliked the woman, her skills as a nurse were unparalleled. Even Sister Loretta, who now sat knitting at the nurses' desk, would show him the utmost care and love. Mirielle needn't worry. Or so she tried to convince herself.

CHAPTER 31

For the next two weeks, Mirielle went about her routine—work in the hospital, card games with Madge and Irene, bedtime stories with Jean—and tried not to worry over Hector. Some days when she'd sneak into the infirmary to see him, he looked better, sitting up in bed and sipping broth or reading the newspaper. Other days he was drowsy, confused, his legs and feet so swollen they looked like tree trunks beneath the blankets.

Payday rolled around at the beginning of August. She'd learned from past months that the day was a celebration all its own at Carville. House orderlies distributed the money, collecting signatures for Sister Verena's meticulous records in exchange for the ten to forty dollars each worker was owed. It might have been an onerous task—tracking down everyone on the list—but word got around quickly, and residents queued wherever their assigned orderly could be found.

Afterward, residents rushed to the canteen and rec hall. The crowd swelled at the far corner of the hall where dice were shot and cards played. So too did the noise—cheers and curses and arguments that, often as not, ended in fisticuffs. In the canteen, stock flew from the shelves as quickly as Frank could replace it. The soda fountain went dry, and the ice chest empty.

Mail piled up for the sterilizer, five and ten dollar bills neatly folded and tucked within the pages of letters by those residents whose families on the outside still depended upon them to eat. Some families wouldn't take the money, Mirielle had heard. Others soaked it in bichloride of mercury as soon as it arrived, then hung it on the clothesline to dry. Those in direst need wasted no time in handing it over to the landlord or grocery clerk, she suspected.

The first time she'd received her pay—thirty dollars, minus fifteen for the wasted ointment in the pharmacy and ruined uniforms—had indeed felt like cause to celebrate. It was a paltry sum considering she'd had more than ten times that amount for pocket money back in California. But that money had been given. First by her father, then by Charlie. This money she'd earned all on her own. The coins felt heavier somehow, the bills crisper. Every time she bought a soda at the fountain or flipped through a catalog, dog-earing items to buy, she felt . . . capable. Able to effect her own ends.

But today, Mirielle didn't feel like celebrating. Not for thirty dollars or three hundred. She avoided the swarm of women around Irene and sat down on the nearby porch steps. Though it wasn't yet ten o'clock, the August air was hot and sticky, and she fanned herself with a palm leaf fan.

"Sorry about the wait, baby," Irene said a few minutes later, grunting and wincing as she sat down beside her. "These old bones ain't what they used to be."

"I'm in no rush."

She handed Mirielle her thirty dollars, and Mirielle scribbled her name. The first few times she'd signed, she'd had to cross out her real name and print the name Pauline Marvin. Now, she hardly had to think about it.

"What you gonna do now that you're a rich woman?" She nudged Mirielle with her elbow. "Oh wait, you always was rich."

Mirielle shrugged.

"You sure are a sad sack lately. Why don't you head over to the canteen and pick yourself out something nice from the Sears and Roebuck catalog?"

"And by nice you mean cheap and common?"

Irene smiled. "There you go, baby. More like your normal high-hatted self already."

Mirielle managed a fleeting laugh.

"You go on, and I'll meet you," Irene said. "I gotta get these signatures back to Sister Verena before she has a conniption fit."

They stood and parted ways halfway down the walk. Mirielle was in no hurry to get to the canteen. She fanned herself as she walked, drawing what cheer she could from flowers and birdsong beyond the screens. It might be hot, but the lawns and trees and gardens colored the colony a vibrant summer green. In this, California's woody palms and pale eucalyptus couldn't compare.

The walkway brought her past house twelve. As always, several men lazed on the porch in rocking chairs, their outstretched legs spilling onto the walkway like hurdles on a racetrack. She knew better than to listen in on their gossip, but she heard one of them mention Hector's name followed by the word *greaser.*

Mirielle stopped. "What did you just say?"

"Huh?" one of the old men grunted.

"Hector's in the infirmary, and you lazy heels are sitting here calling him a greaser?"

The man gave a snort. "I told you she had a thing for spics."

Mirielle's fingernails dug into her palms. It wasn't that she hadn't heard such words before. She'd uttered them a time or two herself. But that was before. Hadn't this disease and its stigma taught them anything? "You'd think, seeing as we're all lepers here, you might find it in your old withered hearts to be a bit kinder."

The men flinched at the word *leper.* She stepped over their outstretched legs and continued on.

"He ain't got no business here," one of the men called after her. "This place is for Americans."

Mirielle didn't turn around. Telling them Hector had been born in California wouldn't change their minds. Instead, she raised her arm and extended her middle finger—the way she'd seen drunken men in clubs do.

Not until she rounded the corner did Mirielle lower her hand. That would show those nosy old men. But Sister Verena was just beyond the bend walking in her direction.

"Good heavens, Mrs. Marvin, what are you doing?"

"Just . . . er . . . stretching my arm. I had a cramp."

"And your finger?"

"A cramp."

Sister Verena stopped. The great wings of her hat cast her face in shadow, but Mirielle could still make out the sour disapproval in her eyes. "See to it that it doesn't cramp again. This is a hospital, Mrs. Marvin. Not a back-alley saloon."

"I'll do my best."

"Why is it that your best always seems to come up wanting?"

Mirielle's jaw clenched, but she held her tongue and let Sister Verena pass, extending her finger again quickly behind the sister's back.

When she arrived at the canteen, it was a throbbing tangle of customers. Only a few cans of sardines and a couple of cakes of shaving soap remained on the shelves. All four of the tables were filled with people sipping Cokes and flipping through newly purchased rags. Mirielle sat on the last free stool at the far end of the counter.

"Sorry, Polly. I'm outta soda," Frank said, stacking empty glasses into the washbasin behind the counter.

"That's okay. I just wanted to take a look at the Sears and Roebuck catalog."

He fetched the catalog from a shelf beneath the counter and poured her a glass of water. "A lagniappe for our champion frog hunter."

"Lagniappe?"

"A li'l something extra."

"A glass of water? That's your idea of a little something extra?"

"This ain't the Ritz, *chère*." He winked and went back to his washing.

Mirielle opened the thick catalog. She missed the creams and tonics she'd ordered from Paris. Cold cream, whitening cream, vanishing cream, eyebrow cream; talcum powder and toilet water; perfume and hair-curling fluid. Cheaper versions of these products were sold in the catalog, but they wouldn't feel and smell the same.

She pulled her wages from her pocket. What from her old life would this buy? A pot of cream? A few cakes of lavender-scented soap? She closed the Sears and Roebuck catalog and pushed it away. Neither a fine perfume nor a cheap imitation would make her feel better. Here she was bemoaning bath products when Hector's family mightn't eat this month. And who knew how long until he'd be well enough to work again.

"Where's that can you put out?" she said to Frank. The What Cheer Club had an old coffee can it occasionally set out for donations. Sometimes the money went to practical concerns like replacement batteries for the radio or new netting for the tennis court. Sometimes the money went to the blind residents or to help fix up someone's wheelchair. She didn't know whether money had ever been raised to send to someone's family, but it seemed just as worthy a cause.

Frank finished drying the glass in his hand, then set it beside the soda fountain and looked at her.

"Hector's been in the infirmary two weeks now," she said. "But he's got a family he supports on the outside. Maybe we could put the can out for him. For his family."

Frank gave a low whistle. "If I didn't know better, I'd say that sounded like altruism."

"Oh, phooey. It's just . . . we Californians got to stick together."

"Usually, the club gotta decide about the can together."

"If you wait, people will burn through their pay, and there won't be any money to be had."

He nodded, slowly, thoughtfully, then withdrew the can from beneath the counter. "Suppose we could make an exception."

Mirielle finished her water and dropped her thirty dollars in the can. She was just about to leave when church bells rang out. Her body stiffened. The sound roiled her stomach more than the god-awful chaulmoogra pills. The bells at Union Chapel and Sacred Heart tolled once on the hour from dawn to dusk. They tolled for mass and Sunday service. When they tolled like this, though, several slow strokes in the middle of the morning, it was a death knell.

CHAPTER 32

Two days later, Mirielle shuffled into one of the back pews of Sacred Heart. Incense stung her eyes, or at least that's what she told herself when they began to water. The priest wore a white tunic and embroidered stole over his black robes. Hector's coffin, a simple affair of unpolished wood, lay on trestles in front of the dais.

What had possessed her to come? Were she not already squeezed into the middle of the pew, Jean and Madge on one side of her and Irene on the other, Mirielle would have fled. As it was, she could barely keep herself from hyperventilating.

She tried to focus on the little things. The stained glass. The flickering candle flames. The notes of the reed organ Sister Katherine played in the corner. The rest of the sisters and several staff members filled a bank of pews separate from those the residents occupied. None of Hector's family was there. Though surely they'd been notified. But even if they'd had the money to come, they never would have made it in time. Hector's body could have been shipped back to California, if his family could afford the expense, including the cost of a sealed metal casket.

Most everyone in the chapel lined up for their wine and wafers, while Mirielle, Irene, and the rest of the Protestants remained seated. The sisters and staff drank from a different chalice than the patients. Even in God's house, the disease separated them.

After the service, the priest led the procession from the chapel to the cemetery on the far side of the colony. Six orderlies dressed in black coats and white trousers carried the coffin. Next walked the sisters, followed by several dozen of the residents.

Mirielle and her housemates trailed at the end. It took conscious effort for her to put one foot in front of the other. Never mind the humid air and buzzing insects, the boggy soil and overabundant green. With each step, she had to remind herself where she was, that this wasn't *his* funeral.

The cemetery lay behind a tidy row of pecan trees. Dozens of squat white gravestones sprouted amid the grass. Irrational as it was, Mirielle avoided reading the stones' simple inscriptions for fear Felix's name would be among them.

The priest sprinkled holy water on the ground where the coffin was to be interred. Two residents waited nearby in the shade of the pecan trees, shovels in hand. After the priest's final benediction, Mirielle and the others took their leave. At the sound of the shovel blades striking dirt, her step faltered. Before she could make it but a few steps beyond the cemetery, she doubled over and dry heaved.

Later that evening, Mirielle made her way to where Frank lived, beyond the walkways and patient houses in a cabin he'd built himself. It was one of half a dozen detached cabins collectively called Cottage Grove. With the help of Mr. Li and Irene, Frank had organized a small remembrance supper for Hector and taken up a collection for his family. Music played on the phonograph, and the smell of frying fish wafted from inside. Mirielle hadn't eaten all day— a smart choice, considering how her stomach had turned inside out at the graveyard. It grumbled now, but Mirielle didn't trust it. She hadn't come to eat anyway.

Mr. Hatch, Madge, and a few others sat on the cottage's wide front porch. Inside, Frank stood by the stove, flipping the fish while Irene cut watermelon at the table. The cabin was tidy—for a bachelor— with a bed, sofa, and mismatched dinette.

"Oh good, Polly, you're here," Irene said, wiping her hands on a brightly colored apron tied over her black dress. "Just in time for supper."

"I'm not staying. I just came to drop off a few things for the collection."

On the small table beside the sofa, a collection of odds and ends had amassed. Mirielle set a gold brooch down beside the packets of buttons, hand-knit hats, seed packets, a jar of honey, and a small envelope of bills addressed to Hector's family.

" 'Course you stayin'," Irene said before Mirielle could sneak out. "Get them tin plates from the cupboard and set 'em by the greens."

Mirielle didn't have the energy to argue. She set out the plates just as Frank hollered to those on the porch. "Eatin's on."

When she turned to leave, Irene was standing between her and the door, a heaping plate of food in hand. "Eat."

"I don't think I could."

Irene thrust the plate into her hand anyway and shooed her out to the porch. Mirielle sat on the steps and stared out at the lawn. She moved the food around on her plate a while before finally taking a bite. The fish was flaky and well seasoned. She waited for her stomach's reaction before taking another bite. When it didn't flip or tighten, she forked up some greens.

She'd eaten most everything on her plate when Mr. Hatch sat down beside her. She'd seen him a few times on the walkways and standing in line in the dining hall but hadn't exchanged more than a nod with him since their conversation in the tea garden all those months ago.

"Your supposed hole in the fence wasn't there when I went looking."

He took a bite of watermelon, spitting the seeds onto the porch. Juice dribbled down his chin. "They close it up from time to time."

"I broke my arm trying to climb over."

"Heard about that." He took another bite, continuing to talk as he chewed. "Shoulda been more careful."

His clothes smelled of must and perspiration. Crescents of dirt showed beneath his ragged fingernails. She knew now from Irene that Mr. Hatch was somewhat of a celebrity around the colony. A consummate malcontent who could always be counted on to raise sand when the high muck-a-mucks instituted a new rule or policy he didn't like. Many of the residents revered him. Others thought him a fanatic and self-serving exhibitionist.

Mirielle wasn't sure what to make of Mr. Hatch, but she didn't want her calfskin shoes to be a casualty of the watermelon seeds rocketing from his mouth. "Can you spit those seeds somewhere else?"

He chewed his next bite of watermelon very slowly, then plucked the seeds from his mouth with his dirty fingers and flicked them one by one onto the lawn. "Better?"

"Marginally."

He laughed. "I like you, Polly. Most women woulda turned their noses up and walked away. You're like me. We ain't afraid to tell it like it is."

Mirielle wasn't sure whether that was much of a compliment.

"Next time you wanna escape, come find me, and we'll go together," he said.

"To the cathouse? No, thanks."

"Suit yourself." He jabbed a thumb toward her plate. "You gonna finish that?"

"It's all yours."

Irene came by with jars of sweet tea as Mr. Hatch swallowed down the last of her fish. Everyone had gathered on the porch. Mirielle and Mr. Hatch stood and joined them.

"To Hector," Frank said, raising his glass.

"To Hector." Mirielle and the others drank their tea.

Louisiana could have its shrimp and gumbo, but the tea she'd be taking back to California with her. Mirielle polished off her glass and went inside for more. Irene stood by the sink, mixing sugar into a fresh pitcher. Frank had come in behind her and sat on the sofa, flipping through his box of records.

"You seemed mighty shaken today," Irene said.

"I . . . it's been a while since I was at a funeral."

"Best get used to it, baby." Irene refilled Mirielle's glass. "We hardly go a month around here without one."

"Don't make it any easier," Frank said without looking up.

"No, I suppose not." Irene wrapped an arm around Mirielle's waist and squeezed. "When I lost my first husband in the Spanish War, I—"

"The Spanish War?" Frank interrupted. "Way I heard tell, it was the War between the States."

Irene let go of Mirielle's waist and threw a dishtowel at him. "You know I ain't half as old as all that." They both laughed. Mirielle tried to join in but found herself on the verge of tears instead.

"I killed my son."

Frank and Irene stopped laughing.

"He drowned. In a swimming pool."

Irene pulled over a chair from the dinette and ushered Mirielle into it. "Baby, that don't mean you killed him."

"I should have been watching him. He was a good swimmer, and I thought the nanny . . ." She shook her head and cradled her midsection.

"Still don't make it your fault." Irene squatted down and handed her a hankie. But even though Mirielle's voice trembled, her eyes were dry. She took the hankie anyway and wrapped it like a tourniquet around her palm.

Frank cleared his throat. "What was his name, your boy?"

Mirielle turned toward the sofa where he sat. She'd almost forgotten he was here but somehow was glad he now knew the truth of it. "Felix Jeremiah West. He was seven and a half years old."

It felt good to say his name, to acknowledge him among the others they mourned. She loosened the hankie and handed it back to Irene. Her fingertips prickled with the return of blood.

Irene swatted Mirielle's knee and stood. "Baby, you can't move on and live your life with all them should'ves hanging over your head."

"Amen to that," Frank said.

"You got any bootleg up in here?" Irene asked him.

He jutted his chin toward the cupboard. Irene poked around the shelves, then pulled out a jar from the very back. Brown liquid sloshed inside. She poured some into Mirielle's tea. "Days like this call for a little somethin' extra." Irene held the jar up to Frank, but he shook his head. She added some to her own glass then stowed it back in the cupboard. "Let's join the rest of them outside where it's cooler."

Mirielle let herself be shepherded back to the porch. The rotgut soured the tea, and Mirielle set it aside, wary of the once-familiar numbness it promised.

"His family will be fine," Mr. Hatch was saying to Madge and Mr.

Li as Mirielle pulled up a chair beside them. "Get along better now without him."

She flinched at his words. But by the way Hector had described the strain his illness had placed on his family, Mr. Hatch was right.

"Hell, all our families would be better off if we were dead," he continued. "This disease, it marks us. Follows us wherever we go. Once a leper always a leper. Only chance our families have is without us."

"That's a load of baloney," Irene said.

"Doc Jack says once it's arrested, the disease isn't contagious," Mirielle said weakly.

Mr. Hatch looked her square in the eyes. "If you think they give two licks about that on the outside, you ain't half as smart as I thought you was."

"That's enough, Samuel."

Mirielle hadn't heard Frank come outside and startled at the sharpness in his voice.

"This day's about Hector," Irene said, then patted Mirielle's shoulder. "And all those we've lost. Not an excuse for more of your bellyachin'."

Mr. Hatch spat and stomped away.

The rest of them sat a moment in silence, the humid air thick between them. Then Irene said, "I remember, this one time, Hector come to the pharmacy to get the chaulmoogra capsules, but when he . . ."

Mirielle stared beyond the lawn at the distant forest. The sun glowed orange over the treetops. She tried to listen to stories about Hector, but all she could hear were Mr. Hatch's words. *Only chance our families have is without us.*

CHAPTER 33

—————

"*Ahem*. We're almost out of needles and syringes, Mrs. Marvin."

Mirielle turned from the window and caught Sister Verena's stern gaze. "Hmm?"

"Needles and syringes."

"Oh." She rattled her head and looked down at the empty supply table. "Right."

The pan of boiling water they used to disinfect the equipment hissed behind her. Beside it on the counter was a towel where Mirielle placed the sterilized needles and syringes to dry. It was an onerous task, keeping the flow of equipment steady, one that required constant attention and careful timing. If they ran out, Sister Verena would scowl, and the residents in line for their chaulmoogra shots would grumble.

Over the past months, Mirielle had become skilled at managing the tempo, moving the used pieces aside, restocking the supply table once the latest batch had cooled, fishing the slender needles and delicate glass syringes from the water, setting them on the towel to dry, boiling away the sticky chaulmoogra oil and blood from a new set.

But today, she couldn't seem to corral her thoughts and tame her attention. She hurried to the back of the room and gathered up the supplies on the towel. All were cool to the touch and had likely been dry for several minutes.

"Here you go," Mirielle said, arranging the sterilized supplies on the table and grabbing the tray of used ones.

She expected Sister Verena to sigh or glower in response. Instead, the woman looked at her with a level expression and said, "My dear, you cannot let Mr. Sanchez's death sadden you to distraction. You must trust he's in the arms of the Lord now, free from pain and suffering."

"Free of this disease, you mean."

Sister Verena nodded.

"Is death our only hope then?"

"You should not fear death, Mrs. Marvin."

Mirielle touched her silver bracelet. She didn't fear death, or hadn't anyway. But now, she wanted to live.

"But no," Sister Verena continued. "I do not believe death is the only hope." She gestured at the room around them—the large bottles of chaulmoogra oil, the X-ray equipment pushed to the side, the privacy screen behind which Doc Jack sat, ready to inject another patient. "It's why we're here, after all. God helps those who help themselves."

"The Bible says that?"

Sister Verena's lips twitched in what might be a smile. "No. Benjamin Franklin, I believe."

Mirielle gave an almost-smile in return and got back to work. She didn't understand why Hector's death had affected her so deeply. It was as if he'd been a tether to her life before, her life in California, and now that tether was broken. She managed to keep up an ample supply of clean needles and syringes as the morning dragged on, but her almost-smile quickly faded and didn't return.

With only a dozen patients remaining in line, Frank shuffled forward for his shot. While Sister Verena's attention was diverted drawing up his dose of oil, he leaned across the supply table and whispered to Mirielle, "Saturday night, hurry up with supper, then meet me under the oaks. Five thirty sharp."

What the devil? Before she could speak, he put a crooked finger to his lips and disappeared behind the screen.

Mirielle wondered over Frank's cryptic words all the next day.

"He knows I'm married, right?" she asked Irene as they sorted pills in the pharmacy. Even if his intentions weren't romantic, if anyone saw them alone together under the oaks, the Rocking Chair Brigade would be spitting gossip for days.

"Hard to miss that shiny gold ring on your finger."

"Maybe I shouldn't meet him."

"Listen, baby, I've known a lot of men in my life. Most of 'em blockheads. But Frank, he's one of the good ones. Just go. It'll be worth your while and then some."

Clearly, Irene knew more than she was letting on.

"Please tell me I won't need to borrow your galoshes again."

Irene smiled. "Not this time, baby."

The next night, despite her misgivings, Mirielle snuck out after supper. The oak tree–studded lawn appeared empty when she arrived. Robins crooned from the branches, and Spanish moss undulated in the evening breeze. She started to turn back when she heard a low whistle.

Mirielle looked in the direction of the sound and saw Frank behind the thick trunk of one of the trees, frantically waving her over. She reached him just as Watchman Doyle strode into view.

"Shh," he said, pulling her to a crouch beside him. His hair, once again slick and tamed, glinted beneath his hat in the golden sunlight. He smelled of sandalwood and shaving soap. They peered from behind the trunk as Watchman Doyle strode along the fence with his watchclock. When he reached the far corner of the fence and headed westward toward the houses, Frank whispered, "Come on."

Before Mirielle could ask where they were going, Frank dashed to the fence. Mirielle hesitated a moment, then followed, her heels sinking into the soft ground as she tried to keep up. By the time she reached the fence, Frank had already clipped several strands of wire near the bottom with pliers he'd pulled from his pocket. He peeled back the section of the fencing he'd cut as if it were the lid on a can of sardines and gestured for her to crawl through.

"I can't run away. Dr. Ross said if I tried again, I'd get another month in jail."

"It's just for the night," Frank said. "We'll be back before anyone realizes we're gone."

After a moment's indecision, she hunched down and scrambled through. Frank followed, then carefully realigned the fence. Without bending down and inspecting each link, Watchman Doyle would never know the strands had been cut. They crept to the edge of the road and waited in the gully until dust plumed, and a Model T truck stopped a few yards ahead. It honked its horn once.

"Wait here." Frank approached the driver, keeping his hands in his pockets until the driver nodded. Frank passed him a folded bill. She realized watching him that Frank was dressed more dapper than usual. He wore a smart suit of worsted gray wool and a curve-brimmed derby hat. He looked like a jaunty city fellow, not an escaped leper. But surely the driver knew. He took Frank's money nevertheless and motioned with his head to the bed of the truck. Frank waved her over and helped her up. A thin layer of straw covered the bed, but the truck rumbled out of idle before she could think twice about sitting down.

The Model T lumbered over ruts and through potholes, jostling Mirielle like ice in a cocktail shaker. Dust choked the air. But she felt a strange lightness, a giddiness almost, at being away from Carville.

"Where are we going?" she yelled above the truck's rattle.

"New Orleans."

CHAPTER 34

⟶≫◦≪⟵

They reached the city just before ten. The streets in the outlying neighborhoods were empty, the windows of the ornately trimmed houses dark. But as they neared the center of New Orleans, automobiles and streetcars and horse-drawn wagons rumbled past them. People crowded the sidewalks.

"I forgot what civilization looks like," Mirielle said. It wasn't just the way it looked. It was the sound of honking horns and jingling shop doors and hollering street vendors. It was the smell of gasoline and restaurants and trash bins. She drank it all in.

Their driver dropped them off at the corner of what Frank called the Vieux Carré. The buildings here were foreign-looking and run-down, their stucco siding cracked and roofs speckled with moss. Standing on the sidewalk as roadsters and touring cars rattled past, Mirielle felt suddenly naked. What if someone caught on that they were lepers? She'd heard stories from other patients about absconders returning to Carville in shackles or at gunpoint. Of townsfolk hurling stones and garbage to chase them away.

Mirielle's skin tightened around her bones. The fruit seller across the street kept glancing their way as he packed up his cart. The whispering trio of women waiting for the streetcar were surely talking about her. The electric street lamp that hummed overhead shone brightly as a spotlight. She fingered the beads around her neck, hoping they concealed her lesion well enough that it wouldn't draw attention.

The Model T sputtered off before Mirielle could suggest they forget their plans—whatever they were—and return to Carville. A man exited a nearby building and walked straight toward them. Panic twisted inside her. He knew. He must.

Frank, however, appeared unconcerned. His shirt and jacket covered the lesions on his forearms, and his misshapen hands were hidden in his pockets.

"Ready, *chère*?"

The man continued toward them. Mirielle clutched Frank's arm. "That man, I think he—" Just before reaching them, the man turned down an alley without heed to anyone. He unbuttoned his pants and pissed on the brick wall.

"Oh." Mirielle hurriedly looked away, hoping her cheeks weren't as red as they were warm.

"No one's gonna notice us here," Frank said.

She released her stranglehold on his arm. "You going to tell me what sort of shenanigans you're up to?"

"Don't worry. Our mission's completely square. Come on."

She couldn't help but laugh. So far, nothing about the evening had been square, but the shadow that had stalked her since Hector's funeral hadn't made it into the truck bed in time to follow her. That was worth whatever mischief Frank had planned.

He led her through the city to the train station. Even at this hour, the grand lobby was crowded with travelers. Electric pendulum lights hung from the high ceiling. Rows of wooden benches filled the room. She heard what sounded like Italian and German as well as French and English as they wound their way toward the far corner of the lobby, opposite the ticket office.

Frank stopped when they reached a bank of telephone booths. He glanced at the large clock above them on the wall. "It's only eight thirty in California. Ya think your family's still up?"

Mirielle stared dumbly at him for a moment. The din around her faded, and her heart beat a ragtime rhythm. She suddenly realized she hadn't brought a purse or evening bag and hadn't any money, but Frank was already thrusting a small bag of quarters into her hand. "Go on. I'll wait for you here."

She closed herself within one of the booths. The phone, the same model as any old public telephone, looked foreign to her. She rattled

her head, took a deep breath, and lifted the receiver. When the operator asked for the number, Mirielle responded without pause. She fed
a dozen quarters into the machine and waited as the line went quiet.
Then the butler's familiar voice sounded through the earpiece.

"Hello?"

Mirielle's throat cinched around her voice box.

"Hello?"

She moved closer to the mouthpiece. "Hello, this is Mrs. Mar—
Mrs. West. I'd like to speak with my husband, please."

After a long pause, the butler said, "Mrs. West?"

"Yes, Mrs. Mirielle Lee West. Can you put Charlie on the line and
fetch the children, if they're up?"

Another pause. "Er . . . yes . . . just a moment, Mrs. West."

The line was silent for an interminably long time before another
voice sounded through the earpiece. "Now see here, I don't know
what you mean by—"

"Charlie, it's me."

"Mirielle? How did . . . where are—"

"New Orleans. I just slipped away to call."

"Slipped away?" He sounded different than she remembered, his
voice strident and thin.

"How are the girls? Can I talk to them?"

"Talk to them? . . . Yes, yes of course." She heard him cover the
mouthpiece, holler for the nanny, then return to the line. "How—
er—how are you feeling?"

"Fine. Great. Healthy as a May morning," she said, but couldn't
help slipping her hand beneath her necklace to touch her lesion.
"How's the new picture?"

"Swell," he said. "Cecil's terrific. The whole production's being
managed in great style."

"And what about working with Miss Thorne? Is she as boorish as
everyone says?"

"Gloria? No, she's been perfectly—wait, Evie's here."

Perfectly what, Mirielle wondered as Charlie handed over the
telephone.

"Mama!"

Mirielle wasn't prepared for the stabbing pain her daughter's
sweet voice inflicted. Tears flooded her eyes, but she willed her voice

steady. "Evie, dearest. It's wonderful to hear you on the line. Have you been behaving for Daddy and the nanny while I've been away?"

"I have, I promise, Mama. When are you coming home?"

"Soon, my love."

"How soon?"

"In a few months."

"Mama, some boys at Kitty's birthday party said you'd gone crazy as a june bug and weren't ever coming home."

Mirielle's heart squeezed. "Don't you listen to them. I'm looking after my sick auntie, and as soon as she's better again I'll be home."

"They pulled my braids, Mama, and said crazy's in the blood, and I'm gonna get it too."

Mirielle curled around the phone. Tears dripped from her chin onto the collar of her dress. "Oh, darling, that's not true. They're just being ornery."

"I hope your auntie gets better soon."

"Me too. Now tell me more about Kitty's party. Did she have a cake and candles?"

"Yes, a great big cake and—"

The operator cut in. "Another dollar to continue your call."

Mirielle fumbled with the bag of quarters, her hands sweaty and shaky. She managed to slip three quarters into the coin slot but dropped the last one on the ground. She bent down, feeling for it atop the dusty flooring while keeping the receiver pressed to her ear.

"Please insert more—"

"Just a moment," she shouted up at the mouthpiece. When she found the quarter and inserted it, Evie's voice returned, midway through her description of the party.

Not long after, Mirielle heard a muffled voice in the background. Evie huffed into the line. "Daddy says I've got to give Helen a turn, even though she's a baby and hardly says two words. Bye, Mama."

"I love you, Evie." Mirielle leaned so close the mouth horn pressed against her face. "You hear me? I love you."

Static was the only reply. She waited with the receiver to her ear. A cooing noise sounded, followed by a string of babble.

"Helen? Helen, it's your mama."

"Say 'Hello, Mama,'" the nanny said in the background. Helen made a few more garbled sounds.

"My sweet baby." A sob slipped past Mirielle's lips. "I'm coming home soon. I think of you every day and—"

A rapping noise sounded on the phone booth door. "You about finished in there?" an unfamiliar voice said.

"She'll be finished when she's finished," Frank said.

"I ain't got all night to wait around in line."

Mirielle leaned in closer to the phone and covered her other ear with her palm. "Helen, darling, you still there?"

"It's me again," Charlie said. He sounded more like himself now, steady and sure. As if the nightmare of the past months hadn't happened. As if he'd rung her from the studio to let her know he'd be home late and not to wait on him for dinner. "This business Evie was talking about, those pesky boys, don't put any stock—"

"I saw the *Picture-Play* article, Charlie."

Silence carried across the line. Her eyes welled again.

"People don't believe it, do they? Our friends. You're telling them it's not true. That it's just a nasty rumor."

"I'm sorry, Mirielle, I never meant . . . I just wanted those muckrakers off my back."

"*You* told the reporters that?"

"They were hounding me night and day."

"Charlie, the entire city thinks I'm crazy now!"

"I had to tell them something," he replied, and then, in a mutter, "It's better than the truth."

Mirielle flinched.

"It's not so bad, darling. Really," Charlie continued. "Half of Hollywood has been to an alienist."

"Visiting a psychotherapist and being locked away in a nut farm are hardly the same thing."

"How long could I go on telling people you were off caring for some sick relative? Besides, the news didn't come as much of a surprise to people. Not considering the way you'd been acting since . . ."

"And how was I supposed to act?" she yelled into the mouthpiece. "Like you? Like everything was hunky-dory and my son hadn't drowned?"

Charlie didn't reply. Before she could apologize the operator cut in again. "Please insert one more dollar to continue your call."

Mirielle upended Frank's bag. Empty. She felt for pockets in her

dress where she might have stowed loose change, remembering be-
latedly the dress hadn't any pockets. She fingered the coin return, but
it too was empty.

"Please, patch me in again, just thirty more seconds."

"I'm sorry, I can't do that," the operator replied.

"I haven't spoken to my family in months. I just want to say—"

"Goodbye." A clicking sound followed, and the line went dead.

Mirielle dropped the receiver. It swung back and forth on its cord
like a pendulum. She lay her head atop the phone box and wept.

Sometime later—half a minute, half an hour, she wasn't sure—
another knock sounded on the door. This one soft and gentle. She
wiped her eyes and stepped outside.

Frank handed her his handkerchief as the next man in line brushed
past them into the phone booth. "Sorry, I thought it would be nice for
ya to talk to your family."

Mirielle blew her nose, a loud, unladylike honking. She felt tired,
gutted, but when she looked up at the wall clock, she saw only fifteen
minutes had passed since they'd arrived at the station.

"We've got another few hours before our driver returns," Frank
said. "I'm guessing ya could use a drink."

"Boy, could I."

"Come on."

CHAPTER 35

———>•◦•‹———

Mirielle followed Frank down one street and up the next. They crossed a grand boulevard with a tree-lined median into the shabbier part of town where the driver had first dropped them.

He didn't pry into her telephone conversation, as if it were perfectly natural to be walking beside a woman with a runny nose, tear-salted cheeks, and bloodshot eyes. The unobtrusive silence had given her time to cobble herself back together. To rebuild the walls necessary to survive Carville. Now she needed distraction. "How often do you sneak out and come here?"

"Not often. I snuck out more in the beginning. I was angry then, and it felt good to flip my finger at the world."

The kernel of a laugh rocked inside her. She couldn't imagine him flipping a finger at anyone. "When did it go away? The anger, I mean."

Frank shrugged. He was a good head taller than she, and the brim of his hat shaded his face from the lamplight. "I still am, sometimes."

"It's a ruse then? Mr. Happy-Go-Lucky."

He took off his hat and ran a hand through his hair, upsetting the smoothed strands. She could see his expression now, his furrowed brow and focused stare. "No. That's me too."

Mirielle frowned. "That's what I hate most. How this"—she lowered her voice even though no one else was within earshot—"this disease cleaves you into two people. Without it, you'd just be . . . you."

"Ya can't let it split ya like that or you'll go mad. Trust me. Besides, even if—" He paused and flashed that earnest smile of his. "Even *when* ya go home, ya won't be the same person ya were before. No two ways about that. With or without the disease, life ain't that damn long. Might as well make the most of it, or try at least. Wherever ya are."

"You sound like a traveling salesman."

His smile turned sheepish. "Sister Verena gave me that advice. Back in the beginning. When there weren't nothing to me but anger."

Their footsteps echoed into the night as Mirielle considered his words. Spice-scented aromas wafted from the late-night restaurants they passed. She couldn't imagine him like that, all anger. And she certainly couldn't imagine Sister Verena giving such kind, sage advice.

"There's no way Sister Verena said 'damn.' "

He laughed. "I might have added a little color to her words."

They turned down an alleyway and stopped before an unvarnished door flanked by rusty trash cans and moldering crates. Frank looked over his shoulder, then knocked four times.

The alley smelled of urine and rotting lettuce. Patches of brick showed behind the crumbling stucco façade. She wasn't a stranger to backdoor entries, but most of the speaks she and Charlie had frequented boasted nicer entrances.

After nearly a minute had passed, the door opened just enough for a flat-faced man to peek his head out.

"What'd ya want?" he said in heavily accented English.

"*Un jeu de billiard c'est tout*," Frank said.

Mirielle followed the man's gaze downward. Frank held a folded bill between two of his misshapen fingers. The man frowned, and Mirielle's heart floundered. He looked between her and Frank with narrow, beady eyes. "*Un jeu de billiard*," he repeated with a snort, then took the money and let them in.

They followed him down a short hallway into a dimly lit, smoky room. A bar ran the length of one wall, fringed with mismatched stools. A billiard table sat to one side of the room, opposite a small dance floor ringed with tables. A band played from a raised platform at the far end. Several couples jigged on the dance floor.

Naked bulbs crowned with tin shades hung from the ceiling. Posters papered the walls, stained with smoke and curling at the edges. Nothing like the cut-glass chandeliers and velvet-dressed clubs Mirielle was used to. The music too was different. Rawer. The partiers' laughter less restrained.

What would Charlie think of this place? Had their telephone conversation felt as strained to him as it had to her? How long would it take them to fall back into step together when she returned?

She followed Frank to the bar, grateful he hadn't chosen a table by the dance floor. He sat down on the stool closest to the wall and ordered them both a drink. Mirielle sat beside him.

"*Salut*," he said to her after the bartender set two highballs before them.

The liquor wasn't as strong as Frank's home brew. But a hefty slug more potent than the gin or champagne she favored at home. She leaned her forearms on the bar and curled her hands around the glass. Evie's voice returned to her as she drank. Helen's cooing. Charlie's silence at the end. Tears smarted in her eyes again.

How dare he spread such lies about her! If she were free, she'd catch the first train home and finish giving him a piece of her mind. She took another gulp of her drink. As the bright liquid spread across her tongue and down her throat, it occurred to her she was free. There wasn't any barbwire fence here. No orderly counting heads. No watchman.

"I—er—I'm gonna freshen up my face." It was a silly thing to say, considering she hadn't brought anything with her. But Frank nodded, perhaps thinking she had a powder puff tucked beneath the strap of her brassiere.

The washroom was a tiny, filthy room with newsprint on the walls and a cracked enamel sink. She splashed water on her face, building up the courage to run. She wasn't sure how to make it back to the train station or how—without any money—she'd manage to book a ticket. But she'd figure those things out as she went. Back home, everyone would see how perfectly sane she was and leave her daughters alone. Charlie could set the record straight with those pesky reporters. Well, not straight exactly, but crooked in a different direction. One that didn't make her out to be a madwoman. Or a leper.

She dried her face on the hem of her skirt rather than the grimy hand towel and reached for the door. Her pulse thudded in her ears.

Her limbs tingled with exhilaration and a touch of fear. She need only peek around the corner to ensure Frank wasn't looking and then—

Frank. Undoubtedly he'd worry for her and come looking. Miss his ride back to Carville. Spend a month or more in that mice-infested jail when he returned. All because he'd tried to help her. And Irene. If Dr. Ross learned Irene knew about the plot, she might get in trouble too.

Mirielle's hand hovered over the doorknob. No, she couldn't run. Not tonight. Not when her friends would suffer for it. Besides, if there was one thing that could be said of Hollywood, it was that nothing remained a scandal for long. She straightened her dress and swallowed the sorrow building in her throat.

The band had taken a break between sets, so the club was quieter when she returned. Voices rose and fell. Laughter. The occasional grunt or shout. The musicians stood beside the stage, smoking and guzzling down drinks. Dancers crowded the bar. Mirielle threaded her way back to her seat. She'd grown so accustomed to Carville with its endless walkways and wide-open lawns that the thick of sweaty bodies made her jumpy.

As she neared Frank, she saw a group of young men drift toward him.

"What kind of freak do we got here?" one of the fellows said.

Mirielle pushed through them and sat down beside Frank. The men's eyes were glassy, their breath heavy with alcohol.

"Excuse me?" she said.

"Not you, doll." The man jutted his chin in Frank's direction. "Him."

Frank's gnarled hands were curled around his glass. A rush of fear traveled through Mirielle like a shudder. Her limbs went cold, and her heart sped.

Frank raised his highball, took a long sip, then set down his drink. He turned from the bar to face the men. "I reckon ya mean my hands?"

"Damned right, I do."

The air grew heavy and electric while the noise of the crowd faded into the background.

"Tell ya what," Frank said, his steady voice drawing Mirielle's eyes back to him. He sat with his back straight and shoulders square.

Formidable, if it weren't for his ruined hands. "I'll tell y'all two stories about how come my hands look like this. Ya gotta pick which is the lie and which is the truth."

The men glanced between one another. Finally, the one with a crooked nose and thin, wormlike lips who'd spoken before said, "All right. Spill it."

"Back in October—nah—November of eighteen, my unit and I were holed up along the Fritzes' right flank somewhere in the armpit of France. Two dozen of us. The rest had been pulled to the main line. It'd rained for days, washing shit and mud into our trench. The bodies we'd buried in the stretch of field behind us filled the air with rot. Better than gas, my buddy said. I wasn't so sure." Frank described rows upon rows of barbed wire. The leafless, poisoned trees. The sporadic pop of gunfire. They'd run out of cooking oil but didn't dare leave their foxhole to cut wood, so they ate their rations cold.

The drunken men's restless shuffling stilled. They listened wide-eyed and slack-jawed. They were too young to have fought in the Great War but old enough to remember meatless Tuesdays, and newspaper headlines, and posters of brave doughboys.

"One of my buddies, a real cutup, was fooling around, doing a little parody of Kaiser Billy, when he accidentally pulled the pin on his grenade."

The men had drifted closer to her and Frank, so close she could hear the sudden arrest of their breathing.

"They say that time slows down at times like that and damned if that ain't true," Frank continued. "My buddy, he dropped the grenade, him. It rolled through the mud, stopping right at my boots."

"What did you do?" one of them sputtered.

"What could I do? It'd explode and kill us all if I left it there. So I picked it up. You only got a good five seconds before they go boom, and I figured I had at least one or two left. I hurled it like a baseball over the bags toward the enemy line." He held up his rough, mangled hands. "It exploded just after I let go."

"It didn't kill you?" the crooked-nosed one asked, even though the answer sat plainly before him.

"I was lucky. Damned lucky. Some of the rainwater must have gotten inside when it rolled through the mud. Dampened the explosion. The sound was enough to spook those Fritzes, though. They charged out of their foxholes into the sights of our gunners. Battle lasted less than an hour. Or so I'm told. I woke the next day in the field hospital in bandages up to my armpits, no memory after the grenade went *bam!*"

Mirielle gasped when he said the last word.

"By golly!" one of the young men said, and then, after a pause, "What's your other story?"

Frank shrugged and picked up his glass again. "I'm a leper."

The amazement in the men's faces turned to confusion. Then Crooked Nose laughed. The others did too. Deep, raucous laughter that filled the heavy silence of a moment before. They slapped Frank on the back and hollered at the bartender for another round of drinks for the war hero and his gal.

They badgered Frank with several more questions about the war before stumbling off to another juice joint.

"War hero, huh?" Mirielle asked when they'd left.

"It wasn't all a lie," he said, flashing her a smile. "But I was the stupid one playing around with the grenade. Five days in a muddy foxhole is enough to make any man stupid. I threw it as soon as I realized what I done, so no one was hurt. And damned if it didn't spook the Krauts outta their holes. That's the only reason I wasn't court-martialed."

He laughed.

"How'd you know those men would believe it?"

His eyes darkened, and he took another drink. "A good lie's always easier to stomach than the truth."

Mirielle looked down at her glass. Nearly all the ice had melted. So too had her anger. Right or wrong, the rumor Charlie had started was something people could choke down. The truth would never be palatable.

She turned to Frank and held up her highball. "To lies, then."

He clanked his glass against hers, and they drank.

The music had started up again, a jazzy rhythm that spread through her limbs like a hot toddy on a cold day. Beside her, Frank tapped his foot in time with the beat.

"You—er—wanna dance?" she asked.

Judging from the way his foot flagged, she'd surprised them both with her words. His gaze cut to the tangle of dancing bodies, then drifted back to her. He held out his hand.

Mirielle took hold before her nerves failed her.

At first, the feel of his uneven skin and curled fingers consumed her attention. On the dance floor, she moved right when he guided her left and stumbled through the easy steps. His other hand felt like a bumpy rock against the small of her back. The song rolled without pause into the next, and after a few swinging bars, she felt herself relaxing. Her hand settled into the hollow of his palm. She was careful not to squeeze too hard, but otherwise soon forgot her awkwardness. He was a good dancer—nearly as good as Charlie—and she couldn't help but imagine what a hot ticket he must have been in the war years. Handsome blue eyes, dark wavy hair, neatly pressed uniform. How the French girls must have swooned.

But then came the disease.

She chased the thought from her brain before it could sour the moment. And soon everything but the music, the sway of their bodies, and the tapping of their feet fell away. They danced two more songs before they had to leave. For those few minutes, she wasn't Polly the leper or Mirielle the cuckoo mother. She was just a body in motion.

CHAPTER 36

⟾•◅

Two days later, Mirielle sat on the edge of the hospital bed waiting for Doc Jack to return with the results of her skin test. Each month, this hour or two while her slides sat beneath the lens of a microscope were the longest she endured. Now, after New Orleans, her determination to rid herself of this disease had turned so sharp she could taste it on her tongue.

She tried to read a magazine while she waited, but the words wouldn't stay put on the page. At last, she got up and began rolling bandages at the back counter, even though it was her day off.

When Doc Jack returned, he pulled up a stool beside her. Mirielle set aside the length of gauze she'd been wrangling and tried to read his expression. It tottered somewhere between serious and ominous. Mirielle groped for her stool and sat before her legs grew too soft to stand upon.

"Is it bad? Were they positive? Maybe you should test again."

"Your slides were negative."

Three in a row! Air flooded her lungs, and the tautness of her muscles eased. "Thank God."

"It's quite remarkable, really. Last month after your reactive episode, I was surprised at your negative test and worried the bacteria would rebound if given time. But it appears they have not."

"Does that mean I'm in the clear?"

"It's certainly promising."

"Then why the straight face?"

"There's still a lot we don't know about how the disease prolifer-ates. Perhaps the fever you experienced during your reaction helped destroy many of the bacilli in your body. But what remains can still replicate and spread."

Mirielle leaned forward on her stool. "Why not induce another reaction then? I could take more iodide pills and—"

"*More* pills?"

"Er—I mean some pills. I could take *some* iodide pills for the first time. You said they can trigger a reaction."

His expression—that of paternal disapproval—was no longer hard to read. "Leave the dosing of medicine to the doctors, Mrs. Marvin."

"Yes, of course."

"Potassium of iodide has been tried in the past to disappointing results. But, I will tell you a new trial has already been approved. We're just waiting on the equipment to arrive."

"A new drug?"

"I cannot say any more, but be on the lookout for a call for volun-teers. I think you'd be a prime candidate."

Mirielle held tight to the secret of the upcoming trial all after-noon and through supper. Afterward she joined her housemates and the rest of the residents in the rec hall for a picture show. The What Cheer Club sponsored the weekly event and maintained the projector—a bulky contraption that whirred loudly as it ran.

During her first months at Carville, Mirielle seldom attended the shows. *New* was a relative term at Carville, and that extended to the pictures, most of which were two- and three-reelers filmed a decade ago. The motley furnishings of the rec hall didn't help. The uneven rows of rockers, straight-back chairs, stools, and wheelchairs crammed in front of the screen couldn't begin to compare to the cof-fered ceiling, twinkling chandelier, and velvet-upholstered seats of the Million Dollar Theater.

But as the long sticky nights of summer stretched on, Mirielle had given in. If she ignored the out-of-tune accompaniment and the cockroaches that skittered back to their hidey-holes whenever the lights went up for a reel change, it was like being home again. Al-most anyway.

Tonight *Judith of Bethulia* was playing. It was strange to see people she knew—Henry, Blanche, the Gish sisters—projected onto a screen here at Carville. It had never felt that way at home. Thank heavens they hadn't played any of Charlie's films. Even though she was still a little cross with him, it would break her to see him like a stranger in shades of gray upon the screen.

During the second reel change, she slipped to the back of the room where Frank was selling candy bars and roasted peanuts. She bought a Baby Ruth, breaking off half for Irene when she sauntered over.

"Doc Jack told me they're going to be trialing a new cure soon," she whispered to Irene and Frank when the line at the candy stand dwindled.

"What kind of cure?" Irene asked.

"He wouldn't say. But I'm signing up."

"Don't get your hopes too high, *chère*."

"Doc Jack seemed very optimistic. Said I was a prime candidate."

Frank shook his head. Their conversation paused as another resident shuffled up to buy a cone of peanuts. When he was gone, Frank turned back to them. "I've been here seven years. Irene, you're what, going on five?"

She nodded.

"They've experimented with dozens of things in my time here—vaccines, oxygen therapy, snake venom, blood plasma, calf serum. Two or three, I've been part of myself."

"And?" Mirielle asked.

"And I'm still here. So is nearly everyone else who let them doctors poke and prod them."

"But if no one volunteers, we'll never find a cure."

"Oh, people will volunteer. Dozens of 'em. You'll be lucky just to make the cut from among so many eager beavers." The lights went out, and the new reel began to whirl. Frank lowered his voice. "Likely as not, y'all will be disappointed."

"That's not a very optimistic attitude." She turned to Irene, who gave a shrug.

"Frank just don't want to see you get your hopes dashed, baby."

"So you're not going to volunteer either?"

"I'm five negative tests away from my diploma. So close I can almost smell that sweet Texas air. I ain't doing anything to mess that up."

"Sweet?" Frank said. "Pardon my French, but I heard it smells like cow shit there."

They laughed, even Mirielle, until someone from the back row shushed them. She and Irene crept back to their seats, but Mirielle found it impossible to get back into the film. Frank could keep his concern. She hadn't forgone her chance to escape in New Orleans just to come back and sit around idle.

A week later, a new piece of equipment was lugged into the women's infirmary. Sister Verena ordered it placed at the far end of the room, then left to supervise the installation of two identical cabinets in the men's infirmary. Mirielle finished scratching down the pulse rate and temperature of a new patient admitted for pneumonia, then snuck over to inspect the contraption. It looked like an oversized coffin raised to table level on four narrow legs. Shiny metal brackets held it together at the seams. At one end of the cabinet was a dinner plate–shaped hole with a narrow shelf just below the opening. Horizontal doors the size of a breadbox were built into the longer sides. When she slid one of the doors open, it revealed an empty chamber with a thin mattress. After walking all the way around it, Mirielle realized it must be designed for a person to lie inside with their head jutting out the hole at the end. Twin gauges sat atop the cabinet like bulging eyes. Standing on her tiptoes, Mirielle saw that one measured temperature and the other humidity. She stepped back and examined the contraption from afar before returning to her duties. An ominous machine to be sure. Half casket, half monster. But wonderfully modern and perhaps just the ticket to finding a cure.

CHAPTER 37

A notice was pinned to the bulletin board in the dining hall the following day. Volunteers wanted for a trial of artificial fever therapy. Mirielle signed up straightaway.

Conjecture about the trial buzzed through the dining hall and beyond. Mr. Li had read about the success of fever therapy in syphilis patients in a recent medical journal. Others had seen similar articles in the newspaper. Naysayers and curmudgeons said volunteers were just as likely to be cooked alive as cured. But that didn't stop sixty others from signing their names alongside Mirielle's.

During her next shift in the infirmary, Mirielle assisted Sister Verena in examining and questioning each of the female volunteers. A new record book had been procured for the purpose and, as each woman slipped behind the privacy screen and undressed, Mirielle recorded their patient number, age, marital status, birthplace, and any family history of the disease. Then Sister Verena would dictate to Mirielle her examination.

"An active advanced case of mixed type, the nodular form predominant," she would say. Or, "An early case of nerve-type leprosy." Then she would go on to describe the location and characteristics of the woman's disease. "Faded macule on the left buttock. Reddish patches scattered over torso. Diffuse thickening of skin over the face. Discrete nodules scattered over arms and legs. Anesthesia of the feet and hands."

Mirielle recorded everything, glancing up from the page every so often to gauge Sister Verena's expression. Of the dozens of volunteers, they were accepting only twelve. Mirielle hoped a slight scowl or smile or twitch of the eye might betray the criteria the doctors were looking for. But Sister Verena's face may as well have been carved of stone.

When they finished, Mirielle herself undressed for inspection.

"May I rely on you to faithfully transcribe for yourself?" Sister Verena asked.

"Of course."

But it was strange to see herself reduced on paper to a number and description of her disease. When Sister Verena got to the spot—or "red, nodular patch"—on her neck, Mirielle's pen wavered.

"Is there a problem?" Sister Verena said.

Mirielle ran a finger over the hideous spot that mocked her each time she looked into the mirror. The other women, whose disease was far more marked than hers, had endured this scrutiny in the hopes of being selected for the trial. So could she. A shake of her pen to convince Sister Verena that the ink had merely clogged, and she wrote down the words.

At the end, Sister Verena asked her the same questions she'd asked the other women. "Are you afraid of small, enclosed places?"

Mirielle shook her head.

"Do you suffer from hysteria or other ailments of the nerves or mind?"

Mirielle fingered her bracelet. Her doctor had asked the same thing after the accident.

"No," she said.

Mirielle waited three days without report about who had been selected for the trial. During her shift in the infirmary, she stared longingly at the fever machine as she was passing out medicine or counting patients' pulses. Every time Sister Verena called her name, her heart jumped into her throat, as she anticipated news about the trial. It plummeted back into her chest when she was asked to sharpen needles or strip the sheets from a dirty bed.

Finally, before supper on Friday, a list appeared on the bulletin board. Not names, but patient numbers. Mirielle pressed through the small crowd that had gathered around the list like a flock of hens, all but blocking the main door and the hungry supper-goers trying to enter. At first glance, she didn't see her number. In desperation, she scanned the list again. Then it appeared. Second from bottom. Patient 367 was included in the trial.

Apprehension gnawed at Mirielle the first day she reported for fever therapy. She approached the horizontal cabinet in the corner of the infirmary with careful, soft-footed steps.

"No need to be afraid, Mrs. Marvin," Doc Jack said, waving her over.

It wasn't fear, precisely, but a sort of weighty anticipation.

"You're feeling well this morning?" he asked as Sister Loretta slipped a thermometer under Mirielle's tongue.

She nodded.

"No stomachache or cough or unusual tiredness?"

She shook her head. Her insides cramped and gurgled a bit, but that was just nerves. And the chaulmoogra oil she'd taken with breakfast.

"Great." Doc Jack made a few notes in the record book, while Sister Loretta took her pulse and blood pressure. Both were slightly higher than usual, but still within normal range. Her temperature, also normal, was recorded along with her other vitals.

"We call it a hypertherm," Doc Jack said, gesturing to the machine. You'll lie inside for five hours as the temperature and humidity are raised. That, in turn, will raise your core temperature, hopefully destroying some of the bacteria in your body. Sister Loretta will be with you throughout the procedure, keeping you hydrated and monitoring your vital signs. Do you have any questions?"

Even without the thermometer in her mouth, Mirielle found she couldn't speak, and only nodded again in reply.

Sister Loretta handed her a hospital gown. "Everything off, dearie. Even your corset."

It had been years since Mirielle had worn a corset, but she didn't bother saying so, and undressed behind the privacy screen. The hospital gown had been hemmed so it fell just above her knees. Undoubtedly there was some medical necessity for this, but she couldn't help smiling. Necessity or not, Sister Verena couldn't be pleased.

When she stepped around the screen, she saw that the lid of the cabinet was raised, leaving only the bottom in place. Her smile fled. Now, instead of a coffin, it looked like a wide, gaping mouth. Doc Jack patted the mattress. "Climb up, and we'll begin."

Mirielle hesitated, the greater part of her wanting to slink back behind the screen. This was for her daughters, she reminded herself. She took a deep breath and walked to the machine. The mattress was little more than a stiff mat, but she clambered up and stretched out her legs. She lay back, then scooted upward until her head rested on a pillow at the far end.

Doc Jack lowered the lid, latching the sides closed with a click. Only her head remained outside of the cabinet, jutting through the small hole at the top. A hole that quickly shrank as Sister Loretta wedged a towel around her neck to seal the opening.

She wasn't claustrophobic, she'd told Sister Verena in truth, and reminded herself again. But when the machine whirred to life, her heart fought to break free of her rib cage. A warm mist prickled her exposed skin.

"It's all right, dearie," Sister Loretta said, stroking Mirielle's temples with her soft fingers. "Just breathe nice and slow."

Sister Loretta wasn't the most skilled of nurses. Even with her thick glasses, Mirielle wasn't sure she could see beyond her nose. Her quickest gait was a shuffle, and she napped as much as she worked. But of all the nurses Mirielle worked with, Sister Loretta was the kindest, and Mirielle was glad she was here.

Steadily, the moist air circling through the cabinet grew hotter. Sweat dripped down the sides of Mirielle's face. Sister Loretta switched on a fan mounted at the head of the cabinet. The cool breeze about her face was a pleasant but fleeting reprieve from the heat building inside.

"How hot is the machine set to get?" she asked.

"Around a hundred and fifty degrees."

"Are we there yet?" The air inside the cabinet felt hotter than it had all summer. And summer in Louisiana was hotter than any she'd known in Los Angeles.

"Oh, no, not nearly," Sister Loretta said, standing on her tiptoes and craning her neck to read the gauge on top of the cabinet. "Another forty or so degrees to go."

Mirielle closed her eyes and tried to breathe slowly as Sister Loretta had instructed. The fan hummed. The machine whirred. The temperature rose.

Every few minutes, Sister Loretta wiped Mirielle's brow with a cloth dipped in ice water. She held a straw to her lips, and Mirielle choked down a salty, lukewarm liquid meant to keep her hydrated.

After several hours, Sister Loretta took her temperature again. "One hundred and five degrees. Just what we'd hoped." She felt along Mirielle's neck to count her pulse. "A little fast, but that's to be expected."

"You'll check again at the end?" Mirielle asked, her voice breathy and low.

"Once every hour unless you start to feel unwell."

So it hadn't been several hours. Only one. Mirielle felt a twinge of panic. Already it was hotter and longer than she could stand. The mattress felt like a rock beneath her. Beads of water dripped from the roof of the cabinet, singeing her skin.

She forced her mind to Evie and Helen. A day with them at the beach. Evie chased seagulls and collected shells. Helen tottered in the sand, holding Mirielle's hand. Charlie lounged beneath an umbrella, smiling and waving at them. They kept far from the water, enjoying only the sound of the waves and the occasional kiss of sea foam at the very edge of the surf. When lunchtime came, she spread a blanket beneath the umbrella's shade, and they munched on sandwiches and cookies.

Felix was there too, eating beside her, his upper lip stained red with fruit punch. Mirielle kissed his forehead, and he didn't make a face or wipe it off as he'd recently gotten into the habit of doing. She turned to Helen and tore off a bite of sandwich for her, careful not to make it too big. Her front teeth were in now, and she made easy work of the food.

When Mirielle turned back, Felix was gone. She whipped her head toward the ocean just as a cry sounded from somewhere near off. "Someone's drowning."

Mirielle leaped to her feet and raced toward the water. Her feet sank in the hot sand. The surf grew farther and farther away even as she ran. Felix's head bobbed and his arms flailed just above the water. Then a wave came, and he vanished beneath the surface.

Mirielle opened her eyes with a start. A metal-shaded lamp hung overhead. She choked on a sob.

"It's all right, dearie. Only a few more hours to go."

When the five hours were up, Doc Jack returned and turned off the machine. Mirielle felt languid and nauseous. She rested in the infirmary overnight, though her temperature and other vital signs quickly returned to normal. When Doc Jack asked the next morning how she felt, Mirielle lied and said she felt fine. Physically, she was fine, though still a bit weak. Her mind, however, remained addled.

"We'll do another treatment next week then," Doc Jack said. "Be sure to rest up."

Mirielle nodded. One treatment down. Seven to go.

October 7, 1926

Dear Mirielle,

You're not still mad about that Picture-Play *article, are you? Your letters haven't mentioned it, so I'm hoping I'm forgiven. With Rudolph's death, everyone's all but forgotten it anyway.*

Production on the new film is grueling as ever. Sometimes I'm on the lot until midnight and am expected back the very next morning at six sharp. So you must forgive my tardy response. Were it not for Cecil and Gloria—whose work is pure genius—and the other swell folks on set laboring just as hard, I might think twice about this crazy business.

Evie and Helen are fine. It's not two months into school and already Evie's top of the class. Her teacher did mention a tendency toward nervousness. Something about plucking her eyelashes. But I'm sure the teacher is overreacting on account of your supposed illness, madness running in families and all. Gloria says such habits are quite normal in little girls. She herself pulled out a few eyelashes as a child, and look how well she turned out.

Helen's saying a whole host of words now—"dada," "Evie" (though it sounds like Ebie), "cup," "apple," "bunny," and, of course, "no." The nanny tried to teach her to say "mama" by pointing at your picture on the wall. It doesn't seem to have worked, though. Now she calls every picture she sees "mama" regardless of who's in the portrait. Last week, Gloria and a few others from the studio were over for drinks. When the nanny brought the girls into the parlor to say good night, Helen pointed at that stodgy old portrait of your grandfather and said, "mama." We all had a good chuckle over it.

I'll write again when there's time. The girls send their love.

Sincerely yours,
Charlie

P.S. How is your health? This fever cabinet you've described sounds like something out of a Jules Verne novel.

CHAPTER 38

⟶➤•◄⟵

"Hurry up, slowpoke," Jean called from the top of the observation tower.

Mirielle stopped at the landing halfway up the steep stairs to catch her breath. She'd been fine after her third session of fever therapy four days ago. Headache, cramps, nausea, and fever blisters notwithstanding. That all was expected and gone by the next day. Now she was just tired, more tired than she'd been at the beginning of the trial.

"I'm coming," she said, clutching the rail. "Can you see any?"

"No . . . yes! Just the tip of one. Hurry up or you'll miss it."

Each step took effort, but Mirielle made it to the top just as a large sternwheel towboat chugged up the Mississippi. Jean scampered onto the bench that surrounded the deck and waved her arms.

"Careful, Jean. Keep one hand on the railing."

Jean didn't listen, so Mirielle grabbed hold of the back of her dress to steady her. Last week, one of the boys had managed to get a passing ship to toot its horn. And ever since, Jean had been crazed with the idea of doing it too.

"Hey!" she yelled, still waving her arms like automobile wipers.

The towboat passed from view without a sound.

"Aw, shucks." Jean jumped down from the bench, and Mirielle let go of her dress. "What d'ya suppose it's like on there?"

"The boat? I don't know. Smelly." Mirielle sat down and fanned herself with her hand. It wasn't as hot as it had been in early October when the muggy air was little better than the fever chamber, and mosquitos seemed to hatch overnight in the stagnant pools of rainwater. But still far hotter than late autumn at home.

"I think I'll be a ship's captain someday," Jean said, lying down on the deck and staring up at the sky. "Or maybe own my own shrimping boat. *Mon père* got a brother down in Cote Blanche Bay who owns his own boat. Says he don't do nothin' but cruise around all day, eatin' shrimp straight from the net. The shrimp and the sea don't care none about the gazeek."

"That does sound nice," Mirielle said. Not shrimping—that sounded especially smelly—but being somewhere the disease didn't matter. "Can I come aboard someday?"

"Yeah, I guess. But you'll gotta do your share. Haulin' nets and the like."

"Aye, aye, Captain."

Jean smiled, her gaze still upon the sky. She pointed up at a bulbous cloud. "Look, a crawdad."

Evie liked to stare at clouds too. She'd find seahorses and castles and ice cream cones where Mirielle only saw smudges of white. Most days, Mirielle could keep them separate, Jean and Evie. They were unalike in almost every way—age, disposition, looks. But then something would strike her. A gesture, an expression, an innocuous habit like staring up at the sky. And Mirielle's breath would catch. Her heart beat a little more insistent.

She lowered herself from the bench and lay beside her. Never mind the dirt and twigs and speckles of moss covering the planks. Never mind her delicate chiffon dress. Never mind the bitter taste of missed chances with her own daughter hundreds of miles away. "Which one?"

Jean pointed again, and Mirielle saw it—the wispy antennae and bulging eyes. She gestured to another cloud. "And what about that one?"

"That's a snail wearing a top hat."

"And that one?"

"A chocolate chip cookie with a bite taken out of it."

Mirielle laughed and pointed at another, a long wispy cloud that bent upward at the end. Jean thought a moment, then frowned. "That's the leg Mr. Macaroni just had cut off."

Mirielle flinched. They watched in silence as the cloud drifted across the sky, stretching and fading.

Jean rolled onto her side to face Mirielle. "What happened to his leg?"

"It got infected."

"No, I mean after. Where did they put it?"

Mirielle didn't know, but she suspected the incinerator. "I think they burned it."

"With the other trash?"

What could she answer to this?

Jean rolled onto her back again. "If I lose a leg or arm, I wanna bury it and mark the spot with a tombstone."

"You're not going to lose anything," Mirielle said. But it was an empty promise. Already, Jean had lost so much. Her family. Her childhood. Her home. Who was to say she wouldn't lose an arm or leg too before the disease was through with her?

"Because of the fever cure they got y'all doin'?" Jean asked.

"I hope so, yes." The smile returned to Jean's face before Mirielle could temper what she'd said with, "Or we'll find some other cure."

Footfalls sounded on the steps, and the deck planks trembled. Mirielle sat up—too quickly. The sky and surrounding treetops rippled as if underwater. Frank and two of the colony's young boys bounded onto the deck. Mirielle didn't know the older boy's name. But the younger one, Toby, she recognized. Not yet six years old, he was the youngest child in the colony. The boys leaped onto the bench and scanned the river.

"You seen any boats?" Toby asked.

Jean scrambled up and joined them on the bench. "Yeah, a huge towboat."

"How come you didn't get it to toot its whistle?" the older boy said.

"You think I didn't try, stupid?" She punched his shoulder. He was smaller than Jean, but near enough her age that if the punch hurt, he wasn't about to show it.

"Maybe they don't like girls."

Toby nodded. "Yeah."

"Enough of that," Frank said.

They all seemed to be swaying along with the treetops. Mirielle closed her eyes.

"Ya okay?"

She recognized Frank's voice and felt his curled fingers on her shoulder. She opened her eyes. The world was still again.

"Fine, thanks."

"Need help up?"

She shook her head and rolled onto her knees, taking a steadying breath before standing. Her legs didn't feel up to the task of supporting the rest of her body, so she wobbled to the bench and sat down. Doc Jack had warned she might feel tired and lightheaded. Maybe it was the hateful bacilli dying inside her.

Another ship passed. All three of the children flailed their arms and hollered. When it drifted out of view without a toot of acknowledgment, their shoulders slumped, and they turned away.

"I bet Donnie was lying," the older boy said.

"Yeah," Jean said as she picked up a brittle leaf that had fallen on the bench and crushed it in her palm. "There's no way he got a ship to whistle."

Toby swung his legs and looked down. "Think it's 'cause they know about our disease?"

"That ain't it," Frank said. "There's lots to worry about on a boat. Ya got your boilers and your engine and your tow. Not to mention the river *tataille*."

"There ain't no river monster," Jean said.

Frank's expression turned grave. "There is. He's cousin of the Rougarou. Prowls the Mississippi from Vicksburg all the way to New Orleans. All the serious boaters know about him."

"I've never seen him," the older boy said.

"Ya don't see him unless he wants ya to. And by then it's usually too late." Frank held up his hands. "One swipe of his claws can cleave a boat in two."

Toby's legs stopped swinging. "Really?"

Frank nodded. "But ya don't gotta worry about him here. He never comes on land."

"What about the swamps?" the older boy asked.

"Nah, he leaves that to the Rougarou and the gators." Frank turned to Mirielle and winked. "And the possums."

She smirked and twisted around to gaze at the river. The boat had left the water choppy, and sunlight glinted off the waves. The river reeds trembled. An egret took flight from the shore. Despite the warm, still air, a chill skittered over her skin.

"You wanna help us look for worms, Jean?" Toby asked. "Frank's taking us fishing tomorrow."

"Only if I can come along," Jean said.

Mirielle turned from the river to see the boy squirm.

"Dunno." He glanced at Frank. "Can girls fish?"

" 'Course we can, stupid," Jean said before Frank could respond. "Race you to the bottom."

Jean took off running toward the stairs. The boys followed, their feet thundering atop the soft wood.

"Well?" Mirielle said when the noise had died down.

Frank came and sat beside her. "Well what?"

"Can girls fish?"

He scratched his chin in mock contemplation. "If frog hunting's any indication, I'd say they can."

"Glad I've done something to advance the rights of my sex."

"What makes ya think I was referring to you? As I remember it, ya about toppled the boat."

She laughed, but with little breath behind it, as if even her lungs were tired.

"How's the fever therapy going?" he asked after a moment.

"Super."

"That so?"

They'd avoided talking about the trial ever since their conversation at the picture show, and it was clear from Frank's voice his skepticism hadn't waned. Mirielle turned away, her gaze crawling over the weathered bench and railing as the silence stretched on.

"What's this?" She ran her fingers over an etching in the wood, noticing similar marks and gouges farther along the bench and up and down the rails. *S.M. & A.H.,* the etching beneath her fingertips read. "Are these initials?"

Frank nodded.

"Lovers' initials?"

He nodded again. The edges of the cuts were smooth and worn. "How long ago were these carved?"

"Hard to say. The tower's been around since the early days, back when it wasn't no marine hospital, just the Louisiana Leper Home."

"But I thought men and women were kept separated back then."

"We was. But you'd be surprised how wily folks can be when they're in love."

He said it as if she didn't know what it was to be in love. Mirielle's father and grandmother had hated the idea of her going around with an actor. For months, she and Charlie had to contrive ways to slip the watchful gaze of her chaperone and meet. She remembered how the mere sight of him set her pulse aflutter. How his touch electrified her skin. How his kiss stole every thought and hesitation from her mind.

"Maybe they're the initials of loved ones back home," she said.

"I suspect some are."

"Are your initials up here?" She looked around. "Surely you've broken your share of hearts here." She said it teasingly, but he didn't chuckle or smile. Instead, he clasped his hands between his knees— no, not clasped, but pressed them together palm to palm—and looked down.

"I didn't mean to be nosy."

"It's okay. I did have a gal once. Before I came to Carville. We started going together in school. She wrote me every week during the war. We were going to marry as soon as I got back and could save enough to buy a house and some land." He paused.

Mirielle hugged her arms around her chest. The sun shone upon them, just beginning its evening descent, but she still felt chilled. "This girl, she changed her mind? Found another beau?"

It wasn't an uncommon story. Boy goes off to war only to come home and find his girl's been untrue. It happened the other way around too. Mirielle knew of many relationships that had ended on account of the war and counted herself lucky that Charlie had been assigned to the reserves and was only gone for three months' training in Washington.

"Oh, she changed all right. But not on account of another fella. I was already having troubles, signs of the disease by the time I got back. I thought it was from the gas and figured it would go away in time. Whatever it was, she said it didn't matter, but that I ought to see a doctor. We had a family friend who was a doctor in New Orleans. He diagnosed me. I was still in the early stages, and he was gonna treat me on the sly. I told my girl and the next thing I know, the sheriff's at my door saying I best get along to Carville or he'll take me there himself. In chains." He sighed, then straightened his shoulders. "Could've been worse."

"Worse?"

"The sheriff kept things quiet. No one in town found out. Spared my family the shame."

"How do you know it was your gal who squealed?"

"The sheriff was her father."

"Oh . . . and that's why he kept it quiet."

Frank nodded. "The whole town knew we'd been sweet on each other. People would assume she had the disease too."

"Did she ever write? Explain herself?"

"Not a word."

"I'm sorry."

He shrugged, but she could tell from the glassiness of his eyes it still wounded him. "I don't blame her for not wanting to marry a leper. But at least she could've said goodbye . . . No offense, but I don't much trust women after that."

"We're not all that way."

He gave a rueful smile. "I'm sure you're to blame for a broken heart or two yourself."

She started to say that wasn't true but stopped herself. She'd gone with a few boys before Charlie who might accuse her of that. Those days seemed like a lifetime ago. No, like someone else's life altogether. She rubbed the pale spot below her thumb. What would that silly, carefree girl think of the woman she'd become?

She shivered, and her teeth began to chatter. The supper bell couldn't be far off, but she hadn't a wink of appetite. Maybe she'd turn in early. When she stood, the tower swayed again like one of its supports had suddenly gone missing.

"Polly, ya all right?" Frank asked. His voice sounded far away.

"Fine," she heard herself say, and took a step. Her legs felt heavy, her knees soft as Chef's butterscotch pudding. The deck listed, rising suddenly to meet her face. She heard a loud *thwack*, then drifted into darkness.

CHAPTER 39

Mirielle awoke wrapped in a scratchy cotton blanket. Lysol and liniment choked the air. The infirmary. Beneath the blanket, her hospital gown clung to her sweaty skin. Her head throbbed, and body ached. She tried to sit up, but dizziness forced her head back to the pillow.

"There, there, dearie. Don't try to sit up," someone said. Through bleary eyes, Mirielle could make out the winged hat and white overdress the sisters wore. Sister Verena? No, this woman's voice was too gentle. She sat down beside Mirielle and drew a wet cloth across her forehead.

"Sister Loretta?"

"I'm here, dearie."

What had happened? How long had she been asleep? She was supposed to take Jean and the boys fishing tomorrow. Or today. Or yesterday. Or maybe Frank was taking them. He knew oodles more about fishing than she did.

Before Mirielle settled upon an answer to any of this, she drifted back to sleep. When she woke again, her head was clearer. She managed to rise onto her elbows without the world spinning. Twilight lit the whitewashed buildings and mossy trees visible through the infirmary windows. Other patients occupied the narrow metal-framed beds around her. One woman tossed and moaned in her sleep. Another lay utterly still, the erratic rise and fall of her chest the only sign she was alive. To her other side sat a blind patient—Agatha, wasn't that her name?—whom Mirielle had cared for many times. Bandages covered Agatha's hands like mittens. Likely her lesions had ulcerated again. Or maybe the surgeon had operated on her fingers in an attempt to stave off bone absorption. Whatever her ailment, neither it nor the bandages stopped the deft motions of her knitting needles. The rose-colored blanket she'd begun when Mirielle last saw her was now nearly complete.

With slow, labored movements, Mirielle propped her pillow against the bed's headrail and sat up. Her mouth was dry and sticky. The spot beneath her thumb was red and raised. A new lesion marred her opposite forearm. Was this because of the fever therapy? No one else in the trial had fallen ill. If anything, their symptoms were improving.

Maybe she just needed more rest between sessions. Sister Verena had cut back her work in the infirmary to one day a week and taken her off shot clinic rotation as well. She could stop helping out in the dressing clinic. It had always been her least favorite shift. The smell of sweaty feet. The gooeyness of the ointment. But Hector came to mind. How his legs had improved even as his kidneys failed. He'd been able to dance again, one last time before he died. It wasn't much, but it was something. And Mirielle had been part of making that possible.

"What's wrong with me?" she asked around the thermometer when Sister Loretta came to check her temperature.

"Keep your mouth closed, dearie." She felt along Mirielle's wrist, her soft fingers probing beneath Mirielle's bracelet. If she noticed the raised scar, her weathered face made no show of it.

"Doc Jack was worried it might be related to the fever therapy," she said finally, after taking Mirielle's pulse. "But then he ran some blood tests and learned that it wasn't."

Mirielle exhaled with such relief the thermometer nearly dropped from her mouth. There was still hope the fever therapy could work then. Still hope it could cure her.

"It's not often we see malaria this late in the year," the sister said.

"Malaria?"

Sister Loretta tapped the bottom of Mirielle's chin. "Mouth closed. A few more doses of quinine, and you'll be good as new."

She smiled, waited a few more seconds, and then plucked the thermometer from Mirielle's mouth. After fumbling through her pocket for her thick glasses, she held the thermometer up and examined the silver line. "Your fever's already broken."

"I can still participate in the trial, though, right?"

"Don't trouble yourself about that now, dearie. Doc Jack will decide when you're well again."

The quinine gave Mirielle strange, vivid dreams. Making love with Charlie only to devour him afterward like a black widow spider. Building sandcastles with Felix at the beach, then watching as the tide dragged him and the castles into the roiling sea. Dancing with Frank atop the observation tower as a funeral dirge played.

Jean came each day after school to visit with her. She climbed onto the narrow, creaky bed and told Mirielle about the possum they'd seen beneath the house, the raspberry custard Chef made for lunch, the two new patients who arrived from New York, one of whom, Jean insisted, looked just like the cinema starlet Clara Bow.

Irene stopped by every evening after supper to fill Mirielle in on whatever bits of house news Jean had left out. Madge had routed everyone at poker again. Mr. Li had replaced the dull needle, so the phonograph was playing right again.

Mirielle looked forward to their visits and the reprieve they brought from her otherwise monotonous day. She slept, worked her way from broth to toast to lukewarm chicken and rice, and listened to the clickety-clack of Agatha's knitting needles. Without these distractions, Mirielle had nothing to do but obsess over the new lesion on her forearm and worry about others she couldn't see.

With her body fighting off malaria, it had fewer defenses to spare against leprosy, Doc Jack had told her. She imagined tiny rod-shaped monsters multiplying inside her. It made her itch and squirm and want to turn her skin inside out so she could scrub the underside clean. The longer she lay in the lumpy hospital bed, the worse these imaginings became until every cell in her body was infected and she welcomed sleep, no matter how troubling her dreams.

On her fourth day in the infirmary, Doc Jack pulled up a stool beside her bed. The quinine had worked its magic and she was feeling nearly as well as she had before that afternoon in the observation tower. She hoped he'd let her take another treatment in the fever cabinet today, so she wouldn't miss a week of the therapy. But when she asked, his gray eyes retreated from her gaze.

"I've consulted with a few other doctors, and I'm afraid you cannot return to the trial."

"Ever?" she managed to ask.

"If we do another trial in the spring, you could volunteer again."

"But I'm feeling fine."

"Your illness with malaria would confound the results of the therapy." Doc Jack must have read her confusion, for he added, "We wouldn't be able to say whether it was the fever chamber or the illness that affected your disease."

"But I . . ." Her voice faltered. She'd done everything they'd asked. Rested. Ate well. Arrived on time for her treatments and endured the cabinet's terrific heat. She didn't want to wait for the next round of trials. That meant more months away from her family. More missed holidays and birthdays and Sunday picnics at the beach.

"You can still be involved," he said. "Since you know the process and have experience in the infirmary, Sister Verena agreed you could monitor the female patients during their treatments and help us keep the records in order."

He smiled as if this would placate her. But she didn't want to watch others get better; she wanted to get better herself.

"The good news is you're well enough today to be discharged. Though you'll have to keep taking the quinine for another three days and stop by every morning after breakfast for a quick checkup."

He patted her hand and stood, lingering by her bedside until she managed a nod and fake smile. Beside her, Agatha's knitting needles chattered away. Mirielle sank down in her bed, smothered her ears with her pillow, and wept.

CHAPTER 40

⟫⟩◦⟨⟪

When Mirielle returned to house eighteen, she changed out of the chiffon dress she'd worn that afternoon at the observation tower. A few spots of blood stained the collar from when she'd passed out and hit her head on the deck. The short walk from the infirmary had tired her, so she sat a moment on her bed before going to the bathroom to shower.

With her housemates away at supper, Mirielle took her time, relishing the plink of water against her skin and soaping away the dried sweat from her body. If only the water could wash away her disease too.

She toweled off and wiped the fog from the bathroom mirror. The reflected woman looked wan and aged with skin the color of congealed chicken gravy. When had lines permanently formed around her mouth and bags settled beneath her eyes? When had her breasts slackened, and hair turned stringy? A thin line of stitches cut across her brow where she'd hit her head on the observation deck. Undoubtedly it would scar.

Mirielle raised her chin and saw the lesion on her neck had grown to the size of a quarter. She clapped a hand over the spot and squeezed her eyes shut to block the return of tears.

What would Charlie think of her when she returned home? Would he even recognize her? She remembered the way he'd hesitated to touch her when they'd parted at the hospital. He'd stood but two feet away and yet never felt so far.

Mirielle opened her eyes and returned to her room to dress. The boatneck line of her collar wouldn't come close to covering the lesion on her neck. She rummaged through her wardrobe, tossing out slips and stockings and girdles in search of a scarf.

At last, at the very back of the wardrobe, she found a silk print scarf and wound it several times around her neck. Her hand lingered on her collarbone, swept the hollow beneath, then lower to the crevice of her breasts. She lay on her bed amid the tangle of underclothes thrown from her wardrobe.

The last time she and Charlie had made love—three, maybe four months before her diagnosis—had been a quick, perfunctory encounter. Before that, three days after Felix's death, they'd come together in a whirlwind of sorrow and desperation that left them sated but all the more broken. Further back though, they'd made love often, with equal measure fire and tenderness.

What she wouldn't give to feel that fire now. For it to be his fingers trailing over her skin instead of her own. She slid her hand lower, beneath the hem of her dress along the inside of her thigh. She closed her eyes and thought of the softness of his lips, the tickle of his stubbly cheek, the smell of his cologne.

The woman in the mirror bullied into her mind. Her flat, wet hair and lusterless complexion. The giant red lesion on her neck. Mirielle's hand stopped before reaching her sex. The image of Charlie wilted and faded. She buried her face in her mattress and screamed.

Not until her voice was scratchy and throat sore did Mirielle peel herself from the bed. She left the underclothes she'd flung around the room lying where they were and headed for the canteen. A soda and—if she were lucky—a letter would cheer her up.

The counter was deserted when she arrived at the canteen, but two of the tables were occupied. Half the women from her house crowded around one of the tables, including Jean and Irene. Mr. Li, his housemate Billy, and a woman Mirielle hadn't seen before sat with them. Frank stood beside the table, recounting some hammy story.

There wasn't space to squeeze another chair around the table. But Mirielle didn't care for company anyway. She grabbed a Charleston Chew from the shelf and sat down at the empty counter with her back to the tables. Laughter erupted behind her at whatever Frank had said. Mirielle considered leaving her nickel on the counter and going back to her room, but she wanted to see if a letter had arrived. She glanced over her shoulder, hoping Frank would hurry up with his story.

Her eye caught on the stranger. She was younger than Mirielle by at least a decade. Her reddish-gold hair fell in waves to just below her ears in the same *au courant* style Mirielle had once worn. Her large, kohl-rimmed eyes twinkled in the overhead lamplight. When she laughed, her red-painted lips parted to reveal small, straight teeth. Jean had been right. This newcomer looked like a Kodak print of Clara Bow.

Mirielle turned around and unwrapped her candy bar. The chocolate-covered nougat was no longer appealing, but she was grateful for something to gnash her teeth on. Even the girl's laugh sounded pretty.

After pulverizing a few bites of the Charleston Chew, Mirielle reached across the counter and smacked the service bell beside the cash register. No one ever used the bell unless Frank was in the back closet unboxing supplies, and its sharp ring cut through the happy chatter like a scythe. Mirielle withdrew her hand, regretting the noise.

"Hey, Polly," Frank said, coming up beside her instead of going around behind the counter. "Sorry, I didn't see ya come in."

"Hey yourself. Do I have any letters?"

"I'll check." But he didn't move. "It's good to see you're feeling better."

"Thanks," Mirielle managed. She couldn't explain the flush of anger she felt, didn't trust herself not to sock him in the jaw and walk away.

"I tried to make a pass by the infirmary to see ya, but ya know how persnickety Sister Verena is about men in the ladies' ward."

She didn't laugh.

Either Frank was blind to her anger or had no sense of self-preservation, for he stepped closer and lowered his voice. "And sorry I didn't catch ya before ya fell. I wasn't expecting ya to pass clear out like that." He brushed the line of stitches across her brow with the pad of his index finger. The tickle of his rough skin sent a pleasant shudder down her spine. Her anger stilled. Their eyes met and retreated.

She pulled back just as the jostle of chairs and clap of footsteps sounded behind them.

"See you in a few, Frank?" Billy said. Frank nodded.

Irene came up and wrapped Mirielle in a bear hug, squeezing all the tighter when Mirielle stiffened. "I didn't know they'd released you, baby. You comin' to roast weenies with us?"

"And marshmallows!" Jean said. The entire crowd had gathered around her and Frank.

"No," Mirielle said, and then, a beat too late, "thanks."

Irene released her after another squeeze. "Suit yourself."

Mirielle watched them leave, Jean clutching the box of marshmallows, Billy and Mr. Li making a gallant show of letting the Clara Bow lookalike through the door first, oblivious to Irene and the other women who followed.

"She's pretty," Mirielle said when they'd left.

"Who?"

"The new girl."

"Oh, Rose. Yeah. She and an older fella just arrived from New York."

Mirielle glanced at the doorway. The group's laughter sounded down the walkway. Soon enough, Rose would run out of kohl to rim her eyes. The laundry's harsh soaps would cheapen her clothes. Her hair would grow out, and there'd be no big-city beautician to cut it back into a cute little bob. Soon enough, the disease would mark her too.

Mirielle set down her half-eaten candy bar, her stomach unsettled. How could she think such awful things? How could she wish them on a girl who was probably just as sad and scared as she'd first been?

She turned back to Frank. "The mail."

"Oh, yeah, let me check." He walked behind the counter and pulled out a shoe box full of letters. "For what it's worth," he said, flipping through the unclaimed mail without looking up, "I think you're pretty too."

So many men had said that to Mirielle over the years, the compliment was like a worn-out nickel—not half as shiny as it once had been. But it caught Mirielle off guard. She loosened the knot of her scarf and said only, "Oh."

After a moment of silence, he pulled a letter from the box. "Here you go. Mrs. Pauline Marvin."

Their fingers brushed as Frank handed her the envelope. Mirielle jerked back, then said too brightly, "Thanks."

Frank cleared his throat. He stowed the shoe box under the counter and grabbed a rag. "I'm . . . ah . . . closing up soon, but you're welcome to stay until I do."

He left to wipe down the tables, and Mirielle opened her letter, too eager to wait until she was back in her room. Two pages were folded inside. The first was a crayon drawing of their house. Mirielle smoothed the paper flat, running her fingers over the waxy colors. Evie had captured the fountain in the drive, the front arcade, even the terra-cotta-potted plants flanking the double-doored entry. Faces peeked out from the second-story windows. Charlie in one, wearing a boater hat and smile. Helen in another, adorned with a pacifier and a single curlicue of hair. Their Persian cat, Monsieur. Evie, a straight line of red for her lips and smudge of blue—a tear?—beneath one of her eyes. The other windows were empty.

Mirielle stared at the picture, wishing her face would somehow appear. But at least she appeared as a thought at the bottom where Evie had written in pencil, *I miss you Mama.*

"Miss you too," Mirielle whispered before setting the drawing carefully aside to read Charlie's letter. It was just a few lines clearly scratched out in haste. Helen was teething again and fussy. Evie was to have a part in the school Christmas play. Production was wrapping up on the new picture. Gloria had invited him and the girls to spend the holidays at her estate in Switzerland. Just the ticket—didn't she think?—to get away from all the gossip for a while.

Mirielle's hands trembled as she folded the letter and stuffed it in her purse. The *swish swish* of Frank's broom sounded behind her. The crackle of the radio from the rec hall. The irregular thud of her heart. An empty glass sat a few feet away on the counter. Mirielle scooted off her stool and grabbed it. It was cool against her palm. Half a sip of soda fizzled at the bottom. Her fingers tightened around the glass. *Gloria's estate in Switzerland. Just the ticket, didn't she think?* Mirielle hurled the glass at the plaster wall behind the counter. It shattered on impact, showering bits of glass over the back counter and floor.

"*Merde!*" Frank said, ducking beneath a table. He glanced furtively around the room, then rattled his head and stood. "Hell, sorry, I thought . . ." He crossed the room to Mirielle's side and gaped at the mess behind the counter. "What happened?"

"My husband's spending the holiday in Switzerland."

Frank looked down at her, his pupils wide and brow knit with confusion. His skin, a shade paler than before, glistened with sweat. Shell-shocked, Mirielle realized. "Sorry about the—er—noise. And the mess. I threw a glass at the wall."

For several more seconds, he stared at her as if she were speaking Chinese. Then he laughed—a loud, full-bellied chuckle that made tears squirt from his eyes.

Mirielle frowned. Her husband spending the holiday with a beautiful woman in Europe was hardly funny. But Frank's laughter was contagious. It unknit her frown and relaxed her shoulders. It tickled her diaphragm until she too was laughing and her eyes leaking.

"They could make my life into a comedy picture it's become so absurd," Mirielle said when she could manage to speak again. The laughter had dulled her anger, leaving her raw and hollow.

"My favorite type of picture," he said.

Hers too. Though maybe not anymore.

Frank fetched the broom and swept while she wiped the back counter. The shards of glass clanked and tinkled when they dumped them into the trash bin. Otherwise the canteen was quiet. The radio in the rec hall had been dialed down to a whisper. The walkways outside were empty.

"Ya cut yourself," Frank said, and Mirielle looked down at her hand. A thin line of blood trickled from her palm.

He pressed a clean, damp cloth over the wound. It didn't hurt or throb or even sting. "Ya ought to have Sister Verena take a look at it tomorrow." He didn't have to say this was how it started—a cut or scrape or burn, painless and forgotten or not noticed at all, later found to be infected, too much later when the entire finger or toe, foot or hand, had to go.

"I will."

He held the cloth to her palm even after the bleeding had stopped. She stared down at his curled, rough hand. What would his fingers feel like against her skin? Not her palm, but the other parts of her still sensitive to touch.

"You really do think I'm pretty?"

The pressure of his fingers eased, but he didn't pull away. "I do."

"As pretty as Rose?"

His eyes narrowed, but he nodded.

She bit down on her bottom lip. "But Rose's got such a stylish haircut and those movie-star eyes."

The struggle between forbearance and desire played out in Frank's expression. A struggle she shouldn't encourage. When he spoke again, his voice was husky. "I fancy brunettes."

Mirielle gave a shy smile and stepped back, expecting him to follow. He did. She retreated another step. And another. Frank mirrored her movements, keeping the narrow distance between them until she was pinned against the counter. The sweet, syrupy scent of the soda fountain mingled with that of sandalwood and liniment. The bloodied cloth slipped from her hand.

He leaned down and whispered in her ear. "Ya sure ya want to do this?"

His breath tickled her neck. A shiver skittered down her arms. She nodded.

Frank's lips moved from her ear toward her mouth.

Mirielle shifted. A piece of glass crunched under the heel of her shoe, the noise jogging her senses. Her surroundings sharpened into focus—the bright overhead lights, shelves of canned soup and cigarettes and chocolate bars, the scuffed floor and mousetrap in the corner. What was she doing?

She ducked away from Frank's kiss and fled.

CHAPTER 41

—◦—

"Did you review Mrs. Roscoe's initial physical assessment?" Sister Verena asked.

Mirielle nodded, clutching the record book.

"And? What do you see?"

She gave Lula a sheepish smile and stepped closer. Mirielle had been poked and examined enough herself to know how naked and vulnerable Lula must feel. The privacy screen cast long shadows over Lula's legs, and Mirielle regretted having to ask her to turn around, like a windup toy, so she could get a better look. The nodules on her legs—described in the initial record as ulcerated and weeping— were scabbed now and only a shade paler than her dark skin.

"Her legs look better," Mirielle said.

Sister Verena frowned.

"Her lesions are scabbed and no longer appear infected."

"Good. Write that down."

Mirielle balanced the record book against her arm and scratched down her assessment.

"What else?" Sister Verena said.

Nothing else had caught her eye, but Mirielle looked again. She didn't know Lula well. Not because she believed any of that nonsense in Mr. Griffith's film. Indeed, Carville wasn't like the rest of the South. The children—white, black, Oriental, Mexican—all attended school together. Anyone was free to sit in the canteen and drink a soda. At movie nights, no one was relegated to the back row.

But segregated houses were enough to keep most of them on hello-only terms.

"I don't see any other changes."

"Read the initial findings."

Mirielle flipped to the front of the record, flashing Lula an apologetic look. Outside, it rained, and the cold air crept into the infirmary. Gooseflesh covered Lula's skin.

"Aloud?"

Sister Verena nodded.

"Diffuse thickening of the skin over forehead, cheeks, and back of the neck. Eyebrows and arm hair missing. Ulcerated and weeping nodules scattered across both legs. Mycotic infections of the fingernails and—"

"Stop," Sister Verena said. She turned to Lula. "Please extend your hands, Mrs. Roscoe."

When she did, Mirielle saw that the tips of her fingernails were thick and discolored, but the lower halves of the nails, the newer part, had grown in healthy.

"Keen observation is the most important part of a sound assessment, Mrs. Marvin." Sister Verena handed Lula a blanket to drape over her hospital gown until her session in the fever cabinet began. "Thank you for your patience, Mrs. Roscoe. Your results so far are quite promising."

Mirielle added *clearing up of mycotic nail infection* to Lula's record, trying not to begrudge her the improvement. If they were seeing such positive changes on the outside, what might the fever therapy be doing on the inside? Was it clearing up the *Mycobacterium leprae* germs as well? Had Mirielle's own disease started to recede before her bout of malaria only to surreptitiously return in the weeks since?

Lula wasn't the only patient in the trial showing signs of improvement. When word got out, the list of the volunteers for the next round of trials would double. Triple. In all likelihood, Mirielle would again be relegated to the sidelines, jotting down assessments and taking vitals, watching others get better and go home while her disease remained.

Doc Jack arrived and readied the fever cabinet. Mirielle helped Lula climb onto the mattress. Once she was positioned correctly with her head beyond the confines of the box, Mirielle lowered the lid, fastening the sides to the base with a click. She remembered the way that sound had made her heart speed, how tight and confining the cabinet had felt around her. The heat, the burns, the nausea. Still, she'd happily trade places with Lula and climb inside.

The machine switched on with a whirr. Doc Jack watched the gauges, taking his leave as soon as the temperature and humidity inside the cabinet began to climb. Sister Verena lingered a bit longer.

"Make sure she remains adequately hydrated," she said to Mirielle. "Check her vitals every hour and notify me immediately of any abnormal results."

Mirielle nodded, not trusting herself to keep the sass out of her voice. After four weeks assisting with the trial in lieu of participating, she didn't need such reminders. She watched Sister Verena cross the room and seat herself at the nurses' desk. The sisters' giant hats accented the slightest movement of their heads, a distracting and sometimes dizzying display. Especially with Sister Loretta, whose neck seemed like a loose spring, her hat like a kite caught in a fitful wind. But Sister Verena's hat never bobbed or rattled or lolled to the side. When she walked, only her feet moved. When she talked, only her lips. When she sat, she might as well be a statue. Somehow, though, her eyes were everywhere.

Mirielle tried to ignore those eyes as she went about her work. She filled a small bowl with ice water and readied several hand towels to daub Lula's brow when she began sweating. Mirielle mixed up a pitcher of saline and water and poured some into a glass with a straw, coaxing Lula to take a sip every few minutes. She tracked the needles as they moved inside the gauges—up, up, up—until they hovered at their set points. But mostly, she sat, watched, and waited.

About halfway through the session, Lula complained of cramps. Mirielle fetched Sister Verena, who drew up a dose of calcium gluconate in one syringe and a quarter grain of morphine in another. She slid open the side door on the cabinet, just long enough to inject them. Mirielle, standing close by, felt the wave of hot, sticky air as it escaped.

"That's the last of the calcium gluconate," Sister Verena said when she'd finished. "I'll have to go to the pharmacy to get some more. Sister Juanita should arrive presently for her shift. I trust you can manage things in the short interim?"

"We'll be fine."

Sister Verena gave a huff. Or maybe it was actually a laugh. Mirielle couldn't tell. She sat back down to watch and wait.

"Talk to me, Polly, will ya?" Lula asked, her voice soft and drowsy.

Mirielle pulled her stool closer. The tiny curls at Lula's hairline fluttered from the gust of the fan. "What would you like to talk about?"

She gave a tiny shake of her head. "Anything."

"All right, let me see . . ." Mirielle dipped a towel in the bowl of ice water. She drew it across Lula's forehead and over her temples, stalling until she could think of something to say. "Paramount's got a new picture coming out in a few months. No expense spared, I'm told."

Since Hector died, Mirielle hadn't uttered a peep about the film. Too dangerous. Too easy for someone to make the connection. But it felt good to talk about it, as if the words had lived too long cooped up inside her. Besides, thanks to the morphine, Lula wouldn't remember. "*My Best Gal*, it's called. Charlie West is the star. Gloria Thorne's in it too and—"

"A love story?"

"No, not at all. A comedy."

"Could be both."

"Well, it's not. It's about a man who—" Mirielle paused. For all Charlie's talk about the picture—the set, the budget, the other actors—he'd not told her what the story was actually about. "It's about a man who wants to join the circus. . . ." Mirielle made up the plot as she went. Clowns and elephants and tightrope walkers. An aging ringleader, a handsome lion tamer, a pitiful bearded lady— played, of course, by Miss Thorne. Lula didn't seem to mind that none of it made sense. Soon her eyes were closed, her breath slow and steady like one asleep.

Outside, the rain continued to plink against the roof and drizzle down the windowpanes. Mirielle leaned closer to the warm machine, resting her elbow on the shelf between Lula's pillow and the half-empty pitcher of saline water.

A comedy. Wasn't that how she'd described her life to Frank? They'd hardly spoken since that night in the canteen weeks ago when he'd tried to kiss her. An awfully fresh thing to do, considering she was married. Mirielle was right to avoid him. But she missed his company. His laugh. The way he made her laugh. And, if she were honest with herself, hadn't she goaded him on?

Her elbow slipped and struck the cabinet. Not hard enough to hurt or wake Lula. But in righting herself, she bumped into the pitcher and sent it tumbling to the ground. It shattered. Saline water and glass covered the floor. Mirielle turned her head toward the desk at the far end of the infirmary, but thankfully neither Sister Verena nor Sister Juanita was there.

"I'll be right back," she whispered to Lula, who was still sleeping despite the clatter of the breaking pitcher.

Mirielle hurried outside, down a short flight of steps to a small shed where they kept the mop and cleaning supplies. The rain dampened her uniform, and mud squished beneath her shoes. Without the aid of sunlight, it took Mirielle several swipes through the darkness to find the dangling light cord. When the bulb flickered on, several cockroaches and a large mouse scurried to the shadowed corners. She tucked the hand broom and dustpan beneath her arm and grabbed the mop and bucket.

On the way back, she slipped in the rain, falling into a muddy puddle. She scrambled to her feet and hurried back to the infirmary. Now she'd have to clean the mess of the broken pitcher *and* find some way to change her uniform before Sister Verena returned.

Once Mirielle was inside, she set down the cleaning supplies and grabbed a towel from the linen cupboard. As she dried off her uniform, a shaking from across the room caught her eye. She dropped the towel and ran to the fever cabinet. The other patients in the infirmary were all sitting up in bed, staring at the rattling machine. Had some gasket or coil inside it busted? Had the water she'd spilled somehow damaged the circuitry?

As she drew closer, Mirielle realized it wasn't the hypertherm that was shaking at all. It was Lula.

"Lula! Lula," she cried, but the woman didn't respond. Her eyes were open, rolled back, so only the whites could be seen. Foam dribbled from her mouth as her head thrashed on the pillow. Something thudded against the sides of the cabinet. A shaking leg? A convulsing arm?

Mirielle hurried to the wall, almost slipping again in saline water, and yanked the plug from the outlet. The whirring machine went silent. She raced back and unlatched the sides of the cabinet, throwing up the lid as soon as the last latch was sprung. A bloom of hot air struck her face. She climbed onto the mattress, doing her best to cage Lula's flailing limbs, holding her until at last she went still.

CHAPTER 42

Mirielle dunked her scrub brush in the bucket of soapy water and raked it over the floor. After Lula's convulsive fit in the fever cabinet, she was no longer allowed to assist with the trial. Lula had recovered, and Doc Jack assured Mirielle it hadn't been her fault, but none of that mattered to Sister Verena, who now relegated Mirielle to the meanest tasks in the infirmary. For the past three weeks, when Mirielle wasn't emptying bedpans or clipping patients' toenails or on her hands and knees scrubbing floors, she was hand-copying *The Principles and Practices of Nursing*. This last assignment, Mirielle suspected, was more for penance than practicality, for it seemed unlikely Sister Verena would let her take a temperature, let alone assist in some medical procedure ever again. Why she didn't just fire her, Mirielle didn't know.

And why didn't she quit? Each day Mirielle thought about it. Before she could convince herself that what she did aided in the pursuit of a cure. But scrubbing floors? Never in her life had she been subjected to this kind of work.

Frank's voice at the doorway of the infirmary made her look up. He handed Sister Loretta a box overflowing with garlands and ribbons. "The What Cheer Club rustled up a few decorations. Thought it might lift patients' spirits."

"Oh, what a lovely idea," Sister Loretta said. "Mrs. Marvin and I will hang these right away."

Before Mirielle could look away and pretend to be working instead of eavesdropping, Frank's eyes found her. He used to smile when he saw her. Wave. Make some stupid joke to get her smiling too. Not anymore. He said goodbye to Sister Loretta and left without a second glance in Mirielle's direction.

She spent the remainder of her shift helping Sister Loretta string festoons of evergreens from the walls and tie Christmas-colored ribbons to the foot of every bed. They trimmed the nurses' desk with strings of popcorn and hung a wreath on the door.

The What Cheer Club had been right. The decorations did buoy the patients' spirits. There were more smiles and fewer call bells as they watched the ribbons and greenery go up. A few of the women even began humming Christmas tunes.

Mirielle told herself to smile and even hummed along in her head, but she might as well still be scrubbing the floor for all the cheer she felt. She'd loved the Christmas season as a girl. As a young mother too. But Felix's death had overshadowed last Christmas and the one before. Never mind the twelve-foot fir tree aglimmer in the great room. Or the dozens of brightly wrapped presents below. Not even Evie's laughter or Helen's squeals of delight had penetrated the darkness. Now, when at last Mirielle was beyond that shadow, her daughters were hundreds of miles away.

On Mirielle's way back to house eighteen after her shift, Irene intercepted her. She looped an arm around Mirielle's waist. "It's a red-letter day, baby!"

"Humph," was the only response Mirielle could muster.

"Ain't you gonna ask why?"

Mirielle suppressed a sigh. "Why?"

"I'll show you."

When they got to house eighteen, the air smelled strangely fragrant. Maybe Irene had finally gotten Jean to stop leaving her dirty socks lying about. She steered Mirielle into the living room. "Ta-da!"

A huge bouquet sat on the side table—red roses and amaryllis, pearl-white lilies and sprigs of greenery.

Mirielle couldn't help but reach out and touch one of the leaves to feel if it were real. "How'd you get fresh flowers delivered way out here?"

"Ain't they somethin'? My son sends 'em every year. Thought I'd put them out here so we could all enjoy them."

Mirielle bent down and smelled one of the lilies. Its scent mixed with that of the roses creating a fragrant perfume that reminded Mirielle of the grand marble foyer in her childhood home. No matter the season, her grandmother kept a bowl of cut flowers on the lacquered table in the center of the room.

Mirielle straightened and rattled her head as if she could somehow dislodge the scent from her nose and, along with it, the memory. Instead, more memories followed. The wonderfully garish bouquet of roses Charlie had sent after their first date. The lily corsages she'd worn at all three of her children's christenings. The flowers that crowded Felix's small coffin at the funeral.

She stepped away and tried again to smile. "They're beautiful, Irene. What a thoughtful boy."

"He ain't that bright or that handsome, but he's good to his mama."

Mirielle started for the door. She wanted to change out of her scratchy uniform before supper. Maybe take a quick nap. Forget about the flowers. The memories. And the fact that Charlie hadn't been as thoughtful.

"Hey! That's only part of my good news," Irene said before Mirielle could leave. "I got the results of—"

"What's that smell?" Madge said, shuffling into the room. She scowled at the bouquet. "Don't like flowers. Never did. Waste of money if you ask me." But despite her protestations, she sat down on the side of the sofa closest to the blooms. "How's your son able to afford such fancy flowers every year anyhow, Irene? He bootleggin' or something?"

The supper bell rang, and several more of their housemates crowded into the living room, waylaid on their way to eat by the grand bouquet. Each one of their *oohs* and *aahs* and *oh my how prettys* nettled Mirielle until she wanted to grab the vase of flowers and throw it through the window. Before Irene could finish telling Mirielle the rest of her good news, talk turned to the upcoming holiday. Would they take a trip to the woods to cut down a tree? Who'd done what with the ornaments they'd made last year? Had Chef said what he was making for Christmas dinner?

Their happy chatter annoyed Mirielle all the more. A spindly little tree from the woods. Moldering handmade ornaments. A heatlamp-warmed Christmas dinner served on chipped enamel plates. A pathetic bouquet of flowers. How could any of that make up for being away from their families, locked away and forgotten?

As her housemates moseyed out of the living room, still chatting, and on their way to supper, Mirielle headed for her room. Irene called down the hall after her. "You comin' to supper?"

"I'm not hungry."

"You sure?"

Mirielle nodded.

"I'll bring you back somethin'. Ain't good to sleep on an empty stomach."

She opened her door and pressed the light switch. Irene was at the door before Mirielle could close it.

"With all that jaw flappin', I didn't get to tell you the rest of my red-letter news."

Mirielle didn't step back or invite Irene into her room. All the day's little irritations had coalesced into a throbbing at the base of her skull. "I'm not much in the mood for—"

"My tenth skin test. It was negative! Got the results just this morning."

Each one of her words was like a jagged spoon, scooping out a piece of Mirielle's insides. Ten tests. Mirielle only had seven with no cure in sight.

Irene's brightly painted smile faltered. "Ten in a row, that is. Only two more to go, baby, and I'm a free bird!"

After another beat of silence, Mirielle managed to peel her tongue from the bottom of her mouth. "That's swell." She started to close the door, but Irene stuck her hand out.

"Swell? That's all you got to say?"

"Yeah, swell. What do you want me to do? Dance around the room? Go tell the other ladies if you want them to howl about the house with you."

"What's wrong with you? You've been a downright killjoy ever since they kicked you outta that trial."

"I hate this place and everyone in it! That's what's wrong with me. Flowers and Christmas decorations don't change the fact that we're lepers. And neither do your ten goddamned tests."

Irene's lips slackened. She took a step back, and Mirielle slammed the door.

CHAPTER 43

———⟫•⟪———

Five days after the argument, Mirielle listened at her door to her housemates' chatter and hurried footfalls. Carville's unvarying routine made it easy to avoid Irene, even though her room was only two doors down. When Mirielle wasn't at work in the dressing clinic or infirmary, she kept to her room. She came late to every meal, arriving just as Irene and the rest of her housemates were leaving.

Tonight, they were off to the rec hall to watch whatever old movie the What Cheer Club had managed to get ahold of this week.

"Don't forget your pillows, gals," Irene hollered. Shot clinic had been that day, and everyone was likely still sore. Without a pillow, the benches and chairs in the rec hall would only make the soreness worse. One more reason Mirielle was glad to be staying in.

The front door opened with a squeal. Mirielle felt the rush of cold air over her toes. The calls of "Hold on!" and "Anyone seen my scarf?" and "Can I bum a nickel for candy?" faded as the door whined shut.

Silence. The very sound Mirielle had been waiting for. She slipped out of her room into the bathroom, pulling her silk kimono tightly closed against the cold air. All day she'd been dreaming about a bath, conjuring the steam and bubbles in her mind to chase away the tedium of boiling needles and peeling apart cotton squares. She turned the tub's faucet as hot as it would go, but lukewarm water dribbled out.

"Oh, horsefeathers!" she said aloud, wrenching the water off and stalking back to her room. Another resident must have burned himself. It could happen easily enough when you hadn't any feeling in your hands. And whenever it did, the top dogs up at the big house ordered the water temperature lowered another few degrees.

Mirielle put away her bathroom caddy—she wasn't going to waste the last of her good bubble bath on lukewarm water—and threw a satin nightdress on under her kimono. Now what? It was too early for bed. She could read. Buff her nails. Play a game of solitaire. What had she done when she first came here? All those hours alone. Not just in jail but after too. When she'd thought Irene and her housemates and everyone at Carville were just a bunch of common bores.

She sat on her bed and occupied her hands with a nail file. The silence now felt suffocating. She really ought to apologize to Irene. Slamming the door in her face had been a bit much. Mirielle wasn't sure where all that silly anger had come from. Trouble was, it boiled inside her still. Every time she passed by the living room and caught the scent of flowers. Every time she heard Irene laughing. Every time she came home to Christmas music playing on the phonograph or new decorations strung on the walls. Of course Irene would be merry. She had a son who sent her flowers and only two tests to go before she could see him again. Mirielle had more than twice that many tests to go and a husband vacationing in the goddamned Swiss Alps.

Really, it was Irene who ought to apologize. For making all that fuss when she knew Mirielle was so blue. It was downright garish the way she'd behaved. And that music, "*Jingle Bells*," "*Silent Night*," she must know it set Mirielle on edge.

She looked down at her hands. She'd filed her nails to blunt nubs and chafed the tips of her fingers raw. White dust covered her lap. She brushed it off and flung the file onto the table beside her comb. If she had to hear "*Adeste Fideles*" one more time, she'd smash the record in two. Even now, the words looped round in the back of her mind.

She needed something to break the silence. Another song. Something that wouldn't remind her of Christmas parties and mistletoe kisses and children's laughter. She got up and went to the living room. Just because she and Irene weren't speaking didn't mean Mirielle couldn't use her phonograph.

She crouched down and opened the cabinet where Irene stored her records, looking for something jazzy and bright. The first few were all holiday albums. Mirielle flipped quickly past them. A brownish-gold label caught her eye. She pulled the record out from the stack. *Gid Tanner & His Skillet Lickers.* One of Frank's hillbilly records? It must have gotten mixed up with Irene's the night they were all dancing on the deck of the observation tower. She slipped it from its cardboard sleeve and placed it on the turntable. A fiddle and guitar medley sounded through the speakers. She'd expected the lively tune to lift her spirits. Instead, her ribs tightened around her lungs. It was impossible not to think of Frank while listening. She lifted the needle and fumbled for the record sleeve.

A sniffling noise sounded in the silence. Mirielle startled, nearly dropping the record. When she turned around, she saw the scuffed tip of Jean's oxfords peeking from behind the sofa. Had she been here the whole time?

"Jean?"

Another sniffle.

Mirielle walked around the sofa and found Jean sitting on the frayed rug with her knees drawn up to her chest. She'd stolen one of the roses from Irene's bouquet. Its red petals lay scattered around her.

"Why aren't you at the picture show?"

Jean wiped her runny nose on the sleeve of her cardigan and shrugged. "How come you ain't?"

All Mirielle's excuses seemed too foolish to say aloud, so she didn't answer. Instead, she sat down, leaning against the back of the sofa. "Tell me what's up, buttercup."

When she said that to Evie, she always got a smile. But Jean's pout didn't budge. "Mrs. Hardee sent me back and said I ain't allowed at no more shows for the rest of the year."

"What did you do?"

"I only told Toby that there weren't no Santa. He started crying like a baby, and I got an earful from Mrs. Hardee."

Mirielle had expected the usual: Jean slipping a cockroach down someone's shirt or throwing peanuts at the screen during reel change. The existence of Santa Claus caught her off guard. "That's not true. Of course there is."

Her hasty response didn't seem to convince Jean, whose gaze was fixed on the rose stem in her hand. She tapped her finger against one of the thorns, lightly at first, then hard enough to draw blood. Mirielle teased the stem from her grasp and set it on the floor.

Jean sucked on her finger, then said, "If Santa's real, how come he never comes to Carville?"

Mirielle floundered for an answer. Maybe she ought to tell Jean the truth. The girl was ten years old now, after all. Everyone had to learn that Santa wasn't real at some point.

"Is it 'cause of our disease?" Jean asked before Mirielle could reply.

"No. Santa Claus doesn't care a wink about such things."

"Then how come?"

Mirielle picked up one of the rose petals. It felt light and soft in her palm like a swatch of fine silk. She couldn't bring herself to say that Jean was right. That Santa Claus wasn't real. Jean had already faced enough hard truths in her short life. What harm was there in forestalling this one? "He probably doesn't know that you're here. That the colony exists at all. It's not an easy place to find, you know."

"I thought he knew everything."

"Most things. Not everything. Have you written him a letter to tell him that you're here?"

Jean shook her head.

"Well, no wonder he hasn't come." She stood and pulled Jean to her feet too. "I'll get some paper and an envelope."

Equipped with all the necessary supplies, Jean sat for several minutes at the living room desk, gnawing on the end of Mirielle's pen between bursts of writing. Mirielle watched her from the sofa out of the corner of her eye, flipping through a magazine and pretending to read. She felt foolish for all her earlier huffing. What was lukewarm bathwater compared to being an orphan at Christmas?

"How do you spell 'presents'?" Jean asked, her fingers smudged with ink.

As Mirielle spelled the word aloud, she realized more fully the impossible task she'd set for herself. Christmas was only three weeks away. How would she get gifts for Jean in such a short time? And what of the other children? There were almost a dozen here at Carville. Santa couldn't just bring gifts for one of them.

*   *   *

The next morning Mirielle walked with Jean to the canteen to drop off the letter for Santa.

"You're missing a stamp," Frank said, glancing at the letter Jean had placed on the counter as he rang up a can of baked beans for another resident.

"Mrs. Marvin said I don't need no stamp if it's going to the North Pole."

Frank handed the resident his change, then picked up Jean's letter. She'd written *Mr. Claus, One Main Street, North Pole* across the front. Frank's eyes met Mirielle's for the first time in weeks. She'd forgotten how strikingly blue and penetrating they were. He turned to Jean. "She's right. Santa takes all his letters COD. I'll be sure that this gets to the sterilizer right away and goes out today."

Jean smiled so widely, Mirielle could see the hole from the missing molar she'd lost last week.

"Off to school with you now," Mirielle said. Jean skipped off, and Mirielle hollered after her, "Be sure to apologize to Toby today."

She slid onto one of the counter stools and said to Frank, "I have a letter too."

She didn't know when Charlie and the girls were leaving for Switzerland. They might already be gone. Two weeks back, she'd sent a card and letter for Charlie to bring along on their trip and to read to their daughters on Christmas morning. She might not be there in person, but Mirielle wanted Evie and Helen to know she was thinking of them, that morning and every morning, and sending kisses across the Atlantic.

Her letter today was a few brief sentences long and addressed only to Charlie. She'd described the situation with the children here and asked him to send gifts and treats. Her hopes weren't high that it would reach him in time. And even if it did, he might disregard her request entirely like he'd done with the fireworks. But Mirielle had to try.

She handed the envelope to Frank, the back of her neck tingling with heat. It was addressed to *C.W.* at the secret post office box they used in Los Angeles, but Frank must know it was for her husband. He took the letter between his crooked thumb and index finger, tossing it into a box with the rest of the outgoing mail without a second glance.

"Thanks," Mirielle said. She stood, then sat back down, fingering her necklace as she tried to work out what to say next. She'd kissed a few men before Charlie, and rebuffed many more. It had been easy in those days. A laugh. A light swat on the shoulder. A playful protestation that the gentleman shouldn't be so fresh. And just like that, the awkward near-kiss was forgotten.

With Frank, it was different. Not even the trusty balm of time and silence had worked.

"Ya want something else?" he said to her.

"No . . . er . . . yes." She let go of her necklace and folded her fidgety hands atop the counter. "Is it too late to place an order in the catalogs?"

"Depends. Ya looking for it to arrive before Christmas?"

She nodded.

"Too late by nearly a week." He grabbed an empty glass from farther down the counter and carried it between his palms to the washbasin. He dropped it in the sudsy water, saying nonchalantly over his shoulder, "Better luck next year."

Mirielle waited a moment, watching him scrub the glass with a dishrag. When she thought he was finished, he held the glass up to the light and started scrubbing again, as if he were cleaning it for President Coolidge himself. She'd ignored enough people in her day to know he'd keep washing until she left. But this wasn't about them, and damned if she'd leave without getting his help.

She didn't bother walking around the counter, but shimmied herself up and over it instead. It didn't go quite as gracefully as she imagined—she wasn't a gymnast, after all—but the canteen was empty and the gamblers in the adjoining rec hall were too far away to see her girdle straps and ruffly chemise. Frank turned around just as she hopped down and was straightening her skirt.

"Canteen patrons ain't allowed behind the counter," he said.

"You didn't seem to mind last time."

His jaw tightened, and Mirielle regretted bringing it up.

"Listen, this isn't about . . . I need your help getting Christmas presents for the kids."

"The sisters knit them sweaters ever year, and Saint Louis Church in New Orleans sends them prayer books."

"Is that what you wanted as a boy? A frumpy sweater and a prayer book?"

"I didn't grow up all rich and fancy like you. We was happy to get anything." He turned back to the washbasin and picked up another glass. "Besides, the club always wraps up a candy bar for 'em too."

Mirielle stepped closer. She'd missed the way he smelled— slightly woodsy with notes of aftershave and liniment. "Frank, please, I know you think I'm nothing more than a high-hatted egoist. Hell, maybe I am. But I'm trying to do something good here. I want Jean and the kids to have one nice Christmas. A happy Christmas where they're just like every other boy and girl and don't have to think about the disease."

"Don't see how I can help."

She reached out and touched his arm, her fingers lingering on the exposed skin below his rolled-up shirtsleeve until he put down the glass.

"Ya are a high-hatted egoist," he said. "But it's a damned nice idea."

"You'll help me then?"

He turned around and faced her. The flint he'd carried in his eyes since their last encounter was gone. "It's three weeks till Christmas. I don't see what we can do."

"There's gotta be some do-good society in New Orleans or Baton Rouge we can write to."

"We've tried that before, *chère*."

Chère. Mirielle wished she didn't like it when he called her that. Wished she hadn't missed his smell. Wished that some small part of her didn't regret the missed kiss. This friendship was a dangerous one. Liable to hurt them both. She realized she was still standing right next to him, close enough to hear the soft inhale of his breath and see tiny nicks beneath his chin from the morning's shave.

She took a step back, reminding herself of the task at hand. "Well, the one thing that can be said of egoists, we're self-deluded enough to try again."

CHAPTER 44

Mirielle sent letters to the Leper Aid Society, the Catholic Church Extension Society, the Provident Association, the Child Welfare League, and even the Rockefeller Foundation, asking for whatever toys they could send.

Then she waited. Her letters would take time to arrive, funds would have to be allocated, gifts bought and shipped. If her request sat unopened for a day or two on a crowded desk, or a board squabbled over how much money to spare, the toys would not arrive by Christmas.

Jean asked several times whether Mirielle thought Santa had received her letter. Each time, Mirielle assured her that he had.

With a week and a half to go, she began making daily calls at the canteen after work. She felt light, almost giddy with anticipation. The faces of those around her mirrored that same hope. Residents, some of whom she'd never seen before at mail call, crowded the counter. Some walked away ebullient, clutching a package or a letter. Others, like Mirielle, shuffled out of the canteen empty-handed, telling themselves tomorrow something would come.

As Christmas neared, her anticipation grew heavy. She tarried in the dressing clinic restocking supplies or lingered in the pharmacy double-counting pills so she would miss the crowds at the canteen. She wasn't the only one whose hope had soured. And it doubled her disappointment to see all the glum faces. Never mind all those residents who didn't bother to stop by for mail call. Who knew nothing was ever coming for them.

The holiday songs playing over the radio, the evergreen tree dressed in ribbons and bobbles standing in the dining hall, the magazine ads with pictures of a fat, cherry-nosed Santa reminded all of them—not only herself, Mirielle realized—of a home far away.

Christmas Eve, Mirielle dressed in her dowdy uniform and headed to the pharmacy after breakfast. What had once been her favorite shift in her work rotation had become dreary and dull since her fight with Irene. They stood side by side for hours mixing ointment or filling capsules or bottling disinfectant, never saying a word to each other.

Mirielle missed Irene's endless chatter. Her crass sense of humor. Her frank advice. Looking back, their argument seemed so trite. The beautiful flowers in the living room had begun to droop and wither. Instead of a lush perfume, they gave off a lingering smell of rot. She suspected Irene was keeping them now out of pure stubbornness. To remind Mirielle of their argument. To remind her that Irene had someone who cared for her, who remembered her at Christmas while Mirielle had no one.

And it was true. Nothing had come from Charlie since Mirielle's last letter. Nothing had come from the societies and associations and foundations she'd written to either. Her only hope was that something would arrive today—a parcel of bonbons and trinkets, a package of yo-yos and checkerboards. But she knew the chance was slim.

"You're both looking very glum for Christmas Eve," Sister Beatrice said to Mirielle and Irene, leading them to the long workbench in the center of the pharmacy where a hodgepodge of jars and bottles awaited them.

Irene snorted. Mirielle said nothing. Their task for the day was to count, measure, and inventory the pharmacy's stock of medicine so Sister Beatrice and the doctors could calculate what they'd need to order for the new year. Mirielle started with a huge bottle of aspirin, pouring its contents onto the workbench and dropping the pills back into the bottle one by one.

What did Irene have to be glum about? Her son had sent her flowers, for criminy's sake. Tomorrow Mirielle would have to tell Jean that Santa didn't exist. Or make up some lie about how her letter must have been incinerated in the sterilizer on its way to the mailman. Either way, Jean would be heartbroken. Far more disappointed than if Mirielle had told her the truth in the first place.

She chucked pill forty-seven into the jar with such force it split in two. Mirielle scowled and fished out the pieces, readjusting her count. What kind of a mother was she to have bungled Christmas so badly? A good mother would have known not to make promises to a child, even implicit ones, that she couldn't keep. Maybe her daughters were better off spending the holidays in Switzerland without her.

The *plink, plink, plink* of pills grated on Mirielle's nerves. Did Irene have to be so loud? Was she purposely trying to count faster than her? Mirielle quickened her pace. Irene shot her a sidelong glare and sped up too. They worked at this frantic pace for several minutes. Soon, Mirielle was no longer counting at all but merely flinging pills into her jar as quickly as possible. Irene capped her jar, scribbled something onto her ledger, and upended another. Mirielle did the same. Pills bounced and scattered.

"Keep to your end of the bench, will ya?" Irene said.

"You're taking up your half and then some."

Irene shook her head. "You always think you're owed more than your share."

Mirielle swiped at the pile of pills in front of Irene, sending them skittering across the workbench. Irene retaliated by scattering Mirielle's pile too. Pills rolled everywhere. Mirielle glared at her, then bent down to pick up the pills that had fallen on the floor.

"My heavens, ladies!" Sister Beatrice said, stalking over. "You must be careful. Mixing up pills could be incredibly dangerous."

Mirielle stood, wiping off the pills from the floor on her apron. "Yes, Sister."

Irene nodded. Hundreds of small white pills were strewn across the workbench. Only on close inspection could Mirielle tell hers from Irene's by the faint groove down the center. They set out sorting the pills in silence.

"A dose of aspirin won't kill anyone," Mirielle said under her breath.

"Mine's calomel. A good bowel purging never hurt no one either."

Mirielle couldn't help but laugh imagining someone swallowing a few laxatives in place of aspirin. "It might actually do those old fops in the Rocking Chair Brigade some good."

Irene snickered. "Or Watchman Doyle."

"Or Sister Verena."

Irene's snickering burst into full-fledged laughter. Mirielle's too. Her eyes teared. From the laughter? From the sudden release of tension between them? Mirielle didn't know and didn't care. She stopped all pretense of squinting at pills and let the laughter come.

"Mrs. Marvin."

Mirielle's throat closed the minute she heard Sister Verena's voice. Her chuckles deflated. Something about the sister didn't seem quite right. Her posture wasn't just stiff but tense. She looked right past the mess of pills.

"I require your immediate assistance."

"What for?"

Sister Verena's gaze flickered to Irene. "I shall explain on the way."

Unease settled in her chest. What trouble had Mirielle gotten herself into now? She untied her apron and shot Irene an apologetic look for leaving her hundreds of pills to sort alone.

Out on the walkway, Mirielle had to scurry to keep up with Sister Verena's clipped pace. She felt a twinge of relief when they turned in the opposite direction of the jail, though Mirielle still couldn't think what she'd done to unsettle Sister Verena so.

"Where are we going?"

"I need you to assist with a case in the operating room."

Mirielle stumbled, then hurried to catch up. "But I've never helped out with a surgery before."

"With God's grace, we won't need to operate."

"Then why—"

"It's a delicate matter, Mrs. Marvin."

When they arrived a few moments later at the operating room, Mirielle realized what Sister Verena had meant by delicate. Elena, one of the younger women at the colony, sat hunched on the steel table in the center of the room, arms wrapped around a swollen belly. The spotlight and mirrors angled above cast her in a pool of blinding light. She sucked in a sharp breath and grimaced. A sheen of sweat glistened on her forehead. Her discomfort lasted less than a minute, then her scrunched face and tensed muscles relaxed.

"My God, she's pregnant," Mirielle said.

"Don't take the Lord's name in vain, Mrs. Marvin." Sister Verena handed her a floor-length smock. "Put this on and wash your hands at the scrub sink."

"But I . . . why me?"

"Sister Juanita usually assists in these cases, but she's sick with the flu. Sister Loretta will join us presently, but I . . . wanted someone with sharper skills here too. Besides, you have experience."

Mirielle gaped. Giving birth and assisting with a delivery were two very different things! "What about Doc Jack?"

"We'll call him at the end. Sooner if the baby doesn't turn."

A nudge from Sister Verena and Mirielle stumbled to the sink. She knew nothing about delivering babies. Certainly not ones who were breech. She'd been in a morphine-induced twilight sleep for all three of her children's births and remembered next to nothing.

Once her hands were washed and smock donned, Mirielle helped Elena change into a hospital gown. Elena gave her a bashful smile and said something in Greek Mirielle took to be *thank you*. Several minutes passed before her next contraction. When it came, Mirielle held her hand and brushed aside her hair when it fell into her face. Fear, more than pain, showed in her dark eyes.

The contraction passed quickly. Sister Verena asked Elena to lie down and listened to the baby's heartbeat with a special stethoscope she pressed to Elena's belly. Next she pressed down as if to feel for the contour of the baby's head and limbs. Mirielle watched her pursed-lip expression and knew the baby still hadn't turned.

"She's only dilated three centimeters," Sister Verena said after sticking two fingers inside her. "Plenty of time yet to go."

Mirielle cranked a lever beneath the table to raise the head so Elena could sit upright in a more comfortable position. How had Mirielle not noticed a pregnant woman walking around the colony? How had she not heard whisperings about it when she passed the Rocking Chair Brigade?

She thought back to the last time she'd seen Elena. It was mid-

September at a picnic the Mexican Club had hosted. Chili con carne and frijoles, a piñata for the kids, burning pyrethrum powder to keep away the mosquitos. She remembered the day so vividly because of Hector's absence. In her memory, Elena was seated at a picnic table with her housemates. She didn't look pregnant. Maybe a bit pudgy, but everyone looked that way in the shapeless dresses the materials office supplied.

After getting Elena a pillow and blanket, Mirielle crossed the room to where Sister Verena was laying out supplies on a tray table. "How long have you known she was pregnant?"

Sister Verena set down a pair of scissors, aligning them carefully alongside a suture needle and thread before replying. "Two and a half months."

"Where has she been since you found out?"

"House thirty-eight."

Mirielle frowned. House thirty-eight was where they locked away insane patients.

"We couldn't very well have her out among the rest of you," Sister Verena said. "Flaunting her immorality."

"What about the father?"

"In jail."

"Maybe they're in love. If patients were permitted to marry then there wouldn't be anything *immoral* about it."

"I did not bring you here to debate morality, Mrs. Marvin." Sister Verena laid a pair of forceps on the tray table with such force it rattled the other instruments. "Now, please see to it that Miss Remis conserves her energy. Keep track of her contractions and alert me when they become more regular."

Mirielle's frown deepened, but Sister Verena's voice—sharp and strangely shrill—told her not to press the issue. For several hours, she stayed by Elena's side, rubbing her swollen feet and coaxing her to rest between contractions. The light peeking between the slats of the window blinds weakened and vanished. The supper bell rang. Elena's contractions grew steadily longer and closer together.

When Sister Verena examined her again, the baby still had not turned. She instructed Mirielle to walk with Elena around the operating room in the hopes that gravity would help the baby right itself.

They shuffled in circles for what seemed like hours, stopping whenever a contraction came on. Mirielle remembered this part, the flare of pain so sharp and sudden it took your breath away, and let Elena squeeze her hand through it, even though it felt like her fingers might break. She asked questions as they walked to distract Elena and keep her calm. When had she come to America? Where had she lived before Carville? Did she have sisters? Brothers? What name had she chosen for the baby? Elena replied in broken English, her thin voice betraying her growing fatigue.

At midnight, the bells of Sacred Heart chimed the start of mass. Sister Verena checked Elena again. Six centimeters dilated. No change in the baby's position. Doc Jack arrived sometime later in a three-piece wool suit that Mirielle guessed he'd worn for church. He took off his jacket and rolled up his sleeves before scrubbing his hands and examining Elena. Then he and Sister Verena consulted in the corner. Mirielle could only hear snatches of what was said—*still presenting breech . . . more time . . . cesarean section*—but the unease in their voices was unmistakable.

"Is everything all right with the baby?" Elena asked her.

Mirielle's chest tightened. She nodded—it seemed like less of a lie—and said, "Just rest now."

As the night dragged on, Mirielle slept in short snatches, awakening with Elena every time a contraction came on. She wiped away the sweat that dribbled down her face and coaxed her afterward to sip juice and water.

At the far side of the room, Sister Loretta prepared a makeshift bassinet for the baby out of what looked to be a metal drawer. She wiped it down first with strong-smelling disinfectant, then wiped it again before lining it with fresh blankets. After that, she dozed.

Only Sister Verena didn't sleep. When Mirielle closed her eyes, she heard her fiddling with the instruments on the tray table or pacing the walkway just outside the door.

At some point, Elena's labor seemed to slow. Or maybe she'd just grown too tired to do more than wince and moan. Then, suddenly, she sat up and screamed.

Mirielle, sitting on a hard stool and resting her head on a wobbly table at Elena's bedside, jolted to her feet. Sister Loretta startled out of sleep mid-snore. Sister Verena, whom Mirielle had heard muttering the rosary, dropped her beads and hurried over.

"Aou!" Elena cried.

Sister Verena lifted the hem of Elena's hospital gown and gasped. Her face went gray. She froze for the span of several heartbeats. Mirielle counted the thudding, loud in her ears while everything else was silent. One, two, three, four.

Sister Verena straightened. When she spoke, her voice came calm and strong. "Sister Loretta, go get Dr. Jachimowski. Tell him Miss Remis's labor has progressed rapidly and that we have a footling presentation."

Sister Loretta nodded and scurried away.

"Mrs. Marvin, lower the head of the bed until Miss Remis is lying flat, then help her flex and spread her legs."

Mirielle did as instructed, cranking the bed into position while Sister Verena told Elena not to push until Doc Jack arrived. Elena groaned and writhed through another contraction. When it was over, Mirielle helped her scoot to the bottom of the table and bend her legs. She eased Elena's knees apart and made the mistake of glancing down. A slimy foot stuck out from where the baby's head should be crowning. Stool, blood, and birthing fluid smeared the sheet beneath her. Mirielle felt cold and flushed at the same time. She shuffled back, knocking into her stool.

"Are you all right, Mrs. Marvin?" Sister Verena said, but her voice sounded far away. The tables and lights grew fuzzy.

A stinging slap across her cheek brought the room back into focus. "Mrs. Marvin, if you cannot do this, you must leave. I cannot attend to two people at once."

Mirielle jogged her head. Her skin still felt clammy, but her legs were steady. "No, I can help."

She wheeled over the table of instruments and fetched a stack of clean towels, keeping her gaze to the floor. Sister Verena listened again with her stethoscope.

"The baby's heart rate is slowing. We cannot wait for the doctor. Elena, you must push with your next contraction. Do you understand me? Push."

Elena nodded, fear bright in her eyes.

"Mrs. Marvin, press down on her stomach." She took Mirielle's hands and placed them on Elena's belly. "Firm and steady through the entire contraction."

"What are you going to do?"

"Pull the baby out."

Sister Verena grabbed a scalpel from the tray table. Mirielle looked away just as she started to cut, widening the birth canal. A few moments later, Elena's belly went rigid beneath her hands.

"Push!" Sister Verena commanded.

Elena exhaled and tensed her muscles. Mirielle pressed down, tentatively at first, then, seeing Sister Verena struggle with the baby's slippery limb, pushed on Elena's belly with all her force. The baby's butt and shoulders slipped out just as Elena's contraction waned. One arm dangled free. The other remained lodged in the birth canal with the baby's head. Elena's upper body slumped back onto the table. Her skin was pale and drenched in sweat. Her legs trembled.

"You've got to push harder with the next one," Sister Verena said, wiping her bloody hands on her smock. "We've got to get the head out."

Mirielle wasn't sure if she was talking to her or Elena. Her arms felt like they were made of pudding instead of bone and muscle. But when Elena's belly tightened again, Mirielle bore down with all her strength. Elena grunted and pushed. Sister Verena pulled.

One of Elena's legs slipped off the table. Her body slackened. "No more," she said, in a wild, pleading voice.

Sister Verena looked at her. "If you do not keep pushing, your baby will die. Is that what you want?"

Elena shook her head frantically.

"Then push."

Mirielle hoisted Elena's leg back into position on the table, then pressed again on her stomach. Elena hollered an inhuman sound but pushed as Sister Verena had commanded.

At last, the head and arm slid out, and the baby's lusty cry filled the room. Elena's grimace broke into a smile as her limbs slackened. Tears leaked from her eyes.

"It's a boy," Mirielle said, smoothing the sweat-drenched hair back from Elena's forehead. "He's perfect. Pink and chubby and . . . perfect."

Sister Verena dried the baby with a towel and wiped his nose and mouth. She cut the umbilical cord and put a knit cap on the baby's head. He stopped crying, though his eyes remained scrunched shut. His hands were closed in tiny fists beside his face. Aside from his dark crop of hair, he looked so much like Mirielle's own babies had. Especially Felix.

Doc Jack arrived just as Sister Verena was wrapping the baby in a clean towel. He listened to the baby's heart and lungs, then pronounced him whole and healthy.

"Can I hold him?" Elena asked, but Sister Verena was already whisking him back to the far table where Sister Loretta had readied his bassinet.

Doc Jack donned a smock over his clothes—a flannel nightshirt tucked into a wrinkled pair of trousers. He pulled a stool up to the end of the bed.

"Bend your legs again, my dear, so I can deliver the afterbirth and stitch you up."

But Elena didn't move. She was crying more fiercely now. "I just want to hold him, just for a minute, please."

"I'm sorry. You know that's not possible," Doc Jack said. "It's for his own good."

"Why can't she hold—" Mirielle stopped. She'd forgotten all about their disease. She walked toward the far end of the room where Sister Verena was with the baby. Surely, a moment or two in his mother's arms wouldn't hurt.

Sister Verena turned and held out her arm. "Stay back."

"But he's her son. Her son, for God's sake!"

"I'm sorry, Mrs. Marvin. It cannot be helped." Sister Verena's voice was thick and husky. "Please, go help the doctor."

Mirielle didn't move from where she stood. The operating room was a mess of sodden towels and scattered supplies. The spotlight above Elena's bed rained yellow light down upon her. The overhead mirrors reflected the pool of blood-tinged birthing fluid at the foot of the table where she lay. The baby fussed. Elena cried.

Mirielle was too exhausted to sustain her anger. It seeped out of her, leaving in its place a blistering emptiness. She walked back to the surgery table and followed Doc Jack's instructions. She couldn't look Elena in the eye—not as she massaged her deflated belly or washed the slickness from her skin or changed her soiled hospital gown.

When Sister Loretta came for the baby, Mirielle couldn't bring herself to look in that direction either. She didn't want to feel any more complicit in this horror than she already did.

CHAPTER 45

———⟫·◦·⟪———

It was morning when Mirielle left the operating room, the sky a deep mocking blue. She heard voices in the dining hall but couldn't imagine eating anything. Not until she'd showered and slept, and maybe not even then. Somewhere amid the houses, one of the residents' phonograph was playing. "*Adeste Fideles*." Mirielle's feet shuffled to a stop.

It was Christmas. Had Jean already woken to find that Santa Claus had forgotten her yet again? Mirielle couldn't bear to see the disappointment in her eyes. She'd already witnessed enough sorrow today to last a lifetime.

Mirielle changed course, following the music. This time, she really would smash the record, no matter whom it belonged to. It was a lie, every song and stitch of ribbon and strand of popcorn meant to convince them their lives weren't pitiful and hopeless.

Her shoes clapped loudly on the walkway. Her family wasn't thinking of her today. Missing her. They were making snow castles and eating raclette. Charlie had probably forgotten the letter she'd written for the girls, left it on the side table along with the spare cuff links he'd meant to pack.

She was lying to herself if she believed otherwise, and Mirielle was done with lies. Life at Carville was meaningless. She realized that "*Adeste Fideles*" was no longer playing. But another Christmas song, just as false and deceiving, sounded now from the opposite direction.

Her entire body ached, and her eyelids begged to close, but Mirielle was determined to silence this noise. She turned the corner and listened. The song seemed farther away now, off in a different direction. She spun around but made it only a few steps before she heard another song. And another. It was as if every phonograph and radio in the colony had suddenly been turned on.

She covered her ears and sank to the ground, weeping. Her body rocked. The cool winter air swept her skin. When she uncovered an ear to wipe the snot dripping from her nose she heard her name over the music. She blotted her eyes on her sleeve and looked down the walkway.

"Mrs. Marvin!" Jean cried, racing toward her. "Come see, come see."

Mirielle stood, alarmed by the urgency in Jean's voice. Had something happened to Irene? To Frank? To one of their housemates?

But as Jean drew closer, Mirielle could see the delight in her eyes. She grabbed Mirielle's hand and tugged her toward the dining hall. "Santa found us, just like you said he would. And he brung me and Toby and all us kids presents. Come see!"

In the dining hall, residents crowded around the Christmas tree watching the children open their gifts. Cast-off ribbons and crumpled wrapping paper littered the floor. Jean showed Mirielle the silver harmonica she'd gotten and the pink and blue swirled lollipop that looked suspiciously similar to those sold at Ocean Park Pier. The twins had each received a doll with moving eyes, a lollipop, and a child's-size tea set to share. Others got stick ponies and toy trains and domino sets. Candy sticks and marshmallow peanuts. Dominoes and bird whistles and lollipops all around. Toby showed off his new teddy bear and Shoot the Crows in the Corn game.

Mirielle stepped back from the happy mayhem and scanned the crowd for Frank. He smiled at her from the opposite side of the tree. Mirielle smiled back. She was pretty sure Charlie had sent the candy and a few of the gifts. They'd gotten that same silly crow game for Felix one year. At least one of the organizations she'd written to must have sent toys too, but there'd be time enough later to find out who. Now all she wanted was to wash and sleep.

When she got to house eighteen, music was playing from Irene's phonograph. Had that been the sound she'd initially heard? It didn't matter, Mirielle decided. She no longer wanted to smash and silence it.

Irene was seated on the sofa in the living room. The vase of flowers was gone. Mirielle hovered at the doorway. Had it been only yesterday they were laughing together in the pharmacy? It felt like years.

"What happened to your flowers?"

Irene looked up. "They was gettin' old."

"They were beautiful while they lasted."

Irene shrugged. Mirielle inched inside the room. "I'm sorry I . . . I'm sorry I said those things. I'm sorry for everything. I was just . . ." She reached for her neck, but she hadn't a string of beads or strand of bobbles to fiddle with. "Jealous."

Irene shook her head and patted the balding sofa cushion beside her. Mirielle sat down.

"You ain't got nothing to be jealous of, baby. I bought them flowers myself."

"I thought your son—"

"He means well, but you know how men are. Blockheads, the lot of them. He gets busy and forgets about his old mama. Got his own kids to think about now too." She twisted the garish ruby ring on her finger. "So I buy 'em myself and pretend they're from him."

Mirielle squeezed her hand. "I'm sure he loves you and would be awfully glad to know you're getting flowers, even if he is too blockheaded to buy them himself."

Irene chuckled. "So what did Sister Verena have you up to all this time?"

Mirielle looked down at her hands. A small smear of blood stained her shirtsleeve. She opened her mouth, but a sob came instead of words. Irene pulled her close. She cried onto Irene's shoulder as the Christmas music played.

January 5, 1927

Dear Mirielle,

I trust the package arrived in time for Christmas. Evie had great fun helping me pick out the gifts. We've been having a swell time in Switzerland. Just the break we needed from Los Angeles and all its blather. The girls love the snow. I bought Evie a pair of skates, and she spends all afternoon on the lake beside the chalet. Don't worry, the ice is quite solid. Sometimes she pulls Helen behind in a sled. You'd die hearing their laughter. Gloria's been a sport hosting us like this in such fine style. Too bad we're needed back at the studio so soon after the holidays.

Your husband,
Charlie

P.S. I read the girls your letter on Christmas. The day wasn't the same without you.

CHAPTER 46

⟫•◦⟪

After New Year's, the tree in the dining hall was taken out to the incinerator. Decorations were unstrung and boxed away for next year. Christmas records slipped under beds or tucked into the back of cabinets. All that hullabaloo Mirielle had hated was gone. And the colony felt naked without it.

She again noticed the ubiquitous white. Government-issue white paint on the buildings and walkways and water tower and benches. White gravestones. White smocks and uniforms, bleached after each wear to remove the sweat stains and blood. Even the sky took part in the conspiracy, shrouding itself in low-lying clouds for days on end.

When Frank mentioned Mardi Gras and some scheme the What Cheer Club had cooked up for floats and a masquerade, she teased him that they lived from holiday to holiday at Carville.

"Whatever will you do if they canceled Easter or Thanksgiving?" she said. It was a misty Sunday morning, and they'd run into each other on the lawn between the chapels.

"*Mais*, we still got Arbor Day and Confederate Memorial Day and Flag Day and Armistice Day," he said, winking at her.

With the stark, dreary whiteness all around them, she understood why he did it. It was an escape from the tedium of their daily lives and the horrors of their disease. It gave the residents something to talk about in the dressing clinic when she unbandaged and cleaned their feet. Something besides their weeping ulcers and nodulated skin. It gave the women in the infirmary something to look forward to when nothing but pain and medicine filled their days.

But Mirielle didn't want distraction. "I'm holding out for the day they hand me my diploma and tell me I'm cured."

He took off his hat and ran his contracted fingers through his hair. The misty air brought out its waves and luster. "Sure, we're all living for that day. Ya just have higher hopes for it coming along soon."

"Fever therapy's the ticket. I saw firsthand how it helped." Never mind Lula's convulsive fit. "When they do the next trial, I'm going to be first in line to sign up again. You'll see."

He nodded, clearly reticent to bring up their old argument. But Mirielle couldn't help but continue, "I refuse to live like you, surviving on distraction because you're too cowardly to hope."

She regretted the words once she said them and waited for a cheeky retort. But all he said was, "I see."

"I didn't mean . . ." She stopped. Why was *I'm sorry* so damned hard to say? They were alone now on the lawn, the other residents who'd milled about after church having been chased away by the nippy air and oppressive clouds. Or had the lunch bell rung, and she'd been too caught up in her thoughts to hear it? She hadn't told him about Elena and her baby. Not even Irene knew. How then could he understand her newfound desperation? "I just don't see the point of trying to make a life here when I've got one waiting on the outside."

"You're lucky then. Not everyone does."

"You do. I see all the letters and parcels that arrive from your family. I see you with them under the oaks every month when they come to visit."

"I can't just think about me."

"That's not fair. I've got two small girls. It's them I'm thinking about."

They walked together to the ramp leading up to the covered walkway. It wasn't raining, but mist had condensed on the roof and dripped from the eaves. He stepped aside, letting her ascend the ramp first, even though there was room enough to walk up side by side. She waited at the top for him.

"Besides," she said, "a cure will benefit us all."

"And how about the disgust people feel at the word 'leper'? Ya gonna find a cure for that too?"

No one need know, she almost said. But a cure wouldn't fix Frank's hands. Or give the blind back their sight. The amputees back their legs. She rubbed the lesion on her neck. If it didn't clear up, she could explain it away as a rash or a burn. Her other lesions too. Many patients weren't so lucky.

"You've got your war story," she said.

Frank looked down at his hands. He clenched and unclenched his contracted fingers. "Yeah, I guess I do."

She stood on her tiptoes and kissed him on the cheek. Not a romantic kiss. Her lips barely lingered on his skin. But she wanted him to know that not everyone in the world looked on him with disgust.

A line formed between Frank's eyebrows as if he were perplexed. Maybe even a bit perturbed, the way a young boy gets when some dowdy old relative smooches him on the cheek. Mirielle laughed and walked away, saying over her shoulder, "You better watch out. I'm gonna help them find that cure, and then you'll have a flock of gals lining up to kiss you."

The next day, Mirielle went to see Sister Verena in the small office she kept between the men's infirmaries. If Mirielle was going to make good on that promise of finding a cure, she needed to be part of the next fever therapy trial. News of Lula's convulsions—exaggerated in the Rocking Chair Brigade's retelling—had made some residents wary. But plenty of patients like her were still desperate enough to volunteer.

When she arrived at the office, she hesitated, wiping her palms on her skirt before knocking. Since that harrowing night in the operating room, she'd tried to avoid Sister Verena—a largely impossible task considering Sister Verena still oversaw her work in the infirmary and clinics. When she couldn't avoid her, Mirielle was all but silent, nodding to her commands, and forgoing her usual interjections like how they really ought to get a radio for the infirmary or try lavender-scented water in the dressing clinic. Every time Mirielle looked at her, she thought of the baby. It was easier to keep her eyes to herself than be drying tears on her sleeve while she worked.

"Come in," Sister Verena said when Mirielle finally steeled herself and knocked. Sister Verena was seated at her tidy desk, jotting something in a ledger. Her large hat made the room feel even smaller than it was, and Mirielle wondered how she managed to move her head without knocking books off the shelf behind her or the crucifix off the wall. "Ah, Mrs. Marvin, I suspected you would come. Have a seat."

Mirielle closed the door and sat. "I'm not here to talk about what you did to Elena and her baby."

"No?" Sister Verena leaned back and steepled her hands. Her nails were short and blunt, filed to match the slender shape of her fingers.

"No."

"Very well. What can I help you with?"

Mirielle had considered what she wanted to say about the fever cabinet and the new trial on the walk over to the office. But before she could get it out, her eye snagged on the ceramic statue of Mary, arms outstretched, perched on top of the bookshelf behind Sister Verena. She'd never understood the papists' obsession with Mary, but this Christmas cast her in a new light. She too was a mother who'd lost her son. Still gazing at the statue, she asked, "Where did you take the baby?"

"Elena's baby?"

"No, Grace Coolidge's."

Sister Verena frowned. "We took the baby to Sacred Heart Orphanage in New Orleans."

"Is that where all the babies go?"

"If there isn't a family member nearby willing to take the child, yes."

Mirielle looked away from the statue of Mary to her interlocked hands. "How can you talk so coolly about something so awful?"

"What would you have us do? Keep the baby? Risk him being infected?"

"You could have let Elena hold him. Say goodbye."

"That would have only made things more difficult for her."

Mirielle glared at Sister Verena. "You don't know that. You don't know the first thing about being a mother. A part of you dies when . . ." She looked away, determined not to cry.

When they'd pulled Felix from the pool, she'd scrambled out after him and snatched him away, holding his wet, limp body to her breast.

Only the doctor had been able to peel her arms away. So many times since she'd regretted letting go, regretted that inevitable passage from before to after where she would never hold him again.

"I know—" Sister Verena stopped. From the corner of her eye, Mirielle saw Sister Verena's steepled hands fold into a tight ball one atop the other, her knuckles streaked white. She drew in a long breath and continued. "I know this is hard for you. God has a plan for the baby, and it's not here. Nor, I think, would you want it to be. Elena, too, will see that in time."

"I wish I'd never stepped foot in that operating room."

"You proved yourself very able that night. The baby might have died were it not for your assistance."

Mirielle hadn't considered that. She'd felt sick about the role she'd played, as if in helping deliver the baby she was complicit in taking him away too. After a moment, she said, "That doesn't make me feel any less awful."

"No," Sister Verena said, reaching out and straightening the ink blotter on her desk. "I imagine not. Life's not that tidy, I'm afraid."

Mirielle glanced again at the statue of Mary, unable to decide if she felt any better in their kinship. She stood and turned to go.

"Your other question, Mrs. Marvin?"

"Oh, yes." She jogged her head and turned around. "The fever cabinet. When will a new trial be starting?"

Sister Verena's brow furrowed.

"I'd like to volunteer again."

"I'm afraid—"

"At least let me help. Doc Jack said I wasn't to blame for Lula's convulsions and I promise not to leave anyone unattended. Not even for a moment."

"We shan't be doing another fever therapy trial. Not anytime soon."

Mirielle sat down again, scooting so close to Sister Verena's desk her knees knocked against it. "But you have to. The results were so promising. Lula was the only one to have a complication. And maybe that was my fault. If I'd been watching better and noticed the first sign—"

"It wasn't your fault, Mrs. Marvin, and hers wasn't the only complication."

"There were others?"

Sister Verena hesitated. "Weak pulse, hypotension, extreme exhaustion, shock, nephritis."

"I'd still volunteer."

"It isn't just the complications. It's been six weeks since the trial ended, and we're not seeing any positive results."

"That's not true!"

"There's no need to get hysterical about this, Mrs. Marvin."

Mirielle forced herself to sit back and lowered her voice. "You had me recording the women's physical findings, remember? Their disease was getting better. No more infections."

"No more *secondary* infections. But eight of the twelve patients' primary infection, that is to say, the leprosy, has gotten worse."

"Worse?"

"Yes."

"But—"

"It would be unwise, not to mention unethical, to subject more patients to the therapy."

Mirielle gulped down several quick breaths. It felt like all the oxygen had bled from the room. She grasped the edge of Sister Verena's desk as if it were a life raft.

"Maybe we just need to try different settings. Less heat and more humidity. Or vice versa."

"I'm afraid not."

Mirielle looked down at the floor, still trying to catch her breath.

"If that's all, Mrs. Marvin, I really must get back to work."

Mirielle stood, using the desk to brace herself until she was sure her legs were steady.

"What about another trial? Isn't there something else the doctors are looking into?"

"They're always investigating options. But nothing else at the moment looks promising."

"What now then?"

She gave Mirielle a doleful expression. "We keep doing what we're doing and trust in God's mercy that someday he'll deliver a cure."

Someday couldn't come soon enough.

CHAPTER 47

⟾⟾◦◦⟽

Irene squeezed Mirielle's hand for the fifth time in as many minutes. If she kept this up, Mirielle would have a bruise by the time Doc Jack returned with Irene's results.

"You don't have to wait with me, baby."

"Would you knock that off? I told you I would, and that's that."

Another squeeze. "Thanks."

Mirielle looked down at the infirmary floor. Near the wall, dried mud in the shape of a footprint clung to the pine boards. Whoever was in charge of washing the floors had missed a spot. With all the recent rain, Mirielle was glad that task no longer fell to her. She no longer had to copy lines from that boring old textbook either. But even on her day off, Mirielle couldn't help but see the smudge on the floor, the water glasses in need of refilling, and the bandages to be rolled.

"What's the first thing you're going to do when you get out?" Mirielle asked.

"Shh! Don't jinx it."

"Sorry." Mirielle shifted. It was the second time this week she'd sat on one of these uncomfortable beds waiting. Her stomach had twisted inside out by the time her own results came back, and she was only up to nine negative skin tests. Irene must feel it ten times worse. She wished she'd brought Madge's playing cards or a magazine for distraction. "Okay, what was the last thing you did, then. Before your diagnosis."

Irene took off her glasses and wiped them on her blue-and-green-checkered shawl. "Milked the cows, I reckon. Fed the chickens."

"You don't remember your last day of freedom?"

"That was over five years ago, baby. But I do remember the doctor. He couldn't get me out of his office fast enough. Like I was a grenade about to pop and spread my disease all over him. What about you?"

"I was fixing my hair for a party and burned myself on the iron. I didn't want to go. Not to the party or the hospital." She fingered her bracelet. "My husband thought I burned myself on purpose or that I'd been too soused to notice the iron's heat. I guess he had cause to think those things."

The earlier part of the day, before the burn and Dr. Carroll's arrival, was a blur. She wished she remembered playing with Evie or holding Helen or even the sound of their laughter from the nursery, but she didn't.

"Tell you what I ain't gonna do when I get home, wear any more of these goddamn cotton stockings from the materials office. Or eat just because I hear a bell. Or turn my music off 'cause Watchman Doyle's comin' round hollering that it's curfew."

Mirielle laughed. "Or wait in line for soap."

"Or read magazines from a year ago."

"Or watch old pictures."

"Or hurry up in the tub 'cause someone else is waiting."

"Or carry around a pillow because your rear's too sore to sit down without it."

"Or hurl up my lunch thanks to those awful pills."

"Or lose to Madge at poker."

Their laughter petered out.

"Or dance in the observation tower."

"Or drink sweet tea on Frank's porch."

Irene took her hand again and squeezed. "You know I ain't gonna forget y'all, baby."

Mirielle nodded. Her friends in California would have said the same thing, though. She didn't miss them or their petty concerns and banal conversation. But she would miss Irene. Terribly. Like part of herself was leaving along with her. "Maybe someday I could bring my daughters to Texas for a visit. They've never seen a real farm."

"That'd be swell." Irene picked at a loose thread on the bedspread. "Don't suppose you'd want someone like me hobnobbing with you and your fancy friends in California."

"Don't be crazy, I'd love for you to come visit."

"They'd think I was nothing but an old bumpkin."

Mirielle took her other hand. "I don't care what they think."

The infirmary door opened, and Doc Jack came in. Irene clutched Mirielle's hands like a bottle of gin on the eve of Prohibition. She drew in a deep breath and didn't let it out.

Doc Jack looked around and grabbed a stool before heading over to them.

"Oh God, he's gonna sit down," Irene said. "That can't be good."

"Sister Katherine and I had a good look at your slides in the laboratory just now, Mrs. Hardee," he said once he was seated. He flipped her chart open across his lap.

"And?" Irene said.

He patted his pockets until he found his glasses and put them on. "And . . ." He thumbed through several pages in the chart, before closing it and looking Irene square in the eye. "And your slides were negative. Not a bacillus in sight! Congratulations, you're being discharged."

Irene didn't move. Only her eyes blinked. Then she let out a loud sob and pulled Mirielle into a hug. "I'm goin' home, baby! Back to my son and my grandbabies. I'm going home."

Mirielle hugged her back so tightly her arms tingled.

"It will take a few days to process your paperwork and . . ." Doc Jack said, but Mirielle was only half listening.

Irene didn't seem to be listening at all. She let go of Mirielle and wiped her eyes on the hem of her shawl, talking over him. "I got so much to do. I gotta write my son and pack up my things and find someone to look after my garden and—"

"That all can wait," Mirielle said. "Let's go tell the girls."

"You think they'll be happy for me?"

Mirielle smiled. "I know they will."

As Irene dallied in the infirmary, hugging Doc Jack and the sisters, Mirielle slipped out and pulled a yellow square of cloth from her handbag. If she stood just beyond the bend in the walkway and looked north, Mirielle could see the back porch of house eighteen. As planned, Jean was sitting on the top step. Not as planned, she was playing her harmonica instead of keeping a lookout in Mirielle's direction. Mirielle waved the yellow cloth high above her head, hoping it would catch Jean's attention.

"What are you doing?" Irene asked.

Mirielle gave the cloth one last flourish before cramming it back into her handbag. "Just swatting a fly." She looped her arm around Irene's. "Let's go spread the good news."

Irene, always a fast walker, practically sprinted back to their house, dragging Mirielle along. When they got there, Irene stopped just inside the door and called, "Ladies, it's payday!" She winked at Mirielle. "That'll get them out of their rooms."

They waited there in the hall, but none of their housemates appeared. It was unusually quiet for this time of the afternoon. Irene strode down the hall, knocking on every door. No one answered. Irene turned around, the excitement gone from her face. "Where is everyone? They know today was the big day."

"Maybe they ran to the canteen. It's nearly mail call."

"All of them?"

A muffled giggle sounded from nearby, but Irene didn't appear to have heard. Her shoulders slumped. Mirielle hurried over and ushered her toward the living room. "Why don't we wait for them in here?"

Irene frowned, but let herself be led. They opened the door to a dark room. When Mirielle pressed the light switch, a chorus of cheers greeted them.

Irene jumped back. She blinked, her mouth agape, swiveling her head to look at Mirielle then back to the crowd of people squeezed into the living room.

"Congratulations!" someone yelled.

"Finally did it," Madge said.

Jean leaped up from where she'd been crouching and hugged Irene, nearly knocking her off balance.

Streamers fluttered from the ceiling. A banner hung on the wall with CONGRATULATIONS IRENE! painted across it. Frank started singing "For She's a Jolly Good Fellow," and everyone, including Mirielle, joined in.

Irene beamed, swiping the tears from her cheeks. When the song ended, she turned to Mirielle. "You did this?"

"I had some help."

"I was the lookout," Jean said.

"Lookout?" Irene asked.

"In case your test didn't go well."

Mirielle pulled the yellow cloth from her handbag along with a green one. "Yellow meant the party was a go. Green meant everyone had to take down the decorations and skedaddle."

Irene smiled and shook her head. "Swattin' a fly, my ass."

Frank handed round glasses of hooch. "Polly, she asked if I could rustle up some champagne, her. I said sure, if she don't mind champagne with no bubbles and a lot of formaldehyde."

Everyone laughed.

"Even a gal with this gazeek can hope," Mirielle said to more laughter.

"So we settled for good old corn juice." He held his cup aloft between his hands. Everyone else raised theirs too, or in Jean's case, her bottle of Coke. "Only the best for our friend Irene. To happy endings."

"To happy endings," they echoed.

Mirielle took a sip of the liquor, wincing as she swallowed. Someone put a record on the phonograph, and a jazzy tune played behind their chatter. Irene sat down on the couch. Everyone crowded around.

"What ya gonna do first once you're out of this shithole?" Madge asked. This time Irene didn't hesitate to answer.

Mirielle hung back, leaning against the doorjamb. She took another sip of her drink, then set it aside. Was it the alcohol burning inside her or grief? It didn't diminish the cheer she felt at Irene's happiness. Somehow they existed side by side.

Frank caught her eye from across the room. His steady smile buoyed her, and she stepped inside to join the celebration.

CHAPTER 48

$\Longrightarrow\!\Longleftarrow$

Mirielle tried not to look at the fever cabinet, now unplugged and pushed into the corner, during her shifts in the infirmary. She thought about stealing a bat from the equipment shed and bashing the machine to pieces. That might lift her spirits. At the very least, it would provide much-needed entertainment for the women in their sickbeds. But then she'd be stuck copying textbooks for the rest of her days if Sister Verena didn't outright sack her.

Today, she'd snuck in her manicure set, and shaped and polished the women's nails between her other tasks. She could finish an entire hand while the thermometer was under their tongue. Sister Verena would likely scold her later for corrupting the women and endangering their souls. But surely a smile was worth something. These women—their throats narrowing with lesions or the cartilage in their noses collapsing or their vision fading—deserved a little frivolous distraction. God and Sister Verena could blame her all they liked. Besides, no matter what she'd told Frank, Mirielle needed the distraction too.

"There, just like the sheen on an automobile," she said when she finished the last woman's nails. She slipped the clear polish back into her pocket along with her emery board, the bottle of cuticle remover, and the tube of nail white she'd used underneath the nails to bleach the tips.

The woman held up her hands, wrinkled with age and scarred from the disease. "Men really go for this kind of thing these days?"

"Sure they do." Mirielle held out her own hands for inspection. Jean had wanted to play beautician last night, and Mirielle's jagged and unevenly polished nails were a casualty of the game. The pale patch of skin at the base of her thumb had been joined by another, this one reddened and raised around the edges. She chalked it up to the stress of Irene leaving. Of the fever therapy failing. Of Charlie's dwindling letters. "Never mind what a fella thinks. We do it for ourselves. Lovely nails are the first step in feeling put together."

The woman grunted and shrugged.

"Does that mean you don't like it?"

"Of course I do. Now, how about a little lipstick?"

Mirielle laughed. "I'm pretty sure that would get me fired."

A call bell rang from across the room, and Mirielle rose to answer it. When she looked back, the woman was still examining her hands, sniffing and even licking one of her nails. Mirielle smiled and got back to work.

But as she was hanging up her apron at the end of the day, the hypertherm again caught her eye. How long would she have to wait until they found a cure? How many birthdays would she miss? How many first days of school? Helen wouldn't even know her when she returned. Evie would remember her only as a depressive and a drunk. Mirielle slouched against the wall. The manicure supplies in her pocket crushed into her thigh, but she didn't care. Not even when she felt the tube of nail white burst. She had so much to make amends for. So much wasted time to recoup. But what if they never found a cure and she didn't get the chance?

Her greatest hope now was reaching twelve negative skin tests. Only three more to go, and she'd be free like Irene. Never mind the risk of relapse or the people she'd be leaving behind. She walked up to the fever cabinet and gave it a swift kick. The machine didn't even tremble, but her shoe came away scuffed and her toe aching.

That evening Mirielle begrudgingly joined her housemates in the rec hall for a picture show. Another distraction for their pitiful lives. Why Irene hadn't hightailed it home yet, Mirielle couldn't imagine. Something about giving her son and his wife time to fix up the farmhouse. Jean's pleading that she stay for Mardi Gras might have something to do with it too. Mirielle was glad for every extra day with Irene, but it also drew out the sadness of her inevitable departure.

During the first reel change, she bought a Hershey's bar for her and Jean.

"Hang around after the show," Frank said to her as she handed him a dime. "I've got something I wanna show ya."

"What is it?"

The lights dimmed and the projector whirred back to life. Black-and-white images flickered on the screen. The accompanist struck a dissonant chord, then found his place in the music.

"It's a surprise," Frank whispered, winking at her.

Mirielle returned to her seat and spent the rest of the picture wondering what sort of shenanigans Frank was up to. Hopefully nothing that involved rickety skiffs and bullfrogs.

Midway through the picture, after the third reel change, Clara Bow strode across the screen wearing a beaded dress and a lot of skin. This was a newer film. Mirielle remembered reading a review of it in the *Times* only a few years back. "There are only about five actresses who give me a real thrill on the screen," the reviewer had written, "and Clara is nearly five of them."

Mirielle had to agree. Not even the cockroaches stirred when Robert Agnew swept Miss Bow into his arms and kissed her.

Mirielle had been on set with Charlie and knew all the lighting tricks and camera angles that went into such a shot. And still she longed to be kissed like that. Even without the backlighting and ac-companiment, it would be magical. Her thoughts strayed back to Frank. She imagined them together in the empty rec hall, the illu-minated screen casting a soft glow. This time, when he tried to kiss her, she didn't run away but met his lips with an insatiable hunger. His arms locked around her, pulling her so close she could hardly breathe. But she didn't care to breathe, only to be kissed. Her hand roamed upward from the small of his back over the swell of his shoulder blades and along his neck, clenching his tousled hair when his lips descended to her throat.

The bright overhead lights flicked on, and just like that, the vision was gone, as if someone offstage had yelled, "Cut!"

"You all right, baby?" Irene asked her. "You're all flushed."

"Fine. It's just warm in here."

"I'll say. This place has got two temperatures. Damned hot and damned cold. The walk back ought to cool you off."

Irene stood, but Mirielle remained seated.

"You coming?"

"No, I . . ." She hesitated. "Frank asked me to hang around after."

Irene gave a lopsided smirk. "Should I leave you my mint lozenges?"

"It's nothing like that," Mirielle said, glad of how steady and convincing her voice sounded. "He probably just wants help stacking the chairs."

Together they roused Jean, who'd fallen asleep halfway through the picture, and she and Irene shuffled out behind the other residents. Mirielle busied herself picking up stray candy wrappers and soda bottles so no one else would take note of her lingering. The last thing she needed was for the Rocking Chair Brigade to get ideas.

"You're not trying to lasso me into helping with the Mardi Gras party, are you?" she asked Frank once everyone else was gone.

"No." A smile tugged at the corners of his lips as he finished packing up his candy cart. Mirielle's stomach tightened. Would that it had been that easy. That innocent.

"So . . . can I help you with the chairs?"

"Not yet." He wheeled the cart into the canteen and returned with a flat square box. She watched as he removed the final reel of the Clara Bow picture from the projector.

"How'd you manage to get such a recent film?"

"I still got a little juice on the outside. What'd ya think?"

Mirielle shrugged, though heat swept into her cheeks again. "It wasn't bad."

"Reckon you'll like this one even better." He opened the box and pulled out another reel of film. "It's a comedy. Thought it might cheer ya up with Irene leaving and all."

"You ordered it just for me?"

His fledgling smile widened. "Call it an early Mardi Gras present."

"You don't give presents at Mardi Gras."

"Guess that's a perk of being locked up in here. Ain't no one around to tell us different."

Mirielle swallowed and watched as he fed the start of the film strip into the projector, once again surprised at how nimble his hands were despite their deformity.

He turned out the lights and sat beside her. She tried not to revisit the kiss that had played out earlier in her mind. His scent drifted over, cutting through the lingering cigarette smoke. Why, when he used the same soap and aftershave as nearly everyone else at Carville, did it smell so good on his skin? Light flicked onto the screen, and she welcomed the distraction. Thank goodness he'd chosen a comedy.

The title of the film flashed in big black letters. Mirielle's heart froze. THE PERILOUS PURSUITS OF PAULINE. The first scene opened with haunting familiarity—the feckless Pauline playing tennis at her grandfather's estate. Mirielle tried to stand, but the muscles in her legs were frozen too. Charlie came onto the screen a moment later, his handsome face boyishly round, just like when they'd met. The remnants of the chocolate bar she'd shared with Jean inched up her throat, bile-tinged and burning.

"I have to go," she managed, first as a whisper, then loud enough to be a shout. "I have to go!" Her legs came back to life with a jerk, and she stood.

Frank reached out, his curled fingers brushing her hand. "Ain't this why ya picked your name? I didn't mean . . . I thought ya'd like it."

Mirielle couldn't answer, except for a sob, and ran out of the room.

CHAPTER 49

Mirielle lay awake all night. She couldn't explain why seeing Charlie on the screen had rattled her so. It was as if she'd been at a party—a small, intimate affair—and an unwelcome guest had arrived, spoiling everything. But whether that guest was Frank or Charlie, she wasn't sure.

As she tried to sort it out, Mirielle realized how divided she'd become, a Dr. Jekyll and Mr. Hyde of sorts, living two separate lives. How would she knit these lives together when the ordeal of her disease was over? They were utterly dissimilar—her life before, her life after. She certainly couldn't go back to the way things had been before her diagnosis. Charlie hated that woman, and—if she were being honest with herself—Mirielle did too. But she couldn't go back to the happy-go-lucky person she'd been before Felix's death either. Time and fate had killed that woman. Mirielle only had who she was now. Perhaps that was why Charlie's black-and-white image on the screen had upset her. It was as if they were strangers again.

"What's eatin' ya?" Irene asked a few days after the picture show night. They were seated on the living room floor, bending old clothes hangers into the shape of wings. Jean and a few of the other children had built a beehive-shaped float out of scraps of lumber and old wheelchair parts for the Mardi Gras parade. Mirielle and Irene had agreed to help with their bee costumes.

"Are you . . . worried at all about going home?" Mirielle asked.

"What's there to worry about?"

"I don't know, that you'll have trouble slipping back into your old skin."

"Baby, I'm the same woman I was when I left. Hair's a little grayer. Tits a little lower. But otherwise I ain't changed."

Mirielle wrestled with the hanger, trying to bend it into something that resembled a wing. How did Irene face everything with such certainty? Maybe she would feel differently if her son hadn't already been a young man when she'd been taken. Or if the marriage to her second husband had lasted. Or maybe she was just a stronger woman.

Mirielle held out the wire-framed wing. Not bad considering she'd never made anything more complicated than a gin rickey before. Perhaps she ought to be more forthcoming with Charlie in her letters. She'd written to him just that morning, wanting to share the good news of Irene's parole. But her pen had stalled after the usual bevy of questions about work and the girls.

Though she'd mentioned Irene in a few previous letters, she doubted Charlie would remember. Did she take the time now to explain Irene was a friend? Her best friend at the colony, if Mirielle were honest. The best friend she'd ever had. Her pen hung above the page dripping ink until Mirielle had to crumple up the letter and start over. Like it or not, life had moved on since her arrival at Carville, carrying her with it. Somewhere along the way, Charlie had been left behind. The seemingly inconsequential details and events she left out of her letters built one upon the other to shape her life here. And she'd never taken the time to go back and explain. Irene was just the name of her house orderly. Jean was just a rowdy girl. Frank was just a nettlesome man with hideous claw-hands. Hector, Madge, Mr. Li, the twins—they didn't even exist in Charlie's conception of her world.

Mirielle set down the wire wing and started on another. Jean came skipping in, tossing her school books onto the sofa and kicking off her shoes.

"How'd you do on your spelling test?" Mirielle asked, though she could guess by Jean's orange-stained lips. Frank kept a box of candy sticks behind the counter for the children when they earned high marks on a test.

Jean grinned, flashing yet another hole where a baby molar had been. "I got 'em all right. Except for one."

"Which one?"

"Mongoose."

"We practiced that one a dozen times last night."

"I know." She looked down and kicked at the edge of the rug.

Mirielle raised herself onto her knees and gave one of Jean's braids a playful tug. "It's better than I ever did as a kid."

"Really?"

"Really," Mirielle said. "I'm proud of you."

"Can I have a candy bar to celebrate?"

"I'm pretty sure you've had enough sweets for today."

Jean turned to Irene. "Pleeeese."

"All right, go grab a nickel outta my purse."

Jean hurried off.

"Just one! I'll know if you take another, you little rascal." Irene turned to Mirielle and flashed an apologetic smile. "I ain't got much more time to spoil her."

"When she's bouncing off the walls tonight, she's your responsibility."

"Thanks!" Jean called skipping out of the house. A moment later she returned and tossed a letter at them. "Forgot to give you this."

The envelope landed between them, facedown. Mirielle's insides tightened. She'd been hoping for a letter from Charlie for weeks, but now she hesitated to pick it up as if he'd somehow seen into her thoughts—her thoughts about kissing Frank—and had written to chasten her. But that was ridiculous. He was hundreds of miles away. Besides, a stray thought or two about another man's lips didn't make her a cheat and a floozie.

She picked up the envelope and started to open it before realizing it was addressed to Irene. "It's for you."

"Hot dog!" Irene said, grabbing the envelope and putting on her cheaters. "It's from my son. Bet the farmhouse is finally ready." She pressed the envelope to her breast and stood. "You mind finishing up on the wings?"

Mirielle's heart squeezed with envy. "The kids might mind when they turn out all lopsided." She managed a smile. "Go read your letter."

CHAPTER 50

Mardi Gras dawned wet and cold. But the foul weather didn't dampen the colony's excitement. Even Mirielle found herself swept up in the gaiety. Before the parade, she helped Jean and the other children into their costumes. Once everyone's wings were straight, stingers pinned, and antennae secure, the children scurried off with their float to join the other paraders while Mirielle and her housemates crowded onto the porch to await the procession.

She heard the clamor of the parade before it came into view—trumpets and drums and noisemakers. Bike horns and footfalls. A slurring of notes that sounded distinctly like Jean and her harmonica. Then the first of the paraders rounded the corner far down the walkway. Several residents with ribbon-festooned bikes and wheelchairs led the procession, passing in a flurry of green, gold, and purple. The musicians followed, heralding the hodgepodge of makeshift floats.

Mirielle and her housemates cheered as they passed. The Mexican Club had created a piñata-styled float out of colorfully painted papier-mâché and a rusty wheelbarrow. Next came a wagon-turned-pirate ship built by house sixteen, complete with white sails and a Jolly Roger flag. Altogether there were eight floats and at least two dozen residents who'd marched with their instruments and bikes. Perhaps Mirielle was partial, but her favorite was the hive and bee children, lopsided wings and all.

After the last float passed, Mirielle and her housemates hurried inside to change for the party. She'd brought four evening gowns with her from California. Four too many, really. She looked over each of them now and tried to remember what she'd been thinking when she'd asked Charlie to pack these. She certainly hadn't envisioned this—the parade and music and party. Ramshackle and rinky-dink, she would have thought then.

She chose a mint-green gown of silk georgette embroidered with beads. It had a wrap-around bodice and V-shaped neckline infilled with flesh-colored silk. A scalloped belt hung hip-level over the straight skirt.

As she shimmied into the gown, she caught the scent of moth-balls. But also something else. She brought the collar up to her nose. Perfume. Cigar smoke. Home.

Perhaps she wasn't up for attending the dance after all. She started to undress, but then Irene appeared in her doorway.

"Whooee," she said. "What a pretty little number."

Mirielle smoothed her hands over the shimmering silk. "It's too much for tonight, I was just going to—"

"No, wear it. You look beautiful." Irene stepped into the room and straightened the dress's seam. "There."

"You look beautiful too," Mirielle said, admiring Irene's dress of blue chiffon. "Where'd you get this?"

"The Sears and Roebuck catalog. You like it? Cost me half a month's wages. I bought it to wear the day I arrive home, but"—her voice broke, and her eyes turned glassy in the overhead lamplight— "well, it's probably too fancy for the dingy Fort Worth train depot anyway."

Mirielle took her by the shoulders and gave the dress a head-to-toe appraisal. "Nonsense. Wear that snappy silk jacket you have, and it'll be perfect for daytime wear. Why, your son will hardly recognize you, you'll be so lovely."

Tears sprung in Irene's eyes.

"I didn't mean to say you're not lovely anyway, only that—"

"I know, baby."

Mirielle pulled her close and hugged her. For the past three days, ever since their talk in the living room, Irene hadn't seemed herself. Maybe all Mirielle's worry about not fitting in had rubbed off. "Never mind what you look like. Your son's going to be so happy to see you step off that train he won't notice what you're wearing. Your grandkids too. It will be like you never left."

Irene stiffened and pulled away. She wiped her eyes and blew her nose with a hankie she plucked from her brassiere.

"And when I get out of this doggone place," Mirielle said, "you'll bring the whole family out to Los Angeles, just like we talked about."

Irene nodded, then drew Mirielle back into a crushing embrace. "I love you, baby. You hear? Don't you ever forget that."

"I love you too."

Irene tugged on her ruby ring until it slipped off her finger. "This is for you."

"I can't take that."

"'Course you can. It's more suited to a big-city sophisticate than a farm girl like me anyhow."

"Irene, you're nuts. Your husband gave you this ring."

"And I'm giving it to you." She took hold of Mirielle's hand and slipped it on her finger. "There. A little remembrance of me."

"You're the one who's leaving and gonna forget all about us here."

"You'll be out soon enough, baby."

Mirielle held out her hand. The ruby sparkled in the lamplight. Maybe the ring wasn't as garish as she'd thought. Even so, she couldn't keep it. The ring was probably worth more than anything else Irene owned. But Mirielle would wear it tonight to humor her. "It's beautiful."

"You bet your socks it is. Now come on, or we'll miss all the to-do."

By the time Mirielle and Irene got to the rec hall, the Hot Rocks had taken the stage, and dancers crowded the floor. Many wore handicraft costumes—pirates and jokers and witches. Others had made paper masks. The tables and chairs encircled the dance floor like at a cabaret club. Ribbons, flags, and multicolored bunting decorated the whitewashed walls. Streamers festooned the water-stained ceiling.

Irene kissed her cheek, then wandered off into the crowd. Mirielle stood alone a moment, feeling overdressed. Then she spotted Frank by the sandwich trays and punch bowl, dressed in the same dapper suit he'd worn in New Orleans. Now was as good a time as any to apologize for running out on him during the film. But before Mirielle could reach him, she was waylaid by Mr. Li asking for a dance.

She danced two songs with him, then a foxtrot with Billy, and a one-step with Mr. Hatch. Jean and the twins joined her for the Charleston and then she caught her breath over a piece of cake with Irene. They laughed at Sister Verena, who stood sour-faced in the corner with a few of the other sisters, and joked she was waiting until the stroke of midnight to silence the band and smudge everyone's forehead with ash.

Something about Irene was still off, though. She didn't ramble on, as she was prone to doing, and her laughter was thin and clipped. Just nerves, she insisted when Mirielle asked. Just nerves.

After a few more turns on the dance floor, Mirielle looked around for Frank. He wasn't seated at any of the tables or hot-footing among the dancers. The cake had been reduced to crumbs, and only a few stale sandwiches remained. She circled the room twice, then asked Irene if she'd seen him.

"I think he went to fetch somethin' from his cabin."

Mirielle decided to go after him. It would be easier to talk without so much noise. Outside, the houses were dark, and the walkways empty. The smell of damp earth hung in the air. A raccoon scuttled across the quadrangle lawn where the old cemetery had been. She caught up with Frank at the far end of the colony just as he was exiting the walkway. He didn't turn around, though he must have heard her footsteps.

"Hey," she called.

He stopped on the bottom step and said over his shoulder, "Hey yourself."

The far-off jangle of music carried across the night air like a whisper.

"Sure was a swell party tonight."

"Ya come all the way here to tell me that?" he said to the darkness that blanketed the lawn and nearby cottages.

"No." She descended one of the steps, then another, rubbing her bare arms against the cold. "The other night—"

"Let's just forget about it."

"No, you're a real peach for doing that for me, and I acted shamefully. It's just . . . I wasn't expecting that, and it reminded me so much of home. Of my life before."

He turned around. The dim light from the walkway cast slanted shadows across his face. "And that's a bad thing?"

"Not bad, just . . . jarring."

He shrugged out of his suit jacket, climbed the two steps that separated them, and draped the jacket around her shoulders. It was warm and smelled of him—soap and sandalwood and liniment. The worsted wool collar tickled her neck the way she'd imagined his kisses would.

"I don't know why I can't stay away from ya, Polly," he said.

"I don't know why I don't let you."

He gazed at her with an intensity fit for the screen. *That's the look!* she could imagine the director saying. *Let's raise the backlighting and zoom in.*

Charlie had gazed at her with that same hunger once, hadn't he? Mirielle couldn't picture it. Even the shape and variegated hue of his eyes were fuzzy in her mind.

Now then, Frank, lean in and kiss her, the director would say.

Mirielle held her breath. On cue, Frank drew closer. Just before their lips met, the thrum of bicycle tires and thud of feet sounded on the walkway. They pulled quickly apart and looked in the direction of the noise. The dance, it seemed, had ended, and the last of the partygoers were trudging toward them. They smoked and laughed and sipped punch from cups they'd filched from the rec hall. Some peeled off toward their respective houses. The others, either too drunk to find their way home or intent on partying the night through, neared Mirielle and Frank. Billy and Rose were among them.

"Frank," Billy said. "You're just the fella we were looking for. Spin us a few records on your phonograph, won't you?"

Frank glanced at Mirielle, then back at the small crowd. "Kind of late for that, don't ya think?"

"It's not even midnight," one of them said. "Mardi Gras hasn't ended."

"I'm tired," Frank said, giving Billy an intent look. "Why don't ya go pester Irene."

But Billy was clearly too drunk to pick up on the innuendo. "She turned in early." He looped an arm over Frank's shoulder. "Come on, old man. We'll not take no for an answer."

Frank sighed and looked at Mirielle, his handsome blue eyes apologetic. "Ya coming?"

She wanted to. Like mad. To dance with him until everyone else tired and went home, then start up again where they'd left off and finally kiss. She handed back his jacket. "I better not."

CHAPTER 51

The next morning, Mirielle slept through breakfast and sprinted to the infirmary to arrive on time for work. In the weeks prior to Mardi Gras, influenza had spread through the colony, and most of the sickbeds remained full. The women asked after yesterday's festivities as Mirielle checked their vital signs and delivered their pills. She recounted the parade and party at least a dozen times, describing the floats and music and costumes and food all with great detail when she saw how it brightened the women's eyes.

"I hope they throw another party next year," one of the women said. "I haven't celebrated Mardi Gras in ages."

"Of course we will."

Mirielle realized only later as she passed out the women's mid-morning snack the mistake of her words. There wouldn't be any *we* next year. She'd be gone from this place, home with her family. Carville would be nothing but a memory.

That ought to make her happy. It did make her happy. As long as she didn't think about those she'd be leaving behind. Jean, Madge, Mr. Li, Frank. Everyone who'd never make it to twelve negative tests, whose only hope was a cure.

Mirielle was so distracted by these thoughts, she tripped on the leg of one of the beds. She managed to catch herself before falling, but not without spilling the pitcher of milk she'd been carrying all over her uniform.

Sister Verena looked up from the stack of records she was sorting and gave Mirielle a sour look. A smudge of ash darkened her forehead, reminding Mirielle that she, along with all the other Catholics, were fasting today. No wonder she was cranky.

Mirielle cleaned up the milk that had spilled on the floor, then hurried back to her room to change. The house was empty when she arrived—Jean at school or playing hooky and the rest of her housemates in the rec hall absorbed in a game of poker or gin. They played almost every morning before lunch, and it didn't surprise Mirielle that Lent hadn't stopped them.

But as Mirielle changed out of her clothes, she heard a soft scratching noise. Not one that started and stopped like a mouse gnawing at the baseboard. But continuous. She crept out wearing only her chemise and followed the sound to Irene's door.

Irene was probably doing some last-minute packing for tomorrow's departure, Mirielle decided. Though that didn't quite explain the noise. She knocked twice on the door. When Irene didn't answer, she let herself in.

The light was off, and heavy curtains shrouded the window. The sharp scent of disinfectant filled the room. The scratching noise sounded from somewhere within. "Irene?"

No reply. Mirielle felt along the wall to the window and pulled back the curtains. Irene lay on the bed facing away from her.

"Get up, sleepyhead. It's nearly eleven."

Irene's room was tidier than Mirielle had ever seen it, but none of her clothes or trinkets had been packed into her trunk. Of the many framed photographs that hung on her wall, only one had been removed. It lay face-up on her nightstand beside her glasses and an opened letter. "How are you ever going to be ready to catch your train tomorrow? I told you I'd help you pack."

Only the steady scratching sound replied. Mirielle looked about the small room for the source of the noise. Irene had dragged her phonograph in from the living room and wedged it in the far corner. A record spun on the turntable, the needle rasping over the label.

"Irene, you're going to ruin your machine." She crossed the room and raised the tonearm. "Never mind your record."

The disc was scratched, and the label shredded. Mirielle lifted it off the turntable and turned toward the bed. "Come on. We'd better get a start on all this if you don't want to miss your—"

Mirielle dropped the record. It shattered on the floor. "Irene!"

Irene's face was frozen in a grimace, her eyes fixed and dull. Foam had crusted around her open mouth. Her tongue was ashy white and swollen to twice its normal size. In her haste to reach her friend, Mirielle kicked over an empty bottle. It rolled on its side, stopping beneath the phonograph. Mirielle's eyes snagged on the label: Lysol.

"Irene! Oh, God. Irene." She sank beside the bed and shook her. Irene's limbs were cold and stiff. She slapped Irene's cheek, watching for a flinch, a breath, a twitch of an eyelid. Nothing.

Mirielle scrambled away from the bed and screamed.

Two days later, Irene was buried beneath the newly leafing pecan trees in the cemetery at the edge of the colony. Mirielle stared at the small white gravestones dotting the yard, engraved with only a name, patient ID number, and death date. Hector's stone and a handful of others stood bright and upright. The rest were speckled with moss and listed with the roll of the boggy ground. It sickened Mirielle to imagine Irene's among them, all the more when she realized it wouldn't be her real name etched on the stone. Mirielle didn't even know Irene's real name. Now, she never would.

The official report listed heart failure as the cause of her death. Mirielle kept the empty Lysol bottle to herself. Irene's death didn't need to become fodder for the Rocking Chair Brigade. Besides, a broken heart fit just as well with the letter Mirielle had found beside Irene's bed. It was addressed from her son and said simply that he didn't want her to come home, however many negative tests she'd had. Like Mr. Hatch had said, once a leper always a leper.

Mirielle felt gutted and numb walking back from the cemetery. How could Irene's son be so cruel? The high, barbed-wire-topped fence glinted in the distance. For the first time, it seemed not only to be keeping them within but protecting them from all the evil without.

A small group had gathered at Frank's cottage, just as they had after Hector's funeral, but Mirielle couldn't bring herself to attend. How could she listen to Frank's phonograph and not hear that scratching sound again? It was enough that no matter where she went, she couldn't shake the mingled scents of death and disinfectant. Couldn't close her eyes without seeing Irene stiff upon the bed.

Instead, Mirielle sat with Jean on the back porch steps of house eighteen, watching the daylight drain from the sky. Jean leaned against Mirielle's shoulder and played her harmonica. She'd taken to the instrument like a natural and practiced every day since Christmas. But this tune—slow and wistful—Mirielle hadn't heard before. The notes tangled like bramble around her heart.

She mulled over every word Irene had said at Mardi Gras. The dress. The ring. Surely by then, she'd made up her mind to . . .

Mirielle couldn't even think the word *suicide* without the weight of it threatening to crush her. She wrapped an arm around Jean and listened to her play. How many deaths had the poor child seen? How many more awaited her?

That night, after everyone went to bed, the silence of the house haunted Mirielle. Her pulse pounded. She breathed faster and faster, but still thirsted for air. She threw on her kimono and peeked in Jean's room once, twice, three times, just to be sure her chest was rising. She turned on both living room lamps and tried to read a magazine. The words were no more comprehensible than Chinese.

A quiet knock at the front door made her jump, and she sat for a full minute unscrambling her wits enough to stand and answer it. Frank stood on the walkway, still dressed in his funeral suit. In the two days since Irene's death, she'd forgotten how close they'd stood on the steps the night of Mardi Gras. Forgotten how tempted she'd been to kiss him. Forgotten everything but how to move and breathe.

"Polly, I reckon ya don't want company but—"

"Mirielle. My real name is Mirielle."

"Mirielle."

Her name had never sounded so comforting. She flung herself against him and wept into his chest. His arms encircled her. She wasn't sure how long they stood like that in the doorway or how he managed to shepherd her back into the living room without releasing her from his embrace. He held her, and they cried together, Mirielle's sobs loud and relentless, his a slow, silent trickle. What a relief not to have to explain her sorrow, anger, and fear. He felt them too.

With their eyes still wet, her lips found his. She kissed him with abandon. Firm and then light and then firm again. He sank onto the couch and pulled her beside him, trailing kisses down her neck. She enmeshed her hands in his hair. His curled fingers slipped beneath her nightgown, sweeping over her skin. She shuddered at his touch. His fingers lingered on her thigh, just above her knee, but went no farther. They kissed until her lips were numb as if they could draw out the sorrow this disease had injected into their lives. Then she laid her head against his chest and fell asleep to the steady sound of his breathing.

CHAPTER 52

———⋙•◦•⋘———

Mirielle awoke in her bed with only a vague memory of Frank carrying her there before he left. Morning shone brightly outside her window. She closed her eyes against the light. The sadness of Irene's death still engulfed her, but last night's panic was gone. Rolling onto her side, she came face-to-face with the framed picture on her nightstand. Charlie. She said his name over and over again in her mind, hoping to stir something more than languid ambivalence. Frank had saved her last night, not by anything he did. His presence was enough. Someday she'd be able to share her grief with Charlie too. But he'd never fully understand Carville and the tragedy she absorbed here.

She shrugged off her blankets and sat up. She was due in the infirmary today for her tenth skin scraping. Any other morning, she would have hurried to shower and dress, eager to get the test done with and hear Doc Jack pronounce her slides negative. Today, even that couldn't liven her step.

Sister Verena greeted Mirielle with her usual pinched-lip expression when she arrived. "You're late."

"Sorry, I was . . . er . . . I overslept." A feeble smile found its way to her lips. Sister Verena would swoon if she knew Mirielle had fallen asleep in Frank's arms.

"Well, Dr. Jachimowski was called away to assist with a surgery."

"I'll wait." She crossed the infirmary to where Sister Loretta was rolling bandages and sat down to help even though it was her day off. The old sister chatted amiably at her while Sister Verena tended to the bedridden patients, eyeing Mirielle suspiciously from across the room.

Doc Jack arrived thirty minutes later, remarking how well she looked during the examination. The lesion on her neck had vanished, and the others remained faint and flat. "Whatever you're doing, keep it up," he said, transferring flecks of skin and tissue from the spot beneath her thumb to the last of his slides. "With any luck, you'll be out of here in just a couple of months."

The lunch bell rang while she dressed after her exam. She decided to wait out her results in the dining hall rather than the infirmary. Chef was serving chicken salad sandwiches with applesauce and greens. She grabbed a plate and sat at an empty table across the hall. A cool breeze rolled in through the open windows, carrying with it the faintest promise of spring. Birdsong mixed with the residents' chatter. Soon her housemates were seated around her. Their conversation foundered, lapsing into long silences until Jean teased her about being a slug-a-bed for having missed breakfast. They all laughed, though it was impossible not to notice the absence of Irene's snorting chuckles.

When Mirielle arrived back at the infirmary, she could hear Doc Jack behind the examination screen with another patient. She returned to the table where Sister Loretta was still rolling bandages and took up another long strip of gauze. This time, the old woman stayed silent as they worked, not meeting Mirielle's eye.

A few minutes later, Doc Jack and Sister Verena emerged from behind the screen. His ready smile faltered when he saw her. He muttered something to Sister Verena before heading to the sink to wash his hands.

Sister Verena walked over, her expression devoid of its usual self-importance. Mirielle's stomach tightened.

"Have a seat over there, Mrs. Marvin," Sister Verena said, gesturing to an empty hospital bed spaced far apart from the others.

"Is something wrong? Why can't Doc Jack talk to me here?"

Sister Loretta eased the partially rolled bandage from Mirielle's grasp. "Go on, dearie. I'll finish up."

Mirielle crossed to the bed but didn't sit down. She watched Doc Jack dry his hands. He joined Sister Verena by the desk in the far corner of the room, and together they walked to Mirielle, a manila chart tucked under the sister's arm. *Patient 367*, the chart's label read. It reminded Mirielle of Irene's gravestone, how in the end they were all reduced to a number.

"Please sit down, Mrs. Marvin," Doc Jack said, his voice unusually somber.

"I don't want to sit."

His gaze dropped to the ground, and he wiped his palms on his lab coat. When he looked at her again, his gray eyes had regained the steadiness she'd seen in them that morning, but none of the cheer. "We identified several bacilli in your skin scrapings today."

Mirielle's legs felt suddenly hollow. "What do you mean?"

"Your test was positive."

Positive? That wasn't possible. She reached back, finding the thin mattress just as her knees gave out. "But you said yourself how healthy I'm looking."

"It's not always possible to predict when and why the disease will flare."

"But I . . ."

"It's nothing to be too concerned over. Only two of the slides showed the disease. I'm confident if you keep taking chaulmoogra oil and minding your health, you'll be running negative again in no time."

"But I'm meant to go home in a few months."

Doc Jack glanced sideways at Sister Verena. "No, I'm afraid not."

Mirielle thrust out her lesion-marked hand. "You've made a mistake. Retest me."

"We don't retest, Mrs. Marvin," Sister Verena said.

"Shut up," she said loudly enough to elicit murmurs from the bedbound patients across the room. "You're glad for this. You've always hated me."

"I don't wish this disease on anyone."

Mirielle turned back to Doc Jack, tears building in her eyes. "Please, this can't be right."

"It is. I had Sister Katherine in the laboratory verify the slides."

"I want to see." She stood, a building rage giving strength to her legs.

"We don't usually allow patients in the laboratory. It's—"

Mirielle brushed past him and out of the infirmary. Footsteps sounded behind her. His? Sister Verena's? Mirielle didn't care. When she reached the laboratory, she flung the door wide and stomped in.

"Show me my slides," she demanded of Sister Katherine.

The woman looked up from her pipette and beaker. "I'm afraid you can't be—"

"It's all right, Nurse Katherine," Doc Jack said, coming up behind Mirielle somewhat out of breath. "Do you still have Patient 367's slides?"

Sister Katherine fetched a set of six slides and turned on the microscope. Doc Jack sorted through the slides before placing one labeled *367 - R hand* beneath the lens. He looked into the eyepiece and adjusted the focus.

When he stepped aside, Mirielle took his place, peering into the eyepiece. A blur of pink and blue showed through the lens. "What am I looking for?"

"*Mycobacterium leprae* is an acid-fast organism," Doc Jack said. "That means it turns reddish-pink when we put dye on the slide. The dye washes away from your regular cells when we add acid, but the bacteria hold on to the dye. We counterstain your cells with methylene blue, but interspersed you should see several rod-shaped specks of pink. That's the disease."

Mirielle looked again. Slowly, the blur of color took shape, and the rods Doc Jack spoke of appeared. Mirielle backed away from the microscope, shaking her head. She bumped into the wall behind her and groped for what she hoped was the door. Instead, her hand struck a shelf. The clank of toppling equipment and shattering glass sounded through the small room.

"Mrs. Marvin, are you all right? Please let's return to the—"

Mirielle found the door and fled from the laboratory before Doc Jack could finish. She ran along the walkway, exiting down the first flight of stairs she found. The steps spilled her out onto the vast oak-studded lawn between the southeast buildings and the fence. Mirielle hid behind a wide, gnarled tree trunk in case Doc Jack or one of the sisters came looking for her. She couldn't bear to return to the infirmary and listen to their falsely positive prognostications. Nothing they said could obscure the fact she was damned to remain here another year longer. A year of missed birthdays and holidays and

Sunday picnics on the beach. A year without holding her daughters and watching them grow.

She slid down the trunk and sat on the moss-covered roots that bulged from the ground. Her hand was already wet when she swiped it over her tear-streaked cheeks. Looking down, she saw blood smeared across her palm. She must have cut herself back in the laboratory. Blood beaded along the edges of the laceration and pooled in the center of her hand. The sight of it transfixed her the way it had in the bathroom the night of her accident, when it dripped from her wrist in a steady stream, staining the bathwater red.

Would it have been better if she'd died that night? She remembered Charlie's frantic, wide-eyed expression when he found her. He'd clutched his hand to her wrist and begged her not to leave him. Would he say the same thing now? A year from now? She thought of Irene's son and wasn't sure.

"Polly!"

Frank's voice startled her. She wiped her bloodied palm on the skirt of her dress and stood. Overhead leaves blotted out the weak afternoon light. Tendrils of moss drooped from the branches. She heard his voice, closer, and held her breath, hoping he wouldn't find her.

"Polly, my God, what's happened to ya?" He reached for her, but she pushed him away, leaving a smear of blood on his shirt.

"Don't touch me."

"You're bleeding. Are you—"

"You did this to me."

"What?"

She closed her eyes and yelled, "You did this to me!"

"What are ya talking about? I ran into Sister Verena on my way to the canteen. She and Doc Jack are looking for ya. Said ya were upset and—"

"I tested positive."

He stared blankly at her a moment, then shook his head. "Your skin scraping? My God, *chère,* I'm sorry." He reached for her again, and this time she let him wrap her up in his arms. His warmth lolled her, his sturdy frame, his soap and liniment scent. She found herself beginning to melt against him and struggled free.

"You did this. I would never have tested positive if we didn't . . . I should never have let you touch me."

He winced as if she had slapped him and took a step back. "This disease don't spread like fleas or lice. Ya know that. It takes years to develop. Ya had it long before ya met me."

Mirielle did know that. She'd heard Doc Jack say so countless times. But she didn't care. "I hate you. You're disgusting. How could I ever have—"

"Ya don't mean that."

"I do!"

"You're a leper too, Mirielle." He held up his ruined hands inches from her face. "The same bacteria that did this to me is festering inside you. Has been for years. And no matter when ya get your parole, it will still be inside ya. A stupid slip of paper from the health service ain't going to change that. And trust me, the people out there"—he gestured to the vacant road and sloping levee beyond the fence— "your family, your husband, they think you're just as disgusting as me."

He stomped away. Mirielle crumpled to the ground and wept.

March 6, 1927

Dear Mirielle,

An invitation was waiting for me when we returned from the Alps from Mr. Mayer. A little party at the Ambassador for a new club he's created: the International Academy of Motion Picture Arts and Sciences. Douglas and Mr. Niblo are members, and I'm thinking of joining myself. Postproduction is almost wrapped up on the film. It should be showing in theaters in May. Shame you won't be able to see it. I have to say, it's one of my finest works.

What's all this business you were saying in your most recent letter about Mardi Gras? Did I understand right that there will be a parade at the facility? I can't imagine how it could possibly come off. Sometimes it seems like you're writing from a college clubhouse, not a hospital. I don't see how such exertions could be good for your health. I suppose as long as the doctors are game, but don't do anything they haven't approved. You know you do tend to overdo things, especially when a party's concerned.

Your husband,
Charlie

March 21, 1927

Dear Mirielle,

    It's been some weeks since we've had a letter from you. Perhaps your latest correspondence was destroyed in the sterilizer. How was the Mardi Gras play? Or was it a parade?

    Have you had another one of those tests? I forget whether they're done at the beginning of the month or the end. It is every month, isn't it?

    Any chance you can get to a telephone again? I know the girls would love to hear from you. I'd like the chance for a word too.

    Write or 'phone soon.

    Your husband,
    Charlie

April 26, 1927

Dear Mirielle,

Whatever has happened to make you stop writing? Without word from you, I've been left to imagine the worst— some terrible turn in your disease whereby you've gone blind or lost use of your hands. What did you say they call it? Claw-hands? Or worse still, that you've had another accident.

It's damned selfish, if you ask me. Leaving us to wonder like this. You might at least make an effort for the girls. I don't know why I'm surprised. You never did care for anyone but yourself.

Charlie

CHAPTER 53

Mirielle moved from one day to the next like a phantom. She slept through breakfast and suppered in her room. At work, she shuffled languidly through her duties. No more haircuts and manicures. No more smiles and conversation. She avoided the rec hall and tennis court and canteen. When her housemates asked if she wanted to play cards or dye Easter eggs or watch whatever old picture the What Cheer Club had rustled up for movie night, Mirielle's answer was always no. Eventually they stopped asking.

On half a dozen occasions, she pulled out her stationery set to write Charlie and share her bitter news about the test. But every attempt ended in a torn-up heap on the floor. Eventually she stopped trying.

And Frank. He hadn't come around to apologize. She certainly wasn't going to be the first to eat crow. Avoiding him was easy. Not thinking about him proved far harder. But eventually she managed to push him from her mind.

Days passed into weeks. Mirielle could feel herself slipping back into the cloud of numbness she'd lived in after Felix's death. She arrived later and later to work, indifferent to Sister Verena's surly gaze and pointed *ahems*. One day she stopped going at all. What was the point? They'd never find a cure.

One evening soon after, Jean barged into her room. She switched on the light, squeezed into bed beside Mirielle, and thrust something into her hand. Mirielle blinked, her eyes adjusting to the light. What time was it? With her curtains drawn, Mirielle wasn't sure. She squinted at the object in her hand. A magazine. *Picture-Play.* The handsome young actor on the cover wasn't anyone she knew.

Mirielle tossed the magazine onto the floor and buried her head in her pillow. She used to know everyone in Hollywood, at least by reputation. The world outside the colony was moving on—her children growing older, her husband more distant—while she was stuck here. A filthy leper. Never to get better. Never to go home.

Jean got up, stomped around the bed, and picked up the magazine. She held it out to Mirielle. "Read."

Mirielle batted the magazine. "Not tonight, I'm tired."

"You said the same thing last night and the night before." She rolled up the magazine and poked Mirielle in the chest. "Read!"

"Go ask Irene—" Mirielle stopped and winced. Irene was dead. Felix was dead. Soon enough, they'd all be dead. She rolled away from Jean and closed her eyes.

After a welcome moment of silence, Mirielle heard a ripping sound. A wad of paper struck her back. And another. Rip. Wad. Rip. Wad. Mirielle didn't turn around or even open her eyes until a thud sounded against the wall. The torn-up magazine ricocheted to the ground.

"Please don't be so loud," Mirielle said.

Jean thundered from the room.

"The light," Mirielle called after her.

But either Jean didn't hear or didn't care because the pesky overhead bulb stayed on. Mirielle didn't have the energy to get up and turn it off, so she pulled the sheet over her head. She'd fallen back into the hazy numbness of sleep when the shrill notes of a harmonica sounded.

"Stop it," Mirielle mumbled, but Jean only played louder. She climbed on the bed and jumped up and down on the mattress, blowing away into her harmonica.

"Stop it!"

"Then get up!" Jean quit jumping and tugged on Mirielle's arm. "Get up, damn it. Get up!" Tears choked her voice. Her fingers dug into Mirielle's skin.

"Mind your language," Mirielle said, but the words sounded like someone else's. Hoarse, flat, empty.

Jean gave up tugging on Mirielle's arm and jumped off the mattress. She yanked the quilt and top sheet from the bed, hurling them across the room. "Get up!"

Mirielle curled up and turned away. "Go find someone else to pester."

"I hate you!" Jean kicked the foot of the bed. The frame whined and springs trembled. But though she had a vague sense that Jean's heart was breaking and that her heart should break in return, Mirielle felt nothing.

"Please get up," Jean sobbed. "I promise not to be bad anymore."

"I don't care what you do. Just leave me alone to sleep."

A door slammed in response. The crying stopped. Mirielle didn't hear Jean's harmonica again.

CHAPTER 54

—➤·◦·◄—

"Jesus, Mary, and Joseph, it smells in here."

Irene?

No, she was dead.

Madge? One of the orderlies? Hadn't Mirielle told everyone to go away? Let her sleep. Leave her alone.

An onslaught of light blinded her. "I don't want the lamp on."

"A little sunlight will do you good."

"Turn it off."

Her window rattled. Birdsong assaulted her ears. Mirielle burrowed beneath her blankets. Her intruder was right. Something did smell. Egg salad? Breaded catfish? Chef's chicken alfresco? "Like I told the last orderly who came by, I'm not hungry."

"I've not come to bring you food, Mrs. Marvin."

Mirielle peeked from beneath the blankets. "Sister Verena?"

"You've wallowed here in self-pity long enough." Her eyes shifted around Mirielle's room, and the wrinkles around her nose deepened, drawing her upper lip into a snarl. "Far longer than I should have countenanced, I see."

"I'm not wallowing. I'm . . . resting."

Sister Verena laughed. "Resting? You haven't left your room in a week." She brushed off a heap of dirty clothes and clutter from the seat of a nearby chair, pulled it close to Mirielle's bedside, and sat down. The thump of the chair legs and rustling of her over-starched skirt hurt Mirielle's ears as much as the birds' chatter.

Sister Verena pinched the corner of Mirielle's bedding and raised it a few inches from the mattress. "When was the last time you disjoined yourself from these moldering sheets and got up?"

"I used the bathroom only a few hours ago." That had been just a few hours ago, hadn't it?

"And when did you last shower or bring your clothes out for the laundry?"

Mirielle peeled the collar of her nightgown from her skin and sniffed. "It's fine. I'm fine. Go away."

"Mrs. Marvin, you're not fine. The orderlies tell me you don't eat. Your housemates never see you up anymore and complain about the smell."

Mirielle cocooned herself more tightly within her blankets. "I don't care."

"I know the news of your positive test was hard to bear, especially coming on the heels of Mrs. Hardee's death, but you'll never get better and make it home to your family if you don't start taking care of yourself."

Mirielle's chest tightened, a strange sensation after feeling so little for so long. She rolled onto her side, away from Sister Verena. The faces in the photograph on her nightstand stared at her accusingly until she closed her eyes.

"You're not the only one who's known disappointment and suffering. Everyone here could tell a tale. We still rise each morning and thank the Lord for a new day."

"We?" Mirielle snickered. "What tale of suffering could you tell beyond having to wear that ridiculous hat?"

Sister Verena was quiet a moment. Undoubtedly fuming with indignation. Good. Maybe she'd leave.

"When you first arrived, I asked you how many children you had, and you hesitated. Said three, then corrected yourself. Did one die?"

The tenderness in Sister Verena's voice surprised Mirielle, and she rolled back toward her. "My son, Felix."

"Mmm . . ." Sister Verena looked over Mirielle's head out the window, her gaze distant and glassy. "I had a son once too. He had bright green eyes and a head of curly red hair the day he was born."

"You had a family before you became a nun?"

"No," she said, still looking away. "The sisters said it best I didn't hold him."

"The sisters?"

"At the home for unwed mothers where I stayed." Her fingers crawled along the rosary beads dangling at her hip until they found the crucifix at the end. "They were right, I suppose. What good could holding him have done. But they did lift him up for me to see. His hair, his eyes, his ruddy cheeks."

"And what then?" Mirielle asked.

"To the orphanage, of course. Newborns have a good chance of being adopted. Better than older children, anyway. I like to think he found a good home."

Mirielle raised herself onto a shaky elbow. "How old were you?"

"Fourteen."

"He'd be a grown man by now."

"Twenty-four years old just last Sunday."

"Have you ever seen him? I mean, since they took him away."

Sister Verena shook her head. She returned her gaze to Mirielle, her gray eyes once again sharp and focused. "I can't imagine that would do either one of us any good. With God's grace, he doesn't even know."

"How can you say that? You're his mother."

"I am not. I am merely the woman who birthed him." Sister Verena straightened and released the crucifix. The rosary fell to her side, the polished beads rasping against her skirt. "In any case, that woman is gone."

Her strange mood the night of Christmas Eve made sense now. "But how could you take Elena's baby when the same thing happened to you?"

"Believe me, Mrs. Marvin, it was not easy. It's never easy. But we must think of the babies, God's beloveds and innocent in all this."

"Why did you tell me this? About your son."

"You asked about my tale of suffering. And I wanted you to see that life goes on whether we like it or not."

Mirielle's elbow gave way, and she fell back against her pillow. Were there no happy stories in this world? "Thanks for the swell pep talk. Now can you please go away?"

Sister Verena frowned and jutted her chin at the slender stack of letters on Mirielle's nightstand. "Do you know how many patients here haven't a family who writes them at all? Patients whose disease is far worse than yours. Who never make it to one negative test, let alone twelve. They still manage to get out of bed in the morning."

"Bully for them."

Sister Verena stood. "The most despicable part of all of this is that you don't see the people you're hurting. Your fellow patients at the dressing clinic and in the infirmary ask when you're coming around again."

That wasn't Mirielle's problem. So why did Sister Verena's words sting so? "Please, just let me be."

"And Jean. It wasn't enough that her father left her. You abandoned her too."

Mirielle sat up. "Who are you to talk about abandoning children?"

Sister Verena's face flushed. Her lips fell open without the benefit of words. She spun around, her skirts swishing and rosary beads clattering, and left.

Mirielle laid down and drew the blankets over her head. Just as her muscles began to relax, footfalls sounded again. Before she could uncover her eyes, a deluge of cold, sudsy water struck her.

For a moment, Mirielle thought she was drowning. Panic surged through her. Foul-tasting water filled her mouth as she screamed. She kicked and clawed at the sodden blankets, desperate to free herself.

The downpour of water stopped long before she managed to untangle herself. Her entire bed was soaked. Water dripped from the mattress onto the floor. She coughed and spat out what little of the dirty, soapy water she hadn't swallowed.

Sister Verena stood over her with an empty mop bucket. "Like I said. It stinks in here. Either you rise, clean this mess of a room, and start eating, or I'll have the orderlies drag you to the infirmary where we'll strap you to the bed and force a feeding tube down your nose. Your choice, Mrs. Marvin."

CHAPTER 55

Mirielle lay on her wet, dirty mattress, raveled in soggy bedclothes, staring at the whitewashed plaster ceiling. Her fingers drifted to her bracelet, finding the thin, raised line beneath. That was one solution. But when she probed beneath the numbness inside her, Mirielle realized she didn't want to die. And didn't want to hurt people the way Irene's death had hurt her. Yet how could she survive another year at Carville without her family? What if it took her longer than that to accumulate twelve negative tests? What if two years became three, four, ten? What if they never found a cure?

She shuddered. The greater part of her wanted simply to sleep. And sleep. And sleep. To exist apart from the world the way she had after Felix's death. The March breeze—no, it was early May now, wasn't it?—licked over her wet nightgown, causing her teeth to clatter. Why hadn't Sister Verena closed the damned window? And that light! Of all the days to be sunny.

Mirielle dragged herself from the bed to the window. The pecan trees were fully leafed now. Magnolia blossoms scented the air. A woolly caterpillar inched across the windowsill. She started to call for Jean—insects always fascinated her—then remembered with shame how horribly she'd treated her.

She started to close the sash but stopped. Sister Verena had been right about the smell. Now that Mirielle was up, she might as well change her wet sheets and nightgown. The window could stay open until she was through.

Once her dirty sheets were changed, she forced herself to shower. No point in climbing into a clean bed with sweat-crusted skin and oily hair. She'd sleep better afterward.

The water jabbed at her overly sensitized skin like needles. The gurgle of the drain deafened her. But little by little, her muscles relaxed. She lathered her soap and scrubbed every patch of skin. The swirl of bubbles down the drain put her in mind of her children's bath time. Of splashing and laughter. Of their soft skin and sweet scent.

Despair washed over her again, eating away at her like the rising tide does a sandcastle. But something else stirred too. An echo of her former resolve. She could still beat this disease and make it home.

She turned off the water and toweled herself dry. Steam fogged the mirror above the sink. Mirielle hesitated before wiping it away. Her reflection was gaunt, bones draped in sallow skin, the occasional ropey cord of muscle. No softness. No curves.

The lesion on her neck had returned. Those on the back of her thighs were red and raised. Her weeks of despondence had cost her more than time. She tried not to think of it. Told herself not to look back. But looking forward through the prism of her reflection was no more comforting.

One day at a time. No, even that was too daunting. An afternoon. An hour. She turned from the mirror, wrapped the towel around her withered body, and headed back to her room. She could get through the next sixty minutes without lying down. Without giving in to despair. That was as far forward as she could look.

The next morning, Mirielle forced herself out of bed with the dawn. She smoothed her sheets and quilt and tucked the edges beneath the mattress, hoping that untucking them would prove a great enough effort to keep her from crawling back into bed midday. She donned her least baggy dress and twisted her limp hair into a low-lying bun. Maybe tonight she'd find the energy to set it in pin curls. But that was looking too far ahead.

Little things taxed her stamina, like dusting her bedside table or bending down to tie her shoes, and she found herself sitting often. But she'd not allow herself to lie down. In the early afternoon, she knocked on Jean's door. No answer. She put her ear to the wood and listened. No rustling inside. Usually Jean hurried home from school to throw down her books and shrug off her cardigan before running out to play with the other kids, but Mirielle hadn't heard a peep.

She had to apologize. The sooner, the better. And somehow make up for shutting Jean out. Mirielle grabbed a hat and started off to look for her. Jean was bound to be cavorting with Toby and the twins atop the observation tower or fighting over the radio dial in the rec hall.

The afternoon warmth surprised Mirielle. But it was May, after all. Winter had retreated without her notice. She huffed her way to the top of the observation tower, only to find the deck empty. The nearby river glinted like a discarded necklace against a velvet green backdrop. Strange to think it had been silently coursing these many weeks, the water it carried when she learned of her positive test long gone to sea. It was darker now than she remembered, high against its banks.

She climbed down and headed for the rec hall. Along the way, passersby greeted her with smiles.

"Missed you in the dressing clinic," one man said.

"Ain't the same without you," said another.

Madge stopped, throwing up her hands. "Look who's risen from the dead!" She tugged at Mirielle's baggy dress and pinched her sunken cheek. "You look the part of death too, dollface."

"Thanks."

Madge winked and shuffled onward, calling over her shoulder, "Still a hell of a lot prettier than the rest of us."

When Mirielle arrived at the rec hall, she found several people crowded around the radio listening to a baseball game. Jean wasn't among them. At the far side of the room, the regular coterie of loud-mouthed gamblers hunkered around their cards and dice. Nice to know not everything changed. She watched them a moment, steeling herself before heading into the canteen. Mail had just been delivered, and people swarmed around the counter while Frank sorted it. He pushed a few strands of hair behind his ear, smiling broadly at something someone had said.

Mirielle didn't want to be caught staring, but couldn't look away. How had she spoken such awful things to him? She drank in his smile, bracing herself for the scowl that would cloud his face when he saw her. But when he glanced up from the pile of mail, his eyes swept right over her, a slight twitch of the lips the only indication he'd seen her at all.

She sat down at an empty table to wait out the crowd. Frank might have seen Jean after school and know her whereabouts. Besides, Mirielle owed him an apology too. A copy of last season's Sears and Roebuck catalog sat on the table. Mirielle flipped through its curling pages to keep her eyes, if not her mind, distracted.

She'd expected anger from Frank. That she could chip away at over time. But if his cool reaction was any indication, his feelings for her—whatever they'd been—had hardened into something not even time could mend.

A letter landed beside the open catalog. Mirielle looked up. Frank stood above her. She hadn't heard him approach or noticed the crowd thin.

"This came for ya a few days back," he said, and turned to go.

"Frank, wait."

He stopped but didn't turn around. "Unless you're fixing to order a soda, we ain't got nothing to say to each other."

Her fingers drifted to her throat, stroking the raised, scaly lesion as she watched him walk away. She hadn't even thought to wear a necklace or a scarf. No point in hiding what she was here. No hiding behind it either. She was to blame for this rift between her and Frank. Between her and Jean. Not the disease. It was up to her to fix it. But first Charlie.

She looked down at the envelope, at the tidy rows of letters and numbers penned in Charlie's hand. His last letter had been awfully tart—not that Mirielle could blame him—but she was surprised he'd written again so soon. Inside the envelope was a single sheet of paper.

May 4, 1927

Dear Mirielle,

Helen is sick. Scarlet fever, the doctor says. She's under care at the hospital. I don't know if you're even getting these damned letters, but as her mother, I thought you should know. I'll write again when I have more news.

Charlie

CHAPTER 56

Letter in hand, Mirielle hurried along the walkway past the morgue and schoolhouse and chapels. At the hedgerow, she hesitated only a second, then marched on to the plantation house.

Inside, an electric pendant lamp lighted a broad foyer and curving staircase. Beyond the foyer, a hallway ran to the back of the house, branching off into several rooms. Sister Verena intercepted her in the hallway before she could find Dr. Ross's office. "Mrs. Marvin, what are you doing here?"

"I have to see Dr. Ross."

"You know patients are restricted from this part of the facility."

Mirielle brandished her letter. "My daughter is sick. I'm not leaving until I speak to Dr. Ross."

"Return to the colony and I will broach—"

"What's going on here?" Dr. Ross appeared in the doorway of a nearby room. Mirielle sidestepped Sister Verena and hurried over to him. "Dr. Ross, thank God, I have to speak with you."

His lips pursed, drawing his mustache together like an accordion. "You're not permitted to be here."

"Please, it's urgent."

He glanced past her at Sister Verena with a reproving glare.

"She's already here, Doctor. Perhaps we can hear her out."

He sighed and retreated into his office. Mirielle followed him inside and behind her Sister Verena.

"My name is . . . well, my Carville name is Pauline Mar—"

"I remember you, Mrs. Marvin. Not many patients break their arm and wind up in jail within their first week of arriving." He sat behind a wide desk in a wingback chair. Medical textbooks lined a nearby shelf. A gilded clock ticked like a metronome on the wall. Everything was neat, ordered, polished. Even the silver-framed picture of his family on the credenza behind his desk sat at attention.

"I just received news my daughter is very sick. Scarlet fever." Mirielle's voice broke, and she blinked back tears. "I need to go to her. I promise I'll return when she's well."

"I'm afraid that's not possible, Mrs. Marvin." He didn't offer her a chair or even use of his hankie.

"Other patients have been granted permission to go home."

"In rare circumstances, yes, I've allowed patients from Louisiana or Texas leave to attend the funeral of a parent or"—he hesitated—"a child."

A sob broke past Mirielle's lips. "Oh God, please don't make me wait for that. I've already buried one child."

"It's not a question of circumstance, Mrs. Marvin, but of distance. In order for anyone to leave, they must have written permission from the health department of every state in which they mean to travel. You're from California, correct?"

Mirielle nodded.

"It's unlikely New Mexico or Arizona would permit such unnecessary travel."

"Unnecessary?" She pointed at the picture behind him. "You're a father. If one of your boys were sick and dying, would you deem it unnecessary to be with him?"

Sister Verena put a steadying hand on Mirielle's arm, then spoke to Dr. Ross. "Perhaps we could inquire with the health departments in question."

He shot her another glare. To her credit, Sister Verena did not shrink back. If anything, her indomitable countenance grew larger.

"We can't go around making exceptions for people," Dr. Ross said. "Word will get out, and they'll be asking for a leave slip for the tritest of circumstances."

"Mrs. Marvin's circumstances are hardly trite."

He ignored her and turned his eyes to Mirielle. "Even if all five health departments agreed, it would take weeks to arrange. By then, your daughter will have likely recovered."

"Or died!"

He winced. "There's nothing you could do for her anyway, Mrs. Marvin. The fever has to run its course. And your disease. Children are particularly susceptible to the bacilli."

Nothing she could do? She was Helen's mother! No one belonged at her bedside more than Mirielle.

"Go back to the colony," he continued. "And try not to worry. Children are resilient."

Her hand curled into a fist at his blithe comment. She itched to scramble over his desk and punch him. But Sister Verena's grip tightened about her arm, as if she could sense Mirielle's intention.

"My apologies for the disruption, Dr. Ross. I'll see Mrs. Marvin back to the colony."

They walked to the hedgerow in silence, Mirielle's pace clipped. If she couldn't get permission to travel home, she'd leave without it.

"Galivanting up to the administration building is not what I had in mind when I told you to get out of bed," Sister Verena said when they reached the hedgerow.

"My daughter is—"

"I understand your concern." Her voice softened. "Believe me, I do."

Mirielle plucked a leaf from the hedge and rolled it between her fingers, watching it crumple and stain her skin green. "What I said before . . . about you abandoning your son . . . I'm sorry. It was an unconscionable thing to say." She dropped the leaf and looked at Sister Verena. "But if you understand my concern, then you must understand why I have to get home."

"Have you considered that going home might do more harm than good?"

"I'd be careful," Mirielle said. The residents talked about ways to keep others safe. Boiling your dishes after meals. Disinfecting the things you touched. Sleeping in a separate room. "I won't even hold or kiss her. I just have to know my daughter's okay."

"Dr. Ross is correct. Children are more susceptible to the disease. But that's not what I'm talking about." Sister Verena walked to a nearby bench and sat down. Mirielle followed. The boughs of a giant oak tree shaded them. Sister Verena's hand disappeared into the stiff folds of her skirt. A moment later, it reappeared from some hidden pocket with a palmful of candy hearts. She offered one to Mirielle. *Be True*, the heart's inscription read.

"I think of my son every day, Mrs. Marvin." She paused, looking down at the candies in her hand. "I gave him up not because I didn't love him, but because I didn't want to burden him with shame. The shame of being a bastard. It was the only gift I had to give him." She offered Mirielle another heart, then flung the rest of the candies over her shoulder into the grass. "Right or wrong, your disease carries a stigma too. Would you risk that on your daughter?"

"No one will find out."

"You cannot be certain. It stands to reason that—"

"I don't care about reason!"

"What about your family here at Carville?"

The residual sweetness on Mirielle's tongue turned chalky and bitter. "I only have one family. And if you try to stop me from going to them I'll . . . I'll . . ." But what could Mirielle do if Sister Verena truly meant to stop her? Escaping through the fence was one thing, but breaking out of the jail was another thing entirely.

Sister Verena cast a furtive glance at the plantation house. "Come with me."

Mirielle followed her through the colony, regretting she'd ever thought to ask permission to leave. When they arrived at the small office tucked between the men's infirmaries, Sister Verena went straight to her desk and began rummaging through one of its drawers. Did she have a key for the jail inside? A syringe filled with morphine to plunge into Mirielle's arm to sedate her? More of those stupid candy hearts?

Something silver flashed in Sister Verena's hand as she closed the drawer. "We cannot change the past, Mrs. Marvin. What we did or did not do. But we can live true to the present." She pressed a heavy medallion into Mirielle's hand.

"What's this?"

"A medal of St. Christopher. He'll protect you on your journey."

"My journey?"

"Tonight at eight, Watchman Doyle will be called to investigate a disturbance on the far side of the colony. The rest is up to you."

CHAPTER 57

As soon as the sun dipped below the horizon and the sky began to darken, Mirielle grabbed the small valise she'd packed and returned to the canteen. As she'd hoped, Frank was alone. He plunged a mop into a bucket of soapy water, then sloshed it across the floor.

"Come back tomorrow," he said without sparing a glance in her direction. "I'm closing up."

"I need your pliers."

His mop stilled. "What?"

"I'm leaving. Tonight."

Frank didn't move. The hum of the radio drifted in from the rec hall. The gamblers' heckling. The early chirping of a cricket or two from outside.

"I'll climb the fence again if I have to. Broken bones be damned. But one way or another, I'm leaving."

He shook his head and resumed mopping. "I'm done doing ya favors."

Mirielle stalked over and grabbed the mop handle. "I'm sorry for what I said to you. It was rotten, and I regret it. But this isn't about me, or you and me. It's about my daughter. I've got to get home to her."

"Ya wanna talk turkey, Polly? Let's talk turkey." His shortened fingers tightened around the mop, and he yanked it away from her. "I knew ya was trouble the first time I laid eyes on ya. Couldn't see beyond the brim of your own hat, you. And even that was pushing it. I knew, and I fell for ya anyway. That's on me. But Jean, she's just a child. No way for her to know what ya are. Now she's off in the wind and who knows what's happened to her. That's on you."

"In the wind? What are you talking about?"

"If ya hadn't been holed up in your room, you'd of heard. Jean ran off over a week ago. Ain't no one's seen or heard from her since."

Mirielle's breath faltered, as if her lungs had forgotten how to expand. The fragmented memories of their last interaction flashed in her mind. The magazine slamming against the wall. Jean jumping on the bed and trying to pull Mirielle up. "Has someone checked the nearby towns? And what about her father? Has he been contacted?"

"Jean was a drop-off, remember? The docs don't know her family name or where she's from."

"But we know she's from a small town. She talked about her father's boat shop and . . . and shrimp fishing in some bay."

"Ya just described half of Louisiana and a good part of Mississippi."

"It's a start. Maybe Irene knows—" Her eyes met Frank's and quickly retreated to the floor. "I mean, maybe one of the other gals at the house knows something. Or the twins."

"Ya think Doc Jack and Sister Verena ain't already asked 'em? Hell, a whole search party went out. Nothing. If you'd been up outta bed, thinking of someone else besides yourself, maybe ya could of helped."

His words stung like antiseptic to a cut. "That's not fair. I—"

"Life ain't fair. A gal like you oughta know that by now." He slammed the mop into the bucket and let go of the handle. Sudsy water spilled over the sides. He stomped behind the counter and bent down. Mirielle heard the clank of glass and metal as he rummaged around.

Jean absconded? Mirielle couldn't wrap her brain around the news. Where had she gone? She was only ten years old. How could she survive out there on her own? "There's got to be something we can do."

Frank stood and held out a rusty pair of pliers. "Worry about yourself. That's what you're good at, after all. Let those of us who actually give a damn worry about Jean."

Mirielle itched to slap him. She did give a damn. So much it hurt to breathe thinking about Jean out there on her own. But what about Mirielle's daughter? Standing here wasn't helping either of them. She grabbed the pliers from Frank's hand and stormed out.

CHAPTER 58

Mirielle walked along the rutted River Road all through the night.
Her heels chafed against the back of her shoes until her skin blistered
and her toes went numb. The levee overlooked one side of the road;
forest and farmland abutted the other. Despite what Frank had said
when they'd gone frog hunting last summer—no panthers in these
parts and that alligators couldn't climb trees—she jumped at every
snapped branch and rustle of leaves.

Just before dawn, an old Holsman motorcar, the kind she remembered from her girlhood when automobiles were still a rarity and
wonder, rattled down the road. The lamp affixed to the front blinded
her, and the dust kicked up from its huge, wagon-like wheels settled
in her nostrils. It lurched to a stop beside her. The driver said something in a thick accent that sounded like an offer for a ride.

"I'm headed to New Orleans," she said.

The driver, an older man with the type of long, bushy beard that
had gone out of style with the last century, reached down to her.

"Climb up in den," he said—or at least that was her best transla-
tion.

The sky had only just begun to lighten from black to bluish-gray.
If this man meant to hurt her, he'd have no trouble of it here in the
middle of nowhere. But she hadn't time to waste. "Thank you," she
said, taking the man's hand.

The engine wheezed, and the carriage rattled. The cracked leather
seat snagged on her stockings. Were it a race, Mirielle would have

put her money on an old-fashioned horse and wagon to win out over this tired machine, but it beat walking.

They arrived at the New Orleans depot midmorning. The bustle and noise set her heart skittering. The handle of her valise was slick with sweat. She told herself it was just fear of being caught, but deep down, she knew that Carville, with its country quiet and earthy aromas and lazy afternoons, had softened her steely, city-girl sensibilities.

The line for the ticket counter snaked through the lobby. Mirielle took her place at the end, her eyes flickering every few minutes to the large clock on the far wall, watching its long, metal hands inch toward eleven.

Below the clock stood the bank of phone booths Frank had taken her to. Her stomach twisted thinking about that night. How kind he'd been to risk a month in jail just so she could call home. His parting words in the canteen bullied into her mind. *Worry about yourself. That's what you're good at, after all.* But Mirielle hadn't walked all night and hitchhiked a ride from a complete stranger because she was worried about herself. Helen was sick and needed her. Where was the selfishness in that?

She'd be careful at home. Wash her hands, boil her dishes, clean with disinfectant. None of the staff at Carville had contracted the disease. Not one in thirty-four years. She'd find a doctor or a pharmacist who could get her chaulmoogra pills. Once Helen was well, their lives could finally go back to normal.

But what if the health department found her? Or one of the doctors or nurses at County General recognized her? Despite its hundreds of thousands of residents, Los Angeles wasn't such a big city when you were the wife of a motion picture star. Mirielle could take care not to spread the disease—it was only feebly contagious after all—but she couldn't do anything about the stigma.

The hands on the clock were nearing noon when she finally reached the ticket counter.

"Destination?" the clerk said.

Mirielle hesitated. "Los Angeles. First-class."

When the clerk told her the price, Mirielle opened her purse and reached inside for her money. Her fingers grazed the delicate silver chain of the St. Christopher medal. She'd assumed the token was

Sister Verena's tacit blessing for Mirielle's journey home. But not a minute before giving Mirielle the medal, she'd been lecturing her on shame and stigma. What had she said of her son? That letting him go was the only gift she could give him.

The clerk repeated the price, but Mirielle just stood there like a mannequin in a shop window.

We cannot change the past, Sister Verena had said. *But we can live true to the present.*

At the time, Mirielle had thought she was talking about Helen's illness. Encouraging Mirielle to go to her. But what if she'd meant something else?

"You gonna buy this ticket or not, ma'am?" the clerk said.

Mirielle ached to hand over the money and be gone to California. She'd hand over her very heart, still beating in her palm, if it meant seeing her girls again. But she shook her head and stepped out of line.

As much as Mirielle hated to admit it, Sister Verena had been right. Even a quick trip home wasn't worth the risk. Not while the world still saw her as a monster. Sister Verena had been right on another point too. Mirielle did have another family to consider. Another little girl who needed her. Jean.

CHAPTER 59

—⋙•◦•⋘—

Shuttered within the telephone booth, Mirielle waited for the operator to connect her to home. The butler answered.

"This is Mirielle. Is Charlie home?"

"No, ma'am, I'm afraid he's out."

"And Helen? Is she better?"

He paused. "Still at the hospital, ma'am."

"Tell Charlie I called and"—her voice broke—"tell him . . ." She ached to say, *I'm on my way home.*

"Ma'am?"

"Tell him I'm thinking of them all, will you please?"

"Of course."

Mirielle hung up the receiver and sagged against the booth wall, too raw inside to weep. Perhaps it was best that Charlie wasn't in. The slightest hint that he'd welcome her home and her resolve would crumble.

Now what? She hadn't slept in over thirty hours, but didn't have time to rest, nor did she trust herself to rise if she did. A meal, though. That would quiet her stomach and clear her thoughts.

She bought a sandwich from a street-side vendor and ate it in the train station lobby. The bread was stale and the meat chewy, but it buoyed her nonetheless. She pulled the St. Christopher medal out of her purse and fingered its raised surface. She'd never been the praying sort and put little stock in the papists' coterie of saints, but she closed her eyes and made a short plea to God that he look after

Helen where Mirielle could not. Then to St. Christopher—whoever he was—that he help her find Jean.

When she'd finished, she tucked the medal away in her handbag and focused on the here and now. With sixty-two dollars in her purse and the authorities soon to be on the lookout, Mirielle couldn't afford to dally. She suspected Jean aimed to get home. But where was home? She tried to recall everything Jean had said to her but quickly gave up. Once Jean started talking, she'd yapped almost as much as Irene. Somewhere in all those words, though, lay a clue.

Mirielle took a deep breath and closed her eyes again. After Felix's death, she'd all but lived in the past. The gin had helped with that, but also thinking of specific things, touchstones like the softness of his favorite jacket or the nutty smell of the warmed milk he drank before bed. She fanned her fingers over the wooden bench and imagined herself sitting on the living room floor with Jean. She recalled the tickle of wind over the nape of her neck and was high up in the observation tower with her again. She fought back the smell of luggage and cigarette smoke, remembering instead the woody scent of the oak tree she and Jean had climbed.

After several minutes of sifting memories, it came to her. Jean had boasted once that people came all the way from New Iberia and Lafayette to buy boats from her father. The names meant nothing to Mirielle, but she found both towns on the glass-covered railroad map on the wall. The Missouri Pacific line out of New Orleans stopped at both, first New Iberia and farther down the line, Lafayette.

Mirielle hurried back to the ticket line and asked for a first-class seat to New Iberia. Upon opening her purse, she begrudgingly changed her mind and bought a coach ticket. The train left a few hours later. As it pulled away from the station, Mirielle's heart squeezed tighter with every turn of the wheels. This was not the course she'd imagined for herself when she'd packed her bag yesterday. That course—and every course she'd imagined before it—led home.

She arrived in New Iberia at sundown. The town was tiny by Los Angeles standards. Automobiles kicked up dust alongside mule-drawn buggies on the unpaved roads. Main Street boasted a gas and greasing station, several grocers, a creamery, two cafés, a theater, a hotel, and a bank. A glance down the intersecting streets revealed a spattering of stately homes with columned façades like the big house at Carville. The rest of the homes were simple shotguns with weathered siding and wide front porches.

She took a room at the hotel and fell asleep as soon as she finished dinner. Strange dreams plagued her through the night—arriving at long last in California but finding her home abandoned and crumbling; jumping into a swimming pool to save Felix only to find that the lifeless body floating on the water's surface was Jean; running from men brandishing chains and shackles, unable to climb Carville's fence to safety.

The next morning, she awoke tired but hopeful. Jean was out here somewhere, and Mirielle would find her. The hotel's staff greeted her warmly when she sat down for breakfast in the dining room and obliged her with answers to her questions about boatwrights in the neighboring towns. She'd hoped it would be as simple as a single name, but the staff listed several well-known craftsmen in the area.

When she asked whether the hotel had a car for hire, they laughed but happily rang around until they found her a ride with Mr. DeRouen, the soda delivery man. She surreptitiously wiped down her fork and glass with a hankie after eating. As feebly contagious as the disease might be, she'd hate to expose anyone else.

When she'd arrived the night before, Mirielle was too exhausted to feel conspicuous. But as she waited in front of the hotel for Mr. DeRouen, the weight of passersby's stares unsettled her. She'd dressed with care that morning, donning a long-sleeved blouse instead of a more seasonal short-sleeved one, tying a scarf around her neck, disguising the spots on her legs beneath dark-colored stockings. Even so, Mirielle had to fight the urge to fold in on herself.

Mr. DeRouen rattled up in a mud-speckled white truck with the bottling company's logo scrawled in red letters across the side. He looked a year or two shy of twenty, but his dark hair and summer blue eyes reminded her of Frank. The likeness settled Mirielle's jumpy nerves while at the same time stirring a vague pain inside her. Would she ever see Frank again? Beyond getting Jean safely back to Carville, Mirielle's endgame was unsettled. Sister Verena was right; it wasn't worth the risk to her family to return home uncured. But could she endure a life of captivity until then?

She accepted Mr. DeRouen's handshake and returned his timid smile.

"Thank you for taking me around. I'll pay you for your trouble."

"Nah, ma'am. Happy to do it."

He helped her into the cab of the truck. "Where ya from, if ya don't mind me askin'?"

Mirielle hesitated. "California."

"That explains it," he said, revving the engine and coaxing the truck into gear.

"Why I talk so funny?" Mirielle kept her voice light despite her renewed self-consciousness.

"Nah." He cast a shy glance in her direction. "Why you're so perdy."

Mirielle tugged on her scarf. To her relief, the rattle of soda bottles as they drove made further conversation impossible. She turned and looked out the side window at the passing sugarcane fields and moss-draped oaks.

Would Mr. DeRouen show her the same kindness if he knew she was a leper? She'd not be "perdy" in his eyes but grotesque. Instead of a handshake, she'd get a boot in the stomach. All the more reason she had to be careful and find Jean soon.

CHAPTER 60

Mr. DeRouen's delivery schedule took them to three towns near New Iberia. At each stop, Mirielle sought out the local boatwright. The first man she met was far too old to be Jean's father. The second too young. The third too dark of complexion. By day's end, her rear was sore from so long and bumpy a drive. Her confidence was similarly battered. She'd have better luck getting French champagne from a backwoods bootlegger than finding Jean's father among so many bayou towns. But she readily accepted Mr. DeRouen's offer to travel with him again tomorrow.

When he dropped her off at the hotel, Mirielle stopped at the telephone before heading up to her room. Her thoughts had strayed often to Helen during the day. Had her fever broken? Was she still in the hospital? Did she remember Mirielle enough anymore to register her absence?

The telephone sat tucked away in a small nook beyond the lobby, offering only an illusion of privacy. Mirielle held the mouthpiece close as she spoke. The butler answered again. No, Mr. West wasn't at home. No news about Helen either. Mirielle hung up the receiver and waited for her eyes to dry before turning around. No need to appear more suspicious than she already did. She'd wanted to leave a number for Charlie to return her call, but the butler, like the rest of the staff and anyone in Los Angeles who read the gossip rags, thought she was locked away in an asylum. Giving him the hotel's telephone number was too risky.

As she climbed the stairs to her room, she told herself Charlie was at the hospital, not out cavorting with Miss Thorne or some other new starlet. Whatever his shortcomings, he'd always been a good father. But that didn't stop her imagination from taking flight with the idea nor her dreams when at last she fell asleep.

The next morning she woke and dressed just in time to meet Mr. DeRouen as he pulled up to the hotel. When Mirielle saw the name JEANERETTE painted in blue lettering on the welcome sign of the first town they visited, her hopes buoyed. It would make sense that a six-year-old girl dropped at the gates of the leper home would choose a name similar to the town where she'd been born. Or maybe she'd been named after the town and hadn't taken an alias at all.

Mr. DeRouen stopped at a small grocer along the main drag of the town. Mirielle hopped out of the truck before the engine stilled.

"Is there a boatwright in town?" she asked the grocer, a lean man with a large mole on the side of his nose.

"Pardon?" he said.

"A boatwright."

Mr. DeRouen, carrying a crate of soda bottles into the store, stopped and made introductions. When he added she was from California, the grocer nodded slowly, as if that explained her brusqueness.

"You might be talkin' about ol' Don Hirsch."

"Does he have a shop nearby? I'd like to meet him."

"Can't."

"I can't?"

"Don died about three years back."

"Did he have a family?"

"He did."

"I'll speak with his widow then."

"Can't do that either."

Mirielle felt her patience slipping. A hurricane could have been swirling above them, and this man would have stood there just as lackadaisically, doling out one sentence of information at a time. "No?"

"I'm afeard not. They moved on outta these parts."

"Do you know where?"

He scratched his nose alongside the mole and watched Mr. DeRouen lug another crate of soda into the store. Mirielle cleared her throat, and his gaze wandered back to her. "No, ma'am. Can't say I do."

When they got back in the truck, Mr. DeRouen uncapped two sodas and handed one to her. "Sure do mean a lot to ya, this boat maker."

She traced the curve of the glass before taking a sip. Coca-Cola and other big companies charged the canteen extra for bottled soda since they wouldn't take back the bottles for reuse. After all, who would want to drink from the same soda bottle as a leper?

"We both care about the same little girl, is all. And I'm hoping he can tell me she's okay."

The road they followed wound alongside the bayou. A few crumbling mansions roosted alongside the fields of sugarcane that stretched out around them. There was always Lafayette, she reminded herself, and its assemblage of small, nearby towns to investigate. Her money would soon run out, but Charlie could wire her more. He would, wouldn't he?

Mr. DeRouen said something, but it was lost behind the rumble of the engine and rattle of bottles.

"What?"

He pointed at the bayou. Beyond the shaggy trees that lined the bank, sunlight glinted off the water. "Mighty high this year," he hollered over the din. "Best you find this boat builder and get gone before it floods."

The next town they came to was far smaller than Jeanerette or New Iberia. A post office, meat market, and general store clustered around Main Street, along with two churches and a brand-new theater. But no shipyard or boat works shop. Mirielle's heart sank. She'd been to filming lots in Hollywood bigger than this town.

A spattering of houses lined the rutted side streets. Beyond that, the swollen bayou.

"Is this the entire town?" she asked when they stopped in front of the general store.

"Yep."

"How come there are two churches? Isn't everyone around here Catholic?"

Mr. DeRouen nodded toward the smaller church built of wood instead of stone. "That one there's for the Negroes."

She'd seen segregation at work since leaving Carville. The sloppy, hand-painted sign above the filling station outhouse that read, WHITES ONLY. The rough-hewn tables behind cafés where blacks were forced to eat. The separate waiting areas at the train station. It wasn't so different in Los Angeles, though certainly less overt. But she'd not appreciated the injustice of it until now.

She climbed down from the cab of the truck more to stretch her legs than for any real hope in finding Jean's father in this penny-sized town. Two older men sat on a bench outside the store, sucking on tobacco. Mirielle decided she might as well ask them about a local boatwright, and, to her surprise, they directed her to a home a mile or so yonder toward the lake. One of them stretched out a tobacco-stained finger to show her the way.

"You'll know it by da big yella barn," he said. "Dat's where he builds dem pirogues."

Boats, Mr. DeRouen clarified, and offered to drive her over once he finished unloading his delivery. But Mirielle told him she'd be glad for the walk, and he agreed to wait for her at the store. Her calfskin shoes were better suited for marble foyers than dirt roads, and the gathering clouds on the horizon threatened rain, but if this boatwright were Jean's father, better to approach him alone.

"Watch out for da gators," one of the men called after her. Mirielle didn't turn around, preferring not to know whether he was serious.

She passed several cottages along her way. Cambric shirts and cottonade dresses fluttered on clotheslines. Women hunched over garden beds or shelled peas on the front porch steps. Children played with popguns and rusty wagons in the yards. One girl, about Helen's age, crawled after a mangy house cat while her siblings shot marbles nearby. Dirt darkened her tiny hands and chubby knees. Her diaper sagged. But she seemed entirely happy, reaching out for the cat's tail just as it bounded away. She giggled and struggled to her feet. After a few shaky steps in the cat's direction, she fell and took up crawling again.

Mirielle slowed and watched the girl until she disappeared around the house, still in pursuit of the cat. Was Helen fond of animals? It pained Mirielle that she didn't know. Pained her all the more when she realized Helen wasn't that girl's age at all. She'd wobbled to her feet and taken her first hesitant step the week before Mirielle left. Or so the nanny had proudly reported as Mirielle poured herself another gin cocktail. How Helen must have changed in the fifteen intervening months. She was walking now. Talking. Eating with a folk and spoon. Would Mirielle even recognize her daughter when she finally made it home?

Of course she would, Mirielle assured herself, and resumed her hurried pace. But Helen had to survive the fever first. If she didn't . . . Mirielle shook the thought from her head. Fate wouldn't be that cruel.

She arrived at the yellow barn just as the building clouds overtook the sun. A small house with a rusted tin roof stood alongside it. Mirielle climbed the creaky porch steps and knocked on the screen door. A woman answered, balancing a thumb-sucking toddler on her hip. Two other small children played jacks on the rug behind her. Were these Jean's half-siblings? They had the same dark brown hair and deep-set eyes that slanted downward at the end. Perhaps Jean's father had remarried.

"Can I help ya?" the woman asked, eyeing Mirielle warily.

"I'm looking for . . ." The men at the general store hadn't given Mirielle a name. "Does your husband build boats?"

The woman nodded.

"Is he here?"

"Out in the barn."

Mirielle thanked her and headed for the barn. She heard the screen door close behind her but suspected the woman was still watching her from the window. A raindrop landed on her shoulder as she navigated the knee-high weeds between the house and barn. Another plinked against the tin roof behind her. The barn door stood partially open. She slipped inside out of the rain.

Four small windows high up in the walls let in the barn's only light, and it took Mirielle's eyes a moment to adjust to the dimness. A long, flat-bottomed boat rested on two trestles. The air smelled of wood shavings and sap and sweat. A man in dusty overalls stood sanding the boat. His cheeks were sun-chapped. Sawdust sprinkled his hair. He glanced up from his work and frowned, his eyes—the same muddy blue as Jean's—narrowing with distrust.

"Whatever you're selling, I don't want none."

"No, I—"

"Not interested in your Methodist God neither."

Mirielle hadn't expected such a greeting and floundered for a response. "I'm not . . . I don't care what God you believe in. I'm looking for a young girl. Jean, she's called. I thought you—"

"Ain't seen her." He turned his attention back to the boat, rasping the sandpaper over the wood in short, rough strokes.

"I haven't even described her yet." Mirielle stepped closer. He was older than the woman in the house by at least a decade, with shallow lines just beginning to show on his face. "Are you her father?"

"Don't know what you're talkin' about."

"She ran away from . . ." Mirielle paused. If she spoke the word *Carville* was she implicating herself? By now, Dr. Ross must have realized she escaped and alerted the authorities. She'd heard stories about absconders being brought back to Carville at gunpoint or in chains. What if this man wasn't Jean's father and turned her in to the local sheriff? "From the—er—hospital over a week ago."

"Don't know no girl from no hospital."

"Carville." Mirielle swallowed. "The leper home."

The man stopped sanding. His chin dropped to his chest and sighed. "*Merde.* You from the health department?"

Mirielle remembered what Frank had said back at the juice joint in New Orleans. A good lie is always easier to stomach than the truth. "Yes." She took another step closer. Outside, the rain had picked up and plinked steadily against the ground. "Have you seen her?"

"She ain't here."

"Are you sure? I just want to know that she's all right."

The man's face pinched up in anger. No, not anger. His chest spasmed, and he began to sob. "I sent her away." He hid his face in his hands so Mirielle could scarcely make out what he said. "My wife, she don't know. And I got the other little ones to think about."

"You sent her away? Where?"

"I don't know where she went. I told her to go back."

"She's a child. It's a miracle she made it this far, and you just turned her out with nothing?"

He wiped his eyes and nose with the sleeve of his shirt. "What was I supposed to do? Times already hard. If word got out that I had a leper for a daughter, no one from here to Biloxi would buy my boats."

"That's no excuse!" Mirielle's voice trembled with rage. "You're her father. You're supposed to love and protect her. Not abandon her."

He turned away and muttered, "You couldn't understand."

"You're darn right I—" Mirielle stopped. She knew all too well about hard choices. She was here, after all, in the middle of Nowhere, Louisiana, while her daughter lay sick, maybe dying, a thousand miles away. And Felix. She knew guilt and regret too. "I'm sorry. I'm not . . . blaming you. I just want to know where she is. When did you see her?"

He scuffed his foot over the dirt and wood chip–strewn floor. " 'Bout five days ago."

Five days? Jean could be anywhere by now.

"I gave her a few dollars and said she could sleep overnight here in the barn."

"Do you have any idea where she could be?"

Jean's father swiped the tears from his cheeks and shook his head.

Mirielle's hopes withered like a cut flower in the sun. Jean hadn't taken her father's advice and gone back to Carville. Mirielle was sure of it. But she had no idea where else Jean might have gone. With only a few dollars to her name, how would Jean survive?

"I'm sorry," Mirielle said. "I have children too, and I . . ." Her throat grew tight.

"You'll find her, won't ya? And bring her back to the hospital?"

Mirielle nodded, though she had no idea now where to look. She remembered the sickening dread that had spread through her when she heard the commotion and glanced at the pool. Surely that was someone else's boy floating facedown. Not hers. Not her Felix. She felt an echo of that dread now. Did Jean's father feel it too? "What about your wife and other kids, could they know anything about where she might have gone?"

"I didn't want her to infect them others." He started crying again. Mirielle itched to lecture him on the low communicability of the disease, but instead she fished through her purse and handed him her hankie.

"Ain't her mama nohow and them's just her half-kin."

"And they don't know about her?"

He blew his nose into her hankie and shook his head.

Mirielle couldn't help but imagine Jean, her braids frayed and stomach grumbling, peeking in through the house window while her father and his new family sat down to supper. The father who didn't want her. The family that would never be her own. Mirielle's heart ached to think of it. Of Irene and Hector and all the others at Carville who'd been similarly erased from their families' lives.

She turned and walked toward the barn door. Now more than ever, she had to find Jean. Had to show her that someone in the world cared. At the door, she stopped and turned around. "Jean said she had an uncle who was a shrimp fisherman. Might he have seen her?"

"He don't live around these parts and don't shrimp no more neither."

"Oh." She stepped out into the rain. It bled through her dress and trickled down her skin.

Jean's father said something she couldn't make out over the rain. She glanced over her shoulder and shouted, "What?"

"Cote Blanche Bay. That's where her uncle used to shrimp. If she was lookin' for him, she mighta gone there."

Water dripped from the brim of Mirielle's hat into her eyes. Jean's father looked as if he wanted to say more. *Tell Jean I love her*, perhaps. He ran his hand along the side of the boat. Dust sprinkled down onto the ground. "I'd be obliged if ya don't come back, now. If something's happened . . . I don't wanna know."

CHAPTER 61

Mirielle hardly felt the rain as she walked back to the general store. But when she arrived and climbed into the cab of the delivery truck, she was shivering so badly she could hear her teeth chattering above the rumbling engine.

She wanted desperately to speak to Charlie, to hear his voice and know that Helen was all right, but when she arrived back at the hotel, the telephone was out of service. After changing into dry clothes and picking at her supper of spicy gumbo, Mirielle retired to her room. She crawled into bed and pulled the quilt to her chin, but still felt the rain's chill.

Part of her hated Jean's father for what he'd done. Part of her understood. She'd made her share of errors as a mother. Grave errors. She rolled onto her side and stared out the window at the moonlit treetops. At least she was trying to make up for them. She hoped it wasn't too late.

The next morning she packed her valise. The hotel clerk pulled out a worn, creased map and showed her Cote Blanche Bay. It wasn't a town, as Mirielle had foolishly thought, but a great body of water that spilled into the Gulf of Mexico. Along the bay stretched over fifty miles of shoreline with numerous river inlets, canals, and swamps. Jean might be anywhere among this expanse. Or somewhere else entirely.

A train left later that morning for Franklin, the parish seat nearest the bay. Mirielle decided it was as good a place as any to continue her search. She drank a cup of coffee in the hotel dining room and tried not to let the near impossibility of her task daunt her. Music played from the radio in the corner, and she focused on that instead, remembering happier days when she and Charlie danced to songs like these in chandelier-lit ballrooms.

A local news program aired next. The announcer spoke of high waters all along the Mississippi, of upcoming horse races, and some political scandal in Baton Rouge. Next came advertisements for Colgate dental cream and Camel cigarettes. Mirielle was only half listening when the news program resumed.

"Word has come of the escape of another leper from the colony at Carville. The leper is described as a woman in her early thirties of fair complexion and average stature. She is not known to be violent but should be considered highly contagious. Local police have a dragnet out for the woman. If you have any information to help in their efforts, contact . . ."

Mirielle froze. Only a few other guests remained in the dining room, but she felt certain their eyes were upon her. Was the radio announcer right? Were the police really after her? She knew better than to trust such sensational news, but her heart beat frantic anyway. Anger stirred alongside her panic. *Highly contagious*—that was complete nonsense. And *average stature.* She hated that word, *average.* She mightn't be considered slight or tall, but certainly *well-formed* or *of ample height* were better ways to describe her.

She set her coffee down slowly, remembering how coolly Frank had handled those men at the speakeasy in New Orleans. The trick was not to look guilty. She stood and exited the dining room, taking care to walk straight despite her trembling knees and to smile at anyone who glanced her way.

Out on the street, Mirielle felt even more exposed. Her feet itched to break into a run. A deep breath and Mirielle started for the train station. It took conscious effort to keep her back straight, head high, and step graceful. But such attentions diverted her mind from otherwise spiraling into hysteria. She checked to ensure that her scarf concealed the lesion on her neck, then forbid her hand from wandering there again.

Halfway to the train station, a face startled her out of her careful comportment. Not among the passersby, but a face on a poster, looking out at her through a pane of glass. Charlie.

Despite her fears that a police dragnet might actually be hunting her, Mirielle stopped and went to the ticket window behind which the poster hung. MY BEST GAL, read the title in bright blue lettering. She pressed her gloved fingers against the glass and traced the outline of her husband's face. He looked exactly as she remembered him, debonair and confident. The color artist had missed the flecks of green in his hazel eyes and painted his lips a little too red, but otherwise it was as if he were right there—in miniature—before her. Miss Thorne was pictured too, but Mirielle spared only a glance for her before returning her eyes to Charlie. What she wouldn't give to have him with her now.

"You wanna ticket for the noon show?" a voice asked.

Mirielle startled and stepped away. An old man stared at her from behind the ticket window.

"A real hit with the critics, that one," he said.

Mirielle smiled. Charlie would be glad. "No, no ticket, thank you." She allowed herself one last look, then continued on to the depot.

The train ride to Franklin lasted only a few hours. Fields of sugarcane, tired plantation homes, and verdant swampland passed outside her window. Every time a fellow passenger looked her way or the conductor strolled down the aisle, Mirielle's insides clenched. But she continued to meet their eyes and smile.

The town of Franklin was about half the size of New Iberia, with moss-draped oaks and fluted lampposts lining Main Street. Mirielle found a hotel and, with the help of the clerk, a boatman she could hire to take her along the inland waterways that fed into Cote Blanche Bay.

She and the boatman left early the next morning, navigating a swollen bayou in a flat-bottomed boat similar to the one Jean's father had been making. The boatman, a Mr. Jessip, was a gnarl of a man with a long, gray-streaked beard and several missing teeth. His accent was so thick she understood only half of what he said. But he handled the boat—a pirogue, he called it, though it looked to her like a canoe—with the grace and deftness of a prima ballerina.

Spring shrimping season had just begun, and they passed several larger boats—twenty feet or more in length—with a single lugsail and taut rigging connected to seine nets. Mirielle had worked out her story the night before. She was in search of a young girl who may have sought work or tried to stow away on a shrimp boat.

"She yer daughta?" Mr. Jessip asked.

"No," Mirielle replied after a moment's hesitation. "My—er—niece. She's been gone almost two weeks, and I'm desperate to find her."

Mr. Jessip called out to fishermen on the passing boats and described Mirielle's predicament. They seemed to understand his garbled speech better than her own "citified talk" so she let him explain. Each time the passing shrimper shook his head or replied with a drawn-out *nah,* her heart sank a little, until, by the end of the day, she felt it throbbing somewhere below her stomach.

She and Mr. Jessip agreed to meet at the dock again the next morning, and she shambled back to her hotel, her legs stiff from disuse and arms itching with mosquito bites. Her telephone call home from the hotel lobby went unanswered, and she spent the rest of the night fretting about Helen and Jean and her dwindling funds. With only enough money to pay Mr. Jessip for two more days' ferrying, she had to find Jean or reach Charlie soon.

The next morning started out much the same as the one before. Mr. Jessip helped her into the pirogue and they started down the bayou with birds chattering in the overarching trees and dragonflies buzzing among the marsh grass. Alligators peeked their long heads out from the murky water and sunned themselves on the banks.

The previous night's worries had lodged themselves firmly at the base of her throat like a chunk of dry bread. Even so, she found herself smiling when a lone bullfrog croaked from somewhere amid the duckweed. Would that Frank could see her now, traveling the swamps and bayous with this strange man, dauntless of the mud and bugs and gators. But the memory of his hard eyes and cold demeanor the night she'd left chased away her smile.

By early afternoon they'd passed more than a dozen shrimping boats. No one aboard the vessels had seen anyone matching Jean's description.

"We go as far as Mud Lake and den turn round," Mr. Jessip said. Mirielle nodded. What would she do if she couldn't find Jean? She couldn't live with herself knowing she'd failed yet another child.

The watercourse widened, and Mud Lake appeared in the distance. Mr. Jessip maneuvered his paddle to turn the boat around.

"Can't we at least see if there are any boats on the lake?" she asked.

Mr. Jessip looked up at the narrow strip of sky visible above them and frowned. "Gettin' on dusk soon."

"Please. Just a quick look."

He sighed and paddled them onward to the lake.

Mud Lake was aptly named. The water, like that of the bayou and canals, was a murky brown. But it made the rest of the scenery all the more striking—the silver moss and verdant cypress, the white egrets and iridescent-feathered ducks, the paling sky and orange horizon. Three boats drifted through the water—two shrimping boats and a smaller pirogue like the one they floated in. Mr. Jessip paddled up to the nearest lugger boat and then the pirogue. Neither had seen anyone matching Jean's description.

The last boat was hauling up their nets at the far side of the lake when Mirielle and Mr. Jessip approached. It was a newer, gasoline-powered boat, Mr. Jessip explained with some admiration, that used trawl nets instead of seine. Three men bustled about the deck—an older man with sun-cracked skin and two younger ones who looked as if they might be brothers. A tangle of fish and shrimp writhed on the deck.

Mr. Jessip called out a greeting, and the old man shuffled to the edge of the boat. Nah, he hadn't seen a girl like Jean, he said, and returned to sorting his catch. Mirielle dropped her head, willing back the tears in her eyes. Her skin was covered with fresh bug bites, her shoes and stockings wet and mud-stained, her muscles stiff and back aching. The task was impossible. The waterways looked much the same to her, but Mr. Jessip insisted they'd covered entirely new territory today. When she'd asked how many more inlets and lakes and bayous there were, he'd given her a rueful smile, and said hundreds of miles. Mirielle hadn't the time nor the money to traverse them all.

Mr. Jessip started to paddle away when one of the young deck-hands called out to them. "I mighta seen her."

Mirielle straightened and turned to the man so quickly the boat beneath her swayed. "Really?" She described Jean in greater detail.

"Sounds about right," the deckhand said when she finished.

The heaviness inside her lifted like a bird in flight. "Where did you see her?"

"Out about the old shipyard near the inlet of the bay."

"When?"

"Seen her a couple times askin' for work. Shrimpin' ain't no job for a girl, though. Especially scrawny as she is."

"Did you see her there today?"

The man took off his cap and swatted it at the cloud of mosquitos descending upon them with dusk's arrival. "No. Yesterday maybe."

Mirielle turned back to Mr. Jessip. "Can we get there from here?"

"Not tonight. It'd take us least an hour to get dere. Twice as long to get back."

"Please. I'll pay you double."

"Mightn't even be her."

"I have to know for sure."

"We're headed that a'way after we finish tying up our nets," the deckhand called to them. "We could give ya a tow."

"Yes, please," Mirielle said, and then to Mr. Jessip, "please."

"Aw, hell," he said, nodding to the man.

A thick rope was attached to the stern of the trawler and the bow of Mr. Jessip's boat. The older man on the shrimp boat barked orders to the other two men, and soon the engine rumbled and they lurched into motion.

The trawler didn't move nearly as quickly as Mirielle had hoped, but their progress was still faster than if Mr. Jessip had been pad-dling. Soon they were gone from the lake and gliding along a nar-rowing waterway. The air cooled quickly now that the sun had set in a great orange fury beneath the horizon. Mirielle held on to the edge of the boat with one hand and wrapped her other arm around herself, wishing she'd had the sense to bring a jacket. It made her worry all the more for Jean, who likely hadn't packed well for her journey. How many nights had she spent alone in the cold?

Mr. Jessip was right; the girl the shrimper had seen mightn't be

Jean at all. Then what would Mirielle do? She shook her head and fixed her gaze forward. Moss dangled from the surrounding trees, grazing the water's surface. It came alive like a troupe of dancing skeletons when troubled by the trawler's wake. Mirielle gripped the edge of the boat a little tighter and tried to keep her worries corralled. Helen, Jean, the police dragnet—there was nothing she could do now but see her choices through to the end.

CHAPTER 62

Less than an hour later, they arrived at the shipyard. Mr. Jessip untethered his pirogue from the shrimping boat, and Mirielle hollered her thanks to the men. She leaped from the boat the minute they docked and hurried toward the cluster of buildings nestled on dry ground.

"I'll be back as soon as I find her," she said over her shoulder.

A few dozen men lingered about the dock and nearby shipyard securing their boats, mending their nets, and unloading the day's catch. They stared at Mirielle with a wide-eyed mix of surprise and suspicion. Not that she blamed them. Her hair had slipped free from the bun at the nape of her neck and jutted outward around the brim of her hat in frizzy waves. Her wool-crêpe dress was mud-splattered and wrinkled from several days of wear. Scuff marks and water stains marred her leather shoes. But she suspected it was her very presence—the lone woman and an outsider to boot—that baffled them.

When she asked about Jean, most of the men only shook their heads and went back to work. A few opened their mouths enough to mutter *nah* or *non*. But one man pointed to a weathered boathouse at the far edge of the yard abutting the swampland.

"Couple of ragamuffins hang out over yonder, begging for scraps when the boats come in. They might know somethin'."

"Thank you," Mirielle said. She hurried down the dock and through the shipyard. Her haste made her all the more conspicuous, but she didn't care. Let these men gawk and chuckle. Twilight was draining fast from the sky. The air smelled of rotting vegetation and fish entrails.

She reached the last boathouse and rounded the corner. Smoke stung her eyes. A fire blazed in a rusted oil drum. Several children were gathered around it, roasting small fish and skewered bullfrogs. The oldest looked about fifteen, a sparse collection of whiskers scattered across his cheeks. The youngest couldn't have been more than six. Their clothes were threadbare and dirty, their faces gaunt and eyes skittish. The oldest boy slipped a jar of turpentine-colored liquid beneath his patched coat.

A few of them could pass for boys or girls, but after a quick glance, Mirielle was certain Jean was not among them.

"Have any of you seen a girl about yea high"—she gestured to the level of her armpit—"with dark hair and freckles?"

The children shrugged and shook their heads, skittish of her gaze. One of them pointed to the swamp and said, "Maybe the Rougarou's seen her." The others snickered.

Mirielle's eagerness fizzled. Either these children didn't know where Jean was or didn't care. Certainly they didn't trust her. Just like the fishermen. She glanced back at the dock. There were a few men she hadn't queried, but how long could Mirielle go on following flimsy leads and desperate hunches? Jean could have left her father's house and decided to become a lion tamer in a circus for all Mirielle knew. Perhaps it was time she faced the truth. Mirielle had failed at finding Jean, just like she'd failed at beating the disease, and failed at being a mother.

She turned around and started back to the boat. The cool, damp air nipped at her skin. She hadn't gone far when the warbling chords of a harmonica sounded. Mirielle stopped. The slow, mournful tune blended with the frog croaks and cricket chirps emanating from the nearby swamp. Every few notes a squeak would break through, or the player would pause between chord progressions the way Jean had done when she first started practicing last Christmas.

Other memories rushed back, carried on the music—Jean playing in the Mardi Gras parade, on the back steps of house eighteen, in Mirielle's room as she bounced on the bed, trying to get Mirielle to rise.

Mirielle spun around as if the tremulous notes were a fishing hook lodged inside her. One of the boys at the smoking oil drum repositioned the instrument against his lips and continued to play. She stumbled over bits of discarded wood and fraying rope in her haste toward the sound.

"Where did you get that?" she asked.

The boy stopped playing and shrugged. "Found it."

Mirielle snatched it from his hands. It was the same size and tarnished silver color as Jean's.

"Hey! Give that back."

Mirielle stepped beyond the boy's reach and cradled the cool metal against her cheek. Despite the crackling fire and humming swamp, the night sounded hollow without the song.

"Give it back, you crazy witch."

Maybe she was crazy. There must be hundreds of silver harmonicas in Louisiana. It was ridiculous to believe this one belonged to Jean. But Mirielle couldn't let go.

"Look, lady," the oldest boy said. "We don't want no trouble. Just give him back the harmonica and be on your way."

Mirielle laughed. On her way to where? Franklin? Carville? Los Angeles? She might as well walk straight into the swamp.

Another burst of laughter and even the oldest boy backed away. The kids' wide-eyed unease made Mirielle laugh all the more, even as tears mounted in her eyes. A lunatic. A witch. A leper. Maybe she was all these things. Above all, a failure.

Mirielle swiped her cheeks and wrested control of herself. She burnished the harmonica on her rumpled skirt and was about to hand it back to the boy when she spied a pair of feet from the corner of her eye. They stuck out beyond a jumble of crates stacked against the boathouse. Despite the mud and scuff marks, Mirielle recognized the colony-issue, black-and-white oxfords.

She brushed past the boys, her heart thudding at the base of her throat. Behind the crates was Jean, lying atop a heap of old netting. Firelight cast her in a pale, flickering glow. Her clothes were stained and tattered, her face sunburned. Several boils—easily mistaken for flea or mosquito bites—rose along her arms.

Mirielle froze. Was she dead? As if in answer, Jean drew in a wheezing inhale. Mirielle crouched down and shook her. Jean moaned but didn't open her eyes.

"You," Mirielle said over her shoulder, catching the eye of the oldest boy. "I'll give you a dime if you help me carry her to the dock."

He frowned. "Who's she to you?"

Mirielle turned back to Jean, brushing a tangle of hair from her clammy cheek. "I'm her . . . we're family."

"A quarter," the boy said.

"Deal."

Mirielle tucked the harmonica in Jean's pocket. Then, she looped one of Jean's arms around her shoulders. The boy did the same. Together, they hoisted her up. Jean groaned. Her legs were limp and her head lolled forward like a broken doll. Her skin was hot and sticky where it lay against Mirielle's neck.

They half carried, half dragged Jean to Mr. Jessip's pirogue. Once they'd settled Jean inside, Mirielle looked around and remembered she hadn't brought her purse. After a moment's hesitation, she unclasped the silver bracelet from around her wrist. The pale scar beneath it stood out against her skin like the glassy, moonlit surface of the bayou amid the surrounding cypress.

She closed her fingers around the bracelet, feeling the filigreed metalwork bite into her palm, then reached out and handed it to the boy. "Here. It's real silver. Don't let anyone tell you it's not. And don't spend it all on booze. Get you and your friends out of this place. Oh, and buy that other boy a new harmonica."

The boy gaped at her. Mirielle settled into the boat and pulled Jean close. She nodded at the bracelet, still dangling in his hand. "Hide it away before anyone sees."

He nodded, his expression dumbfounded, pocketing the bracelet just as Mr. Jessip untethered the pirogue and shoved off.

"She's been like that goin' on two days now," the boy said from the dock. "Said she didn't have no family, so we didn't know where to take her. Thought you was from the orphanage, otherwise we woulda—"

"It's all right. I understand." Mirielle lay her cheek atop Jean's head. She smelled of sweat and musty fish netting. "She's going to be fine."

It was a lie. As much for the boy's benefit as her own. Mirielle turned from the shipyard, looking past Mr. Jessip into the darkness as he paddled them homeward.

CHAPTER 63

It was past midnight when they arrived back in Franklin. Mr. Jessip helped Mirielle carry Jean to the hotel. He tried to refuse the money Mirielle handed him—double the day's fee, as promised—but she insisted, even though it left her with less than twenty dollars to get Jean and her back to Carville.

Jean shivered beside her through the night, despite the blankets Mirielle heaped atop her. The next morning she was feverish again. Mirielle drew her a bath, remembering from the nursing textbook Sister Verena had forced her to copy not to use water that was too cold. She lugged Jean to the tub and hoisted her in with a splash. The water turned cloudy and brown from weeks' worth of dirt. Her eyes fluttered open as Mirielle began gently scrubbing her down.

"Mrs. Marvin?"

Mirielle's throat tightened at the sound of her voice. "It's me."

"Are we home?"

"No, but we're on our way."

Jean rested her head on the lip of the tub and closed her eyes again. She flinched and whimpered as Mirielle drew the washcloth over her boil-covered arms and legs. A leprous reaction, Mirielle was sure of it. Inflamed nerves protruded beneath her skin. The whites of her eyes were crisscrossed with red. If Mirielle didn't get Jean back to Carville soon, she could go blind or even die.

They managed to make it to the train station, Jean leaning heavily on Mirielle as they walked. There was no direct route to New

Orleans out of Franklin and none at all until the next morning. But if they caught the next train coming through the station, changed lines in Lafayette and again in Opelousas, they could be in Baton Rouge by nightfall.

Mirielle upended her purse on the counter, handing over the last of her crumpled bills and most of her coins to pay the fare. The platform rumbled, and a whistle blared to signal the train's approach. She swept the remaining change back into her purse along with the tickets and hurried with Jean to the edge of the platform.

Jean slept through the first leg of their journey, stumbled through the crowded depot in Lafayette at Mirielle's side, and fell asleep again once they'd boarded the second train. Oaks and cypress and towering evergreens passed outside their window in a blur of green. When the train slowed to collect more passengers at the tiny village depots along the route, pink azaleas and pearly magnolia blooms took shape amid the green.

Under different circumstances, Mirielle might have admired their beauty. The lush Louisiana landscape offered sights entirely different from coastal California. But every flicker of movement within the train car yanked Mirielle's gaze from the window. A rustle from Jean, and Mirielle's stomach clenched with worry that her condition was worsening. A sidelong stare from a new passenger, and Mirielle's mouth went dry with fear that the police dragnet had found them. To keep herself from fidgeting with her scarf, she slipped her hand inside her purse and fingered the few remaining treasures inside. Irene's ring, hidden safely inside the inner pocket. Sister Verena's St. Christopher medal. The remaining coins that jangled at the bottom.

The Opelousas depot was even more crowded than Lafayette. Mirielle clutched her purse and valise in one hand, Jean's clammy fingers in the other as they shuffled inside to wait for their next train. Hurried passengers and scuttling porters crisscrossed their path. Women herded their broods of children this way and that, too distracted to hush them when they hollered or comfort them when they cried. Men bullied past without a pardon or tip of the hat.

Not a single seat was open inside the station, so Mirielle propped Jean up against the wall. "Wait here."

She filled a paper cone with water from a jug in the far corner and brought it to Jean, who managed several sips despite insisting in a weak voice that she wasn't thirsty. Mirielle drank the rest on her way to the telegraph counter. Her thoughts raced as she waited in line. She needed to alert the sisters of her and Jean's arrival in Baton Rouge without arousing suspicion from the operator or anyone else who might see the telegram. She wanted to return to Carville by way of ambulance, not police paddy wagon.

Her turn at the counter arrived before she'd come up with a ruse the hospital staff could decipher. At three cents a word, it had to be short.

"Address," the woman at the counter said without looking up from her machine.

"U.S. Marine Hospital Sixty-Six, Carville, Louisiana."

The woman's quick fingers froze at the word *Carville*. She glanced up at Mirielle with narrowing eyes. Mirielle's heart leaped from one beat to the next. She fled the woman's gaze, looking down and fishing through her purse as if she had more than loose change and a silver medal inside. St. Christopher, set in relief with his flowing robes and gnarled walking staff, struck her with an idea. She squared her shoulders and met the woman's eyes.

"Did you get that address?"

"Ah . . ." The woman quickly finished typing. "Yes. Go on."

"Dear Sister Verena. Stop. Sister Jean and I will be returning from our . . . retreat at Sacred Heart Cloister this evening at six. Stop. Send transportation to the depot in Baton Rouge. Stop." Here Mirielle hesitated. She had only one shot at making sure Sister Verena understood. "Saint Christopher travels with us. Stop. Yours in Christ. Stop. Sister Pauline."

The woman's eyes remained pinched. "You don't look like any nun I seen."

"We're—er—from a liberal order," Mirielle said, doing her best to impersonate Sister Verena's superior air. "God cares about what we do with our lives, not what we wear."

The woman's expression turned perplexed. She pushed her glasses farther up her nose and counted the words of Mirielle's telegram. "A dollar seventeen."

Mirielle handed over the money, her heart still beating off-tempo. Not until she walked away and heard the woman say, "address" to the next customer was Mirielle satisfied they'd make it onto the train unmolested by a mob or the police.

With only seven minutes left until their train arrived, Mirielle checked on Jean, who'd slid from standing against the wall to sitting. She dabbed at the sweat along Jean's brow with her hankie. "Hang in there. We're leaving soon."

Jean's eyelids fluttered open, and she nodded.

"Sister Verena will be waiting for us at the station when we arrive." At least Mirielle hoped so. She kissed Jean's forehead. "I've got to make a quick telephone call. I'll be back in a jiffy."

A bank of three telephones stood along the far wall beside the water jug. The stalls were walled off one from the other but had no doors to block out the lobby noise. Mirielle pressed the receiver to one ear and cupped her hand over the other to muffle the din.

"Hello?" a voice said when the operator connected the call.

Mirielle's lips failed her. She hadn't expected an answer, let alone Charlie's voice over the line.

"Hello?" he said again.

"Charlie? It's me, Mirielle."

When no response came, she said his name again.

"I'm here. I—er—the butler said you'd called."

"Half a dozen times. How's Helen?" she asked, holding on to her breath as she awaited his reply. She couldn't endure it if—

"She's fine. Home from the hospital and on the mend."

Mirielle turned away from the mouthpiece and let out a happy sob. "Oh, thank God. I wanted to come to you but—"

The screech of slowing train wheels sounded from outside.

"Where are you?" he asked.

"I can't talk now, but I promise to write when—"

"You haven't left the facility again, have you?"

"I'll explain everything when I—"

"Did you get my last letter?"

The urgency in his voice gave her pause.

"Of course I did. That's how I knew Helen was ill."

The train blared its whistle as its screeching wheels came to a stop. "I've got to run, Charlie. Give Helen and Evie my love and—"

"I sent another letter and . . . well, just read it."

The clamor in the lobby grew to a near-deafening level as disembarked passengers crowded inside. Mirielle had to go or she and Jean would miss the train, but her feet wouldn't move.

"What does it say?"

He made no reply.

"Damn it, Charlie! What does it say?"

"I never blamed you."

"Blamed me for what?"

"His death wasn't anyone's fault."

"You can say his name, Charles. He'd want us to say his name."

"I wasn't the one who fell apart whenever someone mentioned him."

"My son died. What was I supposed to do?"

"*Our* son, Mirielle, and anything would have been better than trying to kill yourself."

She flinched and clasped her wrist.

"There! I've said it," he continued. "You want to call things by their proper names? How about this: suicide."

"At least I cared! You were back at the studio a week after his funeral."

The line was silent for several seconds.

"Look, I never should have brought it up. I just wanted you to know that wasn't the reason."

Mirielle glanced at the clock above the lobby door. One minute until the train departed. "Reason for what?"

"Read the letter. You don't need to sign anything. It's already done."

Mirielle's stomach dropped, and her hands went cold. The train's whistle blared again.

"Charlie, I . . . I don't blame you either," she said, and set the receiver back in its cradle.

CHAPTER 64

⟴

Mirielle staggered with Jean to the platform just as the train was set to depart. She pushed Jean onto the first step of their car and grabbed hold of the railing. The train lurched into motion. Jean swayed as if she might fall backward, landing them both in a heap on the platform. Mirielle dropped her valise and planted a hand on Jean's back to keep her upright. With her feet still on the platform, Mirielle stumbled alongside the accelerating train, her grip on the railing loosening. Did she let go and retrieve her valise? The clothes and shoes and jewelry she could live without. But the beachside picture of her and her family could never be replaced. Her fingers strained to hold on to the slick metal railing. Jean's weight pressed against her other hand. Her purse dangled from her wrist.

A backward glance at her valise, and Mirielle leaped onto the train's step. Only her toes gained purchase. She tottered backward, her fingers slipping from the railing. The platform fell away, and the blur of gravel several feet below flashed at the periphery of her vision. Just as she was about to fall, the conductor appeared in the doorway above. He grabbed hold of her wrist. Once she was steadied, he yanked both her and Jean up the stairs and inside, muttering a string of curses.

All the coach seats were taken except one. Jean drifted back into unconsciousness before Mirielle could fully settle her into the seat. Her face was flushed and hot to the touch. The whites of her eyes were colored entirely pink. Her breath had grown raspier, and Mirielle feared lesions had erupted in her throat. Thank God they had only one leg left of the journey. When they arrived in Baton Rouge, Sister Verena would be waiting. They could begin treatment right away in the back of the ambulance, even as it jostled down the River Road.

Mirielle found a place nearby to stand, holding on to the handrail that jutted from the top corner of the bench seat. Tears threatened in her eyes. Tears of exhaustion and frustration and mourning. But she held them back, not wanting to cause a greater scene than she already had.

She had other pictures of Felix, though none were quite as dear. She'd write Charlie to send one right away.

What had he been trying to say to her over the telephone? Had he truly not blamed her for Felix's death? She had blamed him, at the time. And herself. And God and anyone at all connected to the event, down to the laborers who'd laid the foundation of the pool. But most of all, herself. The tears became harder to stem. She fanned her face, hoping only to appear overly warm.

The train listed, and Mirielle bumped into the shoulder of the woman seated beside her. "Excuse me," Mirielle said.

The woman scowled and said nothing. She smelled of pickled cabbage. Someone else nearby smelled of barn dust. Another of cooking grease. Mirielle tried not to breathe in too deeply, regretting she hadn't the money for first-class tickets.

A laugh bubbled inside her. It slipped out before she could clamp her lips to stop it. Surely she stank as much as these apple-knockers. Stank of sweat and swamp water and musty silk.

A few of the passengers glanced in her direction. With effort, Mirielle composed herself. Laughing was no less conspicuous than crying. She couldn't afford to do either until she and Jean were safely on their way to Carville.

When the train finally arrived in Baton Rouge, Mirielle stepped aside and let the other passengers alight before rousing Jean.

"I don't feel good," Jean muttered as Mirielle looped an arm around her waist and hoisted her up.

"I know. We're almost there."

Jean teetered a moment, then collapsed back onto the seat. Mirielle sat down beside her, looped Jean's arm around her neck, and stood with her again. They wobbled off the train and onto the platform.

People buzzed thick as mosquitos about the station, pushing carts piled high with luggage. No, not just luggage, but crated chickens and clinking chinaware and mismatched chairs. Was it always this busy here? Two men struggled to unload a piano from one of the baggage cars. A young boy led a goat through the crowd. Women carried enamel vases and wall clocks beneath their arms.

With Jean's weight heavy against her, Mirielle picked through the horde. The lobby and front curb were equally congested. She rose onto her tiptoes and scanned the street. No ambulance. She looked for the orderlies' white uniforms and sisters' spread-winged hats but saw neither among the thick of travelers.

She stepped back beneath the eaves of the station and propped Jean against the brick wall to wait. After nearly an hour, the rate of trains stopping at the station slowed, and the crowd thinned. Darkness had crept across the sky from the east, but the western horizon still glowed a peachy orange. Uncertain from which direction the ambulance would come, Mirielle kept watch up and down the street. Jean sat cross-legged beside her on the ground, resting her head against Mirielle's leg.

A man in a cheap cotton suit came up to her. He nodded to an outmoded and mud-speckled taxicab across the street and asked if she needed a ride. His breath smelled of garlic and tobacco. "No, thank you," she said, looking past him. Any moment the ambulance would arrive. He shrugged and shuffled on.

Another train pulled up to the station, and a swarm of passengers disembarked. The glow of twilight faded. Street lamps flickered on. The policeman who patrolled the station strolled by for the third time. As before, Mirielle flashed him a *nothing-is-amiss* smile even as her heart pounded. This time, he didn't smile back.

"Afraid ya can't loiter here, ma'am," he said.

"Oh, don't worry, we're not loitering. Our ride should be here any minute."

He glanced down at Jean and frowned. Mirielle tensed. Had he noticed the outcropping of boils on her arms? Would he realize they were lepers?

"She sauced?"

Mirielle gave an uneasy laugh. "Heavens no. She's just a child. Tuckered out from our journey is all."

"What's on her arms?"

"Er . . ." Frank's easy demeanor that night in the bar flashed to her mind again. "Strawberries. Would you believe it? She's allergic to strawberries. We've just come from Opelousas where a friend made the most delicious berry pie—mulberry and cherry, I thought—but darned if there weren't strawberries in there too." Mirielle nodded down at Jean. "She ate two full pieces before I realized and—"

The policeman waved her off. "Just see that you ain't here when I come back."

Mirielle watched him saunter away, her tautly wound nerves slowly unspooling. Where was Sister Verena? Maybe she hadn't gotten the telegraph or had misunderstood Mirielle's meaning.

Jean stirred beside her. She needed to get to Carville where Doc Jack and the sisters could care for her and soon. Every moment they waited here, the worse the reaction became.

Across the street, Mirielle saw the cabbie loitering by his car and waved him over.

"I'll take that ride now," she said.

He flashed a brown-toothed smile. "My pleasure. You and the girl?"

"Yes."

"It's fifty cents a mile. Where ya headed?"

"Fifty cents? That's more than double the cost of a gallon of gas!"

"Most of the filling stations are running dry on account of the flood, so I figure it's a fair markup."

"Flood? What flood?"

The cabbie gave her a curious look, then peeled a battered sheet of newsprint from the sidewalk. MISSISSIPPI FLOODING IMMINENT, the headline read.

That explained the hordes of people at the train station and hum of uneasiness in the air. She looked up and down the street for a more reputable conveyance, but the few other remaining cabs were already engaged. Jean moaned behind her.

"Fine. You know the way to Carville?"

The cabbie held out his hands and backed away. "Whoa now, you two ain't sick, are you?"

"At fifty cents a mile, you're not entitled to questions," she said with more bluster than she felt.

"A dollar."

"That's robbery!"

"A dollar a mile, and ya gotta pay up front."

Mirielle crossed her arms and raised her chin. "You're mad as a hatter if you think I'm gonna pay that."

"Suit yourself." He crumpled up the newsprint and threw it at her feet before turning away. "I ain't inclined to be helpin' no filthy lepers anyhow."

She fought the urge to smack the back of his head with her purse. Or holler after him that he was the filthy one. A dollar a mile! She could hire a shiny new limousine for less than that. If she had any money.

A wheezing breath sounded behind her as Jean shifted position on the hard sidewalk. From the corner of Mirielle's eye, she spied the policeman less than a block away, strolling back in their direction.

"Wait!" she said.

The cabbie turned around, and she stepped down from the curb. "I can't pay you up front, but I promise once we arrive, I'll get you your money."

He shook his head. "No deal."

Mirielle opened her purse and raked her fingers along the satin lining, hoping to somehow find a stash of bills she'd missed before. Instead, her fingers brushed against the St. Christopher medal. "What about this?" She held it out by the chain for him to see. "It's pure silver."

The cabbie drew close and examined it, fingering it with callused, tobacco-stained hands. His pungent breath made her cringe. He brought the medal to his mouth as if to bite it, but Mirielle yanked it away.

"Well?"

"Nah. I couldn't get more than ten clams for a piece like that. And Carville's at least a thirty-mile drive. Got anything else in that pretty little purse of yours?"

Mirielle shrank back. "No."

"Too bad." He jutted his stubbly chin in Jean's direction. "Looks like she could really use a doctor."

"If you were a decent sort of fellow, you'd take us then."

"Yeah, but I ain't."

"That's for doggone certain." As she shoved the St. Christopher medal into her purse, the back of her hand scraped against something hard tucked inside the inner pocket. Her empty stomach clenched and twisted. But one glance at Jean and Mirielle knew what she had to do.

"What about this?" She slipped Irene's ring from her purse. The ruby glinted in the lamplight.

"Now we're talkin'." The cabbie moved close again, his dirty hand reaching out. Mirielle winced in anticipation, as if he were not only taking the ring but a piece of her flesh with it.

Before he could pluck the ring from her palm, a voice sounded some distance behind her. "Whoa there."

CHAPTER 65

Mirielle closed her hand around the ring. A man, backlit by the yellow glow of street lamps, reined his horse and wagon to a stop beside her. Shadow obscured his face. A fresh rush of panic skittered from the tips of Mirielle's fingers to her core. Was he part of the police dragnet out to find her? She glanced back at Jean, calculating how far the two of them could make it before this man overtook them. Considering Jean could hardly stand, let alone run, they wouldn't make it far.

"This gal giving ya trouble?" the man said to the cabbie. The familiar timbre of his voice lingered in Mirielle's ear.

"We was just engaged in a little business deal," the cabbie replied.

"Like the devil we were!" Mirielle thrust Irene's ring back into her purse alongside Sister Verena's medal. "Extortion is more like it."

The cabbie scowled at her, then turned to the man in the wagon. "She and the girl are lepers. Tried to get me to take 'em to the colony at Carville."

"That so?" the man said. "Best ya run along then. I'll take it from here."

"You gonna report 'em?"

"Something like that."

The cabbie eyed Mirielle's purse as if he had a mind to snatch it and run. Her fingers tightened around the straps. She was tired and hungry and damned if she wouldn't smash his toes with the heel of her shoe if he took a step closer.

Perhaps he read the defiance in her eyes, for he turned and saun-tered toward his taxicab. Mirielle waited until he was a safe distance away before turning back to the wagon. Whether the man meant to report her and Jean or shackle them in chains and drive them back to Carville himself, she didn't care to find out. She took a backward step toward the sidewalk where Jean sat.

"You fixing to walk back to Carville, Polly?"

Mirielle stopped. The man took off his bowler and ran a gloved hand through his mop of wavy hair.

"Frank?" She rattled her head and stared up at him. "What the devil are you doing here?"

"Good to see ya too." He hopped down from the wagon and handed Mirielle the reins. "Keep him steady while I get Jean."

What Mirielle had thought to be a horse hitched to the wagon was actually a donkey. The same donkey she'd seen a hundred times cart-ing supplies and gnawing on clover at Carville.

"Where's the ambulance?"

"Didn't have enough gas to make it here and back."

Frank hurried to the sidewalk and scooped Jean up in his arms. She moaned when he laid her down in the wagon bed but otherwise didn't stir.

"She don't look good."

"I found her like this yesterday near Cote Blanche Bay. I think it's a leprous reaction. She's got a fever, new lesions, inflamed nerves—"

"Cote Blanche Bay?" He regarded her with an expression Mirielle couldn't read. "What the hell made ya think to look there?"

"It's a long story." She climbed into the wagon. Frank sat beside her and took the reins, giving them a shake to spur on the donkey. They rode in silence through the city, Frank deftly navigating down one street and the next. Mirielle hazarded a glance in his direction but still couldn't read his face. The day's worry seeped out of her, leaving behind emptiness and exhaustion. She longed to rest her head against his shoulder. To close her eyes and forget—for a few fleeting minutes—all the day's trials and those yet to come. But Frank's tight jaw and stiff posture kept her away.

"How come you came and not one of the orderlies?" she asked as they passed the last of the city's street lamps and turned down the River Road.

"Sorry to disappoint."

"No, it's not . . . I'm so grateful I could kiss you."

"Best ya didn't," he said without humor.

"It's an expression."

"Ya might catch more of the gazeek."

"Stop it, Frank."

"Just a friendly warning."

But there was nothing friendly about it, and Mirielle almost wished she'd taken her chances with the cabbie. "What I meant was, how did you know to find us at the station?"

"Two escapees decide to give up life on the lam and come in. Ya think that's gonna stay secret long?"

"Jean didn't have much say in the matter."

Frank glanced over his shoulder at the bed of the wagon where Jean lay. "No, I reckon not." He turned his gaze to Mirielle. "But you did. Thought ya'd be long gone to California by now."

The mention of home made her insides ache. She could have left Jean to his care, and stayed in Baton Rouge until she found her way to Los Angeles. But then what? Until she was cured, the risk to her daughters—be it from the disease or the stigma—was too great. "I guess a life on the lam wasn't for me."

Frank stared at her for several more seconds, the intensity of his gaze making her skin prickle. Then he turned his eyes back to the road. He explained that he'd heard about Mirielle's telegram from the Rocking Chair Brigade, who'd heard from Madge who'd overheard the sisters discussing it in the infirmary. He saw Sister Verena leave with one of the orderlies in the ambulance just before supper.

"But they was back before I'd even finished dessert," he said, navigating the donkey around a pothole. "Guess they ran into someone along the way who warned them off going. Said there wasn't gas to be found anywhere in the city. The ambulance couldn't make it there and back without refilling, so they turned around, them."

"They were just going to leave us stranded there?"

"Nah. Mr. Li heard from Billy who heard from Norma that Sister Verena planned to see about borrowing Doc Jack's car in the morning. But I figured, why fuss about with gas when we got this perfectly good ass and wagon."

Mirielle smiled in spite of herself. For once, Carville's voracious rumor mill had worked in her favor. The city lights had fallen away behind them. Forest crowded one side of the road and the sloping levee the other. The wagon's headlights swayed in time with the donkey's plodding step, casting a roving pool of light before them. "Sister Verena gave you her blessing to come get us?"

"I wouldn't put it quite like that. But with everything going on, I figure she won't be too cross about it."

Mirielle snaked her arms around her midsection. Things would have to be pretty bleak for Sister Verena not to mind.

One of the wheels hit a bump, and the wagon listed. Jean groaned.

"How'd ya manage to find her?" Frank asked.

Mirielle told him the entire story—from her decision at the train station in New Orleans, to finding Jean's father, to her trek along the waterways and bayous with Mr. Jessip. She could tell from Frank's questions he knew the area, at least by reputation, and was surprised a city gal like her had managed so well on her own.

In turn, Frank described how he'd snuck the wagon past the gatehouse right under Watchman Doyle's nose.

"But why?" she asked.

"Why what?"

"Why you?"

"Like I said, sorry to disappoint."

"You know that's not what I mean."

He turned away, fixing his gaze on the levee that loomed alongside the road. "Water's high high. Highest on record, they say. Rose four inches just in the last day." He talked of sand boils, weakened levees, flooding in the parishes to the north, and Mirielle didn't press further about why he'd come. She didn't fully understand the gravity of the situation until he mentioned that two barges had been anchored a few miles upriver from Carville in case the levee failed and the hospital flooded.

The wagon tottered over a rut in the road, and Mirielle clutched the sideboard to keep from falling out. "That could really happen? The hospital flood?"

Frank shrugged, but his tight grip on the reins betrayed his worry. "They say our levees are among the best along this whole course of the river."

"But if they break?"

"If it happens upriver a ways, we should have a few hours to evacuate. If the levee breaks at our peninsula, the water will sweep away everything."

"Including the colony?"

Frank nodded. "Including the colony."

They rode the rest of the way in silence.

CHAPTER 66

They arrived at Carville well past midnight. Watchman Doyle startled awake when Mirielle rapped on the guardhouse window. He rattled his head and rubbed his eyes, not seeming to recognize her. Had she changed so much in the past week? She patted down her frizzy hair and nodded to the wagon waiting in the drive. "It's me, Pauline Marvin. I'm back with Jean." She hoped by not mentioning Frank, she might save him a month's punishment in the clink. Mirielle hadn't such hopes for herself, but once Jean was safely to the infirmary, she didn't care.

Watchman Doyle opened the gate as Mirielle clambered back into the wagon. They drove straight past the administration building without a backward glance, following the road on the staff side of the reserve until they reached the lawn that abutted the ladies' infirmary. Frank carried Jean inside with Mirielle hurrying beside him.

Sister Loretta had the unlucky assignment of night shift and was seated at the nurses' desk when they burst in.

"Put her here," Mirielle said to Frank, pointing at a vacant bed. She turned to the sister, whose expression waffled between shock and alarm. "She's been feverish for a day and a half, maybe longer. I think it's a reaction."

Sister Loretta drew close to the bedside. After a quick examination, she nodded.

"Shall I draw up some potassium antimony?" Mirielle asked.

"Yes, good idea. I'll go fetch Sister Verena."

Mirielle hurried to the sink to scrub her hands while Sister Loretta scurried out.

"Anything I can do?" Frank asked.

"No. You'd better go before Sister Verena arrives." She finished washing her hands and grabbed a towel to dry them. When she turned from the sink, he was already striding toward the door. "Frank."

He stopped and looked at her expectantly.

"I . . . um . . . thanks for the ride."

Disappointment flashed across his face, and she regretted not saying the words that had first come to mind. *I love you.* He gave a curt nod and was gone before Mirielle could rally her courage.

She watched the door close, aching to follow him. Instead, she drew up the medicine into a syringe and returned to Jean's bedside. She removed Jean's clothes, revealing the full extent of her ghastly illness. Many of the lesions that covered her arms and legs had erupted and oozed milky fluid. Her inflamed nerves jutted like strung rope beneath her skin. When Mirielle pulled back Jean's eyelids, the pink mucosa of her sockets was dry and the whites of her eyes just as red as they'd been that morning.

She readied some betadine and cotton squares so Sister Verena could give the injection as soon as she arrived, then hurried to the medicine cabinet to mix some antiseptic solution for Jean's eyes.

Before Mirielle had finished, Sister Loretta returned with Sister Verena. Sleep crusted at the corners of her eyes, and her winged hat sat askew. She glanced at Mirielle with only a flicker of surprise, then turned her attention to Jean. "What's her status?"

"I think it's an advanced reaction. Fever. Neuritis. Iridocyclitis. Ulcerating lesions of the limbs and nasal passages. I've drawn up three cc's of potassium antimony and am mixing up an antiseptic wash for her eyes now."

"Good, very good, Mrs. Marvin. I'll take over from here."

"Shall I wake Dr. Jachimowski?" Sister Loretta asked.

Sister Verena laid her hand across Jean's forehead, then probed along her swollen nerves. "Not yet. Just keep an eye on the other patients." She turned to Mirielle. "Finish with the antiseptic, then fetch a basin of cool water and a sponge. We need to bring down the fever."

Mirielle nodded. She knew the situation was urgent, but Sister Verena's steady presence helped settle her nerves. They worked in concert for several hours, speaking little. Mirielle wetted Jean's eyes with antiseptic and sponged down her feverish body. She cleaned her oozing lesions and mixed a thin paste of trichloracetic acid to smear over them. When there was nothing left to do but watch and wait, she pulled up a chair alongside the bed and cradled Jean's hand in her own. Sister Verena sat beside her.

"She won't go blind, will she?" Mirielle whispered.

"It's too soon to tell."

"And her neuritis?"

"She'll need surgery to strip off the nerve sheaths if the swelling doesn't go down. Dr. Jachimowski will decide about that in the morning."

Mirielle looked out the infirmary window. The night sky was a pale predawn purple.

"You should get some sleep," Sister Verena said. "And a shower."

"But I—"

"You can come back and help again when you're rested."

"You're not gonna throw me in jail for absconding?"

Sister Verena's lips twitched in what might have been a smile. "Not tonight."

Mirielle stood and retrieved her purse from beside the sink where she'd left it. She was halfway to the door when she stopped and turned around. Withdrawing the St. Christopher medal from her purse, she walked back and handed it to Sister Verena. "Thank you."

"I'm glad he saw the two of you safely home."

"How did you know I'd go in search of Jean, not back to California?"

"I didn't." Her long, slender fingers closed around the medal. "I just had faith."

Mirielle nodded slowly. Maybe that was the best any of them could do. Too bad her own faith was in such short supply. She started for the door, making it only a few steps before Sister Katherine rushed in.

"Another bulletin from Dr. Ross," she said, panting and waving a piece of paper above her head.

Sister Verena scowled, stalking over and plucking the paper from the sister's hand. "There's no need to cause a scene." But as she read the bulletin, her expression darkened.

The sisters gathered around. Mirielle inched closer too.

"What does it say?" Sister Loretta asked.

"The levee at Plaquemine Point is about to break." She handed the paper back to Sister Katherine, her gaze fixed on the distant wall. The others stared at her expectantly. One of the patients several beds down from Jean gave a wet cough. Another stirred and moaned.

"We need to ready the patients," she said at last. "Everyone must have a pillow, blanket, and change of clothes set aside should the order for evacuation be given." She took a few steps toward the door, the other sisters following behind like goslings, then stopped abruptly. "We'll need several days' worth of food and medicine set aside too. Stretchers arranged for blind and bed-bound patients. A ramp built from the road to the top of the levee for those in wheel-chairs. And then there are our patients in the infirmary. Someone needs to remain here and—" She turned and collided with the gaggle of nuns behind her.

Mirielle would have laughed, had the situation not been so dire.

"Sister Katherine, wake the rest of the personnel and inform them of Dr. Ross's bulletin. Sister Loretta, you . . ."

Mirielle listened as Sister Verena doled out orders, noting how the infirmary staff grew fewer and fewer. At this rate, no one would be left to care for Jean and the others.

"I'll help," Mirielle interrupted. "I can spread the word among the residents."

Sister Verena regarded her with a wary expression, but at last nodded. "Take care not to start a panic."

CHAPTER 67

Panic had already taken root without the residents even knowing about the perilous conditions at Plaquemine Point. The early risers whom Mirielle passed on the way from the infirmary were so concerned with the swelling river that they didn't even ask where she'd been and why the devil she was back. Under normal circumstances, gossip like that was better than being first in line for Christmas dinner. Heeding Sister Verena's words, she didn't say anything about the bulletin but told them to go back to their rooms and expect an update from their house orderlies soon.

A quick tally of the houses—twenty-four in all, plus the half dozen cabins of Cottage Grove—and Mirielle realized she'd never make the rounds quickly enough alone. She fingered the outline of Irene's ring through the smooth fabric of her purse. With her take-no-guff attitude, Irene would be just the ticket in a spot like this.

Mirielle shook her head and forced back her sorrow. Who else could help? Madge was far too brusque. The rest of her housemates too flighty. Mr. Li, too soft-spoken. She hesitated at a juncture in the walkway, her eyes sweeping past the houses and trees to the far lawn. There was one person everyone in the colony respected. Now was no time to second-guess her feelings and avoid him.

She knocked three times on Frank's door before he finally answered. His wavy hair stuck out at all angles from his head, and one cheek bore the reddened imprint of his pillow. He'd donned a pair of wrinkled trousers but nothing else.

"What time is it?" he asked, squinting in the dawn light.

"Listen, I—"

"Something happen to Jean?"

"She's the same. It's too soon to know"—her voice faltered—"how things will turn out."

"Then if ya don't mind, I'd just as soon hit the hay again."

"I need your help."

He patted down his wild hair, his blue eyes looking past her. "I'm done helping ya, Polly." He started to close the door, but she wedged herself into the jamb.

"Wait, it's the river."

He let her in and set a pot of coffee to boil, throwing on a shirt and shoes as he listened to the news about Dr. Ross's bulletin. Between gulps of too-hot coffee, they divided up the houses, then set out to spread the word. Mirielle stopped by her own house first to drop off her purse and change her bedraggled clothes. The building seemed as one-dimensional as a movie set without Jean running down the hall or Irene crooning along with her phonograph in the living room.

Musty smell aside, Mirielle's room was just as she'd left it. Her empty nightstand caught her eye, and she thought of the picture she'd left behind at the train station, her last real tether to her life before. Tears sprung to her eyes, but she blinked them back. There'd be time to nurse her pain later. If they survived the flood.

She resisted the call of a hot shower and her pancake-thin mattress, staying just long enough to change into clean clothes and notify her housemates about the bulletin.

One of the women broke into tears when Mirielle delivered the news. Another scampered to the attic to fetch her suitcases, even as Mirielle reiterated that they'd only be allowed to bring along a pillow, blanket, and change of clothes.

The next house took the news little better. Clouds rolled in, and it began to rain before she reached the third house on her list. The droplets fell lightly and far apart. But the faint *plink . . . plink . . . plink* against the windows and atop the roof drowned out her assurances that the levee had not yet broken, and Sister Verena only meant for them to be prepared.

"Where will we go?" one of the residents said.

"There are two barges ready to take us aboard."

"How will we all fit?" another asked.

"I'm sure they've made the appropriate calculations."

"You know who'll be left behind if it's a choice between the staff and us lepers," the first woman muttered.

"No one's leaving anyone behind. There's plenty of room for all of us," Mirielle said, raising her voice above the murmurs, though she didn't actually know anything about the barges and how many people they would hold.

It took all morning to notify the rest of the houses. "Remember, the walkways will be crowded," she heard herself say over and over again. "Don't push or shove. Make way for those carrying stretchers and pushing wheelchairs."

When she'd finished her rounds, Mirielle returned to her room and flopped onto her bed without bothering to undress. But the patter of rain against her window kept her awake.

She gave up and dragged herself to the shower. She soaped every inch of her body. The sweat and dirt and grime of travel swirled with the sudsy water down the drain. The lesions and scars remained. She dressed without taking inventory.

Outside, swollen, gray clouds blanketed the sky, but the rain had paused. She stopped by the infirmary and found Jean still asleep and febrile. A damp cloth covered her eyes. The medicine had reduced the swelling of her nerves, though, and staved off surgery. At least for now. Mirielle sat with her for several minutes, stroking her hand and listening to the small radio one of the sisters had smuggled in. In between advertisements for Ivory dish soap and Wrigley's chewing gum, a deep-voiced newscaster reported flooding from Illinois to Louisiana. Hundreds of people had died or were missing. Country folk fled to the cities. Baton Rouge alone had over a thousand refugees.

In their back and forth between the sickbeds and the supply cabinets, the sisters and orderlies dallied by the radio, listening too. Plaquemine Point still held, the newscaster said, but several more weak points had been found in the levee, one at Southwood six miles away and another at the tip of the peninsula where the colony lay. One of the sisters gasped.

Before they could hear anymore, Sister Verena strode into the infirmary and switched off the radio. Everyone scattered to their tasks while Mirielle was shooed away with bundles of gauze and medicine to take to the schoolroom, where all the evacuation supplies were being stockpiled.

After dropping off the supplies, Mirielle climbed the observation tower. The view from the top struck her cold. Only the tips of the riverside trees showed above the turbulent gray water. It lapped at the plank buttresses and stacked sandbags that capped the levee. Upriver, two huge barges rocked with the current.

All around was chaos. Automobiles rattled along the River Road, suitcases and boxes spilling from the trunks, chests and furniture tethered to the roofs. Trucks and wagons carted dirt to shore up cracks in the levee. An airplane flew overhead.

"Just like war times."

Mirielle startled at the sound of Frank's voice and turned around. He'd managed to smooth his hair since last she saw him, and his cheeks were clean-shaven. He held out a letter. "This came while ya were gone."

Charlie's neat lettering marched across the envelope. She hesitated before taking it. "You're making personal mail deliveries now?" She put the letter in her pocket and turned back to the river. "This morning you all but slammed the door in my face."

"About that . . . guess I owe ya an apology."

"You don't owe me anything. I'm the one who made a mess of things."

A bell rang from within the colony. Mirielle jumped, her entire body tensing before she realized it was just the supper bell. Neither of them moved toward the stairs.

"*Mais la*," Frank said, after a strained silence. "Guess I'll leave ya to your letter."

"Wait." Mirielle took a deep breath, her eyes still trained on the swollen river. "Do you remember that night in the rec hall when you played *The Perilous Pursuits of Pauline*?"

He came and stood beside her at the railing, propping one foot on the bench. "Didn't make it but a few minutes into the first reel, as I recall."

"One of the actors—Charlie West—he's my husband." Mirielle

slipped a hand into her pocket, her fingers tracing the raised edge of the stamp. She knew without reading it what the letter said. "*Was* my husband. He's divorcing me."

The flatness of her voice surprised Mirielle. She ought to be choked up or crying. But at least one of them deserved to be free. And knowing Charlie forgave her, that he'd never blamed her at all, gave her a certain bittersweet freedom as well. Maybe at long last, she could forgive herself too.

Frank stood beside her in silence as another truck full of sandbags lumbered up the levee. A breeze troubled the leaves and excited the river's dark water into waves.

"I'm sorry, Mirielle. Truly I am."

She looked down at the tower's rotting guardrail and traced the crooked initials of some long-forgotten lovers. "Are there any happy endings?"

Frank didn't reply. A raindrop struck the deck beside them. Then another. Mirielle waited, listening, but no more droplets fell. The gray sky above them seemed to be waiting too, holding its breath.

"Come on," Frank said. "Let's get some supper."

As they started down the creaky stairs, the sky exhaled, releasing a torrent of rain. They hadn't yet reached the bottom when a cry sounded above the downpour. "We're coming," she muttered. It sounded once more, and Mirielle stopped, her foot hovering over the last step. It wasn't the supper bell tolling again, but the sharp call of the evacuation whistle.

She met Frank's eyes, and they ran toward the colony. Wind blew the rain sideways, droplets pricking her skin, even as they made it to the covered walkway.

"Head for the barges," Frank said. "I'll make sure everyone here gets out."

"Don't be a cluck. We'll split the houses like before."

He frowned, but she hurried off before he could protest.

CHAPTER 68

Mirielle's heart hammered in her throat as she ran from house to house. Residents scurried past with their evacuation bundles. She rallied a small group to help the blind patients, then continued on.

Her last stop was house eighteen, where Madge was herding their housemates out to the barges.

"You coming, dollface?"

"I just have to get my bundle," Mirielle said. "I'll be right behind you."

But when she got to her room, Mirielle realized she'd been so intent on getting everyone else ready that morning that she'd forgotten to prepare an evacuation bundle for herself. She glanced around at all the things that had once seemed so important—her wardrobe full of dresses and shoes and hats, her collection of creams and makeup, her silver comb and brush set. If the flood did come, it would all be lost. She wadded up a blanket, fished Irene's ring from her purse, and untaped one of Evie's drawings from the wall. Everything else would have to remain.

Outside, rain continued to fall. Every drop seemed to carry with it the power to swell the river to the breaking point. She fought the tide of stragglers on their way to the barges as she headed to the infirmary.

When she got there, Jean was gone. Had someone already taken her to the barge? Amid the chaos, no one could say for sure. Mirielle made a second sweep through the infirmary, half expecting to find

Jean crouched behind the medicine cabinet or beneath the dusty old hypertherm, as if this were a game of hide-and-seek. But all the obvious nooks and crannies were empty, and Jean was in no condition to play.

Someone must have already moved her, Mirielle decided, despite her unease. She helped Sister Loretta lift one of the last remaining patients into a wheelchair and pushed the woman through the rain toward the barge.

"Are we going to die?" the woman asked as Mirielle struggled with the chair up the slick planks to the top of the levee.

"Of course not," Mirielle grunted, hoping she sounded more confident than she felt.

Dusk had fallen, making the crowded barge even more difficult to navigate. At one end, a low-slung roof supported by thick pillars sheltered the deck. The sisters had congregated the other infirmary patients there. Mirielle helped the woman she'd wheeled aboard onto a low cot beneath the roof's shelter and covered her with a musty, war-issue blanket. She searched the other cots. But Jean was still missing.

Mirielle's heart beat with growing fierceness. The rain stopped, but the deck remained wet and slick. Only a hint of twilight filtered down through the scrim of clouds. She wound her way through the throngs of residents, asking after Jean. Some were too forlorn to answer. Others hadn't even realized Jean was back. No one said they'd seen her. Mirielle tried to leave the barge to go back and search the colony, but Watchman Doyle wouldn't let her off.

By the time she circled back to the makeshift infirmary, Mirielle's breath came quick and shallow with worry. Jean hadn't appeared, and at any moment the levee might break and water surge at them. Anyone not aboard would drown.

Mirielle swayed, sick at the thought. Had all her efforts been in vain? Then, in the last row of cots, she saw a small figure hidden beneath a heap of blankets. She hurried over, holding her breath as she yanked the covers away. Jean lay curled asleep on the cot. Mirielle gave a sob of relief. After rearranging the blankets and sponging Jean's cracked lips with water, Mirielle sank to the floor beside her.

Night's cold fingers ruffled her damp clothes and crept along her skin. She draped her own blanket over her shoulders and stuffed her hands into her pockets for warmth. Charlie's letter brushed her knuckles.

A nearby oil lamp, flickering with the barge's sway, offered just enough light to read by, and Mirielle pulled the letter from her pocket. Rain had soaked through the envelope, blurring the ink. But she could still make out most of the words. She prepared herself for more vitriol. Instead, Charlie's letter—what she could read of it—was surprisingly tender. Yes, he'd filed for divorce, concealing the true reason, of course, to stave off a Hollywood scandal. But he wrote that he'd always love her and would continue to receive her letters for the girls. Someday, he said, they could tell them the sad truth of why she'd gone away. His final words surprised her the most.

> *I could tell from your letters you'd come to yourself again, made a second life despite your ghastly circumstances. You inspired me to do the same. It's what Felix would want for us, after all. I'm only sorry we couldn't do it together.*
>
> *With Love,*
> *Charlie*

Mirielle folded the ink-smudged letter and tucked it back in her pocket. Jean stirred on the cot beside her. She straightened Jean's blankets and stroked her cheek. For once, her skin wasn't hot or clammy. Her breath came soft and easy.

Had Mirielle come to herself again like Charlie said? Made a second life? Whether or not the flood spared Carville, there was still no cure for their disease. What kind of life was it when you lived caged behind a fence, an outcast from the rest of the world?

She laid her head on the edge of Jean's cot and closed her eyes. This certainly wasn't the life she would have chosen. But Charlie was right; it was a life nonetheless. And she was lucky not to have to go through it alone.

At dawn, she awoke to find the barge still securely tethered to the bank and the colony, with its wire fence and warren of whitewashed buildings, still standing. Jean's cot, however, was empty. Mirielle queried the sisters, but none of them had seen her scamper off.

"What about the levee?" she asked.

"It broke in several spots along the western shore," Sister Verena said. "But our side to the east, God spared."

Relieved, Mirielle went in search of Jean. The rain clouds had vanished with the night, and a fine mist hung over the water. She picked her way among the residents, some still sleeping, others sitting in quiet awe as the sun rose over the river.

At the far tip of the barge, Mirielle found Frank and Jean seated together, staring out at the water.

"About time ya joined us, *chère*," Frank said.

She sat down beside them and wrapped her arm around Jean's shoulders. "Shouldn't you be resting on your cot?"

"Can't see anything from there," Jean said. Her voice was raspy, but the whites of her eyes clear. "I wanna be front and center when we take off down the river."

Mirielle started to say that the barge was securely moored and the levee safe. But she closed her mouth around the words. It was a nice thought. Sailing downriver to the wide-open gulf. Out to where their disease didn't matter. Her arm tightened around Jean. She caught Frank's eye and smiled. Maybe someday.

EPILOGUE

Carville, Louisiana
1942

Mirielle readied another syringe of Promin as the last patient sat down at the treatment table and rolled up his sleeve. She handed the syringe to Doc Jack, who swabbed the patient's skin with betadine, then carefully inserted the needle into his vein. Recent trials with sulfanilamide and diphtheria toxoid had proven unsuccessful, but this new drug was different. After a few months of daily injections, patients' nodules and lesions began to disappear. They had more energy and better appetites. There were side effects, of course. Anemia, dermatitis, allergic reactions. But for once, the drug's promising results outweighed the risks.

A minute's slow injection, a bandage, and the patient was up and ready to leave. Nothing like the hours-long treatment they'd endured in the fever cabinet all those years ago. Mirielle put away the extra supplies and loaded the used needles into the autoclave. Though her shift was technically over, she climbed the infirmary stairs to the roof where several patients sat in the shade of a great arbor, enjoying the late afternoon breeze. She'd promised to set one of the women's hair in pin curls before leaving—soft waves and rolls were all the rage these days. Besides, Mirielle welcomed any distraction from her creeping worry about tomorrow.

From this height, the entire grounds of Carville were visible. The magnolia trees preened with blooms, and the oaks stretched their gnarled boughs across the lawns. A flurry of construction had taken place in recent years. The vast, two-story infirmary with its lovely rooftop arbor had gone up nine years ago and could no longer be considered new. Last year, a modernized dressing clinic was added on. New patient housing built of concrete and stucco, two stories high with interconnected arcades, replaced the old wooden houses and walkways. Best of all was the theater in the new rec building. With velvet curtains and cushioned seats, it reminded Mirielle of the movie palaces in Los Angeles. It still struck her every time she saw a once-familiar face on the screen. Many of her old acquaintances, Charlie included, hadn't survived the arrival of talkies. She still saw his name occasionally listed in the credits as a screenwriter or assistant producer and felt a certain tenderness. But no longer guilt or regret.

She finished with the pin curls and left the patients on the roof to their lounging. On her way home, she stopped by house fifteen. Two of the rooms had been repurposed as a publication office and workshop for the colony's new monthly magazine, the *Star*. There, she found Jean working at the mimeograph machine.

"Tante Polly," Jean said, maneuvering her wheelchair around the table, papers in hand. She'd lost both her legs to infection a few years back but navigated her chair as nimbly as a shrimper steers his trawler. She handed the newly printed pages to Mirielle. "What do you think?"

THE STAR, read the banner. *RADIATING THE LIGHT OF TRUTH ON HANSEN'S DISEASE.* Inside were articles about the upcoming Hospital Day celebration, fundraising efforts for the Red Cross, and the American Legion Junior League baseball game. There was a ladies' page and letters to the editor. Even Dr. Ross had contributed a piece on the new sulfone drug they were trialing in the infirmary.

"Looks great." She handed the pages back to Jean. Depression had dogged Jean after losing her legs. Mirielle had been at her side through it all, but it was Jean's work with the magazine that had brought the spark of life and mischief back to her eyes.

The supper bell rang, and Jean tossed the pages onto the workbench beside the mimeograph. Toby poked his head in from the office. He smiled at Mirielle, then locked eyes with Jean. Without a word, the two of them took off racing toward the dining hall, the wooden wheels of Jean's chair barely missing Mirielle's foot.

"Don't forget about tomorrow," Mirielle called after her.

Jean glanced over her shoulder and smiled. "I wouldn't miss it."

Mirielle trailed Jean out of the house and watched her and Toby speed away, their laughter echoing down the arcade.

She passed dozens of other residents on their way to the dining hall as she headed home. Many were new since her arrival and considered her an old-timer. There weren't many of them, the old-timers, left. Madge and Mr. Li had joined Hector and Irene under the pecans. Every day she passed the growing rows of white headstones and felt a pang of loss.

The smell of frying catfish wafted from the cabin as she mounted the steps. An Andrews Sisters medley sounded from the record player.

"Just in time, *chère*," Frank said when she entered. "Supper's almost done." The skillet popped and sizzled as he flipped the fish. His eyesight had worsened over the years such that even thick glasses hardly helped, and she worried about him at the stove. But he seemed to adapt to his dwindling vision as adroitly as he'd adapted to his crippled hands. He was among the second round of patients trialing Promin. While it couldn't improve his sight or reverse the decades-old damage to his hands, she watched and rejoiced as every day he grew healthier.

She kissed him on the cheek, but he pulled her into a full embrace, releasing her to set the table only when the skillet began to smoke. She washed a bowl of strawberries from their garden and poured them each a glass of tea. Her tea was famous around the colony, but no matter how Mirielle tried, it never tasted quite as sweet as Irene's.

Frank's catfish, however, was as moist and flavorful as the first time she'd tried it. She ate a few bites but found her stomach unwelcoming of the delicious food.

"Tomorrow ain't nothing to worry about," Frank said. "You'll see."

"It's been so long." She turned and looked out the window, absentmindedly patting her graying hair. "Too long, maybe."

"Nonsense, *chère*."

The record ended, and Frank rose from the table to change it. Mirielle picked at her fish but didn't brave another bite. Maybe tomorrow wasn't such a good idea after all. Her gaze drifted to the cabin's far wall where an assemblage of photographs hung beside yellowed drawings. Below sat shoeboxes crammed with letters. After a telephone was finally installed in the canteen, she'd rung monthly. But were pictures, letters, and phone calls enough to overcome the time and distance between them?

When the music resumed, it was no longer the Andrews Sisters' swinging harmonies, but the jaunty fiddle and guitar rhythms of Frank's old honky-tonk music. He returned to the table and held out his hand. "Dance with me."

"Don't be silly, we haven't even finished supper."

Frank didn't move. Mirielle sighed and took his hand. They danced in the small space between the kitchen and sofa. Mirielle's feet dragged at first, her thoughts far away. But soon her step livened, and she found herself laughing. When the next song played—a slow, crooning ballad—Frank pulled her close.

"Your food is getting cold," she said, even as she laid her head against his shoulder. She closed her eyes and felt the worry drain from inside her. Ten years they'd been married, and his steady presence was still a refuge. Even today, couples couldn't wed in Carville's chapels, and some doctors on staff threatened to sterilize patients who snuck out through the hole in the fence to marry as she and Frank had done. Luckily, cooler heads like Doc Jack prevailed. She and Frank had spent a month in jail after they returned but had lived together in his cabin ever since.

The next morning, Mirielle dressed with care. She sat at her small vanity and stared at her reflection. It had been ages since she'd cataloged the lines and blemishes that marked her skin. Her disease had never advanced as far as many patients' had. A few years back, she'd accrued eleven negative skin tests in a row before the insidious bacilli appeared on her slides again. Now, it wasn't a question of beauty or disease, but whether she'd changed so much as to be unrecognizable. Frank insisted she hadn't, but Mirielle wasn't sure. Her life at Carville had been a happy one, but everyone here had their scars. If not on the skin, then on the inside.

They met Jean on the lawn beneath the oaks and waited. Jean took out her harmonica and played while visitors trickled down from the plantation house. One song became two, three, four. Despite the shade, Mirielle's skin grew sticky with sweat.

Maybe they weren't coming. Maybe they'd changed their minds.

Was it Mirielle's imagination, or had Jean's playing become slow and mournful?

Then another car puttered down the River Road, stopping at the guardhouse, before turning down the drive toward the big house. Mirielle squinted, trying to make out the passengers as they stepped from the automobile. Sister Verena greeted them and gestured toward the oaks.

"Is it them?" Jean asked.

"I . . . I'm not sure," Mirielle said, even as her bones hummed with certainty. The new visitors crossed the lawn toward the hedgerow. Mirielle's breath caught. Evie's face had thinned, and her figure filled out. Her hair—the same chestnut shade as Charlie's—was done up in the latest style. She was no longer a girl but a woman now, as sweet and lovely as she'd been sixteen years before. Her companion, Mirielle recognized too. Less by sight than by heart's pull. Helen.

Mirielle ran. Through the dappled shade of the oaks, past the chapels, all the way to the hedgerow. There she hesitated. But her daughters did not. They rushed past the barrier and into her awaiting arms.

AUTHOR'S NOTE

The inspiration for this story came from a small book I stumbled upon at my hometown library: *Carville: Remembering Leprosy in America* by Marcia Gaudet. In my mind, leprosy, or Hansen's Disease as it's preferentially called today, was a disease of far-off places and long-ago times. I didn't realize the disease had once been endemic in parts of the United States or that between 150 and 250 new cases are still reported here each year. More than facts and figures, I was struck by the stories of those sent to Carville. Their sufferings and triumphs. The stigma they endured and fought to change. *The Second Life of Mirielle West* is based on these stories, no one person's in particular, but on themes and events described by many. While the characters were born from my imagination, their circumstances are grounded in truth and history.

Carville began as the Louisiana Leper Home in 1894. Two years later, sisters from the Daughters of Charity arrived to help care for the patients. In 1921, the United States Public Health Service took control of the site, and it became the national leprosarium. Until the late 1950s, it was legal in most states to forcibly quarantine people with Hansen's Disease. The majority of these patients were sent to Carville, many never to be released. After decades of failed remedies, Carville physicians pioneered a new treatment in the 1940s—sulfone drugs—which finally led to a cure. Eventually, patients were no longer forced to remain on site for care and treatment. But years of illness and discrimination are not easily overcome, and several patients chose to live at Carville until their deaths. Today, the site is used by the Louisiana National Guard and home to the National Hansen's Disease Museum. I highly recommend a visit.

I strove to represent Carville and the lives of those who lived there as accurately as possible. To this end, I read memoirs and letters, histories and medical texts. I scoured old maps and perused articles in the Carville-produced magazine, the *Star,* and its predecessor, the *Star Sixty-Six.* But on two points, I did take liberties. Fever therapy was trialed on Carville patients in the manner described in the story, but not until the 1930s, a few years after the book takes place. And while the Mississippi did flood in 1927 and two large barges anchored near Carville for evacuation, they were never actually boarded. I hope the reader will forgive these minor embellishments.

In writing this story, I learned many things about the disease, and about my own biases and misconceptions. Hansen's Disease is a bacterial infection. Contrary to popular belief, it is not very contagious. In fact, ninety-five percent of adults cannot catch it, as their immune systems readily fight off the bacteria. It is not the same disease referenced in the Bible. It is not the result of uncleanliness or an immoral lifestyle. Today, it is treated at outpatient clinics using a combination of antibiotics taken over one to two years.

Those curious to learn more can visit the museum website, https://www.hrsa.gov/hansens-disease/museum, or check out these books: *Carville: Remembering Leprosy in America* by Marcia Gaudet, *Alone No Longer* by Stanley Stein, *Miracle at Carville* by Betty Martin, *A Disease Apart* by Tony Gould, *King of Microbes* by Johnny Harmon, *Out of the Shadow of Leprosy* by Claire Manes, and *Carville's Cure* by Pam Fessler.

ACKNOWLEDGMENTS

Every book is its own journey. Sometimes, an author may feel like she's navigating alone, but there are always guiding hands at play—prodding, questioning, teaching—and the book, in the end, is much the better for it.

Elizabeth Schexnyder, curator of the National Hansen's Disease Museum in Carville, Louisiana, thank you for assisting me with my research. Your commitment to honoring the lives of Carville patients and staff inspired and humbled me.

Michael Carr, my agent, thank you for your honesty, your belief, and for pushing me toward a better story. My editor, John Scognamiglio, you give me freedom to create, while never failing in your support and wisdom. Thank you. And my thanks to the entire team at Kensington without whom this book would never find its readers.

Early readers Tonya Todd, Marycourtney Ning, and Veronica Klash. Thank you for all you bring to my writing and to my life.

My A Group: Jenny Ballif, April Khaito, Angelina Hill, Wendy Randall, and Amber Ornelas Frederick. Your sound advice never fails. Your support gives me wings.

The Garcia family. *Estoy muy agradecida por su ayuda.*

Writing this book reminded me how very precious family is—those you're born to and those you find along the way. Steven and all those closest to my heart, thank you for sharing this journey with me.

THE SECOND LIFE OF MIRIELLE WEST

ABOUT THIS GUIDE

The suggested questions are included to enhance your group's reading of Amanda Skenandore's *The Second Life of Mirielle West*!

DISCUSSION QUESTIONS

1. What assumptions did you have about leprosy before reading this book?

2. Patients at Carville fought for decades to promote the name Hansen's Disease over leprosy because of its strong, negative connotation. What power, if any, does language hold in erasing stigma?

3. Who was your favorite character in the story and why?

4. Mirielle begins the novel a broken, selfish woman. But through her experiences at Carville, she is able to grow and heal. Are there instances in your own life that may have been unwelcome but forced you nonetheless to change or grow?

5. How is Mirielle's approach to motherhood different at the beginning of the story than at the end? How does her approach compare to modern views of motherhood?

6. When Elena's infant is whisked away to the orphanage, Sister Verena tells Mirielle it's for the infant's own good. Do you agree?

7. The title of the novel implies something akin to a death, followed by a rebirth for Mirielle. What moment would you identify as her death? At what point did her new life begin? Was it a gradual process or an immediate change?

8. Frank believes that hope is as essential as medicine in surviving their disease. How big a part does hope play in a struggle, particularly a struggle for survival?

9. For half a century, patients at Carville lived without the right to vote or marry or leave the confines of the hospital. Which of your freedoms would you most hate to give up?

10. In the aftermath of Carville and the tragic quarantining of Hansen's Disease patients, society continues to grapple with pandemic infectious disease (think of HIV and COVID-19). In what ways have we as a society progressed in dealing with these diseases? In what ways have we remained stagnant? Does stigma still play a role?

Connect with  U s

Visit us online at
KensingtonBooks.com
to read more from your favorite authors, see books
by series, view reading group guides, and more.

for sneak peeks, chances to win books and prize packs,
and to share your thoughts with other readers.

facebook.com/kensingtonpublishing
twitter.com/kensingtonbooks

Tell us what you think!

To share your thoughts, submit a review,
or sign up for our eNewsletters, please visit:
KensingtonBooks.com/TellUs.